DEGREE OF GUILT

Baby of the Bailey series - book 1

Dan Cogan

Man of Mystery Publications

Copyright © 2024 Daniel Patrick Cogan

The right of Dan Cogan to be identified as the author of this work has been asserted by him in accordance with the Copyright, Designs, and Patents Act 1998 and other copyright laws.

All rights reserved.

No part of this publication may be copied, reproduced, transferred, distributed, leased, licensed or publicly performed or used in any way, except as specifically permitted in writing by the author, as allowed under the terms and conditions under which it was purchased or as strictly permitted by the applicable copyright law. Any unauthorised distribution or use of this text may be a direct infringement of the author's rights and those responsible may be liable in law accordingly.

This is entirely a work of fiction. The names, characters, and incidents portrayed in this work are entirely the creation of the author's imagination. Any resemblance to events, localities, or actual persons, living or dead, is purely coincidental

ISBN-13: 979-8-3041-2484-3

Dedication

While I was getting towards the end of writing this book, my beautiful sister Yuli and my brother-in-law Natan were killed in a car crash. This came as a complete shock to me, and I was utterly devastated. The fact that there is a major character in the book whose wife and children were also killed in a car crash, makes it all the more poignant.

Their tragic deaths reminded me how important it is to spend as much time with those we love, and constantly let them know that you love them.

So now I dedicate this book to Yuli and Nati, beautiful people, taken from this world too soon.

*"Lovely and pleasant in their lives,
And in their death, they were not divided."*

CONTENTS

Title Page
Copyright
Dedication
Prologue

1	2
2	5
3	11
4	15
5	19
6	23
7	28
8	30
9	34
10	36
11	38
12	40
13	42
14	44
15	46

16	48
17	52
18	54
19	58
20	60
21	62
22	65
23	68
24	72
25	76
26	81
27	85
28	87
29	90
30	95
31	101
32	106
33	112
34	115
35	117
36	121
37	124
38	128
39	132
40	135
41	139

42	144
43	147
44	152
45	157
46	161
47	165
48	167
49	169
50	171
51	172
52	174
53	179
54	181
55	184
56	186
57	191
58	193
59	199
60	204
61	211
62	214
63	221
64	223
65	225
66	227
67	229

68	231
69	233
70	235
71	237
72	242
73	243
74	247
75	250
76	253
77	255
78	260
79	261
80	263
81	264
82	270
83	273
84	275
85	280
86	284
87	286
88	288
89	291
90	292
91	296
92	300
93	302

94	304
95	306
96	311
97	316
98	319
99	322
100	324
Epilogue	330
Acknowledgement	334
About The Author	336

PROLOGUE

Saturday, 23 September, 2023

Even at eight times magnification, it was hard to read the face of Soraya Wallace.
If the eyes are the window to the soul, then yours are more like distorting mirrors, thought the blonde, lowering the binoculars.

As Soraya flicked a silver strand of hair away from her green eyes, an excited scream, from a four-year-old bundle of energy, punctured her thoughts.

"*Over here! Over here!*"

Little Mikey was far too excited to wait, for "Nana" to decide which of them to throw the frisbee to.

"*No! Over Here!*" countered six-year-old Ariadne.

Moments of happiness like this had lately taken on a new importance for Soraya, since Walter's diagnosis. She had tried to keep things close to business-as-usual, for the sake of her heavily pregnant, and recently separated, daughter Huette. But with hindsight, the ending to this warm afternoon would seem almost like a cruel joke.

As the frisbee flew out of her hand towards Mikey, Soraya mouthed the words "next time" to a crestfallen Ariadne. It was not enough to avert a moment of silent protest, as Ariadne walked off to play with her doll. But the lure of the game proved too much for the six-year-old to resist. Well, the lure of the game *and* a few words of warmth and wisdom from her beautiful and ever-loving grandmother.

Way off in the distance, their innocent recreation was being monitored by a woman somewhat younger than Soraya's 65, but about ten years older than Huette's 30.

Soraya felt a twinge of guilt just for being here. After lunch,

Walter had opted out of today's visit to Hampstead Heath, citing fatigue, leaving Soraya, Huette, and the children to their frisbees.

His absence contributed to the one note of uneasiness, marring Soraya's enjoyment of the afternoon. She hated having to make the choice: to go with her daughter and grandchildren to the Heath or stay at home with her husband. She had tried to persuade Huette to stay at the house and let the children play in the garden instead, thinking that Huette in her late stage of pregnancy would welcome the chance to avoid a long, tiring session on the Heath. But the children would have been deeply disappointed to be deprived of their weekly outing.

In the end, it was Walter who decided. He told them all to go to the Heath and let him stay and rest. He would probably take a nap. Such was Soraya's unease, that she had come close to arguing with him, indeed, to insisting that she would stay with him and let Huette take the kids to the Heath. But Walter, a retired professor of statistical mechanics, who could be an uncompromising figure even in his infirmity, gave her a look that brooked no dispute.

So, off they went, Soraya putting her unease on the back burner, distracted by the childish chatter. And back and forth flew the frisbee, the children's excitement rising with each throw and catch.

As time drifted by, the sun sank behind the late afternoon clouds. A glance at Huette was all that it took for Soraya to realise, that while the children were still bursting with energy, her daughter was desperately tired. Hardly surprising considering that Huette had just passed her eighth month of pregnancy. Soraya found herself silently cursing the man who had walked out on Huette five months ago, taking his blonde floozy, his laptop, and his programming skills on the road to become a so-called "digital nomad".

What sort of a selfish git walks out on his pregnant wife?
But Soraya, wasn't going to dwell on that.
It's better to be supportive than angry.

So she gave Huette a look and pointed to her watch. Huette appreciated the message, and after a word to the kids – who quite naturally whined and protested – they proceeded to the parking area. Soraya started packing away the toys and blanket, while Huette strapped the children into the spacious Land Rover that had served her for 12 years. As Soraya and Huette strapped themselves into the front seats, Ariadne, chattered away about an imaginary tea party with the squirrels while Mikey squirmed for a glimpse of the sun, now hidden behind the clouds.

Meanwhile, the woman with the binoculars was hastily making a phone call.

You stand there in the garden staring at the rear door that leads to the kitchen, lured there by words like "I know you killed Raymond" and "Walter will betray you."

The door leading into the kitchen is closed, and presumably locked. Yet it stands there in front of you, offering a tempting target. It wouldn't take too much effort to kick it in. Or to smash the glass and reach inside, where the key is probably already in the lock.

No, it wouldn't take any effort at all. And even if it makes a noise, in this quiet neighbourhood, no one is going to do anything about it, unless they're sure that something is amiss. The worst that could happen is that they look out of a window and see you.

And so what? What would they actually "see"?

You're covered from top to toe in workman's overalls. Even the protective hood is pulled up. How much of a view would they have? And for how long? And how much would they *remember*?

And how good a description could they give?

And as long as you made a clean getaway, how would you come into the frame anyway? You were careful about how you got here. You walked through the Heath. And you would walk back the same way. And the Heath has many exits – not to mention a total absence of CCTV. By the time you exited, you would look completely different.

No, they'd never catch you.

Then why do you hesitate? Have you suddenly developed an aversion to murder?

No, of course not!

What stays your hand is pragmatism. You cannot go in *now*.

Soon, yes. But not now.

With everyone safely belted up, and Soraya at the wheel, they set off towards the house in Hampstead Garden Suburb, where Soraya and her husband had made their home. The drive was filled with the children's chatter, recounting the day's adventures, some factual, but mostly the fiction borne of the fertile imagination that only children possess.

XIII

Soraya was surprised to see an olive-green van in the driveway when they arrived at the lowered kerb. On the side of the van were the words: *Calvin Coffey Construction.*

The van struck no more than a mildly disquieting note with Soraya, as she parked the Land Rover on the road outside. But when she climbed out of the driver's seat, her sense of foreboding grew, as she noticed that the front door to the house, usually firmly shut, hung slightly ajar. Seeking reassurance, she looked back at Huette.

"Maybe Dad forgot to lock it," Huette murmured, hoisting Mikey out of his car seat.

Soraya's sense of unease only grew as she approached the door. It was still just a sliver of doubt, an instinctive sense that something was amiss. But the unease turned into a jolt as the door flew open and a figure burst through the doorway, colliding with her and knocking her a few steps back.

A muted scream emanated from her throat. But she gathered her wits quickly enough to take in the sight of the man. He was in his forties, with curly dark hair, tall and defined in his musculature, his numerous pockets overflowing with builder's tools. Trying to make sense of his sudden appearance, she looked round at his van parked conspicuously in the driveway. All would have been perfectly in order, if Walter had said something to her about a builder coming. But he had told her a very different story – a story of fatigue and needing to rest.

"Who are you?" Soraya demanded, trying to keep her voice steady.

The man paused, his eyes flicking towards Huette and the children, a fleeting look of something akin to sadness, or even regret, passing over his features.

"It's best not to go in," he said, his voice low. It was an ominous warning that sent waves of panic through Soraya. She also recognised the fear in the man's tone, and a claw of suspicion gripped her.

Who was he? She wondered. *What did he want?*

But what she *asked* was "Why?" followed by: "What's happened?"

She tried to go round the man, but he moved backwards and sideways to block her path. She moved back the other way, and this time, when he tried to block her way with his arm, she pushed the offending arm away and made it to the doorway. In what seemed like desperation, he grabbed her wrist, more forcefully than he intended, but then immediately released it, possibly aware of the legal ramifications of his actions.

But she didn't go into the house immediately, whether out of fear at what she might see or concern for her daughter and grandchildren. Instead, she half-turned, met the man's eyes and demanded in a tone of anger and confusion: "What's going on?"

Calvin turned, so that his back was to the children, and in particular the boy, who was becoming noticeably irritated. Then he mouthed the words "he's dead" in a such a way that Soraya could discern it, while the younger woman and the children could not. But Soraya was not to be stopped. With a strength born of fear and determination, she brushed aside his arm again, turned to the door and went in, her heart pounding.

And then she saw the sight that she had dreaded. Walter, her husband, lay sprawled across the floor, his skull brutally smashed in, a bloodied hammer discarded nearby almost like a callous afterthought.

The room spun around Soraya, as she tried to grasp the reality of what she was seeing.

She stumbled outside to see the man still there, now talking to a crying Huette who clutched the children closely, a protective barrier against the horror. Soraya's grief erupted into rage, a primal scream tearing from her throat.

And then, choking on her words, her eyes brimming with tears, she demanded: *"what the hell have you done!"*

Monday 18th March, 2024

1

"So just to be clear," said Emily, carefully baiting the trap, "you arrested Mr Campbell because he was walking slowly."

"That is *not* what I said."

"Very well then, Constable Edwards, in your *own* words."

"I said I arrested him because he was slowing down the traffic *by* walking slowly."

At twenty-four, Emily's youth seemed at odds with her self-confidence. But that self-confidence was something of an enigma. Not evident at first blush, it emerged in the form of a sting-in-the-tail. The first time she walked into a magistrate's court as a barrister, she was mistaken for a secretary. That's what delicate features do for you. High cheekbones and soft, fair complexion have a disarming effect. She was Fay Wray to everyman's King Kong.

However, even in the crown court, the barrister's gown draped over her tailored black suit, and the wig concealing her chestnut hair, did nothing to add that extra layer of gravitas. People just didn't take her seriously, until her jaws closed on some unsuspecting witness.

Now in her "second six" – the second half of her twelve-month pupillage – she had right of audience in magistrates and crown courts. This meant that she was allowed to take on minor cases under the guidance of Nigel, her supervisor, or "pupil-master" as she mockingly called him, recapitulating the archaic terminology from the days when he had been her father's pupil in chambers. Minor cases, for most pupils meant bail hearings and pleas in mitigation. In other words, cajoling judges and bargaining with prosecutors.

But Emily had managed to snag a real peach of a case, defending a climate change activist in a group prosecution at Southwark Crown Court under the recently enacted *Public Order Act, 2023*. Despite the prestige of the case, Emily had been unable to shake off the charge of "nepotism" – whispered behind her back in St Jude's Chambers – or the "Baby of the Bailey" moniker that she had picked up as a child, running wild and wreaking havoc there, much to her father's embarrassment.

Sidney Campbell et al were charged under Section 7, which made it an offence to "do an act which interferes with the use or operation of any key national infrastructure in England and Wales," if the act was *intended* "to interfere with the use or operation of such infrastructure" or "reckless as to whether it will do so."

In this case the "key national infrastructure" was a public road, and the motive was a Just Stop Oil protest. They were, of course, guilty as hell. But, before going to prison, or being saddled with exemplary fines, they wanted to use their day in court to draw attention to their cause and the reasons *why* they had broken the law, in the hope that at least some good might come of their sacrifice.

But His Honour, Mr Justice Dawson, was having none of it. At a pre-trial case-management hearing he had squelched that plan by ruling that neither the defendants, nor the Crown, could say anything about *Just Stop Oil*, or the demonstrators' cause, in the presence of the jury.

Had the protesters spoken openly to the police about their motives at the time of the arrests, or during their police interviews, they could have introduced this evidence in court as a matter of course, and there would have been nothing the judge could do to stop them. But, not realising how the system worked, the protesters had stood by their right to remain silent, and this played into the hands of the judge.

"At the time of his arrest, or immediately prior thereto," Emily continued, "was Mr Campbell looking around?"

"Looking around?" Edwards repeated, wary of a trap.

"Yes, you know. Looking at his surroundings, as if trying to get his bearings."

Mr. Justice Dawson leaned forward.

"Miss du Lac, you're surely not suggesting that your client didn't know where he was, are you?"

"That is *exactly* what I am suggesting, Your Honour."

Emily was all too aware of the judge's eyes upon her body, mentally undressing her, even through her formless barrister's robes. She had faced sexism before of course. What woman hasn't? A keen practitioner of parkour, free-running, and even basic Krav

Maga, she was routinely described as "fit" by her fellow pupils in Chambers. This meant, however, that she was at the height of her vulnerability to that toxic mind-set.

But sexism from a person in a position of authority was a whole different ball game, all the more so because it fell short of sexual *harassment*. Though perceptible to her, it was not overt enough for her to make an issue of it. More of minor frustration than a game changer.

"Pesky" was how her mother would have described it.

That was Mum – mistress of the art of British understatement.

"Very well," said the judge airily, leaning back.

PC Edwards seemed unsure of whether it was his turn to speak, so the judge nodded to him, reassuring him that it was okay to answer.

"Well, I *suppose* he was looking."

"Then I put it to you, that my client was simply lost, when you arrested him."

"He never *said* he was lost," Edwards replied, more than a little confused.

"Well once you arrested him, he was facing a stressful situation, was he not?"

"I suppose so."

"So how can you be sure," asked Emily, her blue eyes blazing with mock indignation, "that the reason he was walking slowly was not simply because he was lost, and was trying to regain his bearings?"

"Well for a start, because of his jacket."

The judge sat bolt upright, his equanimity visibly shattered, as indeed was that of prosecutor Maurice Jordan. For PC Edwards had just opened a door that the judge wanted to maintain firmly shut.

2

"I arrested him at the scene, and he was brought to Wood Green Police Station for questioning."

DI Jane Cherry was above average height for a woman. Two decades ago, she had been on her school's field athletics team. She had dropped out of competitive sport when she joined "The Force" because she knew she was never going to make it to the top-flight as a discus thrower and wanted to concentrate on her police career. But even now, she retained her athletic build and was formidable to look at.

"And did you question Mr Coffey that afternoon or evening?"

The Crown case was led by Hayden Blair KC, a barrister in his late fifties of formidable repute, who was known to the ladies of the bar as the "silver fox".

"No, neither. We postponed the interview till Sunday morning to familiarise ourselves with the facts. That allowed him to get a good night's sleep."

It also had something to do with the fact that it was a Saturday, and they were still processing the drunks from Friday night. She had, in fact, asked him some questions at the crime scene itself. But since these questions weren't asked under caution, Calvin's replies wouldn't have been admissible. However, she had repeated the questions at the formal interview and covered much the same ground.

"And for the benefit of the jury, you can confirm that this exhibit is a true and authentic recording of that first interview?"

"Yes."

They were in Court Number One of the Old Bailey, before Her Honour Judge Mary Braham. Braham had been appointed circuit judge just after her 41st birthday, sitting on the south-eastern circuit, which was based at the Old Bailey. Now, five years later, she was presiding over the case of Rex versus Calvin Coffey.

Defending Calvin was Nigel Farringdon KC, the head of St

Jude's chambers and former pupil of Emily's father Sir John du Lac. Widely recognised as being on a par with Hayden Blair in legal circles, Nigel was instantly recognisable. His sharp dark eyes, set against a complexion of rich ebony, exuded a keen intelligence, and his closely cropped hair highlighted the strong lines of his face, including a well-defined jaw and high cheekbones. Now, in his late forties, Nigel had "known" Mary Braham from their student days at King's College London. But their brief common history would bring him no favours.

He sat facing the jury, with the witness box at his one O'clock and Judge Braham on the bench further to his right. Next to him sat Ian Silverman, his "junior" counsel (recently turned 30), who had been feeling a bit queasy that morning.

Calvin Coffey sat in the dock to his left, beyond immediate communication. At times like this, Nigel wished that British courts could be more like their American counterparts, where the client sat next to the lawyer, so that client and barrister could confer with one another when necessary.

Not that Calvin had proved particularly communicative in his last legal visit, or indeed in *any* of his legal visits.

"Let us now see the recording of the interview," said Hayden Blair.

Blair then used the trackpad on his computer to activate the recording that played through the court's Evidence Presentation System onto the screens in front of the jury, judge, and counsel. Within seconds, the screens were filled with the interview room at Wood Green Police Station, where Calvin had been questioned, taking the jury and Nigel back in time, to that moment when the police probed their suspect for the details of the crime.

"This interview is being recorded at Wood Green Police Station, commencing at ten, twenty-one on September the twenty fourth, twenty twenty-three. I am Detective Inspector Jane Cherry, based at Wood Green Police Station. Also present are Detective Superintendent Chryseis Pines, PC Briggs, Calvin Coffey, who is under arrest on suspicion of murder and Brian Smith, the duty solicitor provisionally representing Mr. Coffey."

Smith was an ex-copper who had earned a law degree a few years ago but never aspired to much. Now approaching 40, he was small in stature and mousy in demeanour.

PC Briggs, with a tad over three-year's experience in uniform, stood silently by the door. He was basically the "muscle", in case Coffey got any ideas about "doing a runner" or flipping over the table.

Superintendent Pines, in contrast was short, rugged and stocky. In the Dickensian era, she would have been Mrs Bumble. In more modern times, she could have been a dominatrix: not the glamorous, leather-clad temptress type, more the big, fat "school ma'am" spanking "naughty" middle-aged schoolboys. At times she even fantasized about such a career change.

"For the benefit of the recording Mr. Coffey, can you confirm your name."

"Calvin Coffey," he replied in an American accent.

Calvin was also in his mid-forties. His hair, peppered with flecks of silver, retained traces of a thick mop of dark natural curls from earlier years. There was something particularly compelling about his rich, dark brown, eyes. They were deep-set and expressive, holding a depth and intensity that could be almost threatening, yet retained a warmth and kindness that could just as easily put you at ease. His musculature was sturdy, like that of a builder, not the bulbous, unnatural frame of a bodybuilder.

"For the benefit of the recording, Calvin Coffey has been arrested on suspicion of the murder of Professor Walter Wallace and has been cautioned under the Police and Criminal Evidence Act, 1984, Code C, Section 10."

Coffey seemed somewhat blasé about what was going on, not cocky or arrogant or even indifferent, just not unduly concerned. Jane Cherry had seen it all before. It didn't necessarily imply that he was innocent, but neither did it mean that he was guilty. That was something she had learned from her mentor (and occasional lover) Chryseis Pines.

"Before we proceed any further, should I call you Calvin or Mr. Coffey, or do you have some other preferred name?"

"Calvin is fine."

"Okay Calvin, first of all could I ask you what you were doing at the home of Professor Wallace this afternoon?"

"Professor Wallace asked me to come and take a look at his loft and give him a quote for converting it into an office or spare room."

"Now this was at Professor Wallace's home in Hampstead Garden Suburb?"

"Yes."

"And where are *you* based?"

Coffey fidgeted somewhat, and Jane's eyes darted sideways to

Chryseis who had shot her a "don't go too fast" warning look.

"I'm based in Sutton."

"That's still London right?"

"Greater London for voting purposes, but a Surrey postal district."

She nodded, as if expressing agreement. Of course, Sutton was distinctly *south* London, whereas Hampstead Garden Suburb was squarely in the north, but in line with her "softly softly" strategy she would let that pass for now.

"Okay can you tell me a bit about what happened when you arrived at the house?"

"I arrived at the house at four something or maybe later. You can check my phone for the exact time. I have an Android phone and I keep the SatNav on all the time, so it'll show my movements on my timeline. Oh, and my van also has SatNav."

"Okay, go on. What happened at the house?"

"When I arrived, the door was slightly ajar. I thought maybe he'd left it open for me, but I didn't want to take any liberties, so I called out and asked if anyone was home."

He paused and looked at Jane's face. But she remained silent.

"There was no reply, so I called out again."

"What did you call?"

"I don't remember. Maybe something like 'Hello, anyone home?'"

"Maybe?"

"I mean, I'm pretty sure it was something like that. In fact, I'm pretty sure it *was* that."

"Go on."

"Well I didn't really want to go in without an invite but..."

"Were you *worried*?"

"Not at that stage. I just don't walk into a place without an invite. I'm from the US, as you probably picked up from my accent. If you do that over there, you can end up getting shot."

"But at some point, you did go in."

"Yes. I guess after a certain point, having come all that way, I figured I'd better go in. Maybe he *had* left the door open for me. Maybe he was hearing-impaired and hadn't heard me. Maybe that's why he left the door open."

"Hearing-impaired? Hadn't you spoken to him before?"

Calvin seemed uncomfortable at this.

"We never actually *did* talk on the phone. All our communications were via email."

"Is that normal? For your trade?"

"No. But it's what he wanted. He said he had a speech impediment."

Jane exchanged another look with Chryseis.

"Okay. So you went in. And then what?"

"Well I kind of looked around and then made my way to the kitchen."

"Why the kitchen in particular?"

Calvin appeared to give this some thought.

"I don't really know."

"Are you *sure* you didn't see anything? Or *hear* anything?"

"No, not that I remember. Maybe there was something subconscious. I don't know."

"And when you got to the kitchen?"

"I saw him lying there."

"Him being?"

"Professor Wallace."

"Oh. Did you *know* it was Professor Wallace at the time?"

"I mean the man whom I *now know* to be Professor Wallace."

"So what exactly did you think at the time? I mean who did you think it was?"

"Oh I was pretty sure it was him. I just didn't know it for a *fact*."

"Did you know he was dead?"

"Oh yes. That I did know."

"Did you touch the body?"

"No. I was careful not to."

Once again, Jane Cherry and Chryseis Pines locked eyes.

"So *how* did you know that he was dead?"

"Well, his eyes were open, but there was no sign of blinking."

"Okay, now we found a hammer at the scene. Was it yours?"

Calvin appeared to stress out at this.

"No it wasn't mine. But I'm afraid I did something very stupid."

He sounded rather sheepish when he said the words. More embarrassed than nervous.

"Thrill me," replied the inspector, in a gently mocking tone, exploiting the moment to build a rapport of humour.

"I actually... well that is... what I mean is... I picked up the hammer."

"You *picked up* the hammer?"

"I'm afraid so."

"In God's name WHY?"

At that point the court proceedings were interrupted by the sound of Ian Silverman throwing up.

3

"His *jacket?*" Emily repeated incredulously. "I don't understand."

In his zeal to make sure that Sydney Campbell didn't slither off the hook, PC Edwards had committed a *faux pas* – a faux pas that enabled Emily to get her foot in the door.

"Why would his jacket prove that he wasn't lost?"

Edwards appeared to be stuttering, but no actual words came from his mouth.

"I mean, did it have a map on it?"

"Miss du Lac," the judge intoned. "I trust you are not being facetious."

"On the contrary, Your Honour. The witness claims that the jacket worn by the defendant somehow prevented him from being lost. I am simply trying to find out why."

"Tread carefully, Miss du Lac," Justice Dawson warned.

She *was* playing with fire now. But she had no intention of stopping.

"So how did his jacket show that he wasn't lost?"

"Because it was the same jacket as several of the other defendants were wearing."

"In what respect? Colour? Fabric? Style?"

"It was one of those Hi-Viz jackets and it said–" He stopped abruptly and looked at counsel for the prosecution. Maurice Jordan tried to shake his head surreptitiously, without the judge seeing.

"Oh, the jacket *said* something, Constable Edwards?" asked Emily with full-throttle mockery in her tone. "Was it one of those new-fangled *talking* jackets perhaps?"

"Miss *du Lac,*" the judge chided.

She brushed it off.

"In your own words, Constable, please clarify."

Edwards hesitated and then spoke in a stumbling voice.

"It said the same... on the back of the jacket... as similar jackets worn by the others."

Emily took a deep breath. The witness had given her the opening that she needed.

Here goes, Your Honour.

"What *specifically* did it say?"

"Miss du Lac!"

"Yes, Your Honour," Emily retorted, smiling sweetly.

The judge turned to the jury usher.

"I'll have the jury out!"

His tone had assumed a new sense of urgency.

As the jury were led out, Emily noticed that the faces of both the judge and the witness had turned bright red. As soon as the door was closed behind the last of the exiting jurors, Justice Dawson turned to Emily.

"Miss du Lac, do not think for a minute that I will deal with this matter lightly because of the high esteem in which I hold your father!"

Emily didn't flinch. But she held her tongue and waited for Justice Dawson to continue.

"Did I or did I not rule before the commencement of this trial – in very clear and unambiguous terms – that the Just Stop Oil movement, and the motives of the defendants, were not to be mentioned in the presence of the jury?"

"You did indeed, Your Honour."

"And did you or did you not just ask the witness a question calculated to encourage him to breach that injunction?"

"Actually no, Your Honour. I simply asked him to clarify an ambiguous answer that the witness had *already given* to an earlier question."

"But such an answer would *inevitably* have led to such a breach, *as you well know*."

"And the alternative would have been to allow the witness's ambiguous answer to *remain* ambiguous – to the detriment of my client's right to offer a defence."

"That doesn't give you the right to disobey my directions!"

"Technically I didn't disobey. I asked a *question*. I never mentioned 'Just Stop Oil.'"

"But the *answer* would have done. It said 'Just Stop Oil on his jacket.'"

"Then the court should have directed the jury to disregard the witness's earlier remark about the jacket."

"You know perfectly well, Miss du Lac, that you launched into this entire line of questioning with every intention of manoeuvring the witness into mentioning the proscribed words."

"I asked questions designed to exculpate my client. The witness should not have mentioned the proscribed words, or the jacket bearing them, and the court should have stepped in timely to shut down him down when he did."

"I think we both know perfectly well that you were luring him into a trap."

"I would challenge the court to find anything improper in my line of questioning."

"Oh really Miss du Lac? The Court may have no power to probe into your instructions. But I have no recollection of this line of defence in your client's defence statement."

"Page eight, paragraph three, Your Honour," Emily replied, matter-of-factly.

Eight pages or more was quite long for a defence statement in a straightforward case like this one. Much of the statement was a long-winded polemic about the damage caused by oil – material that the judge had subsequently ruled inadmissible. But there on page eight, the judge found it, buried three quarters of the way down a long, rambling paragraph. The paragraph was cleverly constructed. Aside from the interminable waffling, it bore an identical sequence of words twice – once just *before* the reference to the defendant being lost, and again just after.

In other words, the paragraph was constructed in such a way as to cause the reader to lose their place and skip a couple of lines, thereby missing the crux of the defence.

"Very well concealed Miss du Lac," said the judge, without thinking.

Emily knew, as soon as these words were out of Dawson's mouth, that she had won the case. For there was no way that he could continue to preside over the case after such a blatant display of prejudice, even in the absence of the jury. And he would be too proud to recuse himself and admit to such judicial bias on the record.

So it came as no surprise to Emily when the judge made it clear to the prosecutor that he would have to allow the defendants – all the defendants – to tell the jury about their motives and thus politicize the trial. Needless to say, this was the last thing the government wanted. This was Dawson's clever way of putting the ball in the court of the Crown Prosecution Service. The prosecutor took the hint and asked that the charges be dropped.

Resisting the urge to punch the air with joy, Emily went over to receive the thanks and adulation of not only *her* client, but the other defendants as well. The barristers for the co-defendants – all of them far more experienced than Emily – were looking at her in awe and envy.

She permitted herself a side glance at the prosecutor, accompanied by a smile.

Still think I got here through nepotism, you bastard?

Maurice Jordan looked away, irritably, as if he had read her mind.

In truth, it was the kind of courtroom trick her father would have used. Despite their estrangement, she was very much Sir John's daughter.

As soon as she left the courtroom, she switched on her phone. It started vibrating immediately. She looked down at the screen to see a message from Nigel that read: "Get round to the Bailey ASAP."

4

Ian Silverman had been checked over by a doctor. After going through what he had eaten recently, item by item, and when the symptoms started, it was diagnosed as a mild case of food poisoning, though it may have been long Covid. The immediate recommended course of action was rest and recuperation, leaving Nigel without co-counsel. Hence his urgent call to Emily.

But getting to the Old Bailey from Southwark Crown Court, on the South Bank of the Thames, wasn't quick without a pushbike or motorbike. Bridges were crowded, while cars and taxis faced traffic jams, diversions and one-way streets. So she walked to London Bridge railway station and took the Thameslink two stops to City Thameslink station, with the intention of walking, or rather *running*, to the Old Bailey.

However, with busy courtroom schedules, especially in the wake of the recent pandemic, Judge Braham was reluctant to delay the proceedings. So the trial of Calvin Coffey resumed while Emily was still in transit.

On the screens of the Evidence Presentation System, Calvin seemed to have shrunk in stature after Inspector Jane Cherry's scathing reaction to his admission that he had picked up the hammer. He was now sitting with his shoulders hunched and his whole torso sunk into the chair. For her part, Inspector Cherry was looking at Calvin like a big sister telling off her little brother for misbehaving.

"I thought I heard someone... an intruder... in another room. I thought I might need it to defend myself."

"You don't exactly look like the kind of man who'd need a hammer to defend himself."

"No but when you're in a room with a body, with a skull smashed in like that."

"But the killer had *left* the hammer there – at the scene."

"Well yes, but…"

"Then why the panic?"

For a few seconds, Calvin was lost for words.

"I guess I was acting on instinct. I didn't have time to reason it through."

"Interesting choice of words that, Calvin," Chryseis Pines intervened. "Reason it through?"

Calvin looked at the superintendent, unsure of whether this called for an answer.

"And *was* there an intruder?"

This was Inspector Cherry, trying to regain his attention.

"No. There was no one." Now he not only *sounded* sheepish, but positively *looked* the part. "I mean I didn't search the house or anything stupid. But there were no further sounds."

A smirk came to Jane's face, possibly a reaction to Calvin not wanting to do "anything stupid."

"I mean there *were* sounds. But I think they were drifting in from the outside."

"From the outside?"

"Through the open windows."

"So you put the hammer down?"

"Yes."

"In the same position you found it?"

"More or less."

Jane looked at the superintendent and then back at Calvin.

"You do know how much harder this makes things, don't you?"

"I'm sorry."

"Okay, then what happened?"

"I thought you knew the rest. I ran out and slammed straight into Wallace's wife."

There was a long pause, while Jane appeared to be looking at some notes.

"Okay. Now, we noted no visible signs of blood on your work clothes, but we'll know more when we get the results back from the forensic lab."

"Well I didn't get too close, but like I said, I picked up the hammer, stupid though that was. So there may be some slight traces of blood, from the hammer, or maybe when I leaned forward to pick it up. I don't remember how close I got to the body."

Jane did the by now familiar meeting of eyes with Chryseis, before giving Calvin her full attention once again.

"I'm going to be honest with you Calvin. There are a few aspects of your story that don't add up. But I want to give you the opportunity to clarify."

Even from a distance, the camera caught the darting flicker in Calvin's eyes.

"Firstly, since when would a man in his seventies want to add a loft conversion to what was already a large house?"

"I don't know. I mean I never asked. At the time of our communications, I hadn't seen the house. In fact, I still haven't, apart from the ground floor."

"Well I *have* seen it. I looked inside the house when the SOCOs were finished."

"SOCOs?"

"Scene of Crime Officer, I think on your side of the Pond, you call them CSIs. And I can tell you, the house actually *had* an office, or at least a bedroom that was being *used* as an office. It also had three other bedrooms, only one of which was in use."

"I don't..." he trailed off.

"Don't know what to say? Or don't believe me? Because, let me spell it out to you Calvin. This isn't the USA. In this country, the police aren't allowed to lie to a suspect."

Calvin stayed silent.

"Walter Wallace and Soraya were both retired. They had *one* daughter, Huette, and she'd flown the nest. Only the ensuite bedroom was in use! And they also had two *large* reception rooms on the ground floor. For an elderly couple with a house that size – not to mention the two vacant bedrooms – doing a loft conversion makes no sense."

"Maybe for overnight guests? Maybe he was going to build a bigger office in the loft and then have his daughter and grandchildren live with them."

Jane looked at the superintendent. Chryseis nodded to her.

"A seventy-three-year-old retired man giving himself another flight of stairs to climb?"

And then, as if on cue, there was a knock on the door and a uniformed police constable entered.

"For the benefit of the recording, PC Wesley has entered the room."

PC Wesley handed Jane a note and then quietly left the room.

"For the benefit of the recording, PC Wesley has left the room."

Jane read the note and then held it so that Chryseis could see it. The superintendent gave her a nod to use the information now.

"I'm afraid I have some bad news for you, Calvin. The forensic

17

computer team expedited their checks on Professor Wallace's computer and phone."

Calvin looked nervous, but only mildly so. Not the proverbial rabbit caught in the headlights type of nervous, just a little uneasy.

"And the bad news is, there isn't a trace of any *correspondence* between you and Professor Wallace on his computer. Or on his phone."

5

"So I guess congratulations are in order, young Emily."

"Er... are you *trying* to wind me up?... Young Emily *my arse!*"

Nigel Farringdon KC's mocking smile said it all. The court had adjourned for lunch, and they were in a café near the Old Bailey.

"When you were born, lo those many years ago, I was your father's pupil – Oh stop rolling your eyes! You're not a bloody teenager!"

"Sorry Nige. I just sensed a lecture coming on and wanted to nip it in the bud."

The thing about Nigel and Emily was that it *wasn't* a normal supervisor-pupil relationship. He had known her since she was a child, and he had grown into something of a big brother to her. While she was running around St Jude's like a pint-sized urban guerrilla, he was spreading his wings under the watchful eye of her father, Sir John du Lac QC, head of chambers. He had witnessed her grow from a precocious child into a confident young woman, in the same years that he had spent clawing his way up the greasy pole of the legal profession, as the first black barrister in St Jude's and now their first black head of chambers.

The son of a Nigerian father and a Ghanaian mother, he had been pushed by his parents to succeed in life. But he had pushed himself way beyond that. And the culmination of that effort was his election six months ago, as head of chambers, which coincided with Emily's arrival at St Jude's, not as Sir John's daughter, but as Nigel's pupil.

"How did Maurice Jordan take it?"

"You should've seen his face."

"He probably felt like he was going up against your father."

"Oh not you too!"

Sir John was no longer at St Jude's. He had moved on to another set of chambers, a long-established set, more befitting his new role as Senior Treasury Counsel, a role in which he prosecuted some of the most serious crimes in England.

While she sipped her orange juice, Nigel cast a quick glance at the wallpaper on his phone, a photo of his wife and two children. It conjured up painful memories. In an instant, a drunk driver behind the wheel of a testosterone-bragging SUV had taken them away from him forever.

For that reason, he had made it clear to the clerks in chambers that he would never represent the defence in a drunk driving case, notwithstanding the ethos of St Jude's. Because it was a whole class of cases that he ruled out, and not just one particular case, his position didn't violate the taxi rank principle.

"Nigel," Emily said gently.

She rarely called him Nigel, preferring the affectionate "Nige" that she always called him as a child. But she did now as she eased him out of his painful memories. He met her eyes briefly.

Yes, Nigel, I noticed... I understand.

His mind came back to the present, to the time and place, to the café.

"I was just going to say, Emily, the way you won your spurs this morning, you can stop worrying about the wagging tongues and the N word."

"The *N word?*"

"Nepotism."

"Gotcha," replied Emily, acknowledging her confusion. "So... about this case?"

"Yes, the case. In a nutshell. A builder arrives at a house where he claims he was hired to do some work – by emails, which turn out to be fake. Door's open already, so in he goes."

"This is his version, I assume."

"Yes. In the kitchen, he finds a body, and a hammer. After picking up the hammer and then dropping it, he runs out and bumps into the dead man's widow, who's there with her daughter and the grandchildren."

"Wait, did you say, 'after picking up the hammer'?"

Nigel nodded.

"What, like, he's never watched a crime drama before?"

"Judge not, that ye not be judged."

"Isn't that the whole point of the law?"

Nigel nodded, with his big-brotherly smile.

"By the way, what happened with Ian?"

"He was feeling queasy all morning, and he threw up in court."

Emily winced.

"Do they know what caused it?"

"The doctor thought it was food poisoning. But it could be long Covid."

"Anyway Nige... the client."

"A builder. Has an American accent. But he's being cagey about his background."

"Maybe I could work my charm on him."

"That's what I'm hoping. But the earliest I could book you a legal visit was Saturday."

"No, wait! I have a flying lesson."

"Cancel it."

He rarely pulled rank with Emily.

"And stop with the puppy dog eyes. The law is a seven-day a week business."

"God, I *love it* when you're masterful!" she gushed breathlessly.

Even without the girlish grin on her face, he knew she was taking the mickey.

"Ah, sweet Emily," he replied, matching her tone of mockery. "When we're alone, you don't have to call me God."

This was too much for her. She whacked his arm with the copy of The Times that a previous customer had so thoughtfully left on a nearby table.

"So, apart from picking up the hammer, and this business with the emails, why's he in the frame?"

"That's pretty much it, really. I mean that and his lack of background. Lives off the grid. Usually works in his local manor – that is Sutton, Mitcham and Cheam. But this time he ventured further afield. And usually most of his clients talk to him by phone, not email."

"I assume we're talking small jobs for people who pay cash for a discount."

"And don't ask for receipts," added Nigel.

"What do the forensics say?"

"Mixed results."

"So, what's the killer fact?"

"What do you mean?"

"Come on Nige. In cases like this there's *always* a killer fact."

"Cases like this?" he echoed, raising one eyebrow, Roger

Moore style.

"Murder cases."

"Considering you've only helped me out on George Stone and this one, I'd say that's a pretty sweeping generalization."

"Quit stalling. What's the killer fact?"

"You've been watching too many American movies Emily."

"Still waiting," she shot back airily.

"The killer fact is that there isn't one. Or if there is, the CPS are in breach of their disclosure obligations. No killer fact, Emily, just a lot of mundane ones that all add up. Plus, the client's story, which *doesn't* quite add up."

"So it's really all circumstantial?"

"Before you were born Emily – come to think of it before *I* was born – more than a few innocent men were sent to the gallows on the strength of circumstantial evidence."

"La-di-da. So I get the lecture after all."

"Just remember why we're called *St Jude's* Chambers."

"Yes, I know. The patron saint of lost and hopeless causes."

Emily's words brought a smile to the face of the blonde woman who was sitting at a nearby table with her back to them.

6

After lunch, Detective Inspector Jane Cherry resumed her testimony. This time it was a recording of the following day's police interview with Calvin Coffey.

But as Jane Cherry recited the names of those present, Nigel noted a change. Calvin Coffey had a new solicitor, their old friend Philip Solomon, instead of Brian Smith, the duty solicitor. Duty solicitors act free of charge and work in police stations and magistrates' courts on a rota basis to give the suspect immediate legal advice. By and large, they are there to help first-time suspects. Career criminals tend to have their own solicitors. However, when a case comes to trial, even a first-time defendant must find their own solicitor, although if the defendant is on low income, they can get one through legal aid.

However, after DI Cherry had confronted Calvin with the absence of evidence on Walter Wallace's phone of any communications between the professor and Calvin himself, it was clear that things were beginning to look grim. So he specifically asked for Philip Solomon.

"I read about you in a newspaper report about that homeless man," Calvin had gushed, when they were given a chance to confer.

He was talking about the George Stone case, one of Nigel's pending cases and one which had been widely reported in the press, before Stone was formally charged and the *sub judice* rules kicked in.

"I figure you'd be someone who doesn't just represent rich people."

Solomon hadn't bothered to explain at that stage about the English legal aid system. They had more important things to discuss.

A tall, lanky man, Solomon could have been a basketball player. He was actually a rabbi's son and had very nearly gone into the family "business". But early-onset atheism, a week before his bar mitzvah, put paid to that ambition.

And so now the interview was about to resume. The police were up against a ticking clock. They had arrested Calvin at 6:47 p.m. on Saturday 23rd of September 2023. That had given them an initial 36 hours in which to charge him, release him or apply for a 36-hour extension from a magistrate. They could release him on police bail or "under investigation". But when it's a serious charge like murder, they sometimes try to put pressure on the suspect by getting an extension from a magistrate to hold them for the full 72 hours.

That's what they had done in this case.

Once they charge a suspect, they must also bring them before a magistrate for a remand hearing. And if they charge them with murder, then they would seek to have them remanded in custody as a matter of course. In England, bail is rarely granted in murder cases, in case they decide to do a proverbial "runner". Even in a country where there is no death penalty and a "life sentence" doesn't actually mean a whole-life-term, murder suspects are considered to be flight risks.

But the police naturally want to know in advance if the Crown Prosecution Service is confident enough to proceed with the case. So they need to wrap up their inquiries well before the 72 hours are up, to give the CPS time to review the evidence.

This meant, the police needed a decision from the CPS by 6.47 p.m. on Tuesday.

So now, on Monday morning, it was the more senior officer, Detective Superintendent Chryseis Pines, who led the questioning. Not because Jane Cherry wasn't up to the job, but because that would signal that the police were upping the ante.

Hayden Blair started the playback of the recording.

"Okay, Mr Coffey, first off I have to tell you that we found some workman's overalls, matching your size, discarded outside the garden hedge at the back of the property."

"But my overalls were in my van." The tone was beginning to show signs of stress. "I was wearing my work trousers and a sleeveless jacket!"

"We took them for forensics, too."

The Detective Superintendent kept her eyes on Calvin.

"The overalls we found discarded behind the back garden hedge in the pathway were positively *splattered* in blood. And it wasn't even dried blood."

"They weren't *my* overalls. I told you."

"Well we'll see if there were any traces of *your hair* on the bloodstained overalls."

"You won't find any."

He said it with surprising confidence. But this meant little. He might have worn a plastic head covering. But they hadn't found one. If he'd had time to get rid of a head covering, he would have had time to get rid of the second pair of overalls, too.

"Or you might have shed some epithelial cells that can be matched to your DNA on the inside of the overalls."

"I never wore *any* overalls," said Calvin. "I think someone's to trying to frame me."

"Frame? In England we say 'fit-up' or 'stitch-up'."

"Well, pardon me for disrespecting the King's English!"

"You didn't ask what 'epithelial' meant."

"So? You think all builders are stupid?"

Chryseis ignored this.

"Okay, Mr Coffey, I need you to help me out with something else. When someone is planning a loft conversion, do they meet the builder and get the quote first, and then apply for planning permission, or do they apply for planning permission first?"

"He didn't need planning permission. A loft conversion is what is called a 'permitted development'."

Chryseis kept her face neutral as she said, "Not in a conservation area."

"What?"

Calvin was clearly thrown by this.

"Hampstead Garden Suburb is a conservation area. In conservation areas you need planning permission for a loft conversion."

"I stand corrected."

"So, returning to my original question. In cases where planning permission is required, *when* would one apply?"

"Usually *after* the quote, and after the client has decided whether to go ahead with the job and *which* quote to go with. Otherwise there's be no point in applying."

"Thank you. That explains why Professor Wallace hadn't even applied."

Calvin's face had returned to neutrality.

"Now let's get back to those missing alleged emails between you and the professor."

"Maybe Professor Wallace deleted them," Calvin suggested, perhaps just a little too eagerly. "Or maybe the *murderer* deleted them. I mean, I've still got them on my email."

"The problem is that the exchange of emails on *your* computer uses the wrong address."

A nervous twitch? Perhaps.

"I don't understand."

"Oh, I think you do, Calvin. You see Professor Wallace's email address is walterwallace nineteen fifty at g-mail dot com. Whereas, you were communicating with walterwallace nineteen L at g-mail dot com."

"So I was set up by the murderer! It's gotta be."

"Set up, yes, Calvin. But we don't think it was by the murderer."

"I don't understand."

Chryseis turned to Jane, letting her do the honours.

"We think it was more prosaic than that. We think you were set up by nothing more than a prankster... as a joke."

"But the professor? The murder?"

Jane Cherry let loose on Calvin.

"Here's what *we* think. You went there in good faith, lured there by a prankster. You normally work in your local manor, Sutton and Cheam. But the prospect of a nice big lucrative job in an affluent North London suburb was so tempting that you didn't stop to question why they'd insist on communicating with you only by email and not using the phone. You must've thought you'd hit the jackpot. You were blinded by greed. And you went there fully expecting to give a fat juicy quote, for a nice lucrative payday. But then you got there and found there *was* no job. And you were angry. You lost your rag."

"You were *furious*," Chryseis added.

Jane continued the double act.

"You couldn't handle the fact that you weren't coming away with the grand prize after all."

"And you needed to take it out on someone," the Superintendent added.

"It didn't matter to you," said Jane, "that Wallace was innocent... that he had nothing to do with the prank. You just couldn't see past the fact that someone had made a monkey out of you. Someone had to pay. Even if it was the wrong man. Even if it was an *innocent* man."

"So you smashed his head in with a hammer," Chryseis threw at him.

"And then you scampered and scurried to clear up the evidence, as best you could."

"Intending to leave and make a clean getaway."

"But you couldn't clear up everything in time," said Jane. "You forgot the hammer."

"And just as you were leaving," the Superintendent concluded, "you walked straight into the wife of the man you had just murdered."

"That's a load of baloney!"

"Is it Calvin?" asked Chryseis Pines. "Why *did* you accept this offer to go and give the quote, when it was on the other side of town? That was way out of your usual work area?"

"Okay, look... The truth of the matter is you called it right on that one. I normally stick to my home turf. But this time, I was tempted by the almighty dollar."

"Dollar?" Jane Cherry inquired.

"Nothing gets past you, Detective."

DI Cherry decided that now was the time to put the question.

"Where are you from? Originally, I mean?"

"I was born in Boston. That's Boston Massachusetts, not Boston Lincolnshire."

"And when did you come to England?"

"When I was sixteen. My parents divorced, and I came here with my mother."

But now it was DI Cherry's turn to drop a bombshell.

"Now that's interesting, because we did a little digging into your background: social media, local newspaper articles and all that... and guess what, Calvin?"

At this point, he looked desperately afraid.

"We haven't been able to find any trace of your existence before last April."

In the courtroom, Emily was watching the video closely, and she noticed that it was precisely at this point that the look of fear on Calvin's face *vanished* – just as quickly as it had appeared.

7

You sit there, staring at the screen, shell-shocked. You have just called up the browser, taking you to the Google search page by default. You only wanted to do a simple search. And when the results came through, you thought you had found what you were looking for.

Yes, it is a 'sponsored' result – in other words, a paid-for link, put there by somebody trying to sell you something. But from the wording of the search result, it looks like you've struck gold. It's *exactly* what you're looking for – a ray of light at the end of the tunnel.

After all the misery and depression following the diagnosis, you actually dare to hope.

So you click on it, and your anti-virus and anti-malware software doesn't block it. The browser takes you straight to the landing page. And the page loads quickly, without stuttering.

Perfect.

But what you see on the landing page hits you in the face and then gnaws at the pit of your stomach.

It says: 'Walter will betray you.'

In a house in Bournemouth, a woman in her thirties was watching a news report about the trial that had opened that morning at the Old Bailey. On the mantelpiece to the side of the television was a framed picture of her late husband. He was looking out at her, smiling and happy. She had taken the picture just after telling him that she was pregnant with their first child.

There were so many things she wanted to ask him. About university life. About the people... about what was troubling him... about...

She would never be able to ask. And all these questions haunted her.

And there were so many questions she wanted to ask the

doctors. But doctors always cover for their own.
If you don't have money, you don't get justice.
"Why you cwying, Mummy?"
It was Liam, her two-and-a-half-year-old son.
She scooped him up in her arms. He was her last reminder of Raymond, who had died horrendously eleven months ago, on the 6th of April.

8

Having made a strong impact on the jury with the police evidence and Calvin's weak and unconvincing performance at the police interview, Hayden Blair was now playing the sympathy card, by calling Walter Wallace's widow Soraya as his final witness of the day.

Soraya's evidence-in-chief – the portion of her evidence that the witness gives under direct examination – was designed to get the jury to think with their hearts rather than their heads. In circumstantial cases like this one, emotional engagement with the jury was paramount.

In the dock, Calvin permitted himself a brief, surreptitious glance up at the spectators' gallery. The only person who noticed was a reporter on the press bench. But the reporter dismissed the thought, because he was too absorbed in his notes for an article about the opening day of the trial.

Soraya testified about the weekend routine, family lunch, her husband deciding not to go with them on this occasion, the outing itself, coming home, bumping into "the defendant" and finding her husband dead. She also testified that Walter had told her nothing about intending to convert the loft into an office or additional bedroom, the very issues that had occurred to DI Cherry when she had interviewed Calvin at the police station. She pointed out that the house already had two unused bedrooms and one bedroom that Walter used as an office.

While Soraya was testifying, Emily was dividing her energies between studying Hayden Blair's technique and making notes for Nigel. Blair made sure that her testimony was thorough and complete, before handing over to Nigel for what everyone expected to be a robust and equally thorough cross-examination.

Emily noticed the gleam in Nigel's eyes as he looked down at the written notes that she had handed him. She knew what that meant. Somewhere amidst all that heart-rending but factually straightforward testimony, lurked a weakness. And when Nigel looked up at Soraya, Emily knew that whatever it was, he had spotted it.

"Mrs Wallace, you have testified that your late husband had not told you about any plans to do a loft conversion. However, you also pointed out that you had two unused bedrooms already. Would it be fair to say that in fact the house was rather big for just the two of you?"

Soraya hesitated, the way partisan witnesses do, when they sense that opposing counsel is baiting a trap for them. She gave Hayden Blair a glance. He avoided making any gesture that might provoke an objection or arouse the judge. But he did meet her eyes for a second and that was enough to allay her fears.

"It was rather big, yes... But we sometimes had overnight guests."

"Sometimes?"

"Occasionally."

"So not very often."

"No."

Emily was sure that his next question would be "when was the last time you had overnight guests?" But then she realised that this would be a dangerous question, because if the answer was a recent date, then it would undermine all the good that came from the previous answers. There was nothing in the files about it, so Nigel probably didn't know. Fishing expeditions can *occasionally* be useful exercises. But, more often than not, such excursions into uncharted territory are a drunken man's walk into the danger zone, because they are fraught with well-camouflaged pitfalls. In general, it is better not to ask a question if you don't know what answer will be given – or at least what the *truthful* answer *ought* to be.

"So, is it possible that Walter was planning on downsizing, but hadn't yet told you?"

He avoided saying "was afraid to tell you." But Emily knew that if Soraya answered aggressively, then he might yet ask that question, playing up the henpecked husband trope.

"But why would he need to do a loft conversion to sell it? We owned it free and clear, and it had a good market value already."

"Oh, you'd looked into it?"

Again, a moment of hesitation.

"In a casual sort of way, yes... we'd been doing that for years."

"So you'd been looking into selling your house?"

Soraya became a bit more defensive.

"It wasn't so much looking into selling it, as such. More like looking up the value of our property on the market, to get some idea of our net worth."

"Is it possible that your husband was thinking not so much about *selling* the house, as *gifting it* to your daughter and her children?"

"Gifting it?"

"Yes, you know, bequeathing it in his lifetime, and either move out or stay, but pay market rent, and maybe building up into the loft so you'd all have more room."

"I don't understand."

"Let me explain, Mrs Wallace. If you leave a property in your will to anyone other than a surviving spouse then it becomes subject to inheritance tax, and your daughter might have to sell it or take out a mortgage just to pay the inheritance tax. But if you – and he – *gifted it* to your daughter and remained alive for seven years thereafter, then there would be no inheritance tax, subject to certain conditions."

He didn't go into the minutiae of married couples pooling their allowances, or taper relief between three and seven years.

"Well if that's the case, then it makes no sense at all," Soraya snapped back. "Because Walter had a terminal brain tumour."

Watching Nigel, Emily was impressed by the fact that he kept his cool and didn't visibly recoil. But they both knew that they had just hit a stumbling block.

Tuesday 19th March, 2024

9

If it wasn't for his dog collar, you would never have guessed that Father Thomas Wyman was a priest. Not that he was one of these trendy "hippy" clergymen either. More "clerical" in another sense – looking like an *office clerk!* Riding the London Underground train to his Camden Town church, he could so easily have been your average office worker: mid-thirties, medium height and build, middle management. Mid-*everything* in fact!

He was only going two stops, but the 31 bus was on diversion and he thought the "Tube" would be quicker.

All the seats were taken, so he stood, hanging on to one of the handrails. As he struggled to hold on, a headline on the folded middle pages of a newspaper caught Father Thomas's attention. It brought back recent memories – memories of a confession he had heard.

Father Thomas never saw faces in the confessional. In his church, it was a traditional arrangement with a mesh screen and the chairs facing parallel to one another, so the penitent and the father confessor were side by side, with the screen between them. Of course, he knew who his regulars were. But at this busy church in this bustling area of London, it was common enough for newcomers to the area, or just plain non-regulars, to turn up here seeking forgiveness, divine grace, or perhaps just some solace and inner peace.

And when they came, their voices were heard. Everyone had their story, and in the confessional, there was no judgement, only patience and Christ's bountiful love.

When penitents spoke, they seldom uttered names, not theirs and not the names of others. It was almost invariably oblique references, like "my sister", "my neighbour", "my boss". In this way the penitents preserved not just their own anonymity but also that of those who formed part of their story or their crisis of conscience. Sheer weight of numbers made it impossible to remember most of the confessions he heard. Not that it would have been desirable if it were otherwise. Who would wish to carry around such tales of petty conflict, or extreme suffering, in their heads? *Christ* was the redeemer; the father confessor was merely the conduit.

But occasionally some parts of the narrative might resonate with the priest, making it harder to forget. And sometimes, even if the name was missing, the role might be enough to learn the identity of one of the parties involved. At least, learn it later, if not sooner.

The headline read: "Pathologist testifies in maths prof murder trial." It was impossible to read the article. The print was too small to read from where he stood. But it triggered memories that left him unnerved.

So, when he got off the train at Camden Town, he bought a copy of the paper and – too impatient to wait – he read it as he walked along to his church, narrowly avoiding bumping into people in the crowded street. But when he stepped into the road to cross diagonally to the other side, the screech of a car horn came a fraction of a second too late to avoid the impact.

10

"The cause of death was an intracranial haemorrhage, caused by the circular skull fracture over a major blood vessel, specifically the middle meningeal artery."

Blair's first witness of the second day of the trial was the pathologist, Richard Hunter, a short man of about Nigel's age who exuded studiousness and meticulous attention to detail. In his career, he'd performed over 300 post-mortem examinations, a fact that the prosecution took great pains to get across to the jury.

"And was that cause of death dependent, or independent, of the other injuries that you described?"

Dr Hunter had already outlined all the injuries to Professor Wallace, illustrating them via the Evidence Presentation System, with close-up photographs, including a ruler held against them to indicate their length in millimetres. At Hayden Blair's request, he also showed them in medium close-up, ostensibly to show them in the surrounding context, but actually to win the jury's sympathy for the victim and reduce any sympathy for the defendant.

Hayden Blair was a master showman when it came to manipulating juries, and although Dr Hunter preferred to think of himself as a consummate professional rather than a crowd-pleaser, he was quite happy to play along with the barrister's request.

"The cause of death from the blow in question was independent of any other blow. That is, it would have caused the death regardless of any other blows. But having said that, at least four of the other skull fractures would *likely* have produced a similar fatal result, either alone or in conjunction with one another, albeit over a slightly longer time frame."

Dr Hunter had examined the body at the crime scene to formally pronounce the victim dead and then carried out the post-mortem at the lab. He put the time of death, based on rigor mortis, lividity and rectal temperature, within an hour of Calvin Coffey's arrival.

Emily had pleaded with Nigel to let her cross-examine the pathologist, and after some considerable soul-searching, he decided that she was ready for her first Old Bailey cross-examination. So, as Blair took his seat, Emily rose out of hers nervously, looking down at the note she had written for herself.

"Brain tumour – no mention – end XM with."

11

Father Thomas Wyman was limping. Fortunately, the bumper had hit him on the side of the leg, rather than the front, so there was no bone damage, only bruised skin and sore muscle.

But it was not the pain in his lower leg that was driving him to distraction: it was the contents of the article. The words he had read left Father Thomas a troubled man. So troubled was he that he had phoned his bishop and asked for an immediate audience to seek advice on a delicate matter of his duties. The cardinal was busy, so Father Thomas settled for a meeting with one of his auxiliaries, the Right Reverend Christopher Deniran.

They met at the *Metropolitan Cathedral of the Precious Blood of Our Lord Jesus Christ* in the *Chapel of the Blessed Sacrament*, entering from the transepts. Beneath its barrel vaulting, Father Thomas explained his dilemma to the auxiliary.

"My dilemma stems from the inviolable sacramental seal of the confessional."

Deniran, a man of African origin who had dedicated his life to God and the Catholic Church, had expected this, based on Wyman's initial urgent request.

"Then put the case as a hypothetical, with no names or identifying details. Tell me only those elements that are necessary to explain your dilemma. If I can answer, I will. If not, I'll take the facts to His Eminence for further guidance."

"All right. First let me put the case that a priest hears a confession of a penitent who has lapsed in his religious observance but is now contemplating his own mortality and seeking to return to the Church in the hope of obtaining divine grace. The penitent confesses to an historic wrong that harmed another man grievously. The penitent was directed by his Father Confessor to tell the relevant authority the true facts of the case and to use his best endeavours to cause the wrong to be righted by telling the true facts to all interested parties – especially the party whom he had wronged."

Father Thomas paused, struggling to find the words.

"Go on," Deniran prompted.

"Sometime later, the Father Confessor reads or hears somewhere that a man – whom he believes to have been the penitent – was murdered."

12

"Dr Hunter," Emily began, "you determined in your post-mortem of Professor Wallace that altogether, a total of *eight* blows were struck with a hammer."

"*At least* eight."

"Indeed so. Therefore, would it be fair to say that the attacker would have been covered with a considerable amount of blood?"

"These weren't knife wounds that would have bled profusely. These were blunt instrument wounds to the skull. They would have produced blood spatter*ing*, but not copious amounts of flowing blood. The bleeding was largely internal."

"But if the blows were administered at close range, then this blood spatter would have been all over the attacker, would it not?"

"The attacker's *clothing*, certainly."

"And we will be hearing evidence that blood-stained workman's overalls were found at the back of the property. Did you have occasion to look at this garment and reach any conclusion as to the cause of the bloodstains?"

"I'm a forensic pathologist, not an evidence technician, but yes, I did look at the overalls. I can say that the pattern of blood spatter on the overalls was *consistent with* the wearer having attacked someone with a hammer."

Hayden Blair KC rose from his chair to address the judge.

"M'Lady, the Crown will be calling expert testimony on the source of the blood."

Even though circuit court judges are normally addressed as "Your Honour," at the Old Bailey it's always "M'Lord" or "M'Lady".

"I'm much obliged to m'learned friend," Emily replied, as Blair resumed his seat.

Turning to Dr Hunter, she asked: "But if the blows were struck to *the head*, and the hammer raised *to head-height*, then would you not also expect blood spatter onto the assailant's face or head?"

"Not necessarily. For example, if the assailant and the victim were moving, relative to one another, then the spatter – though expected in itself – might *miss* the assailant."

Hunter was doing what Nigel called "the wriggle" – refusing to acknowledge the point that the cross-examiner was putting and tailoring his answer to make it more favourable to the side that had called him. This wasn't altogether professional, but it was understandable. Hunter was used to hearing his words distorted by clever defence counsel in the past. And he could be expected to do all that was reasonably possible to stop it happening now.

But Emily had to pin him down, because no blood had been found on Calvin.

"You say 'not necessarily' but my question concerns the balance of probabilities. So let me ask again – let me, rather, *rephrase* my question. *If* the suspect *were* the assailant, would you – *on the balance of probabilities* – expect to find blood spatter on his head?"

The long pause, and then... reluctantly...

"On the balance of probabilities... yes."

In the spectators' gallery, the blonde woman who had been watching Soraya and her family on Hampstead Heath was now watching Emily with some amusement, fully aware of what was about to happen.

"One final question Dr Hunter. You testified in your evidence-in-chief that your post-mortem examination was thorough and complete."

"That is correct."

"And do you stand by that now?"

Emily was warming to this, enjoying the thrill of baiting the trap.

"Of course."

Now she went for the jugular.

"Then why didn't your post-mortem report make any mention of the fact that Walter Wallace had an inoperable brain tumour?"

"Because he didn't."

13

In the Metropolitan Cathedral, Father Thomas took a deep breath, struggling to find the strength to continue.

"Now, a man has been arrested for *another* similar murder. But this man may very well be innocent, and yet *another* person may very well be guilty. The name of that other person is not known to the Father Confessor, but may lend itself to discovery, if certain steps are taken. Such facts and particulars as I *do* know of this case came to me by way of the confessional and as such – by my understanding – they are protected by the inviolable sacramental seal."

"Oh boy," said Deniran, exhaling deeply as if exhausted by what he had heard. "We all pray that the day will never come when we're tested on the limits to the sacramental seal – especially in cases where there's a danger of an extreme miscarriage of justice. Or worse still, a danger to human life. Fortunately, these cases are rare. If a penitent is truly seeking grace, he will do as his confessor tells him."

"I think he may have *started* to act on my counsel, and *that* might have set in motion a chain of events."

"Whatever may have caused it, you are right in your understanding. The sacramental seal *is* inviolable; therefore it is absolutely forbidden for a confessor to betray, *in any way*, a penitent, whether in words or in any manner and for any reason."

"Without exception?"

"I'll put it to His Eminence. But in the meantime, I can only refer you to paragraph 1467 of the Catechism: 'Given the delicacy and greatness of this ministry and the respect due to persons, the Church declares that every priest who hears confessions is bound under very severe penalties to keep absolute secrecy regarding the sins that his penitents have confessed to him. He can make no use of knowledge that confession gives him about penitents' lives.'"

To Father Thomas, this felt like a knife twisting in his gut.

"I don't know if the defendant is innocent. But what am I to do *if he is convicted?* What am I to do to make sure that no miscarriage of justice takes place?"

"As a Father Confessor, you owe a duty of secrecy to the penitent. You may have a general duty to others, but not at the expense of your primary duty to the penitent. If you can find a way to protect the innocent or hold the guilty to account – *without disclosing, in any way, what the penitent told you* – then it is a laudable act to do so. Indeed, you are *morally bound* to do so. But the sacramental seal remains inviolable. There are no exceptions."

14

"What just happened in there?"

Emily was shaking from the confusion and humiliation of the courtroom debacle. They were in the robing room, and while Nigel was putting away his robe in his locker, Emily was sitting on a chair by a table, barely able to move.

"These things happen, Emily. The trick is to take it philosophically."

"*Philosophically?* I've just been made to look a complete fool in open court, for fuck's sake!"

Nigel reached out towards her, as if about to physically comfort her. He stopped himself just in time.

"It's not a complete disaster. For a start--"

"*Like fuck it isn't!* I attacked a prosecution witness, and he demolished us! Demolished *me!*"

"Yes, but in the process we exposed a false statement by another prosecution witness."

"I don't see how..."

And then... she *did*. She remembered what Soraya had said.

"*Walter had a terminal brain tumour.*"

"Soraya?" Emily whispered, as if the word alone explained everything.

"Go on," said Nigel encouragingly, prompting her to follow through.

"She must have been lying."

"If it was a lie, it would have been a very stupid one."

Emily took a moment to think about it.

"You think her husband lied to *her?*"

"It's a possibility."

"Then all the time he said he was having treatment he was doing something else? Like what? An affair?"

Nigel pondered this.

"He wouldn't be the first man in his seventies to have an

extra-marital affair."

"There's a 'but' in your tone."

"The *but* is that if he told her he was going to the Royal Free Hospital for treatment, would he have gone alone? Would she have *let* him go alone?"

Emily thought about it again.

"Maybe she drove him to the hospital and dropped him off. Then he went in but then slipped out for a quickie with his bit on the side."

"I don't think she would have just dropped him off there. I think she would have gone in with him. Waited for him in the waiting room or maybe the cafeteria. If he *was* having an affair, it would have been an arse-backwards way of going about it."

"Maybe he was shagging a nurse."

"You're *still* over-egging the pudding, Emily."

"So what do *you* think?"

"I haven't a clue. That's what we need to find out."

"But how? We can hardly ask a dead man."

15

"There was something of a bombshell surprise in the trial of Calvin Coffey for the murder of Walter Wallace, the maths professor found beaten to death in his home in North London last September. Here's our reporter Robert Donnoly for the details."

The picture on the screen changed from the news studio to the outside of the Old Bailey. And standing in front of the building was a youngish, eager-looking reporter.

"Yes, Janet. As you said, a bombshell revelation in court this morning. It all started yesterday when Soraya Wallace, the victim's widow, testified about finding her husband's body and disputing the defence suggestion that he had been planning on having a loft conversion done on their marital home.

"Calvin Coffey, the defendant, had said in his police interview, that was read out in court, that his presence at Professor Wallace's house was to give a quote for a loft conversion that the professor had requested. That was when we had the first glimpse of a potential clash of testimonies, because Soraya Wallace claimed, under cross-examination, that her late husband had no plans to do any building work on the house and was suffering from an inoperable brain tumour."

The woman in the house in Bournemouth was sitting tensely in her living room, her eyes transfixed on the television screen as Donnoly became animated while delivering his report.

"Then, this morning, pathologist Richard Hunter testified in considerable and sometimes *gruesome* detail about the many hammer blows struck against the late Professor Wallace's head. It was at that point that the fireworks really began. Cross-examined by Emily du Lac, whom we are given to understand is actually Nigel Farringdon's *law pupil*, Dr Hunter was asked about the brain tumour, which he hadn't mentioned in his testimony yesterday. The pathologist responded by denying that there was one or even that there had been.

"This of course clashed with the testimony that Soraya Wallace had given yesterday, claiming that her late husband had been receiving palliative care for his condition at the Royal Free Hospital."

The woman watching the television screen felt herself sliding into an almost catatonic state. As the last of her strength ebbed away, she pressed the button on the remote, cutting off the sound and wiping the television screen.

16

When they returned to the courtroom after lunch, Nigel entered a motion to subpoena the late Professor Wallace's medical records. Hayden Blair knew that there was nothing to be gained by opposing the motion. The matter had to be resolved one way or the other, so he supported the motion. His one caveat was that the trial should be allowed to continue in the meantime. He had other witnesses available to testify, and if the witnesses weren't called promptly, the whole case management and court schedule would be thrown out of whack.

This time it was Nigel who was forced to agree and bow to the inevitable, so he informed the court that he was "ready for m'learned friend to call his next witness," and with those words, the game went on.

A series of witnesses were then called to establish chain of custody over the DNA samples from the hammer, which the pathologist had previously identified as the murder weapon, and the various reference samples that were to be used in the case for the purpose of incriminating the suspect and eliminating others.

The SOCO who had placed the hammer in an evidence bag at the crime testified to confirm his actions and identify his signature on the bag's label on which he had also recorded the date and time. The assistant at the pathology lab who had taken three reference samples from Wallace's cadaver testified to that. The police specialists who had taken DNA reference samples from Calvin, Soraya, Huette and the children, also testified, confirming their actions.

Then, gathering it all together, the Crown's next witness was Oliver Steele, the lab expert who had run the DNA analysis, a short, pudgy man who seemed to have given up any fight he might have had against belly flab. He was dressed casually, and his moustache looked more than a little unkempt. Emily looked at him, weighing up his likely impact on the jury. If they were to judge him by his looks – as juries sometimes do – he would carry considerably less weight than he carried on his short frame. But when he spoke, he had an air of authority that belied his lack of any striking positive features.

The first thing he did, in his evidence-in-chief, was describe how he had opened the bag, and taken several swabs of blood from the metal head of the hammer as well as swabs from the wooden handle. All these swabs were then compared to reference samples from Professor Wallace and Calvin Coffey.

Although DNA was now universally accepted in the courts and legal systems of virtually all developed countries, certain basics had to be explained to the jury every time. So Hayden Blair, who had worked with Steele before, invited the expert to explain how DNA testing works. In response, Steele talked and flipped between slides, via the Evidence Presentation System, to show the jury what he was describing.

"There are certain particular sequences of DNA that vary from one individual to another more than the rest of the DNA. It's these particular sequences of DNA that we use to catch the bad guys."

This little snippet of homespun phraseology wasn't particularly well-liked by judges, and it sometimes earned a judicial reprimand. But in this case, it passed under the radar without comment.

"Could you explain how this is done?"

Blair and Steele were now working together like a well-oiled machine.

"We look for short sequences of DNA that are repeated several times in a row at particular locations. These are known as Short Tandem Repeats or STRs. Let's take a look at an example."

Steele tapped on the trackpad to show the next chart.

"This one happens to be a classic example."

A smile came to the faces of some of the jurors when they saw a sequence that could have been a transcription of someone coughing.

G-A-T-A G-A-T-A G-A-T-A G-A-T-A G-A-T-A G-A-T-A

"This is a very famous sequence at a location – or locus, as we say. We refer to this locus as D7S280. It is sometimes used to teach how forensic DNA testing works. In this example, we see the sequence G-A-T-A" – he spelled it out letter by letter – "repeated six times."

He paused for a couple of seconds.

"A sequence of this kind is called an allele. At any given locus you have a pair of alleles that might be either the same or different. That's because we get half our DNA from one parent and half from the other. So a person might have that sequence six times in one allele and eight times at the other. Or they might have identical sequences at both."

"And how do these differences distinguish people?"

"Well different people have *different numbers* of repetitions of *that particular* sequence, GATA, at *that* locus. Indeed, in just that one particular locus – D7S280 – the number of variations of the sequence can vary between six and fifteen repetitions."

Now Hayden Blair performed his next party trick: playing the stubborn sceptic.

"But surely between six and fifteen means a mere... er... (he pretended to do the maths) *ten* possibilities, does it not?"

"Yes indeed," Oliver Steele confirmed.

"So then, in a world of eight billion people, there must be millions of people who match that sequence?"

"Yes indeed. But we don't just look at one locus. We currently look at *thirteen different locations on the DNA sequence*. And we could look at even more. At any *one* locus, the number of Short Tandem Repeats may be the same for many people. But once you start looking at all thirteen loci – all of which are *independent* of one another – then the likelihood of two people having the same DNA is much smaller by far."

"Now could you explain how you match or distinguish DNA?"

"We compare the *crime-scene sample* – in this case the handle of the hammer – to the reference samples of *both the victim and the suspect*. If we find an allele in the *crime-scene* sample that matches the number of repetitions in the *suspect's* reference sample, then we call that an *inclusion*. Conversely, if we find even *one* allele in the crime scene sample that didn't come from the suspect *or the victim*, then that's an *exclusion* and the suspect is thereby eliminated."

"But let me ask you this," Blair followed up. "What if it's the other way round? What if there's an allele in the *suspect's reference* sample that isn't found in the *crime-scene sample*?"

"That's *not* an exclusion because whereas a reference sample is a *complete* sample of the person's DNA, the crime scene sample can easily be *incomplete*. In other words, there may not be enough good DNA in the crime scene sample. That's actually quite normal. DNA can be degraded. The process for extracting it may fail to extract everything. There's even a name for it: allele dropout."

"But doesn't that make the results uncertain? Call them into question?"

"It's all about probabilities. We take not one, but *thirteen different loci* on the DNA sequence. If we find, firstly, no *exclusions*, and secondly, *enough inclusions to make the likelihood of two randomly selected people having the same inclusions infinitesimal*, then we may safely conclude that the DNA came from the suspect. Unless of course the suspect and the victim had similar DNA and the inclusions could come from either."

"Okay could you tell us how you would go about identifying where particular DNA in this case came from – or rather, from whom?"

Steele flipped to another slide showing a grid of the 13 loci and the number of short tandem repeats at those loci in the crime-scene sample and the reference samples of Professor Wallace and Calvin Coffey. In the row marked "Crime scene – hammer handle", some of the cells were empty.

"The results showed that all the blood on the *head* of the hammer came from Wallace, none from Coffey and none from any other contributor."

"So the blood came from Professor Wallace."

"Yes."

Another slide came up on the Evidence Presentation System.

"Can you tell us what this is?"

"Yes, this shows a comparison between the skin secretion DNA on the handle of the hammer and the reference samples from Professor Wallace and the accused. In this case we can see eight inclusions of the accused's DNA for the eight that we found on the handle. This means that it was his DNA. No exclusions."

Again, he didn't quantify it. The probability was astronomical, but it would be more effective if it came out under cross-examination. The effect would be devastating.

"Thank you. No further questions."

Hayden Blair KC sat down.

17

Restlessness had driven Ruth Morrison to the Upper Gardens, a wilder, more rugged and overgrown terrain than the manicured, short-trimmed grass of the Lower Gardens or the tidy but longer grass of the Central Gardens. Unlike the Lower Gardens, which practically bordered on the seashore, the crisp Bournemouth air carried the fresh smell of the trees and grass after a thunderstorm, rather than the salty sea air. The walk was intended to offer her solace – a reprieve from the doubts and fears in her mind since the latest news report.

Walter Wallace – Professor Wallace – bludgeoned to death in his London home.

Such an implausible coincidence. But WAS it a coincidence? It has to be. And yet…

The more that emerged in the trial, the less likely that it was *merely* a coincidence.

The serenity of the surroundings did little to calm her. Through a tangled mess of questions, her heart raced, assailed by "what ifs" and "supposings". She had hoped the police would see the connection when she phoned them, that they would reinvigorate the stalled investigation into Raymond's death and link it up with Walter's. But their brusque dismissal stung her, leaving her feeling more isolated than ever.

As she looked around now, she realised that she had walked aimlessly, barely noticing the vibrant green of the gardens. Families laughed around her, but their sound was muted and muffled by her fears and doubts. The sound of children wafted towards her from between the nearby trees. It reminded her that she soon had to pick up little Liam from the carer who looked after him during the day, so she could work from home without distractions.

She had sought solace here before, in the days following Raymond's death. But today, the gardens provided no comfort, only a backdrop to the chaos raging inside her. Reaching a secluded bench by the gently babbling River Bourne – though it was really more of a brook than a river – Ruth sank down. She watched the water flow, aimless and constant, and wished she could follow it into the sea and be carried away somewhere pleasant and tranquil.

Her hand trembled as she reached into her pocket, retrieving her mobile phone. She stared at it, debating. Finally, with a resigned sigh, she dialled the familiar number, her heart hitching as the dial tone echoed in her ear.

"Hi Ruth."

The voice on the other end was warm, a stark contrast to the chill that had taken root in Ruth's bones.

"Hi Petula," Ruth's voice was a strained whisper.

Petula's tone shifted immediately, concern lacing her words. "Ruth, darling, what's wrong? You sound terrible."

Ruth hesitated, the weight of her fears pressing down on her.

"It's... It's about Raymond. I watched the news today, about the murder trial... the maths professor... Walter Wallace. It's just so similar, Petula. And the police... they won't listen. They say there's no connection."

18

Emily watched tensely as Nigel rose from his seat to cross-examine Oliver Steele. Calvin had admitted to picking up the hammer, so it would be dangerous to try shaking Steele too hard. That would merely make his testimony look more important than it was.

"Mr Steele, you stated that there were no exclusions on the handle of the hammer."

"Yes."

"Meaning that no alleles were found matching third parties."

"Yes."

"Also, none matching the deceased, Professor Wallace?"

He said this in a deliberately tentative way, as if he were unsure and wanted to hear it from the expert.

"There *were* three that *also* matched Wallace. But the other five were exclusions of Wallace."

"Is there any reason to preclude the possibility that some of those alleles attributed to Calvin Coffey could have come from an unknown third party?"

"Not in my opinion."

"Now there is something called noise, I believe: contamination of a crime scene DNA sample that comes about from the process of increasing the DNA sample in the lab to make it workable for test and comparison purposes."

"Yes, but these were not noise."

"You mean the eight that were attributed to the defendant?"

"Yes."

"But were there any *other* alleles, on the handle of the hammer, that you considered to be noise?"

"Yes."

There was a slight strain in Steele's tone now.

"Let's take a look at the *graph* of your comparison, not just the printed numbers. So that we can see that noise for ourselves."

Oliver Steele was starting to look a bit uncomfortable as Nigel brought up the relevant slide on the screen.

What's he doing? Emily wondered, wary of Nigel walking into another trap.

"And could you point out the…"

Nigel peered at the graph.

"Could you point out the three highest peaks of those alleles that you have dismissed as noise?"

Steele was squirming as he did so, because all of those peaks were above a certain horizontal line that appeared on the graph.

"What is that horizontal line, Mr Steele?"

Steele's voice was reduced to a hoarse whisper as he replied: "It's the noise threshold."

"But those peaks that we've just looked at are *above* the noise threshold? So how could they possibly be noise?"

"First, I need to explain that because it's so hard to get touch contact DNA, we have to set the sensitivity of the equipment that measures the strength of the samples towards the *higher* end of the scale in order to get meaningful results. But in the process, we amplify the noise."

"And so how do you get rid of that amplified noise?"

"By manual elimination… by an expert."

"So you mean an expert looks at the graph and *decides* that those alleles are noise and can therefore be dismissed."

"Yes."

"And in this case the *expert* was… yourself?"

"Yes."

"Okay, could I ask you now to point out the four *weakest* out of the eight alleles that you *identified as inclusions*?"

He was reluctant. He was *more than* reluctant. But he was trapped. There was nowhere to run. Oliver Steele highlighted the four weakest alleles that he had attributed to the defendant.

Nigel had chosen the number four for a reason, and everyone in the courtroom could now see why, including the jurors.

"But aren't these four alleles – that you claimed as *inclusions* – in fact at a *lower level of intensity* than the three highest of those alleles that you *excluded as noise*?"

On the screen, Nigel used a colour highlighter to illustrate how the peaks of the three so-called "noise" alleles, as Steele had called them, were sticking their heads out above the four that matched Calvin.

"See!"

"I still believe that those four are genuine inclusions."

"Oh, you *believe*, do you?"

The tone was now overtly sarcastic. Nigel pressed on.

"Well, what if we, say, apply your own noise threshold *consistently* and treat these four so-called inclusions as noise, in the same way that you yourself treated those three other peaks as noise?"

"I believe it was Ralph Waldo Emerson who said that consistency is the hobgoblin of little minds."

He was trying to be clever, but on this occasion, he had outsmarted himself.

"He actually said 'A *foolish* consistency is the hobgoblin of little minds.' But he meant that a wise man is ready to *reconsider* his beliefs, not that a wise man can *hold* contradictory beliefs at the same time. That would be what George Orwell called *doublethink*."

Emily scribbled a quick note to Nigel. It read: "Now you're showing off!" It brought a smile to Nigel's face – a smile which only added to Steele's fear of what was coming next.

"Returning to my question then," Nigel pressed on, "we would get not *eight* inclusions for the defendant's DNA, but only *four*, w*ouldn't we*? And that would substantially reduce the likelihood that the DNA uniquely identifies the defendant?"

"Yes, but like I said, I don't think we should do that."

"All right," Nigel said, trying to sound accommodating, "let's try it the *other* way. Let's *keep* those four alleles as inclusions and *not* treat them as noise. But in that case, we must then count the three high peaks, instead of blithely dismissing them as noise. And if we don't get inclusions and don't treat them as noise, what do we get then?"

"I don't know."

The desperation in Steele's voice almost made Emily feel sorry for him.

"Oh yes you do. You know *exactly* what we get. We get three alleles, on the handle of the hammer, that do *not* belong to the defendant or the deceased. In other words, *three exclusions!* Three alleles in the crime-scene sample indicating that the hammer was handled by a person or persons *unknown*."

"Yes, but that wouldn't completely exonerate the defendant. It *could* mean that the hammer was handled by another person *in addition* to the defendant."

Nigel half-turned to the jury and repeated Oliver Steele's words, slowly.

"The hammer was handled by another person *in addition* to the defendant."

Then he turned back to the witness.

"*Thank you*, Mr Steele. No further questions."

Nigel sat down to Emily's unabashed, smirking delight. She had just watched a master at work and could think of only two words to describe it: *Job done*.

In the spectators' gallery, Father Thomas looked on, equally impressed and somewhat relieved.

19

"Ruth, listen to me." Petula's voice was firm, commanding, even through the phone. "We need to meet. Can you come in to London tomorrow?"

Ruth glanced around, the paranoia that had been her constant companion whispering that eyes were on her even now. "I... Yes. But Petula, the police said –"

"Forget what the police said," Petula interrupted, a rare edge to her voice. "This is important, Ruth. More important than you know. But you mustn't tell anyone about this, understand? Not where you're going, not who you're seeing."

A shiver ran down Ruth's spine, not from the cold but from the gravity in Petula's tone. "I understand," she murmured, a mix of fear and trust battling within her.

"Good. I'll text you the place and time. Be careful, Ruth. We're going to get to the bottom of this, I promise you."

The line went dead, leaving Ruth with a tense feeling of anticipation mixed with dread. She pocketed her phone, her gaze lingering on the flowing water. Petula's words had thrown her a lifeline, but her feelings were tinged with fear. She knew that Raymond had been a troubled man before he died. But it wasn't because of his health; it was because of something that had happened long ago.

Wednesday 20th March, 2024

20

Emily had arrived at St Jude's before 8.00 a.m. and by the time the other three pupils had drifted in, she had spent almost an hour sitting at the big table in the open plan office, comparing Soraya's statement with Huette's, looking for even the slightest discrepancies.

One of the things she'd learned about the practice of law was that everything needed to be checked and double-checked. It was all too easy to overlook a single word or phrase – a small thing that could make a big difference. And in many cases, those significant words looked quite innocuous, at first glance.

Just then her phone rang. It was Nigel. Even when they were both in the office, he used his mobile and called hers directly. It made sense really. He might be on the move between rooms, and she might not be at her desk.

"Yes, Bwana," she answered.

"Don't be cheeky."

Like... when was I ever anything else?

"Has it arrived?" she asked, brushing off the reprimand.

"Yes. And I think you might like to see it."

"What does it say?"

"Why don't you haul your proverbial up here and find out?"

He nearly said "lazy ass" or even "sexy ass", but either would have been crossing a red line. As it was, their occasionally flirtatious banter was more than a little risqué.

For Emily, the curiosity was unbearable. So, notebook and pen in hand, she swept out of the open-plan office, where she sat with the secretaries, clerks and the other three pupils, and made her way to Nigel's office, one flight up.

In fact, Emily was pretty sure she knew what the answer would be, as she walked briskly down the corridor – what it *had to be*. Soraya Wallace had been misled by a cheating husband who was playing some sort of devious game with her. The only alternative was that an experienced pathologist had overlooked something as major as a brain tumour.

She took the stairs two at a time, with a sense of growing anticipation and excitement, and walked along the final stretch of corridor to Nigel's. Entering without knocking, she sat down opposite Nigel. And that's when she got the feeling that something was wrong. As he tapped the desk with his index finger, Nigel's unflappable demeanour was not quite as composed as usual. Emily mirrored his concern as her eyes locked onto the stack of printouts.

"According to these," Nigel began, his voice steady – by conscious effort – "Professor Wallace *was* undergoing palliative treatment for a terminal brain tumour."

21

The coffee shop was a stark contrast to the bustling London street outside. Newly reopened after refurbishment, it was now brighter and more airy, albeit at the price of the long double-sided table with USB ports, that sat centre stage, where young people used to sit with their laptops for hours on end. The big table had been replaced by a long thin bar where customers could still sit with their laptops, but only on one side. Even the wood of the chairs and table legs was brighter, with light pine replacing dark walnut to make for a more reflective, light-drenched ambience.

In other respects, the café had become less comfortable for lingering. But it still catered to the same clientele. The aroma of freshly ground coffee beans and the soft murmur of hushed conversations created a cocoon of tranquillity. Petula had chosen this place for its anonymity, a spot where she and Ruth could blend into the background, their thoughts and muted conversation their only company.

Petula arrived with a flurry of scarves and an infectious smile. Their friendship had been forged in the days following Raymond's death. Petula was a bereavement counsellor whom Ruth had found via a notice on the board at the funeral parlour. They had several sessions in Ruth's home and had remained friends ever since.

As they settled into the crisp new seats with their hot drinks – tea for Ruth, coffee for Petula – Ruth's hands trembled slightly, betraying her inner turmoil. Petula reached across the table, her touch reassuring. "Ruth, darling, talk to me. You look like you've seen a ghost."

Ruth sighed, her eyes meeting Petula's.

"I told you," she began, her voice barely above a whisper. "It's Raymond and the professor... the similarities. Petula, they're uncanny."

"But you knew that before, honey. Why the panic now?"

"It's not just the way they were murdered. It's the fact that they both had brain tumours. When I heard that report from the trial about Wallace having one too, it was like... I don't know. I mean, like... you couldn't make it up."

"Now hold on. Slow down a minute, Ruth. According to what I read on the Internet, the professor's wife *thought* he had a brain tumour, but then the pathologist came back and said he didn't. So it's not the same as in Raymond's case, right?"

"Yes, but that's what's been bothering me. I saw the pathologist's report after... after Raymond was killed. And I don't remember any mention of the tumour there either."

Petula inclined her head, thinking about this.

"Well, did you check? I mean did you go back and –"

"I can't find it."

"What do you mean you –"

"I mean I lost it. Or maybe I threw it away."

"You think someone stole it?"

"No of course not. I mean it's probably somewhere. Or maybe I *did* throw it out. I don't know. But I can't find it."

"Do you remember who the pathologist was?"

"No I don't."

"Could it have been –"

"It wasn't the one at the Old Bailey. I know that. I mean I'd've remembered if it was."

"But you're sure it didn't mention the tumour."

"Yes – I mean no. I'm not sure of anything."

Petula's mind raced, the pieces falling into place with a clarity that was almost frightening.

"Ruth, this is important. You need to see that report again. There could be something, a detail, anything that was overlooked or... or deliberately omitted."

The suggestion of deliberate omission was like a cold splash of water, jolting Ruth from her reverie of despair. She had been a passive spectator in the aftermath of Raymond's death, leaving the investigation to the professionals. But Petula's words ignited a spark, a flicker of resolve and determination in the darkness.

"I've tried," Ruth admitted, her frustration evident. "I looked everywhere for my copy of the report, but it's gone. I can't find it anywhere."

Petula's response was immediate, her voice laced with determination. "Then you must ask for another copy. Demand it, Ruth. As Raymond's widow, you have every right to see it. And if necessary, you should speak to the pathologist directly, ask him about the discrepancies, the tumour... everything."

The very thought of confronting the pathologist, of stepping back into the maelstrom of questions and accusations, filled Ruth with dread. Yet, there was a part of her, perhaps the part that had survived the unimaginable, that knew Petula was right.

"You're stronger than you know, Ruth," Petula said softly, her hand squeezing Ruth's. "And you're entitled to some straight answers."

The weight of the decision lay heavy on Ruth's shoulders as they parted ways that afternoon. The London streets seemed to slow around her, each step towards the tube station a step closer to a decision she knew she could no longer avoid.

The journey back to Bournemouth was a blur, the landscape passing by her window a reflection of the turmoil within. By the time the familiar sights of Bournemouth came into view, Ruth had made her decision. She would confront the past and talk to the pathologist.

Then she remembered something from the meeting with Petula. She had forgotten to ask her at the time about an object she had seen in Petula's open shoulder bag. It seemed too big for opera glasses. But she couldn't think of *any* reason why Petula would carry a pair of binoculars.

22

"Professor Wallace *was* undergoing palliative treatment for a terminal brain tumour."

The words hit Emily like an explosion. As if to underscore the point, Nigel gestured towards the MRI scans attached to the records.

"I didn't know you could read brain scans, Nige."

He nodded tolerantly.

"I can read the accompanying reports."

Emily weighed it up.

"If Wallace was terminally ill, it means he was telling the truth to Soraya."

"And *she* was telling the truth in court."

"And *that* means we can rule out adultery as the motive behind his murder."

"Let's put that in proportion, Emily. It means we have no *specific* reason to believe that it *was*. But it also means that Richard Hunter was mistaken – *hugely* mistaken. Which in turn means that at least we can discredit him about the time of death."

"How could an experienced pathologist like Hunter screw up like that?"

"Overwork? Professional stubbornness? Take your pick."

"So what do we do now? Recall Hunter?"

"I don't think Braham will let us. Hunter already testified in unequivocal terms. We'll have to break the tie with a second postmortem."

"A review of the P.M. material? Or a full-blown exhumation?"

"A review will hardly tell us anything. If they removed brains from two cadavers on the same day, and got them mixed up..."

Emily gave this some thought.

"Hold on a minute. If they got two brains mixed up, then they would probably have put the wrong one back inside Wallace when they released his body for burial."

"That can be resolved by DNA."

"I wouldn't put it past Blair to object on faux humanitarian grounds or compassion for Soraya."

"Oh, he probably will. That's why I sent Hunter's pathology scans to the consultant at the Royal Free. If he tells us they're different people, then they'll have to do a second post-mortem."

"Did you tell him it was urgent?"

"I did. But he's a busy man. The other thing Blair might try is arguing that we should have applied for a second post-mortem within twenty-eight days."

Emily perked up at this.

"Ah, I'm glad you mentioned that, 'cause I think I've come up with grounds for a counter-argument: material non-disclosure."

"Specifically?"

"I was looking at Soraya's original witness statement just now and she didn't say anything about her husband having a brain tumour. The first time she mentioned it, was in court."

"Excellent."

Emily remembered something.

"Could I…"

She wanted so badly to ask.

"Could you… what?"

He could see the youthful enthusiasm in her eyes.

"Well, I'd like to make up for what happened with the pathologist, in cross-examination."

"And?"

He wasn't going to make it easy. She had to be hungry for it.

"Well, I was thinking that maybe *I* could argue before Braham. I mean I spotted the conflict of testimonies– *both* on the *prosecution* side. I spotted the material non-disclosure. We've got medical records that contradict the pathologist on a major issue. *And* a monumental failure of disclosure obligations. It's a slam dunk."

"I thought that wasn't allowed in netball."

Nigel was giving her his big brother smile.

"I played basketball too."

She was referring to her sporting activities at the North London Collegiate.

"You'll have to brush up on the Coroners and Justice Act."

"I will."

"And I'll test you."

"I'll be prepared."

"Okay, just don't get too cocky."

She scrunched up a sheet of paper and threw it over the desk into the bin next to him, like a basketball shot.

"I won't."

Just then, the phone rang. Nigel answered.

"Yes?... Oh, put him through."

Emily heard a muffled voice on the other end of the line. She managed to pick out a word here and there but didn't quite get the gist of it. What she *did* get, however, was the reaction on Nigel's face.

When he put the phone down, he looked shell-shocked.

"What is it? asked Emily, on the edge of her seat."

"That was Doctor Fletcher, from the Royal Free. He says it's a different brain."

23

"The medical records and brain scans from the Royal Free Hospital clearly show that Walter Wallace *was* suffering from an inoperable brain tumour."

Although there was no jury in the courtroom, Emily was aware that many eyes were upon her in a major case in which a serious point of law was being argued. And she was still only a law pupil.

"The need to resolve the clear and fundamental clash of factual claims as between the pathologist, Dr Richard Hunter and the hospital consultant, Dr Simon Fletcher, M'Lady, is the most compelling reason for granting an exhumation order.

"Regarding the normal twenty-eight-day grace period for requesting a second post-mortem, I would remind the court that at the time of trial preparation and case management, there had been *no disclosure* of any claim by *any* prosecution witness that the deceased was suffering from a brain tumour. The first inkling the defence had regarding the tumour was an off-the-cuff remark by Soraya Wallace from the witness box.

"Turning now, M'Lady, to Dr Hunter's evidence. The defence concedes that the pathologist removed the brain from Walter Wallace's cadaver. We concede also that in addition to some surgical dissection, he conducted a magnetic resonance imaging scan on a brain at some point, and that he *believed* in good faith that said brain was the one he had removed from Walter Wallace's cadaver.

"However, we gave Dr Fletcher sight of the post-mortem report, including the brain scan, and he compared it to his own ante mortem scans of Professor Wallace's brain. His *unequivocal* conclusion was that the brain that was scanned by Dr Hunter was *not* that of Walter Wallace. The only alternative is that the man being treated at the Royal Free, under the *name* of Walter Wallace, was an imposter.

"We submit that this clear contradiction, as between the claims of Doctors Hunter and Fletcher, makes it impossible to determine who is right and who is wrong, without conducting a second post-mortem comprising, specifically, an exhumation of Professor Wallace's body *and* a second scan of the brain. We also need a DNA analysis of tissue from the brain to confirm that the *right brain was placed back into Professor Wallace's body before burial.*"

Nigel gave Emily an approving nod as she sat down. Judge Braham looked over at Hayden Blair who was making a show of shuffling his notes.

"Mr Blair?" the judge intoned.

"Thank you M'Lady. Firstly, I would point out that Dr Hunter is one of the most eminent pathologists in the country, if not the world."

"But Dr Fletcher is no *less* eminent in *his* field, Mr Blair," said Braham, "and as counsel for the defence has pointed out, we *do* have a major discrepancy on our hands."

"Indeed so, M'Lady, and I cannot give any definitive answer to that question. But perhaps it might be helpful if instead of an exhumation, we simply give the scans that Dr Fletcher took to Dr Hunter. It may be, that notwithstanding Dr Hunter's initial view that the deceased never had a brain tumour in the first place, and Dr Fletcher's view that he had one that was incurable, there was a tumour that underwent some kind of spontaneous remission."

Judge Braham was having none of it.

"I see nothing to be gained by that, Mr Blair. Dr Fletcher was quite unequivocal that the scans taken by the pathologist were *not* those of Walter Wallace. Either Dr Hunter agrees with Dr Fletcher that the two scans are from *different people*, or he believes that it's the *same* brain, but holds that Fletcher's opinion regarding the tumour to be wrong. Either way we need to resolve the matter once and for all."

"But aside from that, I would still urge Your Ladyship to consider the immense distress and psychological trauma that an exhumation would have on Professor Wallace's widow."

As if to underscore the point, Blair looked over again at Soraya.

"But I *want* to know!" Soraya blurted out.

It was quite out of order for her to address the court without being asked. And some judges would have been angry at the outburst. But Judge Braham well understood the pain and suffering of a widow.

"To be clear, Mrs Wallace, what is your preference on this matter?"

"I want the truth. I want to be sure." Soraya spoke in a strong voice, without tears. "If there was a mistake in Dr Fletcher's diagnosis, I want to know it. And if the *pathologist* was wrong, I want to *know* that too."

The judge turned to Blair.

"I think in view of that statement, the last of your objections falls away, wouldn't you agree Mr Blair?"

"I do," said Blair, in the tone of a reluctant groom at a shotgun wedding.

"So I will direct the coroner to exhume Professor Wallace's remains at the earliest possible date and conduct a new brain scan and a DNA comparison of tissue from the brain to confirm that it was the brain of Professor Wallace."

Blair realised that if the results showed that the brains *had* been mixed up, then his case would collapse. Technically, he'd have to seek fresh instructions from the CPS. But in practice this trial would be over.

However, Judge Braham wasn't quite finished.

"In the meantime, I am bound to indicate that I am mindful to halt the current proceedings and discharge the jury."

Nigel was on his feet.

"M'Lady, if the proceedings are to be halted and a new trial ordered, I would ask the court to consider granting bail, as we do not know when the trial is likely to be resumed in the face of the current backlog."

"I won't consider bail, Mr Farringdon, notwithstanding the exceptional circumstances. The charge is murder and the client's background is virtually unknown."

"In that case, may I suggest that instead of a stay of proceedings and jury discharge, we simply adjourn the trial until we get the results of the second post-mortem."

Blair, who had been sitting there looking somewhat morose, snapped out of it and reverted to his combative stance.

"M'Lady, could *I* in that case suggest that if m'learned friend is concerned about delays, while his client languishes in gaol, we do *not* delay the proceedings any further. We have already fallen behind schedule, as a result of previous delays which – I concede – were not the fault of the defence. But all the more reason to avoid *further* delays. Aside from the impact on the defendant, another delay would cause considerable inconvenience to the jury and would likely be disruptive of case management and the scheduling of *other* court proceedings at a time when we are still recovering from the impact of Covid. I suggest therefore that we continue this case in the meantime, while we await the results of the second post-mortem."

He took his seat, newly invigorated, with a bold and confident look on his face. Mary Braham looked over at Nigel.

"May I suggest a compromise, Mr Farringdon? We will continue until close of business today and then adjourn until Friday morning, by which time we should have the results."

"Very well, M'Lady," Nigel replied reluctantly. "But could I, in that case, request that we adjourn until this afternoon so that I may explain what's going on to my client?"

Judge Braham looked over at the wall clock to check the time.

"I have several mention hearings in the queue, so I think we can manage that, Mr Farringdon."

24

"How are you holding up?"

That was Emily. Neither being born into privilege, nor seeing the effects of crime on the victims, could cause her to lose her natural compassion for the man in the dock. Even if they were guilty as hell – and more often than not, they were – they usually had a backstory that mellowed their culpability.

"Okay," said Calvin, managing what might almost have passed for a smile.

"No one giving you any hassle?"

"One of the old lags told me they had a mock trial before I even got here, to decide whether I was the victim of a stitch-up or the spawn of Satan. They opted for the former."

It was a four-way meeting in the holding cell: Emily, Nigel, Philip Solomon and Calvin Coffey himself. Coffey seemed somewhat downbeat, but relaxed. However, Emily knew that it was better not to read too much into this. The first two weeks in prison for the first-time offender (or suspect) are the worst. Being "banged up" is an inherently frightening experience for a newcomer. But after two weeks, they start to make friends – with a few exceptions.

"Look, we've got a lot of ground to cover," said Nigel, "so we need to get on with this."

Everyone nodded their agreement. Nigel proceeded to explain in detail how the issue of the brain tumour impacted the case, from the point of view of both the *time* and the *cause* of death. Making it clear that their best hope was if it was the pathologist who was wrong.

"But what if the doctors who were treating Wallace were wrong?" asked Calvin tensely. "I mean what if there *was no tumour*?"

Nigel explained that if that were so, then he would demand an investigation into how such a mistake could have come about. It wouldn't necessarily help the defence, but it would highlight human fallibility in general and muddy the waters.

Calvin appeared to have something else on his mind.

"Listen, I was remanded on the twenty-sixth of September, and we're coming up to the twenty sixth of March. Don't they have to let me go because of the Custody Time Limit?"

Nigel shook his head.

"The CTL only applies until the jury is sworn in."

"All right, but in that case, what if you argue that the prosecution case is so tainted by the contradictory evidence that the case can't proceed, surely?"

"There's no way they'll throw the case out. The most we can hope for is that they'll discharge the jury and restart the trial. And that might not even be the best thing for our case. Better to keep the jury and play on their damaged faith in medical science."

"But if they restart the trial, doesn't that have some effect on the CTL?"

"Unfortunately not. The rule is that once a trial on indictment has commenced, the CTL stops. Even if the trial has to be stopped and the jury discharged and a retrial ordered, the CTL remains stopped. It doesn't apply either to the trial period itself or to the period between a stopped trial and a retrial."

"So they can keep me banged up as long as they like?"

He sounded like a man who had lost all hope.

"Not 'as long as they like.' But until the proceedings are completed. Unfortunately there's no statutory limit on how long the proceedings can take. The Home Office guidance, based on a leading case called *Leeds and Wardle*, holds that in cases where a trial is halted and restarted with a new jury, the judge should be vigilant to protect the interests of the defendant, by fixing a speedy retrial or considering a grant of bail or even a stay of the proceedings."

"Can we get a stay on grounds of unreasonable delay? And the fact that it was the prosecution that screwed up?"

"If the pathologist screwed up, maybe. If Fletcher screwed up, no."

"What about bail?"

"Under Section 25, Criminal Justice and Public Order Act 1994, a person charged with murder will only be granted bail in exceptional circumstances."

"Aren't these exceptional circumstances?"

"I think so. But it's what the judge thinks that counts."

"What about all that being 'vigilant to protect the interests of the defendant by fixing a speedy retrial.'?"

"If it turns out that the pathologist was wrong, and if Mary – Judge Braham – orders a retrial instead of halting the proceedings, I'm sure she'll do her best to make it speedy. But speedy is a relative term. There's a massive backlog in the courts. And it's not entirely due to the pandemic. It's partly due to government policy, lack of expenditure and many other factors."

Now Emily realised why Blair had been so insistent about going ahead with other witnesses. He didn't want to be held responsible for any delays in the proceedings.

Calvin looked at Nigel as if he wanted to say something. But he held his tongue. Then his head dropped. Now it was Emily's turn to look at Nigel. He nodded surreptitiously in case Calvin saw. Then she leaned forward and touched Calvin's arm gently and spoke quietly.

"Our biggest handicap is the fact that there's virtually no record of your background going back beyond April of last year."

"How would that help me?"

"It's more a case of the absence of any record *not* helping. No one knows if you're a criminal or an illegal migrant. I mean... okay, you've said you're an American. But the prosecution hasn't disclosed any indefinite leave to remain in the UK, which they surely would have found. And we haven't been able to find a British birth certificate."

"I actually *do* have indefinite leave to remain. The Home Office has probably lost it, like all that documentation they lost from the Windrush immigrants."

"Except," Emily added, "that it could be rather hard proving it."

Emily remembered that the scandal had broken in 2018. If he remembered it, then they could push back his timeline in the UK at least six years.

"So what are they going to do? Deport me? Apart from my accent, they've got proof I'm an American."

"Is that what you're worried about? Deportation?"

"Hell no! Let's just say that when I'm ready, I'll fill you in on the blanks. Right now, I just want to get this case over and done with."

"Well..." Emily hesitated. But this time she continued *without* looking at Nigel. "For all we know, what you're holding back might make your case worse. In fact, that's the only reason you'd have for holding it back."

A flash of anger flared across Calvin's face. But it took only a second to subside. And then he was back to his old, friendly self.

"Look. Just do what you can. I won't hold it against you if it's not enough."

Only when the three of them were halfway down the corridor, did they talk amongst themselves.

"He's acting," said Emily. "And acting badly, at that. I've got this funny feeling,"

"What?" asked Nigel with a grin. "A funny feeling that he's holding something back?"

She elbowed him gently.

"About his *reason* for holding back. I don't think he's afraid at all. I get the feeling that he's enjoying the position he's in right now. Like it's some big drama and he's the leading man holding centre stage."

25

Hayden Blair's witness, after lunch, was Lorraine Epstein, a data systems and electronic communications expert whom the police regularly called in, to assist their own in-house specialists.

With her sharp, observant hazel eyes, she exuded an air of confidence as she testified first to her qualifications: Bachelor's at Cambridge, direct doctorate at Imperial, and post-doctoral research at the University of Strathclyde.

She didn't mention that it was at Strathclyde that she had learned to put on a variety of Scottish accents, almost at will. It served her naught, professionally speaking, but she found it a useful skill for amusing various partners in a string of sapphic relationships that invariably ended when new jobs required her to relocate.

With her credentials established, she proceeded to the facts of the case. Using her own laptop and the court's Evidence Presentation System, she explained that she had analysed the contents of the hard drives on the personal computers belonging to Professor Wallace and Calvin Coffey, as well as their mobile phones, email accounts, WhatsApp accounts and various other communication channels.

She had found no evidence of anything on any of the professor's devices to show that he had any contact with Calvin Coffey or made any requests for a quote for a loft conversion. Nor were there any signs on his hard drive, cloud storage, web browser history or recent search history that he had done any research about those subjects. She talked quietly, using layman's language, making the complex seem simple.

"Just to be clear," asked Blair, "was there any sign of any *deletions* from his browser history? Or any signs that he had visited any websites dealing with loft conversions or, for that matter, anything to do with building, construction or remodelling?"

"No, none."

"Did you look for any other signs that he might have looked at home repairs or refurbishment on the web? I mean apart from the browser history and recent search history?"

"Yes, I also looked for temp files that might also preserve evidence of such browsing."

"And was there, or were there, any?"

"There were many temp files but all about mathematics. Nothing about building, remodelling or refurbishment."

"Okay, now let us turn to the laptop and phone belonging to the *defendant* Calvin Coffey. What can you tell us about that?"

Lorraine explained that she found evidence of Calvin Coffey engaging in extensive correspondence about doing a loft conversion in a house in Hampstead Garden Suburb, with a man *claiming* to be Walter Wallace but from a different – albeit similar – email address. She explained that setting up an email address similar to someone else's was a trivial task.

"And could an expert in your field trace the location or identity of the sender?"

"Well, first let's cover the basics. Everything connected to the public Internet has a unique address called an IP address."

She had learned, from past experience as an expert witness, testifying before lay people, not to go too deep into the rabbit hole, unless one of the parties wanted to dig deeper. So she didn't go into IPv4 and IPv6. IP address was enough for now.

"Secondly, every email message contains something called a message header. This contains the IP addresses of all the Internet Service Providers that passed the message along towards its designated recipient, as well as the IP address where it started. This is usually the IP address of the sender. But not always."

Again, she didn't go into static versus dynamic IP addresses. Nor did she delve into the fact that long messages are broken up into packets, and that each packet has its own header and the packets might arrive out of order, but are assembled at the other end, when they arrive.

"The third is that there are many organizations that provide what are called VPNs to customers. VPN stands for Virtual Private Network. Now if you are connected to the Internet via a VPN and you send an email, the service provider of the VPN strips away your IP address and puts one of theirs in its place. And one of theirs can include an IP address in another country. In fact, most of the major VPN providers allow their customers to *choose* which country they want to connect via."

"And do the VPN providers *retain* a record of the IP address that they stripped away from the message?"

"Some do, some don't."

"And in cases where they do, presumably it can be recovered from the service provider."

"Yes, although in many cases, the providers are uncooperative with law enforcement, and the information can only be obtained by court order. However, in this case I was able to establish that the person on the other end of the messages to and from the defendant was using a VPN registered in Panama. The VPN has points of presence in many other countries. But they have a no-log policy that has been verified by a Big Four accountancy firm. This means that they do not retain logs of the data, so even *they* do not know the original IP address of the user."

"So would it be fair to say that there's absolutely no way of knowing who the defendant was talking to?"

"That's correct."

"Indeed it could even have been himself."

"Don't lead your own witness, Mr Blair," said Judge Braham. "If you have no specific evidence and wish to speculate, save it for your closing speech."

"I apologise, M'Lady," said Blair. Then, turning to Lorraine, he asked: "Regarding the *telephone* data of Professor Wallace. Can you tell us what you found?"

"I checked the numbers called against information supplied by the police and--"

"M'Lady, for the benefit of the jury, the witness is referring to a statement made by Soraya Wallace, listing phone numbers known to her from her husband's contact list."

"Thank you," said Judge Braham. She nodded to Lorraine to continue.

"And I was able to identify all but two mobile phone numbers that Wallace called, one on the 4th of April 2023 and the other on the 5th of April and then again on the 22nd of September, the day before he died."

"And that is in your report?"

"Yes."

Blair handed copies from the agreed bundle to be given to the jury. The judge and Nigel already had copies. Over the next few minutes, Blair talked her through the calls to the unidentified numbers, their dates, times and durations. And then, he was finished.

"Thank you, Miss Epstein. Wait there please."

As Nigel rose to his feet in a deceptively cumbersome manner, Emily wondered how he would play it this time. They hadn't really discussed a strategy for this witness, because they'd been so focused on the second post-mortem issue.

"Miss Epstein, did you look at the timings between the defendant's emails and the replies from, shall we say, the 'fake' Walter Wallace."

"Yes. I did."

"And could you tell us in each case – Coffey first, Wallace second, and then Wallace first, Coffey second – what were the shortest, longest and average times?"

They both knew the answer already because it had been in her witness statement.

"The average timing interval between a message from Professor Wallace and a reply from Mr Coffey was around two hours. The shortest being 14 minutes and the longest being just over five hours. In the case of the reverse timing, a message from Coffey followed by a reply from Wallace, the shortest was fifty-six minutes and the longest was about three days. I calculated the mean average to be a tad under seven hours."

"So in terms of the human element, the patterns were very different."

"M'Lady," said Blair, rising quickly out of his seat, "the witness is not a psychologist."

"I think her expertise is enough to allow the question, as phrased by counsel."

"I would say the patterns were *very* different and quite distinct. The defendant was quick to respond to the messages he received, but the counterparty was slow to respond to the defendant."

Although she was a prosecution witness, she didn't make the slightest attempt to sugar-coat her answer for the benefit of the side that called her. Her job, as an expert witness, was to give her testimony factually, and let the chips lie where they fall – to use the original and correct form of the saying.

"Thank you, Ms Epstein. No further questions."

In the spectators' section, Father Thomas was watching in awe, as Nigel made his point, with just a couple of questions.

The judge addressed the courtroom.

"In view of the hour, I think we shall adjourn until Friday, when – hopefully – we will have the results of the second post-mortem. Are there any objections?"

Needless to say, there were none. What Judge Braham *didn't* say was that she had a backlog of five case management hearings that she wanted to clear.

But something was nagging at Father Thomas – the words of the cardinal's auxiliary, the Right Reverend Christopher Deniran.

"If you can find a way to protect the innocent or hold the guilty to account – *without disclosing, in any way, what the penitent told you* – then it is a laudable act to do so. Indeed, you are *morally bound* to do so."

So wrapped up in his thoughts was the priest that he didn't notice the woman sitting just a few feet away from him, her eyes transfixed on Calvin Coffey. A woman called Petula.

26

"If you can find a way to protect the innocent or hold the guilty to account – *without disclosing, in any way, what the penitent told you* – then it is a laudable act to do so. Indeed, you are *morally bound* to do so."

It was impossible to escape Bishop Deniran's haunting words. Not just a "laudable act," but "*morally bound to do so.*"

The sacramental seal was one side of the coin. But the duty to do all that was in his power to put matters right was the other.

"*You see that a person is considered righteous by what they do and not by faith alone,*" warned James. "*As the body without the spirit is dead, so faith without deeds is dead.*"

So now, this evening, Father Thomas Wyman was sitting alone at a corner table in a rather noisy pub, his posture relaxed yet attentive, dressed casually, not wanting to attract attention to himself. His eyes, calm and introspective, occasionally wandered through the window, but mostly stayed fixated on the entrance. A cold lager sat in front of him, beads of condensation tracing down its side, untouched, as he waited patiently.

It wasn't long before Patrick entered the pub. Patrick (*not* Paddy) was his nineteen-year-old nephew, the quintessential "nerd". His hair barely hinted at hurried combing, let alone meticulous styling. Dressed in what could be considered the unofficial uniform of a computer science student, a plain, somewhat wrinkled t-shirt with a picture of Einstein, paired with comfortable jeans, he wore old sneakers that had seen better days. His glasses were as "square" as his personality, although he would have been quick to remind people that they were actually rectangular. They were also slightly oversized for his face, dominating his youthful features and magnifying his keen, curious eyes.

The backpack casually slung over his right shoulder along with his jacket, housed a laptop (Linux not Windows or Mac), an iPad, an iPhone, *and* an Android S23 Ultra phone, as well as various pocket-sized hacking tools with names like the *Flipper Zero* and the *USB Rubber Ducky*. He also had a change of clothes and a bathroom kit for overnight stays. He found it too constrictive physically to wear the backpack on his back with his arms through the straps. Wearing it that way made him feel not only physically uncomfortable, but also psychologically vulnerable. But his devotion to his academic pursuits made it *de rigueur* for him to carry around at all times.

Despite his somewhat dishevelled appearance, there was an undeniable sharpness to Patrick – a quickness in his step, an alertness in his eyes. He scanned the pub and upon spotting Father Thomas – or "Uncle Tom" as he jokingly called him – a smile broke through his reserved exterior.

Upon noticing Patrick, Father Thomas offered a warm, welcoming smile in return. The priest's presence exuded a sense of calm and kindness, providing a silent reassurance. Despite their differences in outlook – the man of faith versus the young man of science – there was an unspoken bond between them, one of family ties and mutual respect.

But Uncle Tom's reason for inviting Patrick to this meeting remained unspoken, adding a layer of anticipation to the encounter.

There followed an exchange of sign language, with Patrick making the hand gesture for a drink. His uncle pointed down to show that he already had one. The younger man pointed to himself and then the bar, to indicate that he was buying one for himself. The priest nodded and Patrick made his way to the crowded bar.

Being a nerd in every sense, Patrick wasn't very pushy when it came to catching the barman's eye in the face of vociferous competition from the regulars. So it was nearly five minutes before the priest's nephew arrived at the corner table, edging through the crowd with his pint of lager. When he got there, he slumped into the vacant seat.

"You made it," said Father Thomas.

"I made it," echoed Patrick, before taking a sip of his beer. "So what exactly is all this about?"

"I need your help tracing someone."

Without missing a beat, Patrick whipped out his iPad and activated the Scribble app.

"Details?"

"The first thing I need to tell you is that I'm not a hundred percent sure of anything. But this is what I think..."

You are preparing a Google search ad for a sponsored result. That means that Google may display it – it's always "may", never "will" – when certain words are entered into the Search Box. In this case, the targeted key words are "brain tumour" and "brain cancer". You can target Google Ads by location. That can mean a continent, a country, a district or region *within* a country, a city, a street or even a radius around a single house.

And that's precisely what you are doing. You are targeting an advertisement on a single house. The text for the advertisement says: "You haven't got long. Make it count." The link on the advertisement, will take whoever clicks it to a website, where you're going to do the *real* work.

You smile as you look at the ad. Together with the parameters it's bound to hit the spot.

But then, you decide to change it. Not in a big way, just one small change.

You add a word.

You add a name at the end.

Thursday 21st March, 2024

27

Dawn was breaking as they entered the East Finchley Cemetery. The small group of men paid little attention to the pair of Cedars of Lebanon trees planted on the front lawn. Instead, they focused on the task that had brought them here with a palpable sense of solemnity and respect.

Clad in dark, nondescript clothing, the Registrar of Cemeteries, a lean, almost matchstick-like figure in his sixties, led the party of men to the grave that he had carefully identified and painstakingly confirmed. As the officer in charge, his task today was to ensure the dignified exhumation of one Walter Wallace.

Wearing gloves and masks, as health and safety rules required, the small team approached a grave marked out by its slightly more recent appearance and a discreet plaque, with the sun beginning to edge its way above the cloud-obscured horizon.

"This is the one," the Registrar said to the Environmental Health Officer. The EHO inspected the paperwork, looked at the grave, then looked up at the Registrar and nodded.

Screens that had been erected overnight surrounded the grave, shrouding it in an intimate cocoon. Strategically placed task lights illuminated the area with a soft, non-intrusive glow, ensuring that every detail was visible without breaking the dawn's gentle embrace.

The exhumation had been scheduled as early in the morning as possible, in order to maintain privacy and minimise the chance of unwanted onlookers.

And so, the team began their painstaking work. Their movements were measured, almost reverential, as they began the process of reopening the grave, adhering strictly to the protocols laid down for such rare occasions. Progress was slow, as they had to be careful to avoid any sort of disturbance that might affect the ground beyond the funeral plot.

Once the original coffin was reached and carefully

uncovered, the Environmental Health Officer inspected the new coffin, ensuring it met all necessary standards for the safe and respectful re-containment of Professor Wallace's remains. He indicated his approval, and the team proceeded with the delicate task of transferring the remains. The original coffin was carefully placed inside the new casket, both to honour the memory and dignity of the deceased and to ensure that hygiene was maintained.

When the new coffin was sealed, the Registrar marked it externally to preserve chain of custody and made a corresponding written note. The EHO nodded for the team to thoroughly disinfect the area around the exhumation site, leaving no trace of the morning's activities.

With the procedure complete, the Registrar and EHO exchanged copies of their respective paperwork, and with that, all arrangements for the onward transmission of the remains were in place. When the coffin was loaded onto a waiting hearse, the team climbed in, including the Registrar, while the EHO made his way to his own car.

As the hearse disappeared from view, the cemetery gradually returned to its former state of tranquillity.

28

Cold. Cold and sterile ... and chilling. Such was the atmosphere in the pathologist's office.

Ruth's hands were trembling as she sat waiting for the pathologist, Harold Finch. It had been nearly a year since her husband, Raymond, was found battered to death by a series of hammer blows. The police had investigated, checking door cameras and CCTV in the nearby high street. Even Ruth herself had been politely questioned in detail as to her whereabouts at the time of the murder.

Frustrating though it was that the murder remained unsolved, she could hardly claim that the police had been remiss or negligent in their duties. They had checked if anything had been stolen, looked through Raymond's computer and phone records. Even delved into his finances and found some anomalies. Anomalies like unexplained sums of hundreds of pounds going into Raymond Morrison's bank account every few weeks.

They had questioned her about it, and even picked up on the flicker of surprise in her eyes when they first mentioned it. She had told them that he probably had a side hustle in addition to his work as a teacher at the local academy school. But she didn't know what it was. Possibly private tutoring. They pointed out that the money had been deposited at various bank branches in cash. She confessed that he might have been paid in cash to avoid declaring it to the taxman.

But then, why would he deposit it? And why at bank branches in London, rather than Bournemouth?

She nearly told them that he had been commuting to London regularly, for treatment. But then she had paused, alerted by some suspicion that she couldn't describe. So instead she waited until they had left her and then looked up the bank statements to check up the dates of the deposits. And when she saw them, she realised that her explanation was no explanation at all. Because most of the deposits were before that – before he had been diagnosed with a brain tumour.

There was, in fact, another reason for her not to interact too closely with the police on this point – too apprehensive to delve too deeply into these payments in the presence of the police. Because she had been afraid that the "Revenue" might come after it and might even say that she was complicit.

So apprehensive was she, that after the police left, and after she had checked the dates, she consulted a solicitor for advice on the extent of her exposure and legal jeopardy, making it clear that she was telling the truth to the police when she denied all knowledge. The solicitor reassured her that, provided she stuck to that line, there was no danger of the taxman coming after her in any criminal capacity.

And as for civil pursuit, the solicitor told her to take it one day at a time. HMRC didn't like garnering bad publicity by raiding a widow's inheritance. Especially after her husband had been brutally battered to death. And the sums involved weren't exactly huge.

But Raymond's death still left her crying out for answers.

Dr Harold Finch, the pathologist who had carried out Raymond's post-mortem examination, looked uncomfortably at Ruth as he settled into the chair opposite her. She had been offered tea, which she accepted, and biscuits, which she politely declined. For his part, Finch chose neither, preferring to avoid making the interaction too social. In truth he just wanted to get it over and done with.

"Mrs Morrison, I'm a bit puzzled. We sent you a summary of the post-mortem report. But I'm not sure that an in-person visit can add anything to what we've put in writing."

"I wanted to ask you some questions. Something that the summary didn't answer."

"What was it?"

"A few months after Raymond's death, a man in London man – a maths professor by the name of Walter Wallace – was killed under circumstances eerily similar to Raymond's. That is, he was bludgeoned with a hammer."

"Yes, I heard about the case. There's a trial on now at the Old Bailey."

"Yes," Ruth replied, weakly.

"Well, I'm sure the police would have considered the possibility of a connection. I'm not an expert on police procedure, but police forces around the country routinely share information – especially about serious crimes, and *certainly* about murder. If they want to contact me at any time, I'm available. And if the CPS want me to compare notes with the pathologist in the London case, I'm available for that too."

"Please bear with me, doctor." Ruth replied, her voice steady despite the turmoil inside her. "You see, the thing is... in the London case, the professor... Professor Wallace, had been diagnosed with an inoperable brain tumour and was receiving palliative care for it at the Royal Free Hospital in North London."

"Like Raymond?"

"Ah, so you *did* find it in the post-mortem?"

"Well I wouldn't be much of a pathologist if I'd missed it."

"But you see, in the case in London, the pathologist *did* miss it."

"*What?*"

"What I mean is... there's a dispute. The pathologist says there was *no* tumour and he has scans to prove it. But the doctor who was treating him says otherwise. And he has scans that confirm the diagnosis."

"And have they *compared* the scans?"

"Yes, and they say the man in the mortuary wasn't the same as the man who was receiving palliative care at the Royal Free Hospital. But the question is which of the scans is the right one for Professor Wallace? So now, they're going to exhume the professor's body."

Finch looked like he was struggling to take it all in.

"That's pretty rare. But what's the connection with Raymond's case?"

"That's what I'm trying to find out. You saw Raymond's tumour. But you didn't mention it in your report."

"I think you're thinking of the report *summary*. I certainly mentioned it in the *full* report."

"But why not in the summary?"

"Because it wasn't relevant to the cause of death."

29

Thursday mornings can be dreary with their not-quite-Friday feel. And so it was when the cadaver of Walter Wallace arrived at the pathology lab from the East Finchley Cemetery.

Richard Hunter was allowed to watch through a CCTV link from his office in the building. But he was not allowed to be in the room when Dr Eleanor Bentley, the lead pathologist in this second post-mortem, did her work. Her assistant, James, a young man with a keen eye and an unshakeable resolve, prepared the necessary instruments with meticulous care.

Walter Wallace's body, or what was left of it after six months under the ground in a coffin, was carefully transferred onto the examination table. The room filled with the subtle, unsettling sounds of zips and snaps as the body bag was opened.

Dr Bentley consulted the notes from the initial post-mortem report, her eyes scanning the details that had led them to this moment. The first examination had revealed the cause of death and documented the cumulative effect of the intense trauma to the brain.

With precise movements, Dr Bentley and James began the delicate process of reopening the skull. The brain was gently extracted from its resting place with precision and care. Dr Bentley cradled it in her gloved hands and placed it in a specialised container filled with a solution to preserve its intricate structures during the scanning process. She covered it with a saline-soaked cloth to prevent drying.

The most delicate part of the operation was done. Now, it was the machine's turn to speak.

The MRI scanner loomed large as they approached its cylindrical chamber. James carefully transferred the brain to a specialised cradle within the MRI. It looked almost comical – the wrinkled pink and grey mass nestled inside the high-tech machine. James positioned the container holding the brain onto the sliding bed of the scanner, ensuring it was perfectly aligned with the machine's exacting specifications. While James secured the cradle, Eleanor entered the specific scan parameters into the nearby computer terminal.

With a few final adjustments, the bed slid smoothly into the chamber, engulfing the brain in the magnetic field that would soon – hopefully – reveal its secrets.

"Okay, here goes," said Eleanor, her voice tinged with nervous anticipation.

They retreated behind the protective barrier, and James pressed the start button. The room was suddenly filled with a loud, rhythmic thumping noise. The MRI was awakening, its powerful magnet humming to life.

Eleanor's brow furrowed in discomfort as the rhythmic thumping escalated. Through the barrier window, they could see the cradle within the MRI slowly slide into the machine's belly, engulfing the exhumed brain in its artificial womb.

The sounds that followed were the relentless rhythmic thumping of the machine, occasionally punctuated at odd and unexpected intervals by long stretches of silence. The minutes ticked by and the tension was palpable as they awaited the results. As the machine hummed, clicked and thumped, layer by layer, the brain was unveiled, each slice a page in a book waiting to be read. The scan took forty minutes, owing to the thoroughness of the settings that Eleanor Bentley had selected.

Finally, with a long, drawn-out sigh, the MRI shuddered to a halt. The rhythmic thumping ceased, replaced by an eerie quiet. Eleanor and James exchanged a glance.

"Okay," she said. "All good."

Stepping out from behind the barrier, they were greeted with the familiar hum of the lab's ventilation system. James retrieved the cradle, carefully removing the brain from the confines of the MRI. It looked unchanged, the saline-soaked cloth keeping it moist and glistening.

Dr Bentley studied the results of the scans. The images were clear, and they answered the first question. The brain bore no signs of the tumour that the hospital had diagnosed.

However, was it the correct brain? Or had there been a mix-up at the lab on the day of the post-mortem?

So now they had to move on to the next phase of their examination.

Back in the lab, under the watchful eyes of Dr Bentley, James used a sterile scalpel to delicately remove a minuscule sample of the brain tissue from the cortex, the outer layer of the brain. The precision of the cut was crucial: only a small amount was needed, and the integrity of the sample was paramount.

The tissue was then placed in a sterile container. This sample would serve as the source of DNA for their analysis. The extraction process began with the addition of a lysis buffer, a solution designed to break down cell membranes and release the DNA into the solution. James then added the enzyme Proteinase K to digest and remove proteins and other contaminants, leaving behind only the pure genetic material.

There followed a series of steps involving the addition of other chemicals called "cutting enzymes" to break the DNA down into fragments followed by electrophoresis, which involved passing an electric current through the samples to separate them by size (which depended on the number of repeated sequences).

The samples were placed in a detector where light of a specific wavelength was shone through the sample and the quantity of light absorption measured. This detection step was what enabled them to measure the number of repeated sequences that enabled them to compare samples.

Parallel to this, the reference DNA taken from Walter Wallace's body months earlier had been processed in the same manner. Its profile was stored in NDNAD, the Home Office National DNA Database, a digital ledger of genetic identities waiting to be matched against new samples.

The moment of truth came as Eleanor Bentley aligned the profiles side by side. Each locus was a mirror of the other, reflecting the same genetic blueprint. Eleanor allowed herself a moment of professional satisfaction as the final locus confirmed the match. There was no doubt left; the alleles at all thirteen STR loci in the brain tissue sample that she had just collected corresponded precisely to those in the reference sample taken from Walter Wallace's cadaver on the day of the post-mortem. The number of repeats was identical.

In statistical terms, the probability of such a match occurring by chance across thirteen different loci was infinitesimally small. This was not just a match; it was a definitive statement that the brain tissue analysed indeed belonged to Walter Wallace.

Back at the central table, James was placing Walter Wallace's brain back into the cranial cavity, so that his mortal remains could be returned to their final resting place once more.

Meanwhile, Eleanor Bentley was pondering the implications, which were significant. The brain scans matched. The DNA matched. Dr Richard Hunter, her fellow pathologist, was vindicated. She turned to the nearest CCTV and gave him a reassuring thumbs up.

Not so lucky for Dr Fletcher, the neurology consultant. He had screwed up big time!

Friday 22nd March, 2024

30

"It has now been clearly established that it was Dr Fletcher who was mistaken, and that the deceased did *not*, in fact, have a brain tumour."

Nigel was addressing Judge Braham in the absence of the jury.

They had been somewhat disappointed – both Nigel and Emily. It wasn't the result they were hoping for. It would have been far better for the defence if there had been a tumour and Richard Hunter had missed it in the post-mortem. That would have blown his evidence sky high, along with his credibility, and made *any* prosecution unsafe.

But the results were incontrovertible, so Nigel and Emily just had to deal with it. After calling Calvin, to keep him informed, they discussed several possible explanations in some detail – both as to their plausibility and the merits to the defence. Out of these discussions, a favourite emerged that Nigel had every intention of pushing in his motion to halt the proceedings.

"This appears to be due to a mix-up with the scans at the hospital between two patients. If so, then the hospital will have to take urgent steps to identify the other patient, who might have been given a false negative and may right now be in urgent need of treatment.

"However, as m'learned friend pointed out previously, Dr Fletcher is one of the most eminent consultants in this field in the country. This gives rise to a much *graver* possibility that there was some deliberate *interference* with the scans. And if so, that means there is a hidden hand at work. And given what we *already know*, that the defendant was lured to Professor Wallace's home by a deceiver – or a 'prankster', as m'learned friend would have it – this calls for some further investigation by the police. Of course, such investigation will necessarily take time. But in the meantime, my client has been languishing in gaol for over six months.

"I therefore move that, in view of the exceptional

circumstances, the trial be halted, and the defendant be released on bail. This will allow the police conduct a proper and thorough investigation into how a most reputable hospital came to misdiagnose the deceased, as well as how the defendant came to be tricked into attending the scene of the crime. We cannot allow the hidden hand of an anonymous interloper to sow the seeds of confusion such as to yield a poisonous harvest of injustice."

Nigel was waxing lyrical and eloquent, which made no sense to Emily, as there was no jury to impress.

"Mr Blair," said Judge Braham, as the prosecutor did his old shuffling notes routine.

"What was all that about?" Emily asked quietly.

"Just feeding a headline to the tabloids," Nigel replied with a winsome smile.

She could see it already, emblazoned across the front page of a "red top": Hampstead hammer horror house 'hidden hand'.

"M'Lady," Hayden Blair began his response. "If it had been the *pathologist* who made the mistake, I would have felt obliged to support m'learned friend's motion. However, Dr Hunter was entirely correct in his post-mortem report. The person who made the mistake – that is the false diagnosis – was not a witness in this case. Therefore, the erroneous diagnosis is not a sufficient reason for halting the trial. If m'learned friend wishes to argue that the diagnostic error has some bearing on this case, he is free to so argue. I won't assert an adverse inference under Section 11."

Section 11 of the Criminal Procedure and Investigations Act 1996, provided that "where... the accused... at his trial... puts forward a defence which was not mentioned in his defence statement or is different from any defence set out in that statement... the court or any other party may make such comment as appears appropriate."

And more importantly: "the court or jury may draw such inferences as appear proper in deciding whether the accused is guilty of the offence concerned."

However, because new evidence had come to light that was previously unknown to the Crown, and therefore not disclosed to the defence, Hayden Blair was waiving his rights under the section, and asking the court to direct itself also to commit to not commenting.

In layman's terms, this meant that if Nigel and Calvin wanted to offer a different defence to the one they offered in the defence statement, they could do so without fear of either the prosecutor or the judge making an adverse comment to the jury.

"Anything to add to your argument Mr Farringdon?"

"Only this M'Lady. If I am to be able to argue the relevance of the diagnostic mistake made by the neurologist, then I am going to need time to investigate its causes. Furthermore, because we are agreed that the defendant was lured to Professor Wallace's house by trickery, and as the source of that trickery has yet to be identified, I submit that the need to identify the culprit for said trickery has become all the more pressing. And the onus for finding that culprit falls entirely on the shoulders of those who have both the *resources* and the necessary *authority* to conduct such inquiries: namely the police.

"Needless to say, all of these investigations will take time. But in the *meantime*, my client is languishing in gaol. Finally, M'Lady, the jury were told that this trial would take two weeks at the most. Instead, it is looking like it will be at least *three to four*.

"For all of these reasons M'Lady, I would ask the court not only to halt this trial, but to release my client on bail and stay the proceedings until the police have been able to identify the person who lured the defendant to Professor Wallace's home – and also until the hospital has been able to provide a credible and comprehensive explanation for the diagnostic error.

"I would further ask, at minimum, that if the police are unable to identify the party who lured my client to the Wallace home, then the charges against the defendant should be dismissed on the grounds that it is impossible for him to get a fair trial."

Nigel sat down, unsure if Judge Braham was moved by his arguments, but at least hopeful.

In the event, she didn't spend any time dwelling on it, or even taking a short adjournment to consider it. She had read the second post-mortem report at the same time as counsel, and she knew what arguments they would come up with.

"At this time – and I stress *at this time* – I am not persuaded that there are sufficient grounds to halt the trial. As counsel for the Crown has pointed out, the error was not made by a witness in this case. However, it is certainly arguable that the misdiagnosis is relevant to the defence. For this reason, I will allow the defence some considerable latitude in raising the misdiagnosis and I hold the Crown to its undertaking to refrain from mentioning or intimating that any such matters were not in the defence statement.

"Finally, turning to the renewed application for bail. It would be quite exceptional to grant bail in a murder case, especially a particularly violent murder such as this one. Moreover, as I have already stated, the attendant risks are exacerbated by the fact that the defendant's background is a complete mystery. He seems to have emerged from nowhere, operated off the grid, worked without a national insurance number on a strictly cash basis and has no discernible past.

"I am not suggesting that this is due to any sort of criminality. His fingerprints and DNA have been checked against the national database and no match has been found. And I am reliably informed that his fingerprints and DNA were also sent to the USA, Canada, and the Republic of Ireland – again with no positive information about a match coming back. Indeed, under his own name, there is no evidence that he has ever had indefinite leave to remain in the United Kingdom. However, given that there is equally no evidence of where he came from, he cannot be lawfully deported. He has not changed his name by enrolled deed poll, and his identity and whereabouts, prior to a year ago, are unknown.

"For these reasons, and under the terms of the Coroners and Justice Act 2009, the defendant will remain in custody for the duration of the trial."

Emily cast a quick glance over at Calvin in the dock. He had taken it well, or at least wasn't showing any sign of distress or anger.

Judge Braham addressed Hayden Blair.

"Are you ready to call your next witness, Mr Blair."

"Yes, M'Lady."

Judge Braham had the jury brought back.

"Before we proceed," she intoned, "I'm going to read to you the results of the second post-mortem and explain to you their significance."

While she did so, Emily studied the faces of the jurors, to try and get some idea as to how they were processing the information. When Judge Braham had finished reciting, she went on to the second part: her interim directions to the jury.

She told them that they were not to speculate on their own initiative as to how or why the hospital came to make the diagnostic mistake in the first place. But they should listen carefully and diligently to any suggestions as to the causes offered by counsel, whether for the defence or prosecution. They should also give all due consideration to any further evidence offering support for any theories or explanations for the erroneous diagnosis or for the emails that led up to the defendant's arrival at the house of Professor Wallace.

With these directions given, Judge Braham told Hayden Blair to call his next witness. The witness was another tech expert who had examined the SatNav in Calvin's phone and the one in his van and confirmed his arrival at the house at the time when Calvin said and a few minutes before his encounter with Soraya outside. This evidence put Calvin at the scene within the timeframe when Wallace died, so from that point of view it was incriminating. On the other hand, it matched precisely the time when Calvin said he arrived and thus corroborated his honesty. Nigel asked a few questions to make this clear.

The next witness was the specialist from the investigation team who analysed and viewed the CCTV evidence from the nearby street CCTV cameras and the door cameras of nearby residents. He was able to establish the time of the arrival of Calvin's van at the time corroborated by the SatNavs. Calvin's van also had a dashcam, and the footage had been downloaded by the police. Again, Nigel simply brought this out on cross-examination. And so with that, the morning session was over, and Judge Braham called the lunchtime adjournment.

While Nigel was putting away his case notes, Emily was looking over at the dock, where Calvin Coffey was being led away by a custody officer. Nigel's voice cut into her thoughts.

"Don't worry. We've got that legal visit tomorrow."

"It's not a legal visit he needs. He hasn't had any family or friends come to see him. It's like no one cares about him."

"You said before that he was playing a role in a drama."

"I still think he is. But I'm wondering if maybe that's all he's got going for him."

"In the meantime, I've got a job for you. I want you to call Philip Solomon and ask him to send an Inquiry Agent to the Royal Free."

"Inquiry Agent" was a quaint British word for what Americans would call a Private Investigator.

"What are we looking for?"

"We need to corner Dr Fletcher and get him to open up about the scan – if we can get him over lunch, we might just catch him off guard."

"I'll get right on it."

Except that she had no intention of doing so. She had other

ideas.

Outside the courtroom, Father Thomas switched on the phone that he had smuggled into the Old Bailey against the security rules (as applicable to visitors) to be greeted by a message from his nephew: "I've got a name – and an address. AND A PICTURE."

31

The hospital restaurant was open to the public, but few people knew it, or even where to find it. Most hospital visitors went to the café or the adjacent Deli Bar for snacks and sandwiches that could be zapped or grilled in two minutes. The restaurant, on the other hand, was where the staff went for proper meals. The more knowledgeable of the visitors knew where to find it, and even though it operated a two-tier pricing system, it was still a bargain. And the food tasted good.

Emily had zipped over to the hospital from court, hoping to make it to the restaurant before Fletcher got there. That way she could tuck herself into the queue right behind him and make it seem more natural. But when she got there, she did a quick visual scan of the place before ordering her food and saw him sitting in the corner alone.

Actually, this might be even better: she didn't want anyone else there or it would be harder to get straight answers out of him. He had barely started on his food. This was also good. It meant that she had time to get some food of her own and then join him with her tray, which would make it look just a bit more natural. If she just turned up empty-handed, it would arouse his suspicions from the get-go. Not that she could completely avoid arousing his suspicions.

She joined the queue and leapfrogged to the section that had the fewest people ordering quickly, realising afterwards that what she took – pizza – would not ordinarily have been her first choice. She walked over to the payment point with the shortest queue, switched on her phone's voice recorder and slipped the phone back into her pocket, just as she got to the front of the queue.

She paid for the food with her debit card – *"no, I'm not a staff member, I pay the full price"* – and then carried here tray over to the corner and slumped into the seat opposite Fletcher, making out like the bottle of Diet Coke on her tray was about to topple over.

It was a move that she had learned in amateur dramatics at the North London Collegiate, and it gave her a quasi-credible excuse for sitting there when there were other free tables available.

"Aaaaaaah Christ!" she blurted out as she staged the manoeuvre.

A little overdone, Emily, but I don't think he noticed.

"Are you okay," he asked, clearly pleased by the sudden appearance of young female company.

"Just about," she replied, restoring the Diet Coke bottle to its upright position.

"Mind if I sit here?"

With his back to the restaurant, he might not have noticed how many other tables were free.

"No problem," he replied with a shrug.

She took a bite of her food and a sip of Diet Coke, in order not to be too obvious. Then she looked at his badge.

"Are you a doctor?"

She was making a conscious effort to dumb it down, try to play to his intellectual ego.

"Er, yes," he said, his tone betraying just the slightest irritation at this intrusion on his lunchtime peace and quiet.

"I figured…"

He nodded and gave her the once-over.

"You visiting someone?"

"Just came in for a blood test."

She hoped he was going to ask for what. That would provide a segue to continue the conversation. But Fletcher returned his attention to his food and ignored her, apart from the occasional surreptitious glance for a pervy eyeful.

Emily knew she was going to make the effort.

"Your name looks familiar."

"What?"

Emily's bar training left her ear finely attuned to intonation. *Confusion? Fear?*

She nodded towards his name badge, not wanting to seem too eager to talk. The idea was that being less verbose herself, she might make him more so.

"What about it?"

"It looks familiar."

He shrugged it off, embarrassed.

"So what were these tests?"

He's not really interested. He's just trying to divert my attention.

"I'm not really sure." She decided to play the 'dumb' card. "I've been getting tired a lot, so my GP sent me. I hope they don't get my results mixed up."

"That's very unlikely," he replied. "Although you wouldn't think so, to read some of the tabloids."

Emily's face lit up.

"That's it!" she said.

"What?"

"Was you in the news the other day?"

His face went bright red. She pressed her psychological advantage home.

"I read something about you. You was a witness in some big murder case."

"I really don't know – I mean yes, but I wasn't... a *witness*."

"I'm sure they said something about a Doctor Fletcher. Something about a neurol... neurol... whatever."

"Neurologist."

"Yeah. They was banging on about it in the *Daily Mail*. There was a mix-up about someone 'aving a brain tumour."

"Look, I know the case you're talking about. But I can't talk about it. It's what's called *sub judice*."

"The thing I don't get is how there could be a mix-up like that? I mean like, don't you do brain scans and stuff like that?"

"I'm afraid I can't talk about it."

He returned his attention to his food, but Emily had no intention of letting up.

"You know what my theory is? I think his results must've got mixed up with someone else's."

"I couldn't say."

"But if they got all mixed-up, and they was treating him for nothing, then someone else might have been told he was all right when he wasn't."

"Look I can't discuss the case – *or* theories about it." He was snapping now. "I came here to have lunch, not to talk about medical cases. If you *were* a medical professional, you'd know that I can't discuss cases outside the scope of professional consulting, even if it wasn't sub judice. Now if you'll excuse me--"

"All right, keep your hair on! Anyway, I've got another theory. Maybe it *wasn't* an accident. Maybe someone done a switch with the results."

Fletcher smiled reluctantly, like he was bowled over by the sheer absurdity of the suggestion.

"That's ridiculous! Who would do such a thing?"

His reaction was helpful. It meant he was rising to the challenge and not sticking to his resolution to keep silent.

"I dunno. Maybe one of the nurses."

"And why would a nurse want to do that?" he asked, his tone still mocking.

"How should I know. Why would a nurse want to kill babies?"

She was referring to a recent case that was still arousing controversy on social media.

"Well at least that's one explanation we *can* rule out."

"What d'ya mean?"

"Simple. These days the records are all computerised. Now if you'll excuse me."

And with that, he picked up his tray, with some of the food still uneaten, and carried it off to the trolley where trays could be stacked for taking to the utility room.

Emily carried on eating her pizza, while removing the crusty edges.

While she was doing that, a group of rather loud and lairy nurses arrived at the table next to hers and started talking at a volume that suggested they wanted to share their conversation with everyone in the restaurant, or at least everyone at the nearby tables.

She noticed from the uniforms that they were in fact student nurses or "associate nurses" as they were now called.

"Chelsey's gonna have a right problem catching up," said one.

"Yeah, I wonder what she's got?" asked another.

She was talking about another student nurse, not the Premier League football team.

"I think they said it was the flu."

"God, she's gonna miss so much."

"Already has. She asked me to take notes for her."

"When's she back?"

"She said Wednesday. Tuesday or Wednesday. I'm not sure."

Suddenly Emily had an idea.

"Excuse me," she said excitedly, turning to the table where the student nurses were sitting. And putting on a posh voice this time, she asked: "That isn't Chelsey Oliphant is it? We were at school together."

A couple of the student nurses looked like they wanted to laugh.

"No," replied the one who said she was taking notes for her.

"Chelsey Slater."

Emily tried her best to look embarrassed. More to the point, she was working on her next big idea. And as Nigel had once told her: "When you get ideas in your head, Emily, you can be quite dangerous."

32

It was 1.55 p.m. and the trial was about to resume. But Emily was nowhere to be seen, and Nigel was getting worried. Worried and annoyed. He had no reason to believe that Emily was in any danger. But she was the kind of person who was perfectly capable of *putting herself* in danger.

"All rise!" intoned the usher.

There was no chance of calling her again. Nigel was hastily switching off his phone and putting it away as Her Honour Judge Braham entered the courtroom. Within a few seconds, the judge sat, followed by everyone else, except Hayden Blair KC, who remained on his feet.

"Mr Blair," Mary Braham intoned. "Are you ready to call your next witness?"

"Yes, M'Lady."

The jury were brought in and when they were seated and settled, Blair called his next two witnesses in succession.

The first was the SOCO who had found the bloodstained workman's overalls, discarded outside the garden hedge at the back of the property. He testified that he had found the overalls, confirmed the authenticity of the pictures taken by one of the photographic officers, showing the discarded overalls in situ. He also confirmed bagging up the evidence and marking the bag for chain of custody. Nigel let his routine testimony pass without challenge.

The second witness of the afternoon was a forensic lab technician who had analysed the blood on the overalls for DNA, a non-binary woman in her twenties with cropped hair and tattoos. She testified that she logged the details from the label on the evidence bag, opened the bag in a sterile environment, took samples of the blood, ran them for blood group and DNA and compared them to the reference samples from Walter Wallace and Calvin Coffey. She confirmed the hard copy of her report that had been included as part of the agreed bundle of evidence.

As to the crime-scene samples from the overalls, she confirmed that, based on the DNA, all of them came from Walter Wallace and none of them matched Calvin Coffey.

Finally, she testified that she had taken tapings from the fabric in the hope of finding hair samples from the person who had worn it, but found none.

There were no surprises in this testimony. Nigel had read it already in the lab report, and the evidence wasn't incriminating. But on the other hand, neither did it exonerate Calvin. There were no bloodstains from *any* third parties. So there was nothing to be gained by Nigel cross-examining and emphasising this absence of evidence. Blair would simply re-examine and bring out the fact that *whoever* had worn the overalls had left no tell-tale signs.

After the witness stepped down, Judge Braham looked at the clock. It was getting on for 3.30 p.m. There was plenty of time for more witnesses, but 3.40 p.m. was the cut-off time, when new spectators were no longer admitted. This would include any spectators who had to leave for a call of nature. So, following her regular pattern, Judge Braham called a short adjournment for ten minutes, telling the spectators that they must be back by 3.40 if they wanted to hear the remainder of the day's proceedings.

Nigel took advantage of the adjournment to try and call Emily. It went straight to voicemail. But rather than talk, he sent her a text message: "Where the devil are you?"

After the adjournment, Blair called his final witness of the day: a bloodstain spatter expert. A man who could have been any age from 30 to 50. He testified that the bloodstain spattering was consistent with the overalls having been worn by the attacker, basing his knowledge of the attack on the description of the attack provided in the post-mortem report, as well as his own observations at the crime scene.

He then went on to describe his observations at the crime scene, using pictures and the display system. He explained how the attack likely played out and how Wallace and the attacker probably moved relative to one another.

Then Blair handed over to Nigel for cross-examination.

But this time, Nigel noticed something. He noticed that Blair seemed slightly apprehensive. Lawyers are not really supposed to let themselves become psychologically vested in their cases. Indeed, that was one of the things that he was trying to teach Emily: the skill of professional indifference. But Hayden Blair was an alpha male. He was programmed to win. And like Emily (who was very much her estranged father's daughter), he took failure personally.

So why is he looking so apprehensive?

Nigel knew he had to be careful. Hayden Blair didn't only know how to argue a case, he also knew how to *act* – at least how to perform for the benefit of a jury.

I have to do it! I have to take a chance.

"I see that it's getting late," he said to Judge Braham, "so I'll be very brief." Then turning to the witness, he asked: "Were you able to determine the relative *heights* of the deceased and the assailant?"

The answer wasn't in the expert's witness statement, so he probably hadn't been able to reach a conclusion.

"Well... determining these things is an inexact science."

The "wriggle" again. That could be a good sign. Like the hand covering the mouth that went with it, a classic sign *not* that he was lying, but that he was being forced to talk about something that he would rather *not* talk about. Nigel cast a quick glance sideways at Blair. He wasn't smiling. He wasn't tight-lipped either, as if he was trying to suppress a smile. That was an even *better* sign.

Let's press on.

"I know, but you *were* able to speak with great confidence about the relative *movements* of the two parties."

"Yes, but that was based upon the bloodstains on the overalls."

"And the walls."

"What? Oh yes, and the walls."

"So what about the ceiling?"

"I don't follow."

"The ceiling. You mentioned in your evidence-in-chief that there were bloodstains on the ceiling."

"Oh... er, yes."

Nigel felt a tinge of excitement now. This witness may have *seen* the blood. But right this minute, Nigel could *smell* blood.

"So if you were able to track the motions of the deceased and the killer in *two* dimensions, based on blood spattering, then all I'm asking you to do is apply that same logic – and that same information – to the *third* dimension."

Nigel paused for a moment to let this sink in with the jury. If the witness didn't answer now, it meant he had something to hide – something of benefit to the defence.

"So, once more, and with feeling, did the blood spatter

patterns on the walls – and the ceiling – yield any information about the relative heights of the killer and the deceased?"

The witness looked ever so briefly at Blair and then, knowing that he had been seen, back at Nigel.

"I would say... purely on a *probabilistic* basis... that Professor Wallace was taller than his attacker."

There was a faint gasp in the courtroom. Because they all knew what this meant.

"And you are aware that Professor Wallace was five feet eight inches tall?"

"Yes, but..."

Nigel knew that he was going to say that people get shorter when they die. This is not strictly true. People get shorter when they age. But in any case, he backed off when he realised that it wasn't his area of expertise.

"And are you also aware that the defendant, Calvin Coffey, is five feet eleven and a half inches? Just under six feet?"

"I... I didn't know."

Nigel was going to ask Calvin to stand up and for the witness to repeat his assessment. But he decided not to. Firstly, the distance to the dock was too far for it to work effectively. Secondly, it would serve no useful purpose. And thirdly, it might go awry. That would undermine all the good that he had achieved already.

"Would you agree – given what you have already stated in sworn testimony – that, *on a probabilistic basis*, it is unlikely that a man of the defendant's height could have been the killer of Professor Wallace?"

The words "given what you have already stated in sworn testimony," were critical. They effectively tied up the witness in knots. He could hardly now say "no" after what he had already testified.

"I suppose so," the witness mumbled.

"You *suppose* so," Nigel repeated.

There was a tense silence from the witness box.

"No further questions."

Nigel sat down.

What he had done was devastating. He was always telling Emily *not* to gamble in cross-examination, when there was the slightest chance of a downside. But this time, Nigel had taken a gamble – and it had paid off. Now it would be up to Blair to salvage what he could.

"Do you wish to re-examine?" Judge Braham asked

prosecuting counsel.

"No, M'Lady."

"Then the witness is excused."

The witness was escorted out of the courtroom. Like other expert witnesses, he was not required to remain there until completion of the trial.

Blair now addressed the judge.

"That concludes the case for the Crown, M'Lady."

Bang on time for the weekend. Blair had been hoping to leave the jury thinking about the prosecution's evidence as a whole, circumstantial, but still strong. However Nigel had punctured that balloon. The last thing the jury had heard – and the only thing that the jury would remember over the weekend – was the prosecution's own expert witness telling them that it was unlikely that Calvin had killed the professor.

The jurors were sent out and told they could go home for the weekend, along with the usual reminders not to discuss the case unless all 12 of them were present, nor permit it to be discussed in their presence, and not to read about it in the press and not to do any research online.

"Will the defence be ready to begin on Monday?"

Nigel stood and answered with quiet confidence: "Yes, M'Lady."

Though in truth, he was hoping that he wouldn't have to. He might just be able to persuade Her Honour that there was no case to answer.

"Then we'll adjourn till Monday morning, nine o'clock."

The court didn't sit with the jury until 10.00, but that first hour was for administrative matters and case management. Judge Braham knew that Nigel would prepare a detailed submission of "no case to answer" and she wanted to allow enough time for it. She could have told counsel to be in at 8.00 when the court opened, or 8.30. But that would have been too much. And with that, the court adjourned for the weekend.

Before Calvin was led away, Nigel looked over at the dock and gave him an encouraging nod. But in any case, Calvin had perked up, no doubt from what he had heard. Nigel felt for him, as Calvin turned to accompany his police guards back to Belmarsh Prison. Belmarsh was a cold, stark place for any man, let alone one who seemed to have no friends – at least none outside the prison.

As he left the court and made his way to the robing room, Nigel switched on his phone. It sprang to life, beeping almost exuberantly at the sound of a message from Emily: "Didn't have time to arrange an Inquiry Agent. Doing some research myself."

33

Emily wasn't lying. In fact, she decided to pass up the usual Friday after-work drinking and partying session, in favour of work, much to the surprise of the other three pupils. But she had the bit between her teeth now, and she was determined to follow through with her plan.

So she sat with her laptop open, along with the add-on triple-screen, and set to work.

First, she logged on to a site that prints lanyards and ordered four "NHS Student Nurse Lanyards" for £1.19 each, two in pink and two in pale blue. It was surprisingly easy. She thought she would have to have them printed specially and risk arousing suspicion as to why a private address would order such an item. But, in fact, it was available off the shelf. She also ordered matching badge holders to go with them.

Earlier that day, in the hospital restaurant, she had already taken a couple of discreet pictures with her mobile phone to give her a clear idea of the layout of the badge itself, as well as the uniform. But just to be sure, she did some searching on the web to make sure she got it right for the hospital trust.

Sourcing the uniform at short notice, on the other hand, was a bit trickier. It took a little more internet searching to find an online retailer that sold the tunic in pale blue with white piping worn by the NHS student nurses at the Royal Free. She ordered it with the logo (to be supplied as a JPG). And with it the matching scrub trousers. The next-day delivery option was £15. But she chose it anyway, hoping that St Jude's would foot the bill.

Then she went to an NHS site to download the NHS logo for the name badge and the hospital logo for the uniform itself. That was a bit trickier. She couldn't find an exact example. So she opened up her graphics program and, working from what she had, she created the badge and the logo file for the uniform. She printed out several badges on white card and trimmed them to size for the badge holder.

With these tasks complete, all she had to do was pray that "next-day delivery" was more than just an idle promise.

Saturday 23rd March, 2024

34

"They *said* they were in contact with the police in London. But I think he was just brushing me off."

"Slow down, Ruth," said Petula. "Just catch your breath and slow down."

Ruth was taking a walk in the Upper Gardens to relax. But despite the sight of the lush, familiar greenery around her, and the sound of the River Bourne rippling as it flowed nearby, she couldn't relax. She was tired... tired and out of breath. She wanted to sit down. But she was too restless to sit still. It was a strange feeling – being both tired and restless at the same time. She used to get these feelings occasionally, as far back as she could remember.

"I'm okay! I'm okay. Just listen! I went to the pathologist and asked him about Raymond. And he told me the tumour was real. So it's not the same as Prof Wallace. But with all those similarities, I went to the police again."

"And what did they say?"

"It was pretty much like the *first* time. They just fobbed me off."

"Wait, they said they weren't going to investigate?"

"They said they were in contact with the Met in London. I got the feeling that if Raymond also *didn't* have a tumour, they might have taken it more seriously. But because he did, they're treating it like it's two unrelated cases."

Talking into her phone, from a busy London street, Petula tried to sound reassuring.

"But if they said that they're in contact with the Met, then at least things are moving."

"Yes, but I don't think they're in any hurry to take the information to the lawyers representing the man accused of killing Wallace."

"I don't understand."

Ruth struggled to find the right words. The truth of the

matter was, she didn't really understand either. It was all just convoluted fragments – pieces of a jigsaw puzzle all jumbled up together.

"If my theory is right," she said, but then trailed off. She didn't really have a theory. "I mean, if I'm right that it's all connected, then whoever killed Raymond, must've also killed Professor Wallace."

"Well, maybe this Calvin, what's-his-face…"

"Or maybe Professor Wallace killed Raymond and then someone else killed Wallace."

"Oh come on, Ruth, you're being ridiculous. A seventy-three-year-old man killed your husband?"

"With a hammer. You don't have to be strong to kill someone with a hammer."

"And then he got killed the same way?"

"I know it doesn't make sense. But I can't think of the answer."

"So maybe it was Calvin. Like I said."

"Well if it was, then you'd think the police would be interested in investigating. I mean, then they should be charging him with two murders."

"Maybe they will," Petula replied, in a calming, reassuring tone. "Let's wait and see what happens."

"Yes, but suppose he's innocent?"

"Who?"

"The man who's on trial for killing Wallace."

"Calvin Conway? I mean Coffey?"

"Yes. Shouldn't he be told? I mean shouldn't his lawyers be told?"

"Yes, but that's the police's job. They have a duty of disclosure. That's the law."

"They said it's up to the CPS, not the police themselves. But the police down here haven't told the CPS. They've only told the Met. And if the Met don't tell the CPS, then the CPS won't know, and so they won't tell the defence lawyers."

"Okay, so how about this, when you're next in London, we can arrange for you to talk to the CPS. All right?"

There was silence on the other end of the connection.

"Ruth… are you there?"

"Petula…" The voice had dropped to a whisper. "I think I'm being followed."

35

She was no longer Emily du Lac, pupil of Nigel Farringdon KC at St Jude's Chambers. She was now "Chelsey Slater" student nurse at the Royal Free Hospital, complete with lanyard, ID badge, and pale blue tunic coat with white trim that included the embroidered badge of the hospital.

So now, camouflaged with a blonde wig, against later identification by CCTV, she was walking down the corridors of the hospital, headed for the Neuroendocrine Unit, holding a clipboard. She was trying not to look out of place or self-conscious. But it was hard. All the more so, since she didn't know exactly what to expect when she got there. As this was Saturday, she hoped that it would be easier to avoid arousing suspicion.

She told herself that it was a big hospital. Nobody at the hospital knows everyone. So if she just looked like she belonged there, then she would be able to quietly blend in. She timed it to coincide with lunchtime, to increase the chances of finding an unattended computer terminal.

The main thing that hospital staff worry about isn't unauthorised access, it's forgetting their password at a crucial time when they need to gain quick access to the patient's medical records. No one wants a colleague to be locked out of the system for precious minutes due to a forgotten password. So in many cases the sign-in details are taped to the underside of the keyboard. Sometimes they even share passwords across an entire department. And sometimes they just don't bother to sign out.

When she arrived in the department, it was not exactly a hive of activity. But then again, it was by no means deserted either. And, most crucially, the receptionist was still at her desk. There were probably terminals in the consultation rooms. But these rooms would be either unlocked or currently in use. She could hardly walk into one, although she had once practised lock-picking and was quite good at it. But she wasn't *quick* at it. And that was important:

she couldn't risk being caught picking a lock by a passing member of staff.

No, she realised, *I'll just have to hang around till she's gone.*

She hovered around, looking at a noticeboard, writing things at random on her clipboard, and generally avoiding drawing attention to herself. Then she heard the receptionist say those magic words to a colleague: "I'm going for lunch."

"I'll be along in about ten minutes," said a nearby colleague.

Perfect! That means the colleague, who knows no one else is supposed to be at the reception desk, won't be here to notice me.

From Emily's point of view, it couldn't have been better.

But even if the user forgets to sign out, the system will automatically sign the user out after a certain amount of time. So after three minutes, Emily strolled over and "accidentally" dropped her pen, so that it fell onto the receptionist's desk. Looking suitably frustrated – in case anyone happened to be paying attention to her – she reached over and retrieved it, at the same time tapping the return key. That would count as activity for the purpose of keeping the receptionist signed in.

However, she might have to do it again... and again. It all depended on the colleague.

She held the pen openly, in case anyone thought that she had stolen something. Then, after a few seconds, she put it away in her pocket to wait out the remainder of the ten minutes.

Those ten minutes seemed like an eternity to Emily, even though they only lasted six in total. The colleague had overestimated.

As soon as the coast was clear, Emily walked round the reception desk and sat at the terminal. The picture showed a scrolling NHS logo. That might just be a screensaver. She moved the mouse this way and that and prayed.

The screen changed, but instead of access to the records, it opened up a modal dialogue box with an invitation to "Enter your username and password."

Drat!

She lifted up the keyboard, praying again, and looked under it.

Yes!

They were there – in all their complexity.

Username: Florence.

Password: Nightingale1

And that was it. A few keystrokes later, she was in. Another student nurse was walking past, giving her a funny look. She tried not to look frightened or out of place, and in any case, seconds later the student nurse was gone.

Focus, Emily. Focus!

She did a search for "Walter Wallace".

Date of Birth?

She had done her homework and knew what to expect. She keyed it in.

The computer appeared to be stuttering or sputtering, or whatever you call it when the machine is struggling to do something but not outright refusing. Computers at public institutions were often like this: using outdated software, overloaded with data and slow to retrieve the relevant records. That's why they always tell you: "Okay, I'll just call it up... the system's a bit slow today."

She surveyed the screen and saw the details of appointments and next of kin and contact details, but nothing else. No actual medical records. No scans. And no way to send the details by email or save them to a device.

Then she realised that this wasn't going to work. They had different systems for appointments and contact details on the one hand and medical history on the other. Even if the terminal was connected to the backend of the medical history details, she could not access it. There was a card-reading device attached to the computer.

I probably need an authorised card to access it!

This wasn't going to work. And so, regretfully, Emily signed out, got up and walked round the desk, just in time to see the student nurse, who had given her a funny look a few minutes earlier.

Emily acknowledged her with a nod of her head and started to walk away briskly.

"Excuse me," the student nurse called out.

Emily stopped, feeling that avoidance of any suspicious action made more sense than hitting the panic button. Whatever the student nurse wanted, it would be better to try and blag her way out of it than to create a scene.

The nurse closed the distance between them as Emily half-turned. It was then that Emily noticed the security guard, who had been walking a few paces behind the student nurse, but in the same general direction.

"Is your name Chelsey Slater?"

It was on her badge, so she could hardly claim otherwise.

"Yes."

Emily stayed immobile and tried to keep her features that way too. But on the inside, she was panicking. Was this girl in the same group?

"'s funny," said the student.

"What is?" Emily replied innocently, with just a tinge of nervousness at the slightly ominous tone in the other girl's voice.

"You don't look like you did last time I saw you."

Okay, she's met Chelsey Slater. But she didn't claim that she knew her.

Emily had to think fast – something she was trained to do as a barrister.

How does Chelsey Slater talk? Is she posh? Middle-class? Working class?

Emily decided to go with working class, matching the cadence of the other girl and the vocabulary and grammar that she associated with it.

"I've 'ad my 'air done different – 'aven't I?"

Would it work?

The security guard was still hovering, but he had stopped a few paces back, still taking an interest in Emily, or maybe in the nursing student.

"Yeah, but not just your 'air. 'Cause last time I saw you, you was black."

Panic time!

Emily turned abruptly, hoping to make a quick getaway. But she caught the student nurse, in her peripheral vision, making a hand gesture. And almost simultaneously, the security guard – a brick house of a man – seemed to "get it" in that single instant.

As Emily tried to close the distance between herself and the outer corridor, beyond the department, she heard footsteps behind her, and she felt a strong man's hand grabbing her wrist from behind.

36

"Okay, Ruth, don't panic... Is there anyone else about?"
Petula was trying to sound reassuring.
"No, Just me. And him. And... *Oh my God, he's looking at me!*"
"Okay, now *listen*! Just stay calm. This is what you do. Walk fast, then look round to see if he's still following you. If he is, then run. Look back again and if he's still following you, then scream."
"Okay... I'm walking fast... I'm walking..."
She was out of breath, both from the fear *and* from walking fast.
"Ruth?... *Ruth?*"
"Okay..." She was panting heavily. "It's okay. I managed to give him the slip."
"You're okay?"
"Yes... I think so... I ducked behind some trees."
"Okay, maybe wait a bit to give him time to give up. If you feel safe there."
"Why would anyone be following me?"
"I don't know, girl."
"Maybe I've stirred up a hornets' nest."
"Don't panic. Stay calm... Focus."
"But..."
"Just listen. You're in a public place and it's daylight. You haven't stirred up anything. It's most likely some loser who follows random women and then gives up or tries another after a while."
Ruth knew the type.
"I'm gonna double back."
"No wait. He's probably lurking still. That type always does. Give him a few more minutes."
"No. I want to find out who he is."
"What?"
"I'm going to double back and follow him."
She sounded so earnest and sincere.

"No, listen, Ruth. I think you've been watching too many spy films."

"Okay, I can see him. He's walking to where I was…"

"Be careful, Ruth."

"Now if I can just get a look at him."

Ruth turned down the sound so that if she got close and Petula spoke, the man wouldn't hear. She knew that to see his face, she'd have to overtake him. But she wanted to be well ahead of him, so he wouldn't see her.

An idea struck her. When she reached Prince of Wales Road, she crossed to the other side of the Bourne and began to continue the walk along a parallel route. She now lengthened her stride to close the distance and overtake him. As she walked briskly along, she felt her phone vibrate in her hand. She looked down to see that Petula had ended the call. But seconds later, as Ruth maintained her relentless pace, Petula called again.

Ruth wanted to answer. She knew that her friend was worried about her. But she didn't want to slow down. She had to get ahead of him – had to see his face. So she shoved the phone into the pocket of her jacket and just kept going at the same relentless pace, ignoring the vibration of the phone.

Finally she came to the narrow gravel-topped footbridge, parallel to the Treetops apartment building. And there he was, sitting on a bench, looking down. He looked tired… and sad.

Maybe it's frustration, Ruth thought. *Because he lost me.*

She walked slightly back, just in case he looked up and saw her.

Perked up with excitement, Ruth took out her phone and noticed three missed calls from Petula, as well as a few messages. She called back, feeling slightly guilty.

"Hi Petula, I'm okay."

No answer.

"Petula, can you hear me?"

Silence.

Then she realised that she had turned the sound down. She turned it up.

"*Ruth, are you okay?*"

"Yes, I'm fine. I can see him. He's sitting on a bench on the other side of the bridge."

"What does he look like?"

Ruth didn't know how to describe him.

"I'd say mid-thirties. He looks tired… worn out."

"Can he see you?"

"He might, if he looked up... Oh and get this, he's wearing a dog collar."

"A *dog* collar?"

"Yes. I guess he must be a vicar. Or a priest."

"A priest? Look, Ruth... I think you should get out of there. Don't let him see you. Just get out of there."

"Why, what's he going to do? Splash me with holy water?"

Petula started to reply. But it was just a single syllable before the sound cut out. Ruth's phone had lost reception. Or maybe it was Petula's.

Regardless, Ruth had made up her mind. She walked back to the bridge and crossed it. Incredibly, he still hadn't seen her. Only when she had completed the crossing and got onto the path, did he look up and see her. And when he noticed that she was looking straight at him – and walking towards him – it was the priest who panicked.

She could see the fear in his eyes. Or maybe fear was too strong a word. Maybe it was just embarrassment. His eyes darted left and right, as if he wanted to run, like he was looking for an escape route. He could all too easily have done so. In addition to the path branching off in both directions, he was also only yards from the exit of the gardens.

But despite the fear or embarrassment in his eyes, he didn't budge. Instead he waited like a lamb about to be slaughtered, as Ruth closed the distance between them and looked down at him, the same way as she looked at little Liam when he was being naughty.

"Why are you following me?" she demanded.

"I wanted to talk to you. If you *are* who I *think* you are."

"And who do you think I am?"

"I think you're Ruth Morrison, the widow of Raymond Morrison."

37

In the sterile, white-walled corridor of the Royal Free Hospital, Emily's heart was pounding against her chest like a drum, leaving her breath shallow and rapid. This was not going to be an easy situation to talk her way out of. She had been caught red-handed, impersonating a student nurse *and* accessing confidential patient data. The charade was over before it had even begun. She could be disbarred. *She could go to prison.* At minimum she would have a criminal record, and she would be ignominiously kicked out of the legal profession.

Even her estranged father – who *wanted* her to succeed – would be on her case about it. After he had "traded in mum for a new model" as she had "so charmingly put it," her ultimate ambition of revenge would be shattered. Revenge, to Emily, meant outdoing the "love rat" in the practice of law. And now that ambition was about to collapse on top of her head. For a moment, she felt tears about to well up in her eyes.

No Emily! A voice from inside her seemed to shout. *You're still your father's daughter. And members of the du Lac family do not lose. Or if they do, they go down fighting!*

The security guard – a brick-house figure with a stern expression that seemed to mock her – clutched her wrist firmly, his grip unyielding.

"You're not going anywhere until we clear this up," he declared.

The mix of authority and suspicion in his tone annoyed Emily. It was like being challenged by her father *and* her mother, all in one go. Yet anger was one thing. Actually doing something about her predicament was quite another.

Clad in the nurse's uniform that she had purchased online, she looked nothing like the young, ambitious law student she was. *Prima facie* – to use that old legal expression much beloved by her father – she appeared as a fraud, an impostor pretending to be someone she wasn't, and for a purpose that may not be nefarious, but was certainly illegal.

Emily's mind raced and she drew deep into her memory to recall the relevant legislation. If she admitted to looking at the computer, she risked not only legal repercussions under Section 1of the *Computer Misuse Act 1990*, but also the professional and personal embarrassment it would cause to Nigel.

Of course she had legitimate reasons for wanting to find out why and how the hospital had made a mistake in diagnosing a brain tumour that wasn't there. But illegally accessing a computer carried a maximum sentence of 12 months imprisonment on summary conviction in a magistrate's court, as well as a fine up to the current statutory maximum.

But how well did the security guard know the law? He was there to protect staff and patients from violent disorder, not to serve as a private policeman with general duties.

"There's no law against dressing up as a nurse," Emily protested, trying to keep her voice calm, despite the growing knot of anxiety in her stomach. "You can escort me out of here. But holding me here against my will, by force, is another matter entirely."

The security guard's eyes narrowed. "We'll see about that. You were accessing hospital records, weren't you?" he accused, his gaze unwavering.

Before Emily could respond, another voice cut through the tension. "Yeah, I saw you," chimed in the student nurse who stood a few feet away. "You was looking at the computer."

This was the real nursing student, the one who knew Chelsey Slater personally, or at least knew her well enough to realise that Emily was not who she was pretending to be.

"You evidently don't know the law," Emily countered quickly, her voice adopting a blend of her own upper-class accent and the more casual tone she'd been using as "Chelsey". "It's only a summary offence, unless there's *actual damage*. Even a copper can't arrest for it without a warrant."

She said this because she didn't want them to delay her departure until the police arrived, which could occur very quickly in a hospital. The only problem was that it wasn't actually true. Under an amendment to the Act, brought in as Section 35 of the *Police and Justice Act 2006*, unauthorised computer access could be tried "either way" – summary or indictment. If the CPS decided to try the case on indictment, in the Crown Court, she could be facing a sentence of up to *two years*. But more importantly than that, the fact that it was triable either way meant that the security guard *could* make a citizen's arrest if, amongst other reasons, he had grounds to believe that she'd escape before a police officer was able to assume responsibility for her.

The guard looked uncertain, his grip on her wrist slightly loosening. Emily seized the moment to press home her advantage. "And even just *holding* my wrist like this is assault. I can 'ave you done for it," she added, her accent now a peculiar mix that reflected both her true self and her assumed identity.

Her words seemed to have the desired effect. The security guard hesitated, his eyes flickering to the silent onlookers who had gathered around the scene, drawn by the commotion. Hospital staff and a few patients watched with bated breath, but no one spoke up. The tension in the air was palpable.

After a moment that felt like an eternity, the guard released her wrist, stepping back with a mixture of frustration and resignation. "Just get out of here," he muttered, not wanting to escalate the situation any further in front of an audience, and worried about possible criminal prosecution for his own actions.

Emily didn't need to be told twice. She turned sharply on her heel and made for the nearest stairwell, her heart still racing, but relief beginning to seep through her veins. As she pushed open the heavy door to the stairwell and began her descent, the cold, hard steps echoed her rapid footsteps, a stark reminder of the reality she was escaping.

She didn't look back. The stairs seemed endless, even though she was only on the first floor, but she welcomed the physical exertion of the staircase and the long corridor taking her towards the exit, her mind gradually clearing with each step. By the time she reached the ground floor and pushed the exit door open, the cool air hit her face like a splash of cold water, shocking her back to reality.

Outside, Emily drew in a deep, shaky breath, allowing the chill to fill her lungs and steady her nerves. She was free – for now – but she wondered what the repercussions would be.

As she walked away from the hospital, her mind was already turning over what to do next. She had to get clear... had to get away from CCTV cameras. Indeed, she had to get away without leaving a trail that could lead the police right back to her if the hospital staff decided to escalate the matter.

Emily du Lac, the law student, the undercover investigator,

the woman caught between two worlds, was on her own once again.

Where can I go that there are no CCTV cameras to catch my trail?

She turned and headed for Hampstead Heath, without looking round – and therefore without noticing that the student nurse who had called her out was now watching her from the distance... and following her.

38

Father Thomas shuffled to one side, making room on the wooden bench. He was close enough to the bin to hear the rustle of leaves around it as the wind darted through the gardens. Ruth took a seat at the other end of the bench, leaving a respectful distance between them, her coat brushing the weathered paint as she settled in.

Despite her newfound confidence, Ruth remained suspicious of this priest. He had sought her out in the strangest of ways. But then again, since Raymond's death, everything had been strange.

"Ruth," Father Thomas began, his voice as soft as the breeze, "before I start, I have to stress that anything shared in confession is protected under an inviolable sacramental seal. But I can tell you that I know of your husband's fate from local newspapers and online reports. For what it's worth, my heart truly aches for your loss."

"I appreciate your condolences, Father," she said, her gaze locked onto the small bridge that she had crossed a minute earlier. "But whatever Raymond told you, it was *before* he was killed."

"As I said, I read about it."

"And what? You recognised his name?"

"Names are seldom mentioned in the confessional. But sometimes details can act like a fingerprint."

"Well, whatever you read, it could never have told you about *my* pain – the pain of finding his battered body on the kitchen floor."

"This isn't the confessional. But if you want to talk about it."

"I took Liam out that day, so that Raymond could work in peace. He worked a lot from home. And when I got back…"

Tears were welling up in her eyes. The priest nodded slowly.

"Raymond's death was a tragedy. And the fact that you still have no closure makes the burden all the heavier. But I wanted to ask you something: are you familiar with the murder of a professor in London called Walter Wallace? And the trial of a man at the Old

Bailey?"

Ruth's eyes lit up at this.

He knows about it too!

"Yes! I've been following the trial. There are so many similarities. I mean the method... battered to death with a hammer... multiple blows... in his own home."

Father Thomas leaned towards her.

"Yes, and the links don't end there, do they, Ruth?"

"You mean the brain tumour? I thought about that too. But that's actually a difference. I've spoken to the consultant and Raymond really *did* have a tumour. But in the trial in London, they said he *didn't* have a tumour. A false alarm or something like that?"

"The *neurologist* in the Calvin Coffey trial actually said that the professor *did* have a tumour. But the pathologist disputed that. And in the end, it took an exhumation and a second post-mortem to confirm that the pathologist was right and the neurologist wrong."

"Well, in Raymond's case, the pathologist hasn't disputed the neurologist's findings. And we're *not* going to have Raymond exhumed."

Father Thomas's brow furrowed, his gaze following the meandering path of an errant leaf as it danced across the bridge.

"I wasn't actually talking about the brain tumour. I was talking about certain... other... facts."

This hit Ruth hard.

"He *told* you?"

"I cannot tell you *what* he told me. But how do you think I was able to connect *your* name to the case in London? What do *you* think was the common denominator?"

Ruth understood. He was straining the limits of the confidentiality of the confessional. He was probably praying in his heart that the heavenly father didn't judge him too harshly. But he *had* sought her out, not the other way round. And she had to know the truth.

"Is it possible," she asked, "that this man accused of murder..."

"Calvin Coffey."

"Calvin Coffey... really *did* kill Professor Wallace? Maybe even killed Raymond as well?"

"I'm a priest, not a policeman. And I've never met the man in person."

"But from the point of view of motive?"

"I'm in no position to know. He could be a guilty man. Or he could be an innocent man whom someone has framed. You and I are just spectators to the events as they unfold."

"But can't we *do* anything? I mean to help him? If he's innocent? Or at least to make sure that the authorities know the full facts and investigate properly? Making sure that they cover all the bases?"

Father Thomas looked weary.

"There's a limit to what *I* can do. As I said, I can't reveal anything that was said in the confessional. But if you're aware of facts that may be relevant to the trial in London *or* to your husband's death, then you should do everything within your power to convey these facts to the authorities."

"Do you think I haven't been trying?"

"And what did they say?"

"They brushed me off."

"I'm sure they have a duty to disclose evidence to the defence."

"They say it's a separate case. No one's been arrested or charged for Raymond's murder."

Father Thomas thought about this for a moment.

"Have you considered taking what you know to the press?"

"The *press*?"

"As a last resort. Or to the Metropolitan police *in London*. Or even the CPS? They also have a duty to disclose evidence to the defence – even if they don't use it themselves."

Ruth shook her head, realising that she had missed a trick.

"Then that's the solution, Ruth. You should go direct to the CPS. Tell them everything you know. Then they'll *have* to take it to the police – *and* the defence. That way *both* sides will know and one way or another the truth will come out. Let the chips lie where they fall."

Ruth was finally beginning to understand the purpose of this meeting, the reason why this priest had sought her out.

"Is that why you wanted to talk to me? To get me to do something that *you* can't?"

He looked away, the lines of his face hardening with resolve.

"I labour under the restriction of my solemn oath, Ruth. But if you're sincere in your quest for justice – and I believe that you are – then you'll stick to your course and disclose everything you know to those who are in a position to do something about it. And I mean *both* the things we've spoken about... *and* the elephant in the room."

The conversation lapsed into silence.

Ruth stood up abruptly, the decision clear in her stance. "I'll go to the CPS. Thank you, Father." Her voice carried a new determination.

As she walked away, Ruth pulled out her phone with trembling hands and put in a call to Petula.

"Ruth, I was worried! Are you okay? What happened?"

"Just let me talk! Listen, I spoke to the priest–"

"You spoke to him? I mean what, like you approached him? Or he approached you?"

"I approached him. I told you I was going to."

"And what happened?"

She recounted the details of the meeting, her words mingling with the soft rustling sounds of the gardens and the babbling of the stream. When she had finished, Petula's encouraging voice came through the phone.

"You're doing the right thing, Ruth. Go to the CPS. Tell them everything."

The call ended, and Ruth pocketed her phone, her resolve strengthened by Petula's encouragement. She took a deep breath, taking in the scent of damp earth and the promise of rain. Then, with her head held high, she set off towards the exit, tapping into her phone: *"CPS contact* details."

39

The student nurse barely knew Chelsey Slater. But she knew that someone had tried to impersonate Chelsey – someone who sounded posh one minute and working class the next. Someone who had tried to access the computer at the hospital. Someone who was trying to hide something. Someone who was up to no good.

It probably wasn't anything personal to do with Chelsey. If she was looking into the hospital computer, it could be anything. But it was Chelsey that she had impersonated.

Maybe it *was* about Chelsey. Maybe Chelsey knew her.

No, then she would have known that Chelsey is black.

Okay, but whatever it was, the student nurse was determined to find out.

So she followed the impostor onto the Heath, holding back a safe distance in the wide-open expanse, in case the imposter turned to look back. Only when the imposter disappeared behind some trees, did the student nurse break into a run.

When she got to the trees, she was about to run past them when she heard something that gave her pause: a voice... the voice of the imposter.

"I'm going to phone Soraya and ask her if she's ready to talk to me."

She's on the phone right now. Talking to someone about "Soraya" – whoever that is.

"Maybe *she* can shed some light on the false diagnosis... Yes, I know she believed it. But now that she knows the truth, maybe she has some ideas. Maybe she can tell us how he came to be tested in the first place."

She was looking into a false diagnosis! That's why she was accessing the computer! So there was a false diagnosis at the Royal Free? In the neuroendocrine unit? But who?

"Okay, I'll call her when I get home?... On Hampstead Heath... I needed the fresh air to clear my head... why would I be out of breath? ...Yes, I *was* jogging..."

Liar liar, pants on fire.

"Okay I'll call you after I've picked Soraya's brains."

Who was Soraya? The patient? A nurse?

"You don't want me to... I thought *you* were the one who told *me* that the law is a seven-day-a-week business, Nige."

The law? What was she, an undercover copper?

"Okay, in that case let's talk about it back at St Jude's on Monday."

St Jude's? A church maybe? But why Monday? Why not Sunday?

The call ended and the student nurse waited half a minute before chancing it round the trees. She poked her head out carefully, just in case the imposter was looking back. But she had nothing to worry about, because the imposter had walked some considerable distance at a brisk pace and was now just a receding figure in the distance.

Shall I follow her? Yes, I think I will.

But the student nurse didn't leave it at that. She still had 25 minutes on her lunch break, and she decided to use it. So as she walked along, she put the phone to her mouth and said "St Jude's, law"

The phone misheard it as "Jude Law" and came up with a whole load of pages about the actor. She tried again.

"*Saint* Jude's... law"

"Do you mean Jude Law?" asked Google.

"*No, Jude's–*"

She broke off, realising it wasn't going to work, hit the back button and then typed in "'St Jude's' law nige."

Google stuttered for a few seconds, but this time it came up with something more meaningful: "Do you mean St Jude's law Nigel?"

She chose *Yes* and got a very full list. The very first item on it was a page from St Jude's Chambers, which she understood from what she saw to be *law chambers*. And on that page, she saw the picture of a handsome, middle-aged black man: Nigel Farringdon KC.

She read on eagerly, while trying to keep pace with the young woman in the distance. It was hard to do both, but she was very determined.

Nigel Farringdon KC was the head of chambers – evidently someone quite important. It said in his potted biography that he had been a pupil of Sir John du Lac QC, the founder of the "set". And it also said "Pupil: Emily du Lac."

Presumably, some kind of nepotism going on there.

But then she noticed that Emily's name was a hot link, so she clicked on it. It pulled up a new page on a new tab. And there it was! A picture of the young woman. A picture of the imposter! True, she was wearing a smartly tailored suit, not a student nurse's uniform. But there was no mistaking the face.

So there she had it: a name and a place of work.

She looked at the time in the corner of the phone screen. It was late. She would have liked to maintain the pursuit and find out where this "Emily du Lac" lived. But she had only 15 minutes to get back and she'd gone quite far into the Heath. She'd have to walk quickly to get back before the official end to her lunch break.

Besides, she had all the information she needed.

The impostor was called Emily du Lac, her boss was called Nigel Farringdon KC. And she was a law pupil at St Jude's chambers.

40

"*Please, just listen!* My husband was battered to death with a hammer. Just like Professor Wallace. But the killer was never caught."

"Both my husband *and* Professor Wallace were diagnosed with brain tumours shortly before their deaths. In Professor Wallace's case, it turned out to be a misdiagnosis. But in my husband's case, it was correct. I've checked that out already. Checked and double-checked."

"I appreciate your call, Mrs. Morrison, but these are things you need to tell the police."
"They knew each other!"

"Raymond was Professor Wallace's PhD student. I mean not at the time of Raymond's death… but before that. And he was also one of the markers for the exam papers that Professor Wallace set… so it's that, plus all the other coincidences."

The recording came to an end.
"And that's it?" asked DI Cherry.
"That's it."
Jane Cherry was talking to Amanda, the case officer in charge of *Rex versus Calvin Coffey*.
"And she identified herself as Ruth Morrison?"
"That's right. The widow of one Raymond Morrison."
"Okay, thank you."
Jane was only the *Deputy* SIO and ordinarily, she would have passed it up the chain of command to the SIO, Chryseis Pines. But the Detective Superintendent had permitted herself the luxury of

a weekend off, for the first time in three months, and Jane realised that this had to be disclosed, or they would be running the risk of any conviction being overturned on appeal.

Normally, the disclosures are made well before the trial starts. However this was new evidence. She could simply pass it on in this raw form. But she knew that there was more to this than just the phone call and the defence would certainly want it.

And the trial was due to resume on Monday morning.

So rather than waiting for Chryseis Pines' return, Jane decided to contact their counterparts in Dorset, in the Raymond Morrison case. They would have people on duty, even at the weekend, and she would impress upon them the urgency of the situation.

At one level, she thought it was a waste of time. She had been convinced from very early on that the murder of Walter Wallace was a one-off spontaneous murder, by an irate, opportunistic builder who "lost his rag" after being tricked into driving across London in pursuit of a job that wasn't there. So what could possibly be the link to this murder in Bournemouth? On the other hand, one thing stuck out from Ruth Morrison's call: she said that her late husband *knew* Walter Wallace and had been one of his students.

That was something that had to be checked out.

So she duly did what was required and requested access to the crime-scene DNA evidence from the Raymond Morrison murder. For the sake of completeness, she even requested Raymond's brain scans taken at the post-mortem and from the hospital.

Once she had all the evidence, she got her analyst officer to go through it, for anything that might seem even *remotely* relevant to the Walter Wallace murder. She wasn't expecting him to find anything and was hardly surprised when he told her that there was no second-party DNA in the Bournemouth crime scene available for comparison.

She thanked him and was expecting him to walk away when he added: "There was one thing though – something rather important in fact."

"Yes?" she said, in the pregnant silence that followed. She had no patience for grandstanding.

"I thought it might be a good idea to take a look at the Morrison brain scans."

"What about them?"

"Well this is going to sound a bit crazy, but my visuo-spatial IQ is way higher than my numerical or verbal reasoning. That's why I'm good at chess."

"Cut to the chase, please."

"Well it seems that I excel at pattern recognition."

"And?" Jane said impatiently.

He carried on speaking, and as he did so, Jane was gobsmacked.

Sunday 24th March, 2024

41

"The truth of the matter is that it ought to be a lot more painful than it feels right now."

Soraya was pouring a cup of tea for Emily when she said this. They were in the living room that Soraya had once shared with Walter. Emily suspected that Soraya would find it a lonely place in the absence of her husband. But right now, it was anything but lonely. In fact, it was quite the salon, as Soraya served Sunday afternoon tea to her daughter Huette, a grey-haired, seventy-something family friend called Seamus Harper (very English despite his Irish first name) and Harper's twenty-something daughter, Tina.

Lost in their own world nearby were Huette's children, Soraya's grandchildren, ignoring the grown-ups as they immersed themselves in their own fantasy world.

While six-year-old Ariadne was entertaining her dolls, pouring imaginary tea into miniature cups from a matching teapot, four-year-old Mikey was engaged in a losing struggle trying to teach his recently-arrived little brother, five-month-old John-John, how to crawl. Mikey himself had started crawling at six months and about a month later was able to pull himself up into a standing position – aided by furniture. It seemed as if Mikey's impatience to explore the world carried over into helping his brother beat his record.

Soraya was relieved that Huette had remembered to bring the play mat. The carpet was clean enough and regularly vacuumed, but carpets are inherently dirt traps harbouring all manner of dust mites and as such do not bode well for babies, who tend to put anything and everything into their mouths.

Emily, recovered from yesterday's excitement at the hospital, had gone to see Soraya by prearrangement, to find out why and how they got that false diagnosis.

"So, have they told you anything at all?" asked Emily.

"Only that they're conducting a full internal inquiry, and they've notified the police."

"This was the administration who told you? Or Dr Fletcher himself?"

"The admin. Specifically the *legal* department." And picking up on the look on Emily's face, Soraya followed up. "That's right. They're now communicating through lawyers. I guess they're afraid of a lawsuit. As if *that* would solve anything."

"Has Dr Fletcher been suspended at least?"

Emily knew full well that he hadn't been. But she could hardly admit that. And in any case, this could be a segue into her next question.

"Not as far as I know."

"I wanted to ask you something, I know this is a bit delicate. Do you still think Calvin Coffey is guilty?"

"To be honest… I had my doubts even at the beginning. He didn't *act* like a guilty man."

"What do you mean?"

Emily was intrigued by this. Soraya had never said anything in her statements to intimate this belief.

"I mean just the way he seemed to show genuine concern when we arrived at the house. It was almost like he was trying to shield us from the trauma."

Interesting.

"Of course it might have been that he had some personal grievance with Walter and he didn't want the rest of us to be affected. But to kill a man with a hammer and then to immediately be concerned about his wife…"

"It wasn't *you*, mum," Huette interrupted. "It was *the children*. He was looking down at *them* when he said 'don't go in.' He was worried *they'd* be traumatised."

"Who are we talking about?" a slightly high-pitched man's voice intruded. Emily looked over to the two-seater, where Seamus Harper was sitting with his daughter.

"Calvin Coffey," Tina explained quietly. "The man who killed Walter."

"I know him," the high-pitched voice continued. "He was cheating, you know."

Emily, looked again at Harper and then at Soraya, who looked more embarrassed than shocked.

"Alzheimer's," Tina Harper mouthed, her expression distinctly downbeat.

Emily nodded, silently communicating her understanding and sympathy.

A shattering sound on the side of the room turned five heads. Little Ariadne had managed to knock a framed photograph off the mantelpiece. Huette flashed with anger, but then brought herself under control, picking up the picture with the shattered plastic frame, and letting Ariadne cry out her tantrum without giving her further attention.

"I'm sorry," said Huette, handing Soraya the picture and frame.

"Forget it," said Soraya, looking at the picture. It was a wedding picture of Huette and her estranged husband Gerald, who had unceremoniously walked out on her. "I should have thrown it out a year ago."

"No, keep it. Please, mum. It was *my* day, even if it meant nothing to him."

Soraya's temper flared at this.

"He's still ghosting you for Christ's sake! Has he sent you a penny since he buggered off to the Caribbean?"

"Mum... *please*... let it go... Just let it go."

The plaintive tone and the looks in both their eyes were heartrending to Emily, and she felt like she was intruding on a private moment – made only marginally more comfortable by the additional presence of Seamus Harper and his daughter.

A few tears appeared in Soraya's eyes. Huette's tone went from angry to earnest and gentle.

"He isn't worth it, mum."

Huette hugged Soraya, to calm her down and whispered in her ear: "And you were right to hate him on sight."

"I *didn't* hate him on sight. Your dad hated him on sight. I guess we should both have listened to Walter."

Emily still felt like an intruder. But without realising why, she found herself talking.

"I don't suppose... I could have his contact details."

Huette's manner became suspicious.

"Whose? Gerald's?"

"Yes."

"Why?"

"I guess it's just for the sake of completeness. I mean did the police ever interview him? Check out his alibi?"

"He dropped out of my life five months before that," Huette replied. "What could he possibly have to do with it?"

"You're right. I'm just thinking we should cover all the bases."

Emily realised what she was asking might be terribly offensive. She was, after all, representing the man accused of killing Walter. But they had already said that they had their own doubts about Calvin's guilt.

Huette certainly wasn't offended. But she was puzzled.

"Do you have any power to interview him?"

"Even the police don't have the power to interview him – unless they arrest him. And even then, he can still stay silent."

"In that case, what's the point?"

"I can at least try. And if I think he knows something relevant to the case and is holding out, we can subpoena him and obtain the judge's permission to question him as a hostile witness."

Huette seemed to think about this for a moment.

"Well that would be great if you could do that. But Gerald has broken off all contact with me. Like mum said, he's been ghosting me since he walked out."

"And that was... a year ago?"

"Eleven months if you want to get technical. 29th of April to be exact. One day after dad got the diagnosis about the tumour. He just packed his bags – Gerald that is – and went off on a Caribbean jaunt with some floozy. *And* set his Facebook status to single."

Perfect timing, thought Emily cynically.

"How does he support himself?"

"Contract work."

Emily raised her eyebrows.

"Computer programming. He's what they call a digital nomad. Freelancing and working remotely. It started even before he walked out on me, during the Covid lockdown. The remote working, I mean."

While this discussion was taking place, little John-John was in the process of finding something on the floor in the corner by the disused fireplace – something very small. And being a baby, he quite naturally put it in his mouth. With the grown-ups involved in their adult conversation and Ariadne absorbed with her dolls, the only one who saw this was Mikey. And to him it was a cross between a source of amusement and a guilty secret.

Monday 25th March, 2024

42

With the excitement of the weekend over, Emily had woken up on Monday morning to a feeling bordering on depression. Compared to the drama at the hospital on Saturday, and the insightful meeting with Soraya and Huette on Sunday, the prospect of Monday morning in court seemed to hold out little hope for anything but the mundane – not bad for a murder trial.

But she managed to drag herself out of bed and get ready for work, make-up and all, just like she had in her student days, and even got to the Old Bailey with plenty of time to spare.

The first hour of the Monday morning session had been allocated to Nigel's submission that there was "no case to answer," and Hayden Blair's all-too-predictable response. However Nigel and Emily were both surprised when the clerk told them that the purpose of the session had been changed to another mention hearing because the Crown had some new disclosures to make that were not previously available to the CPS.

After the obligatory short wait – to reaffirm the lines of authority Emily suspected – the usher intoned "All stand!" and Her Honour Judge Braham arrived. They all duly stood, bowed their heads towards the Royal Coat of Arms and waited until the judge was seated. Emily and Nigel then sat down, while Hayden Blair remained on his feet.

"Mr Blair," said Judge Braham, inviting the prosecutor to proceed.

"Thank you M'Lady. Firstly, I should preface what I have to disclose by saying that this information literally only reached the Crown Prosecution Service late yesterday."

Blair then proceeded to outline the details of the murder of Raymond Morrison, the fact that Morrison had also been diagnosed with a brain tumour, albeit a real one in his case, and the fact that Morrison and Wallace knew each other previously, through Morrison's PhD studies under Professor Wallace's supervision and his work as an exam marker for Wallace.

He apologised most profusely for the failure to provide this information timely and could only say that it was the two separate police forces themselves that appeared to have failed to appreciate the full significance of these similarities. He added that he was sure there was no deliberate malintent on the part of the compliance officers of either the Met investigative team or their counterparts in the Dorset Police incident room investigating the Morrison murder.

It was at this point that Her Honour Judge Braham stepped in to ask the question that Emily was itching to ask.

"Could you explain, Mr Blair, how and why the CPS eventually and belatedly came to realise that these facts were indeed relevant?"

Blair proceeded to ramble and dissemble, explaining that it involved different police forces, that the Morrison murder was not yet before the CPS, because no one had been arrested, let alone charged – also, there were material differences between the cases, such as the fact that in Raymond Morrison's case the tumour was real, etc.

Emily felt a tingling sensation at this, sensing that the trickle of almost reluctant revelations dripping from Hayden Blair's lips was a prelude to something rather more substantial.

"Indeed it was only because Raymond Morrison's widow Ruth contacted the CPS that the two police forces were alerted to the possibility that the cases were related. At that point, M'Lady, the Metropolitan police and their counterparts in Dorset coordinated their efforts and compared notes. This led to a significant discovery. Specifically, one of the evidence analysts in the London team compared the brain scans of Morrison and Walter Wallace."

By now Emily could feel the rumble with growing excitement, as if it were about to turn into an avalanche.

"Cut to the chase, Mr Blair," Judge Braham intervened, losing patience.

"Through that comparison, M'Lady, it was determined that although the Morrison scans differed substantially from the *post-mortem* scan of Walter Wallace, the *hospital* scans of Morrison and Wallace were *identical*."

The moment of opened mouthed silence that followed, gave way to Mary Braham's voice.

"What do you mean 'identical'?"

"I mean, M'Lady, that apart from the embedded name, date of birth and NHS number, the two scans are identical."

And seeing the blank look on the judge's face, Blair reiterated: "It's the same scan, M'Lady, with the identity details and metadata modified."

"But how is that possible?"

"It appears that it's the same *brain*."

"Yes, I *got* that!" Judge Braham said irritably. "But how is *that* possible?"

Blair was sweating now. And he was usually the epitome of "Mr Cool".

"Well we don't yet know exactly."

"Do you know whether the matching scans are in fact of Professor Wallace or Raymond Morrison?"

"Yes, that we do know, M'Lady," replied Blair, with obvious relief that he was able to provide at least some solid, specific information. "It would appear that the *original* is the Morrison scan. How it came to have entered the system at the Royal Free Hospital as that of Walter Wallace, is now being investigated by the police."

43

Hayden Blair's surprise revelation, welcome though it was from the defence point of view, had thrown something of a spanner in the works. Nigel had been all set to lead the morning's proceedings with his formal submission that there was no case to answer. He had prepared his arguments carefully, over the weekend, based on the evidence the Crown had presented in court. And he had practised them in front of the mirror, Winston Churchill style.

But now the Crown had dropped a loose joker from the bottom of the deck. And so Nigel was sitting at one of the tables in the robing room, hastily revising his arguments accordingly, in the half-hour adjournment that Judge Braham had granted.

Meanwhile Emily had seized upon the initiative and decided to follow up on the written portion of Hayden Blair's disclosures. The file that Blair handed them had not redacted Ruth Morrison's phone number. So Emily – without asking Nigel's permission – decided to give her a call.

But not from the robing room. That would be indiscreet. The robing room at the Old Bailey is quite large, and there were other lawyers constantly wandering in and out. But also, Nigel might not approve. He was a meticulous planner, and he would want to work out a strategy for what questions to ask her and in what order. Already Emily was keeping things from him – like her visit to the hospital in which she had effectively committed a criminal offence which could have ruined her career had she been identified. And if she told Nigel, it would compromise *his* position. He would be legally obliged to report the matter to the police *and* the Bar Standards Board.

Of course, phoning Ruth Morrison was a trivial matter by comparison. But now that she had got into the habit of withholding things from Nigel, it felt perfectly natural to do so again. She could always tell him afterwards, if she managed to glean any useful information. So she quietly slipped out of the room and made her way to the foyer, where she found a suitable place to stand out of earshot of anyone else. She briefly considered stepping outside the building altogether. But that would have meant going through security again on her return. And that – combined with the early spring rain – made it a less than attractive prospect.

Taking a deep breath, Emily picked up the phone and tapped in the number that she had copied from the file. It rang for a few seconds before a woman's voice answered.

"Hello?" came the reply, the tone suspicious.

"Good morning, is this Ruth Morrison?" Emily asked, keeping her own tone professional yet cordial.

"Yes, speaking. How can I help you?"

"My name is Emily du Lac. I'm one of the lawyers representing Calvin Coffey... the defendant in the case of Professor Wallace's murder. I understand you've heard about the case and noticed similarities with... with your late husband's death."

Ruth's voice was steady, tinged with a hint of curiosity. "Yes. Who is this again?"

"Emily. Emily du Lac. Please call me Emily."

"Okay... Emily."

A bridge of trust was slowly being built. Emily continued.

"We've been told by the Crown Prosecution Service about Raymond, and the similarities to Professor Wallace's case. But firstly, I just want to thank you for picking up on those similarities and pushing the police into action. If it hadn't been for you, we would never have found out about any of this."

There was a slight pause before Ruth replied, her tone softening.

"Thank you, Emily. I always knew there was a connection. I'm just relieved that someone's finally taking it seriously."

Emily was encouraged. She pressed on.

"I was hoping to discuss something specific that might help us understand the broader picture of these crimes."

"I'm not sure what more I can add to what I told the police."

We're still not quite there yet, thought Emily.

"What I was wondering was if you know how your husband's brain scan came to be entered into the system at the Royal Free as that of Professor Wallace?"

Ruth gasped slightly. "No, I... I had no idea. I didn't know anything about that. I... I mean, I knew that Professor Wallace was given a similar diagnosis... and that it turned out to be a mistake. But what was that about Raymond's scan?"

Emily realised, in that moment, that although Ruth had picked up on the similarities, she hadn't been informed of these latest developments.

"It seems that your late husband's brain scan was in some way doctored–"

She cursed herself for that clunky choice of words.

"Altered, I mean, and entered into the system as that of Professor Wallace."

"That's... terrible. How do you know about this?"

"When the Dorset Police and the Met compared notes, they looked at the scans and spotted it."

"Does that mean the same person did *both* murders?"

Emily understood what was playing on Ruth's mind. She was desperate for answers – desperate for closure. But the truth was, Emily didn't have a clue.

"It's too early to say. But it means that there's a lot more to this case than meets the eye."

Ruth seemed almost lost for words.

"There's... I don't even know how to describe it. But there's one thing I remember. Raymond's smartphone was stolen when he was murdered. In fact, the police initially thought the murder was a robbery gone wrong. Then the phone turned up, literally discarded somewhere in the Central Gardens. And they checked it. But it had been reset to factory settings."

Emily's mind was racing ahead with the implications of wiping a smartphone.

"Do you know if Raymond had been in recent contact with Professor Wallace before his phone was stolen?"

"I don't know."

Emily picked up on the hesitation, like Ruth wanted to add something but decided not to. And then Ruth *did* add something.

"I got the impression that there were things in Raymond's past that he didn't like to talk about."

Emily felt a buzz of excitement. *A juicy morsel. But what else?*

"Anything in particular?"

"There was something from his past, something he felt he needed to atone for."

By now, Ruth had Emily's undivided attention.

"*Atone* for? Like what?"

Ruth's voice lowered, her words slow and thoughtful.

"After he got the diagnosis, he said that it was divine punishment. I asked him for what? But he wouldn't say."

"You mean something that he felt so guilty about, that he couldn't talk about it?"

"Yes. At least not to me."

"You mean he talked to someone else?"

If so, Emily desperately needed to know who.

"In his youth, Raymond was a Roman Catholic. And you know what they say about Catholicism. You can lapse, but you can never completely lose your faith."

"What... did anything *specific* give you that impression?"

"He had to go into London for part of the treatment."

"This was at the Royal Free?"

"No, UCH."

University College Hospital.

Emily made a mental note to check if UCH was part of the same NHS trust as the Royal Free.

"Sorry. You were saying."

"Well, like I said, he was a lapsed Catholic. And while we were up in London, we took a trip to the Regent's Canal and Camden Lock. And while we were there, he decided – it seemed like it was on impulse at the time – to go into a church there. And then, again apparently on impulse, he went into the confession booth and spoke to the priest. I waited a few yards away to give him some privacy. But this was... like... I think... his first confession in years. And he was in there for a long time. I mean he wasn't just getting things off his chest. I think he was seeking forgiveness."

Emily's mind was racing now. She had seen a priest in the spectators' section of the court.

Could it be the same priest? And why would he be following the case?

"Do you happen to remember which church it was?" Emily murmured, jotting down notes. "It might help us understand more about his state of mind or find more witnesses."

"More than that. I was approached by that priest on Saturday."

"*Approached by the priest?*"

"He got his nephew to help him track me down. I think his nephew is a bit of a computer nerd or something. Anyway, he tracked me down and approached me."

Emily's mind went into overdrive. She was picking up on the words "computer nerd". Whoever had hacked the hospital computer system must have had some formidable computer skills.

"And what did he say? I mean did he tell you about what Raymond had said?"

Emily would have been surprised if the answer was yes, but she had to ask.

"He couldn't say. They're not allowed to reveal anything that's said in a confession."

"Then why did he contact you?"

"Basically to urge me to reveal all that I know to the police. And when I told him that I already tried and they brushed me off, he told me to go direct to the CPS."

"Do you remember the name of the Church? In Camden Town."

"I think it was called 'Our Lady of Hal' or something like that."

"And that's where he spoke to the priest?"

"Yes."

"And did you notice any changes after that? In his behaviour I mean?"

"Yes. He seemed a bit secretive after that. Like he was going out alone and wouldn't let me come with him. And he became very careful with his phone after that. He always kept it password protected and locked. I knew the old password, but he changed it."

"Anything else?"

"Raymond felt guilty about the injustice, whatever it was. I think he just wanted it to end. And I hope this helps."

"It certainly does... And Ruth, I just want to say thank you. And I mean it. I know this must be hard for you."

"Thank *you*, Emily. Please, do whatever you can." Ruth's voice thick with emotion. "I just want the truth to come out."

"I'll do my best."

With the call ended, Emily quickly looked up the Church of Our Lady of Hal and found their website. It listed several of the priests, but only had a picture of the parish priest, and it wasn't him. But several others were named in their Contacts page. She looked them up one by one, in Google searches, selecting the *Images* tab.

It was third time lucky. She found herself looking at a picture of the priest she had seen in the visitors' gallery of the courtroom: Father Thomas Wyman.

44

"M'Lady, it had been my intention to present a long and detailed submission that there was no case to answer. However, in view of m'learned friend's surprise disclosure, I would now like to put before the Court a *separate* motion that the charges against the defendant be dismissed."

Emily had caught Nigel as he exited the robing room, so there was little time for comparing notes as they made their way swiftly back to the courtroom to avoid incurring the judge's wrath. But Emily had carefully sanitised what she passed on about her phone conversation with Ruth. She echoed what Ruth had told her about Raymond's conscience troubling him after the tumour diagnosis. However, she held back the part about the priest and the fact that she had identified him and seen him in court. She was slowly hatching a plan to follow up on that – Emily style – and if he didn't know what she was planning to do, he could hardly tell her not to.

In any case, she sensed that Nigel had not taken it all in and that he was squarely focused on his courtroom arguments.

"Prior to this morning, the defence was unaware of the murder of Raymond Morrison, unaware of the similarities between that murder and that of Walter Wallace, let alone of the fact that this Raymond Morrison was a student of Walter Wallace."

Nigel, for his part, hadn't had time to tell her what he was planning. She knew, of course, his prepared arguments for the half-time submission, because she had helped draft those arguments. But she knew nothing of his plan to move, separately, that the case be thrown out on account of the belated prosecution disclosures.

"From the early stages of this case, we were concerned about the fact that Professor Wallace had been diagnosed with a brain tumour, which – it turns out – was an erroneous diagnosis. But at the time, we were unaware of how this could have happened. Now we have been told that the brain scan of one of Professor Wallace's students was somehow uploaded into a hospital computer system, culminating in a false diagnosis."

"This in turn suggests – *more* than suggests, *proves* – that there is a hidden hand at work in this case. Probably the same hidden hand that lured the defendant to Professor Wallace's house. And very probably the hidden hand that slew Raymond Morrison in a crime almost identical to this one. We do not know whose hidden hand that was, but there has been no suggestion that the defendant in this case murdered Raymond Morrison."

Emily had grown to love this phrase "hidden hand" that Nigel kept using. It was an incredibly powerful phrase, but so far it had left the judge unmoved. On the other hand, if it came to the crunch, she knew that he would use it on the jury too, and probably even *before* his closing speech, in order to avoid letting Blair get in with the first blow, which might give the impression that Nigel was merely borrowing his opponent's phraseology.

"So, in summary, as things stand now, we know the following. Firstly, we know that someone impersonated Professor Wallace by email and lured the defendant to the home of Professor Wallace, but we don't know *who*. Secondly, we know that six months before Professor Wallace was battered to death with a hammer, his former doctoral student was battered to death in precisely the same manner. Again, we don't know *by whom*, but there has been no suggestion that it was the defendant. Thirdly, we know that this former doctoral student was diagnosed with a brain tumour and that subsequently so was Professor Wallace. And we know that in the case of Professor Wallace it was a false diagnosis."

He paused for dramatic effect, despite the absence of a jury.

"Finally, we know that the *reason* for the false diagnosis was because someone copied or downloaded the Morrison brain scan, modified the identifying details and then somehow hacked the computer system at the Royal Free Hospital and uploaded the modified scan, passing it off as that of Professor Wallace. *Again* we do not know who did this."

Emily had known Nigel for so long that she could read his body language. He was now about to round off his argument.

"So we know that at least *four* actions of a nefarious nature – two murders, one impersonation and one computer hacking incident – have been carried out by a hidden hand. We do not know who is the *owner* of that. But what I ask is this: if we can all agree that there *is* a hidden hand at work, pulling the strings, can we be confident that there is genuinely a case to answer? In the face of so much concealed fact and detail about which we know very little, can the Court reasonably demand that the defendant be required to answer such flimsy evidence? I think not.

"For these reasons, M'Lady, I move that the charges against the defendant be dismissed and a verdict of Not Guilty be entered on the record."

Judge Braham thanked Nigel for his brevity, though Emily was unsure if this was sincere or sarcasm. Then the judge turned to Hayden Blair and invited him to respond.

"Thank you, M'Lady, I will be equally brief, if not more so.

"Whilst the murder of Raymond Morrison is similar to that of Walter Wallace, there is no clear-cut evidence that the two crimes were the work of the same person. And even if they were, there is *equally* no clear-cut evidence that the defendant is innocent of the Morrison murder. Absence of evidence of guilt is not the same as evidence of innocence. The Morrison murder is currently an unsolved crime. It is only recently that the police have even been made aware of the similarities and are thus in a position to investigate *this defendant* in relation to the Morrison murder. As matters stand, Mr Coffey has certainly *not* been eliminated as a suspect in the Morrison case.

"As to the subterfuge relating to the false diagnosis, I would draw your Ladyship's attention to the fact that at no stage did the diagnosis, or indeed Professor Wallace's medical treatment, form any part of the Crown's case. Nor has m'learned friend been able to show any *link* between the diagnosis and Professor Wallace's subsequent death. The cause of death was multiple hammer blows to the head. From what I understand, even Morrison – who *did* have a tumour – died of hammer blows, not the tumour that afflicted him. In the case of Professor Wallace there *was* no tumour, just a false diagnosis. But Wallace did *not* die from a diagnosis. He died as a result of serious and violent assault. M'learned friend is trying to muddy the waters with these extraneous factors. But so far, he has been singularly unable to establish any connection between these extraneous factors and the death of Professor Wallace. Accordingly, the Crown most emphatically opposes the defence motion.

"Moreover, if the defence needs time to look into these new disclosures, then we suggest that *this* trial be halted, but that a new trial be set at the earliest convenient opportunity."

You're covering all the bases, aren't you, you bastard? thought Emily.

When Blair sat down, Emily tried to read the judge's face.

Reading judge's faces was partly a game with Emily. But it was also a form of self-training – a useful skill. In this case, it was hard to call. Blair appeared to have made short shrift of Nigel's arguments, if one looked at the case from the point of view of the Crown's evidence.

But on the other hand, Nigel had established the existence of a hidden hand that had not been investigated, let alone identified. If the case against Calvin had been backed up by forensic evidence or eyewitness testimony, that might not matter. But the prosecution case wasn't just circumstantial, it was – as Nigel had described it – quite flimsy. At least that was the way Emily saw it.

But it was how the judge saw it that counted. Judge Braham had several options, in fact.

She could grant Nigel's motion and halt the trial with prejudice, entering a Not Guilty verdict on record.

She could halt the trial and order that the charges be allowed to lie on file, while the police investigate the matter further. There was certainly plenty to investigate – and the police had better resources to investigate these matters than the defence.

She could halt the trial and set a date for a new one. That would cause serious delays in the management of other cases, which would be deeply unpopular with many lawyers and defendants, given the backlog of cases that had built up already due to Covid-19. It would also be unfair to Calvin, unless he was granted bail, as it would require that he sit in gaol for longer, deprived of his freedom, despite the fact that he had not yet been found guilty of any offence.

Or she could allow this trial to continue and let the defence work with what they had.

But the one thing she could *not* do was grant a long delay in the current trial. It would be unfair to the jury if they had to sit around doing nothing, while the defence looked into these matters. For that reason, Emily was sure that the judge would either throw the case out completely or order a new trial with a new jury.

And now, like the rest of them, she was about to find out.

Judge Braham spoke, slowly, choosing her words carefully.

"I have to confess that I am troubled – *deeply* troubled – by what has happened today. These new disclosures have opened something of a Pandora's box, and the defence now finds itself having to work blind, facing new information at short notice, while the entire Crown case stands on an uneven foundation of shifting sands.

"The eloquently argued defence motion presents the Court with something of a dilemma. On the one hand, we cannot deny the defendant's right to a fair trial. Nor can we allow the defendant to spend an inordinate amount of time in gaol, with the matter of guilt or innocence unresolved."

Emily's excitement was rising.

She's going to let him go. YES!

"On the other hand, we cannot simply allow a crime such as murder to be taken off the table, on the grounds that mistakes were made in the investigative process. Indeed that is why the double jeopardy rule was amended quite a number of years ago: so that mistakes by the CPS would not deny justice to an innocent *victim* of crime. In such circumstances, we try to seek the middle ground, to balance the interests of justice for all sides, whilst being ever mindful that a defendant has fundamental rights that the law holds inviolable.

"But in seeking this middle ground, we must not forget that granting bail for a defendant on a murder charge would be exceptional. Furthermore, we cannot overlook the fact that the defendant's background is largely unknown. Indeed he seems to be a complete enigma, with no record of his past beyond a year ago, or less. And this naturally raises the issue of an elevated risk of flight or at least non-appearance at trial."

What are you saying?

"I am therefore not persuaded by the defence arguments that it would serve the interests of justice to grant the motion at this time. But nor may I safely conclude that there *is* a case to answer until I have heard and carefully considered the *full* defence submission and the Crown's response. Therefore I am not going to grant this motion in its current form at this stage in the proceedings. But I will take these arguments together with any further arguments the defence may wish to present in its final submission."

Judge Braham looked over at the clock.

"As we have now spent a lot of time on this matter, I will hear the *full* defence submission and the Crown's response after lunch. The court is adjourned until two o'clock this afternoon."

Emily was looking at the judge with no effort to conceal her contempt.

Thanks for the lifeline bitch!

45

By the time they reached the robing room, Emily had calmed down.

"Will you need me to help with the submission arguments?"

Nigel could tell that Emily had something on her mind.

"No, they're all done. I just need to get them across. Go and enjoy yourself. I'll see you at two."

I know what you're going to do, Nigel. You're going to take a stroll along the embankment and mope – sorry "reminisce" – about Joanie and the children.

She realised that it was uncharitable to dismiss his lingering grief. Grieving is a very personal process, and it was not for one who hadn't experienced such a devastating personal loss to decide how someone who had should deal with it. Emily had never known this kind of grief. She had known the pain of estrangement from an adulterous father, but not the pain of bereavement. And she had enough maturity to understand that it was a very different sort of pain.

Nigel often used to meet Joanie in the Embankment Gardens and even on the other side of the Thames, by the Royal Festival Hall and the rest of the South Bank Centre. Sometimes they'd even meet the children there, as they were allowed out of school at lunchtime.

But all that was in the past. Now, all Nigel had was his memories. They were painful... and happy... and bittersweet.

The case was exhausting. But once he had his arguments lined up, he didn't like to spend too much time going over them or even dwelling on them. After lunch, he'd come into court, recite the arguments and then hope that Judge Braham would buy what he was selling.

So she wasn't surprised when Nigel had readily agreed to her going off at lunchtime, before this important afternoon session, to do her own thing. He assumed that she would be meeting one or more of her fellow pupils from St Jude's. He had no idea that she had an agenda of her own – one that did not involve the other pupils. Instead she found the cheapest restaurant she could find, ordered the first item that caught her eye, and set to work.

Setting to work, on this occasion meant opening her laptop and setting up a Wi-Fi hotspot with her phone. The restaurant had its own Wi-Fi, and she could have used it. But she never trusted public Wi-Fi networks, and even using a VPN offered no guarantees. Also, since she had learned about TunnelVision, a new hackers' attack on VPNs, she decided to avoid public Wi-Fi networks and connect through her smartphone, as the Android operating system was immune from the TunnelVision attack.

She signed in to Facebook and searched for Huette's husband Gerald. Something that Huette had said was bugging her. Gerald Shannon had walked out on her eleven months ago, just about the time when Calvin Coffey first showed up. Now obviously there was no way Calvin could be Gerald. Huette would have recognised him. But it did seem like an awfully strange coincidence.

When Nigel had first told her she was going to be his junior in the case, she immediately set to work using her Gen-Z social media skills, to find out everything she could about her client. Despite formidable effort, she had found nothing at all about Calvin on social media going back more than eleven months.

But now, she was hoping she'd have better luck with Gerald Shannon. And sure enough, his name came up – multiple times – at her first port of call. In a community with two billion members, it was a common name. So she made a few false starts before finding the right one. At least she *thought* it was the right one. The picture matched what she had seen at Soraya's home. But the status was set to "single". Not "it's complicated" – *single*.

Then again, anyway you looked at it, he was a rat. So why should you expect him to behave like anything other than a rat?

The good news was that his profile wasn't hidden. His life was an open book. There were a few posts about Huette and the children, as well as pictures. But you had to scroll down to see them. Because his latest posts were about the great time he was having in the Caribbean, with a fit, busty blonde who looked barely out of her teens, but who gave her age as 27, when Emily clicked on her link. Unlike Gerald, the blonde – whose name was "Candy Sweet" of all things – had only joined Facebook 10 months ago. Just *after* Gerald had left Huette, interestingly enough. So she didn't have much visible history. And what little she had, consisted mostly of regaling anyone, who might be interested, with tales – probably exaggerated – about the great time she was having with her current "sugar daddy".

Yes, that was what she openly called him!

Emily took an instant dislike to her, remembering how her own father had walked out on the family when – after a string of short-term affairs – he finally decided to go the whole hog and shack up with some bimbo barely ten years older than Emily.

She clicked back to look at Gerald's profile. The pictures were similar to the ones on Candy's own profile. Except that in both cases, they appeared to be pictures of Candy more than those of Gerald. As if she was vain and narcissistic enough to want to show pictures of herself, while he at least had the discretion to hide behind the camera, snapping away at his floozy, instead of displaying his beer belly and balding head to a world that almost certainly wasn't interested.

It made perfect sense really. He bucked up his ego more by showing the "hot chick" in his life than advertising the middle-aged manspread that he had acquired. The fact that she was probably only interested in him because of his money – which he *should* have been paying to Huette in child support – didn't matter, as far as feeding his ego was concerned.

While eating her lunch, Emily continued to look at Gerald's Facebook page, noting that his entries had in fact been few and far between, until he ran out on Huette and hooked up with Candy. Emily could imagine what was happening: a midlife crisis and now a young woman comes along and helps him recapture his youth – or at least, the *illusion* of his youth.

Periodically, Emily flipped back to Candy's page and her preening and posing before the camera, before returning to Gerald's. She didn't know what she was hoping to find. He was touring the Caribbean – Bahamas, Bermuda, Cayman Islands (tax implications, anyone?) – and bragging about what a wonderful time he was having. It wasn't clear who he was bragging to. He didn't appear to have acquired any extra friends since his newfound life as a mock-single man. And his old friends were mostly just ignoring him. It may have been simply that his posts were not showing up on their feeds. The Facebook algorithm only feeds new posts to friends who have recently interacted with earlier posts. Once they stop reacting, at some point, the algorithm stops feeding them and the later posts dry up.

Still, Emily thought it odd. Why wasn't he tagging his friends if he *wanted* attention? Or why was he posting all these pictures at all, if he *didn't?*

At some point, Emily realised that she was just going over the same material, and there was nothing more to look at – at least nothing more from the period after he had walked out on Huette. She also realised that time was getting on and she'd better head back to the Old Bailey.

So she asked for the bill, and it was while the waiter was getting it that she noticed something odd about one of the few pictures of Gerald himself. It was a good quality picture, in high resolution, and he was apparently staring straight at the camera – "apparently", because he was wearing sunglasses. But the thing that Emily noticed was the reflection – in Gerald's sunglasses – of the woman who took the picture. The face and features were hard to make out, because the woman had the sun directly behind her. Not unusual in itself: a good photographer keeps the sun behind them, so that the subject of the picture is well lit and clearly visible.

The problem was that while Gerald was looking straight ahead at the camera, *his shadow*, like those of other people and objects in the background, *stretched off to the viewer's left, or Gerald's right.*

46

"To summarize, M'Lady, the defendant offered a reasonable explanation, at the time of his arrest, for the presence of his DNA on the hammer. His own hammer, along with most of the rest of his tools, was in his toolbox in the van. The lack of blood spatter on the defendant or his clothes suggests that he was not the attacker. The absence of defendant's hair on the overalls, that were clearly worn by the attacker, suggests that my client had not worn the overalls.

"It follows therefore that the attacker, who *did* wear the overalls, was someone else. The Crown's expert on blood spatter distribution, conceded that the attacker was probably shorter in height than the deceased, whereas the defendant is some three and a half inches taller."

Nigel was rounding off his submission that there was no case to answer.

"As to the circumstances that brought the defendant to the crime scene in the first place, I will not dwell on that, as it is agreed by both parties that the defendant was lured there by some unknown person who posed as Professor Wallace.

"However, I wish to briefly address the Crown's contention that the defendant has a *motive* for killing Professor Wallace *because* he was tricked into going to Wallace's house. I can only say that aside from this argument being pure conjecture, it amounts to saying that a motive may be inferred, *not* because of a wrong done *by* the defendant, but rather because of a wrong done *to* him. That is, M'Lady, in my humble submission, akin to a dagger plunged into the heart of British justice.

"Finally, I would remind Your Ladyship of my earlier arguments pertaining to m'learned friend's belated disclosures. Even if those arguments were deemed inadequate *in themselves*, they should be taken into consideration now, in conjunction with the arguments in support of this submission, as Your Ladyship promised. And in conclusion, I submit that the effect of these facts, taken as a whole, is that there is no case to answer."

And with that, Nigel sat down.

Emily was watching Judge Braham carefully, again trying to read her.

"Mr Blair," Mary Braham prompted. "Does the Crown wish to respond?"

"Briefly, M'Lady," said Blair.

"The Crown concedes of course that the case against the defendant is circumstantial. As m'learned friend pointed out, there were no eyewitnesses to the events themselves. And indeed no one overheard screams or shouts that might enable us to definitively conclude that the attack took place after the defendant arrived at the house."

Or BEFORE he arrived, you sneaky bastard! Emily's mind was screaming.

"However, there are many pieces of the puzzle that fit together neatly to demonstrate that the case against the defendant is somewhat stronger than m'learned friend has implied."

Hayden Blair looked down at his notes, even though he had memorised them. After a pregnant pause, he continued.

"Firstly, as to *means*, the defendant was a builder who possessed several hammers, and indeed his DNA was on the murder weapon, which he *admits* he handled."

"Secondly, as to *motive*, the defendant normally worked in his local area, south of the river, but on this occasion, motivated by greed – *which again he himself conceded in the police interview* – he decided to accept what he thought to be a lucrative job in North London. So greedy was he that he decided to do the job on the strength of a few emails, without even bothering to talk to the client by phone. To any reasonable man, the client's refusal to provide a phone number, or to talk by phone, should have been a red flag. Yet, so blinded by greed was the defendant, he ignored this warning sign and drove all the way across London in pursuit of this imaginary job. The Crown's theory is that the defendant lost his temper when he discovered that there *was* no job after all. Now that may be just a theory, but it is a theory supported by strong circumstantial evidence.

"Thirdly, as to *opportunity*, the defendant arrived at the house at a time that clearly coincided with the time when the murder was committed.

"Thus the defendant possesses that holy trinity of

incriminating factors: means, motive and opportunity. And while the Crown concedes that means, motive and opportunity do not *necessarily* prove a man guilty of a crime, the effect of these factors – when there are *no other suspects* – is so greatly amplified, as to leave little room for doubt.

"Finally, regarding the belated disclosures and m'learned friend's much vaunted 'hidden hand' theory, I would point out that this too is merely speculation. I can only say that even if the defendant was a victim of a prankster, the sole effect of the prankster's actions would appear to be to have provoked the defendant into an act of murderous violence. Spontaneous violence, I concede. But violence nevertheless – and *fatal* violence at that. Whilst the owner of that 'hidden hand' may be, in some way, *morally* culpable of contributing to the tragic stream of events, *all* the evidence suggests that the defendant is *legally* culpable. Thus he should be held to account, or at least put to proof and held to answer the compelling evidence against him."

And with that Hayden Blair KC sat down looking confident that he had prevailed.

In fact, Nigel Farringdon KC looked equally confident. But these appearances were nothing more than acts, to impress the ladies and gentlemen of the press.

The truth of the matter was that neither of them had a clue which way the judge's decision would go. But they were about to find out.

"I have no need to retire to consider the eloquent arguments of both sides. It would be wrong and unfair to keep the defendant waiting. Firstly, as I have already stated, much about this case troubles me. Not merely the paucity of evidence, but also the behaviour of the Crown with respect to its disclosure obligations. It is clear to me that the Crown's evidence offers many areas of vulnerability that the defence may wish to attack. But as things stand, the Crown's evidence is sufficient, when taken as a whole, to establish a prima facie case. Accordingly, I rule that there *is* a case to answer."

Judge Braham looked over at Nigel.

"Will the defence be ready to start tomorrow morning?"

On the inside, Emily was fuming.

Nigel was more stoic. He would have liked the chance to look into the new material that Blair had disclosed. And to give the police the chance to investigate too. Indeed he would have been in a good position to *demand* it. Or even take up Hayden Blair's suggestion that they halt the trial and call a new one. But Judge Braham had made it clear that she had no intention of granting bail, and this would mean that Calvin would be locked up even longer. And with the backlog in the courts showing no signs of abating, who could say *when* the trial would restart. The defence was boxed in on all sides.

So he decided to make the best of a bad situation.

"M'Lady, as the Court is well aware, the defence has obviously been caught by surprise regarding these *belated* Crown disclosures. However, in the face of Your Ladyship's steadfast refusal to grant the defendant bail, the defence will use its... *best endeavours* to start tomorrow morning."

He had made his point for the record. But the tone was as harsh as he dared without risking contempt of court.

So, not quite so stoic, Emily concluded.

47

"Are they part of the same NHS trust?"

Calvin asked the question earnestly, as if trying to make sense of it all.

The spontaneous legal meeting was Emily's idea, more to give Calvin some encouragement and moral support than anything else. Huddled together in the small holding cell, Emily and Calvin were seated, while Philip Solomon and Nigel were standing.

The scan had originated at the Royal Bournemouth Hospital. But University College Hospital in London held a copy.

"I checked it out," Emily explained. "The academic buildings on the Royal Free campus that used to belong to the Royal Free Hospital School of Medicine, merged with UCL Medical School way back in 1998. But the NHS trusts are separate."

So the elephant remained in the room.

How did Raymond Morrison's brain scan come to be inserted into Walter Wallace's medical records?

"Is there any way of finding out how it happened?" asked Calvin. "I mean are the police even looking?"

Emily was doing something on her phone. So it was left for Nigel to answer.

"They *are* looking." The tone was reassuring. "But there's no guarantee that the hacker left a trail. I mean, you heard the evidence about the emails. Whoever is doing all this, knows their business."

"Hello Ruth. It's Emily."

Nigel and Calvin looked round to see Emily on her phone.

"I wanted to ask you a question. What was the number of Raymond's phone – the one that was stolen?"

She struggled with a pen and notebook as Ruth replied.

"Okay thank you."

When she ended the call, Nigel was looking at her as if to say:

"What was all that about?"

"Sorry guys. I just had a hunch."

"And?"

She was flipping through something on her phone. Suddenly her face lit up.

"I was *right!*"

"Care to share it with us?" Nigel prompted.

"The number that Professor Wallace called on April the 4th... it belonged to Ruth's husband."

48

Unlike her parents' house in Hampstead Garden Suburb, Huette's modest two-storey house stood on a quiet, leafy street corner in Camden. Its pale facade was partially obscured by lush greenery, a mixture of yellow blossoms and climbing ivy that softened the lines of the brickwork, with a small front garden enclosed by a wooden picket fence.

The rooms inside would have been well-lit by the large, white-framed windows, but for the overhead stretching branches of a large tree on the corner. A tall streetlamp stood at the other corner, while similar houses lined the rest of the street.

Although Gerald's freelancing as a computer programmer had proved lucrative at times, they had struggled to get onto the property ladder. Amidst bouts of recession and unemployment for Gerald, and low-paid temp secretarial work – punctuated by unpaid maternity leave – for Huette, there had never quite been a "right time". So their choice of house proved to be a compromise between needs, desires and costs.

It was centrally located, but serene. It offered easy transport links to the business and commercial centres in London, but its location on a working-class council estate, and its modest size, made it accessible to their equally modest finances.

It was not a new build, and when they bought it, they were all too aware that it had suffered from decades of dilapidation. But they had spent a chunk of money, that they could barely afford, on doing it up and modernising the interior, adorning it with a modern, tasteful touch.

Inside, it had only two small bedrooms, one for the parents – now reduced to a single parent – the other for all three children. They had known when they bought it that at some point, when the children were older, they would have to sell up, and probably move out of town, if they were to have any chance of finding something bigger. But for now it would have to do. Until he built up a list of clientele and repeat business, Gerald had to be close to the financial centre in the Square Mile and the commercial centre in the West End.

Of course, since his untimely departure, none of this made sense anymore. Huette couldn't afford the mortgage and that thought was driving her to distraction. But right now, she had other worries.

Specifically John. Little baby John, or John-John as Michael called him. He was acting cranky. Normal for a baby, perhaps. But this had been going on since yesterday. And she had tried everything. He didn't want to sleep. He didn't want to interact with her or with his siblings, and perhaps most significant of all, he didn't want to eat. He wanted neither food nor the comfort of the nipple.

And he was crying the whole time.

Huette was at her wit's end about this too. Since Covid, it was practically impossible to get a doctor's appointment. Of course she could take him to the A&E room at UCH. But it wasn't really an emergency, and without Gerald to look after Ariadne and Michael, she'd have to take them with her.

She decided to give it another day, to see if he improved. And in her mind, she silently cursed Gerald.

49

Judge Braham had given them till tomorrow to make any adjustments they needed to their defence in light of the latest CPS disclosures, but they had a lot of work to do in that time. So Emily and Nigel waved off Philip Solomon and hailed a taxi to take them back to St Jude's. Nigel was lost in thought, but once in the taxi, it was Nigel who spoke first.

"Okay I'm going to draw up a petition for habeas corpus."

"She'll never grant it."

"No, but I want it on record."

"You're already planning an appeal?"

"Just covering the bases."

"You know she's being *bloody* unfair!"

Emily felt tears in her eyes. And she realised how unprofessional this must look. Lawyers are *not* supposed to get emotional about their cases.

"It may not come to that. Their case is full of holes. And Blair's just given us loads of points of attack if we throw everything at them."

"Then why waste time on habeas corpus?"

"It'll put her on the defensive. She won't want to *look* biased."

"Would you be ready to go nuclear?"

Emily was asking if Nigel would consider a motion for recusal on grounds of bias.

"If I had grounds."

"You studied law with her."

"That's not enough."

"Well she's consistently ruling against you."

"Not really. She was ready to order a new trial."

"While keeping Calvin banged up."

"She has the Coroners and Justice Act on her side."

Just then, Emily's phone rang. She looked at the screen.

"It's Ruth."

"Take it."

She took it, while Nigel looked on.

"Hello, Ruth."

"Oh hi. It's… I mean Hello Emily. Listen there was something I remembered that I wanted to tell you."

She proceeded to tell Emily about the money going into Raymond's bank account on a regular basis – in cash. When she had finished, Emily asked the question she had been itching to ask from the first sentence.

"Do you have any idea where the money came from?"

"At first, I thought he was just doing a spot of private tutoring and concealing the income from the taxman. But now I think he may have been getting it from Professor Wallace."

"But why would Professor Wallace be paying him money?"

"To keep him quiet."

50

It was round about mid-afternoon that the call came through to the Crown Prosecution Service. After the caller had navigated the labyrinth of "Press this if you want that," they finally got through to a human being.

"I'd like to talk to the person in charge of the case of the R versus Calvin Coffey."

"May I ask what it's regarding?"

"It's about the case of the R versus Calvin Coffey."

The caller realised that the voice changer they were using might be making it harder for the other party to hear them.

"Do you know the name of the person you wish to speak to?"

"If I did, I would have *said* the name."

The caller was becoming increasingly irritated.

There followed the usual routine of the call being transferred several times – each time the caller stating what they wanted and being told that they needed to talk with someone else.

Eventually the caller got through to the right person.

"Okay listen – the reason I'm calling is because I have some information about the defendant in the case of R versus Coffey that the CPS isn't aware of. The defendant is supposedly a builder called Calvin Coffey. But his name wasn't always Calvin Coffey. And he wasn't always a builder."

51

Sitting at home in the evening, Emily was feeling restless. Back in chambers, she had done everything Nigel had asked her to do in the case, following up on the conversation with Ruth and looking into the hospital trusts. But there was something else nagging away in her head.

She was still holding off telling Nigel what she had discovered about Gerald Shannon. But after seeing that manipulated picture on Facebook, a theory was taking shape in her mind. It was too early to say exactly, but the ideas were flowing thick and fast.

So what she decided to do now was check out the pictures of the eponymous "Candy Sweet" to see if she had any past, before she hooked up with Huette's husband. There were several good reverse image search sites that didn't require a paid subscription: TinEye, Yandex, PimEyes, Google Reverse Search. She decided to start with TinEye.

She picked a very clear and sharp beach shot of Candy from Facebook and pasted it into TinEye. Within seconds, it declared "No Match". Next she tried it on PimEyes. It found several similar images and one exact match, but in each case only the first part of the URL was visible. To get the whole address, you had to pay $15 (US) or twice that for a monthly subscription.

No, thank you.

Next up was Yandex. It came up with lots of similar images – with hotlinks to websites. But no exact match. And some of the links just took her to commercial sites that wanted to separate her from her money.

This is getting frustrating.

But she knew that this sort of thing required patience and persistence. So then she tried Labnol. And they came through in spades. Original picture on the left; single, exact-match result on the right. The URL was truncated with the now familiar ellipsis because it was too long. But a click on the link took you to a new page on the same tab, showing the full URL in all its glory. And that too was a hot link. She clicked on it, and it took her to the website – a travel blog no less.

And it wasn't any "Candy Sweet". It was called **peripateticblonde.travel**.

An effing travel blog! He's been copying pictures from a travel blog and pasting them onto his Facebook page... and manipulating the images.

Then Emily remembered that Gerald Shannon was a computer programmer, and he probably also had skills using programs like Photoshop. So if he wanted to lift an image, strip away the background and paste it into another location, it would be no big deal for a man of his skills. And if, for example, he wanted to insert an image onto a beach, where all the shadows were pointing towards the left, he would have to isolate the image, insert it onto the background layer and then create the shadow pointing in the right direction to match the other people and deckchairs, etc.

And that was precisely what he did with his own image: created the illusion that he was somewhere that he wasn't.

But why?

In an instant, the answer came to her.

To conceal where he WAS. In other words, TO GIVE HIMSELF AN ALIBI.

And a man would only give himself an alibi... if he *needed* one.

But if there's no connection between Gerald Shannon and the blonde, then who was the woman reflected in his sunglasses? The woman who had taken the picture of him?

An accomplice?

Okay, but who was she? And what's the motive?

The shape of the woman's body was all too familiar. But she couldn't see the face, because with the sun behind the photographer the woman appeared only as a silhouette... sil... sil...

Huette!

52

Miles away, despite the urgency of the case, Nigel was trying to take his mind off the case by working in the garden of his detached house in Hampton, a quiet, leafy suburb of west London. Working in the garden, in this case, meant breaking up a few old wooden pallets that he had acquired free of charge from a neighbour, and turning them into frames for raised beds that he would use for planting vegetables. So his current labours were more akin to woodwork than to gardening.

The garden had always been Joanie's domain. Sometimes she roped him in to do the DIY stuff – turning their broken old freezer into a worm bin for composting. But planting potatoes in oversized buckets or using the wood from old pallets to make raised beds for onions, carrots and peppers? *That* was her job. He always wanted to do it, and sometimes he helped out. But gardening didn't suit his schedule, as he often had to work weekends. When he told Emily that the law is a seven-day business, he wasn't lying.

It was a phone call from Emily now that cut short his current labours – and reminiscences.

"Nige, listen, I think I've figured it out!"

"I'm fine Emily. How are you?"

"What? Look, it's… I mean… sorry. Hi, Nige, how are you?"

"I'm fine. And I'm sure you're fine too."

He wasn't actually angry, nor trying to teach her manners. He was just trying to get her to slow down and catch her breath. She was clearly hyper, and desperately eager to tell him something. But she had to learn to control her emotions. At times, she was still that toddler accompanying her dad to St Jude's. And his reaction was like getting her to sit on the naughty step for two minutes in order to calm down.

"Okay, okay. Look, just listen. I did some digging into Huette's husband. You know the one who supposedly walked out on her."

"*Supposedly?*"

"Yes. I mean that's my theory."

Over the next few minutes, she outlined her social media research on Gerald Shannon, the doctored picture of him on Facebook, and the stolen pictures of the woman from the travel blog. When she got to the end, she fell silent, breathless.

"Okay... okay," said Nigel, also breathless from the exertion of listening and reeling from the information overload." Still trying to take it all in, he asked: "but what's your theory?"

"Theory?"

She was mentally drained from the effort of telling him.

"You said you had a theory. I mean what does it all add up to?"

He regretted asking her, wondering how long she'd be bending his ear for *this* time.

"I think they were working together – Gerald and Huette I mean."

"To what end?"

"To get the house."

"Specifically?" He was being laconic now, and quite deliberately.

"I think they hacked the hospital computer. I mean Gerald did, using his computer skills. To trick her dad into thinking he had a brain tumour. So they could get the house."

"And how exactly would that work?"

"Well if he thought he had a brain tumour, then he and Soraya might move into some sort of protected or sheltered accommodation or a care home or something, and gift the house to Huette and Gerald and their children."

"Yes, but that didn't happen, did it?"

"I know and that's why I think they killed him."

"*Hold* on a minute! *Who* killed him? And how and why?"

"Think about it. They must have heard about Raymond from Walter or Soraya, and used his scans to trick Walter – or rather his doctors. But Walter was a stubborn man. Everybody says so. And presumably he didn't want to gift the house. So then they must've realised that more drastic action was called for."

"More drastic action meaning...?"

"Murder."

"Go on."

"Okay, so, she decided to kill her dad – presumably thinking that Soraya would be more pliant and easier to manipulate. But they needed alibis. And more than that, they needed to make sure that nobody even suspected. Especially not Soraya. So they came up with this plan in which Gerald appeared to walk out on Huette for some floozy. And then went abroad. Hence, the phoney pictures on his Facebook."

"Why not real pictures?"

"Because he still had to be in this country – to actually do the murder I mean. Otherwise he'd've had to leave Britain, sneak back in to commit the murder without it showing up on border control, then sneak out again without it showing up, then come back openly as the prodigal husband."

"None of this makes sense, Emily. How do you sneak back in undetected?"

"That's my point. You can't. Or at least it isn't easy. But if you never left in the first place, then it's easy. But you still have to create a record of being abroad if you want an alibi. Hence the fake pictures on Facebook."

"And what about a departure record?"

"There won't *be* any. I mean there's no passport control on your way out."

"No but the carriers scan your passport when you check in. And again when you board the plane."

"But they don't share it with border control."

"Not automatically. But the record is there."

Emily thought about this.

"There are ways it could be done. At some airports, they board via the Tarmac. That's what happens at Luton. Then you could slip away from the other outgoing passengers and mingle with other passengers from an incoming flight."

"And again have to go through border entry."

"Okay, but what if you have dual nationality? You could have two passports with slightly different spellings of the name? You could exit on one and re-enter on the other."

This time it was Nigel who was silent for a few seconds.

"Yes, I suppose that *could* work. But why go to all that trouble?"

"Well, first of all, if they appear to have split up, then nobody would suspect them of being in league with one another. Gerald would have the skills to hack the computer, but no motive for committing the murder. Huette would have the motive for committing, but with an alibi she wouldn't be in the frame. That's why Huette had to be on the Heath with Soraya and the kids – to have a watertight alibi."

Nigel was listening attentively now. Emily could really be

onto something here.

"Go on."

"Okay, but now here's where it gets tricky. If they were still together – I mean, if they hadn't broken up, and if Gerald just made some excuse for not going along to the Heath, he'd be the prime suspect from the get-go – and so would Huette. This way she has a cast-iron alibi, and nobody suspects her. And nobody thinks Gerald had anything to do with it, because as far as everyone else is concerned he's gallivanting across the globe with his floozy."

"But what about the Raymond Morrison killing?"

"That's probably what gave them the idea. Both the tumour diagnosis *and* the murder."

"But what's the endgame? I mean now Soraya owns the house. That doesn't put them any nearer to owning it."

"I think it does. With her father dead, Huette'll probably find it easier to manipulate her mother."

"And what about Gerald?"

"If my theory is right, at some point he'll return, all humble and apologetic and he and Huette will be… 'reconciled.'"

"I don't think Soraya will accept that."

"Okay, so maybe Huette'll flip the order: first get Soraya to sign over the house to her and the children, prevailing on her goodwill and playing up the helpless single mother. Or maybe she'll remind Soraya that the sooner she signs it over to them, the more certain they are to avoid inheritance tax. Then, *after that*, Gerald makes his grand return, once Soraya has signed on the dotted line."

"Okay. It's plausible, I'll grant you. But what about Raymond? Who killed him, and how does that fit into the overall scenario?"

"That's the one thing I can't answer. But maybe Raymond's death is entirely separate. It happened in Bournemouth, remember – away from London. Maybe it was some sort of a local matter."

"And Calvin?"

"They needed a fall guy."

"So you think they set up our boy?"

"I'm sure of it."

Tuesday 26th March, 2024

53

It was breakfast in the Shannon household and while Ariadne and Mikey were tucking into their cornflakes, Huette was fighting a losing battle with baby John in his highchair, trying every way she knew how to get him to eat.

She had tried breastfeeding him. And it worked briefly. But not for long. But then he started crying again and nothing she could do gave him any comfort. Once she had him seated in the highchair – and even *that* had been a struggle – she tried some strawberry yoghurt. He wasn't interested. Soft mashed fruit? Same result. Waving toys in front of him and singing "The Wheels on the Bus." *Nothing.*

Finally, in despair, she spoke to him as if he could understand her.

"Oh John-John. I wish you could tell me what's bothering you."

It was just as well that she said it, because it produced a reaction.

"He eated a sim card."

This was little Mikey, who had just finished his cornflakes.

"*What?*"

Mikey looked frightened, because Mummy sounded angry.

"What did you say, Mikey?"

She mellowed her tone consciously, to get him to repeat himself.

"He eated a sim card."

Huette's mind was in a whirl.

"When? Where?"

She was back to sounding frantic. But this time Mikey answered anyway.

"At Nana."

Her mind went back to Sunday and her visit to her mum, when John had been crawling on the floor and she was talking to

that young female barrister representing the man accused of...
And John had started acting cranky soon after that.

Huette turned to Ariadne. At six she was likely to have more understanding than four-year-old Mike.

"Did *you* see him swallow anything?"

Ariadne shook her head. Huette turned back to Mike.

"You're sure he swallowed a SIM card?"

Mike nodded, as if he too no longer trusted his voice.

"Okay, we're going to the hospital."

54

"So what are we going to do about it?"

Emily was being her usual, eager and enthusiastic self. She had arrived at St Jude's early and excited, all bright-eyed and bushy-tailed. But Nigel had called her to say that he was running late and would go directly to the Old Bailey. So now, here they were, in the robing room, getting ready for the big day in court – the day when the defence would finally open, and the jury would get to hear Calvin's version straight from the horse's mouth.

"Do about what?" he asked.

She was about to show her irritation, when she noticed that he seemed distracted. And she well knew why. He was thinking about Joanie and the children once again. It was still too raw. At times like this, she wondered how he managed to come into work at all.

She waited a decent interval before replying: "About my theory."

"At this stage, there's not much we can do."

"We could always call Huette as a witness. Maybe ask Judge Braham if we can treat her as hostile?"

"We haven't got enough to justify that. And anyway, what are we going to ask her?"

"We could start off with the direct approach. Like… 'where's your husband?'"

"We could. But I don't think we'd get very far – even if Mary let us."

"Oh, so it's Mary now!"

"I always knew her as Mary. It's hard to call her M'Lady in court. I practically have to bite my tongue to stop myself calling her by name."

"So are we just going to let it slide? I mean we've got *evidence* that Huette is lying."

"But she hasn't lied in court."

"That's because nobody *asked* her about Gerald. If we *call* her, we can *ask* her. And then, if she lies, we've got her."

"But first we'd have to justify re-calling her. And then we'd have to justify asking her questions about her husband. And even if we can establish that the pictures on his Facebook page are fake, that doesn't mean it has anything to do with her – or that she knows anything about it."

"At least we can put her under pressure."

"Yes, and alert her to the fact that we're onto her and Gerald."

Emily was pouting.

"Besides," Nigel added. "Like I said, there's no way the judge'll even allow it."

"So we're just going to ignore the most likely explanation for the murder? Because we're afraid of the judge?"

"I didn't say that. We just have to keep our powder dry. For now."

"For *now*?"

"When we get back to Chambers, I'll call Philip Solomon. In fact, maybe I'll even do it at lunchtime."

"Call him and what?"

"And ask him to hire an Inquiry Agent to look into it."

"You mean a private detective?"

"Yes. We need to establish something more solid. Like proving that Gerald either never left the UK or left and came back. And maybe we can establish that Huette is still in contact with him."

"What's he going to do? Put a tail on her?"

Nigel was shaking his head with a beaming smile.

"Those American movies again."

"Seriously. How *are* we going to get her? If I'm right, and her husband never left the country, it's pretty damn hard to prove a negative."

"We do have another avenue of attack, Emily."

"Which is?"

"Well assuming that you're right, I don't think Soraya knows what they did."

"You mean we should tell her?"

"Not at this stage. She's going through enough pain at the moment."

Emily realised that Nigel was bound to sympathise with a grieving widow, despite his professional duty to their client.

"But if we can build up enough of a case to be sure *ourselves*, then at that stage we might have to make a move to get her onside before we go nuclear."

Emily nodded, feeling a thrill of excitement, but now a twinge of concern crept in: Soraya *was* emotionally fragile.

Nigel was now fully berobed.

"You ready?" he asked Emily, casting her a sideways glance.

"Uh-huh."

"Then here goes. Once more into the breach– "

"*Be serious, Nige!*"

55

With no one to look after them, Huette had to bring the other children with her. That meant she had to strap John into the carry seat and Michael into the small, blue booster seat. Ariadne was old enough to strap herself into her slightly larger pink booster seat.

But that was only the beginning. The traffic on the way from Camden Town to Warren Street was congested, and then she had to find a parking space. Not necessarily a legal parking space, just an available one. She found one in Grafton Way and parked there but didn't have the time or presence of mind to check if it was a loading bay or a disabled bay. She put her father's disabled badge in the window for what it was worth, and prayed that if a traffic warden came, she would only get a penalty charge notice and not get clamped or, worse, towed away.

Then she unstrapped Mike and John's carry seat, while Ariadne unstrapped herself, and proceeded on foot to the A&E department. Ariadne was cool about the whole process, seeing it as a grand adventure. But Michael was tired and didn't want to walk, throwing a tantrum when he found out that he wasn't going to be pushed along in the buggy.

Huette knew that she couldn't carry Mike while carrying the baby in the carry seat. But try explaining that to a tired four-year-old. So she told Ariadne to hold Mike's hand and not to let go under any circumstances. The only time she was worried was when they had to cross Tottenham Court Road. It was a main thoroughfare, and the traffic could be unforgiving. Fortunately there were traffic lights and pedestrian signals right by the intersection where Grafton Way met the main road.

They had to cross Grafton Way again on the other side, to get to A&E, but that was also regulated by traffic lights and pedestrian signals, so they breezed through that without too much stress.

Once inside the hospital, she followed the signs to the children's emergency department, which was separate from the main A&E. Finally she arrived at reception.

56

It was ten o'clock on the morning of Tuesday 26th of March, when Calvin Coffey finally got to testify. He was sworn in and then Nigel proceeded to lead him through his evidence-in-chief.

"Could you tell the court about your business – what you do, how you operate and how you find clients or customers?"

Lead was perhaps the wrong word, as strictly speaking, the lawyer who calls a witness – including his own client – isn't allowed to ask leading questions directly.

So after "You are Calvin Coffey of such and such an address" and an affirmative reply, the questions became open-ended.

Calvin explained that he was a builder, a jack-of-all-trades: bricklaying, carpentry, plumbing, glazing, plastering. He was even a qualified Gas Safe Registered gasfitter and electrician, he added proudly. He did small jobs, either alone or brought in someone else, variously on a percentage partnership basis or for fixed wages. The jobs could be anything from internal repairs to loft conversions and building extensions, such as conservatories.

He advertised through leaflets and fliers, trade directory listings, word-of-mouth and display ads in shop windows or on the notice boards of DIY shops and such like. He did have a simple website consisting of about three pages, plus a contact form that sent initial messages through to his email. But he admitted that very few clients came by that route.

Yes, he was American and *yes* he had been living here for quite a while, legally. He didn't go into what he was doing before a year ago and Nigel didn't push him for it. That wasn't his job. And in any case, it might backfire: Nigel didn't know what he would say, whether it would be true or not and whether – if true – it would be helpful or damaging.

During his testimony, Calvin was trying to look at the jury, as Nigel had told him to beforehand. The jurors are the arbiters of fact. So a witness is supposed to address the jury when giving evidence and not the lawyer who asked the question. However, there is a natural tendency on the part of witnesses, to look at the lawyer, when giving evidence especially the defendant, looking at his own lawyer. Judges tend to let this slide without comment, unless the witness actually looks round at the judge and *away* from the jury.

However, on cross-examination, opposing counsel will often take advantage of this to interrupt the defendant and say something like: "Oh *not* to me: to the jury." This is *not* because the jury can't hear the testimony perfectly well. It's a deliberate prosecutor tactic to break the flow of the defendant and take him out of his stride, so that he becomes disoriented and nervous. This then makes his subsequent testimony less convincing.

Nigel had warned Calvin that Hayden Blair would do this, given half an excuse. So they practised testifying, using random facts unrelated to Calvin's case.

"Now turning to the events of Saturday, the twenty third of September 2023, could you tell us please, how you came to be there?"

Over the course of the next few minutes, Calvin outlined the story of how he was contacted via email by the man he thought to be Professor Walter Wallace and asked for an estimate for a loft conversion, how Wallace insisted on communicating only by email, claiming that he had a speech impediment, how Wallace had sent him a few poor-quality pictures and how he had arranged to go to the house to make an assessment with the intention of giving a firm and binding quote.

"And did you go there?"

"Yes, on the afternoon of Saturday the twenty third of September, last year."

"And how did you get there?"

"I drove. In my van."

"Does your van have SatNav?"

"Yes. And a DashCam."

"And were these operating at the time of the journey?"

"Yes."

"For the whole journey, or only part of it?"

"The whole journey."

"So there's a record of your entire journey."

"Yes. Both an MPEG of the road journey *and* the SatNav record – both from the built-in SatNav on my van and my phone."

The judge looked up from her notes.

"Are these in the agreed bundle Mr Farringdon?"

"Yes, M'Lady."

Nigel stated the reference for the record.

"Now, Calvin, could you tell us what happened when you arrived at Professor Wallace's house."

"Yes. As I told the police, the door was slightly ajar when I got there, and my initial thought was that he'd left it open for me. However I wasn't sure, so I called out something like 'Hello, anyone home?' And then after a few seconds I called it out again."

"So you called it out twice?"

"Yes."

"And did you get any answer?"

"No."

"So what did you do next?"

"I pushed the door open with my hand, my right hand I think, and strained to hear any trace of movement, or anyone saying anything. Then I went in."

"Okay. So you were in the house. What did you do then?"

"Well... first, I kind of looked around in the entrance area. And then I made my way to the kitchen."

"The kitchen in particular? Was there any reason for that?"

"Well it's interesting, because when I gave my police interview, I wasn't really sure why I went to the kitchen. But upon reflection, I realise why."

Emily was listening to Calvin's testimony, and his choice of words, with an uneasy feeling – a feeling of mild scepticism.

"And why was that?

"Well the doors to the other rooms were closed, whereas the kitchen door was open. And light was coming in via the kitchen. So it was as if the kitchen was an extension of the vestibule. It was the logical place to start, if you see what I mean."

"And when you entered the kitchen, could you describe what you saw."

"I saw the man whom I now know to be Professor Wallace lying on the floor."

"And what state was he in?"

"He was dead. And bleeding."

"Bleeding?"

"I mean there was a lot of blood. On his head and upper body. And on the floor. I mean the pictures shown by the prosecution pretty much show what I saw at the time."

And how did you know he was dead?"

"As I told the police. His eyes were open, but there was no sign of blinking. So I concluded that he was dead."

"Okay, now in your police interview, you were asked about a hammer that was found at the crime scene?"

"Yes, it was lying near the body. And I heard someone or something, that appeared to be coming from inside the house. I realised afterwards that it had probably come from outside, through an open window. But at the time, I panicked. And because there was a body lying there – a badly battered body – I kind of picked up the hammer in my state of panic."

"And to be clear, the reason for this was?"

"To defend myself – in the event that the murderer was still there and might try to harm me."

"But you're not exactly a small man are you Calvin?"

"Leading, M'Lady!" Hayden Blair interjected, rising swiftly to his feet."

"I think I can take judicial notice of the defendant's physique," said Judge Braham, introducing a note of judicial levity into the proceedings. The lawyers and court staff chuckled, while the jurors seemed oblivious to the humour. The prosecutor resumed his seat.

Emily noticed that Calvin looked uncertain of whether he was still supposed to answer. But before she could prompt him with a nod, or Nigel by word, he decided to speak.

"With hindsight, I realise it was a stupid thing to do. And I acknowledged as much to the police. But it was a moment of panic."

"And then what?"

"Well after a few seconds, I realised that there was no one there, or at least that if there was, they would probably be looking to make an escape. And in any case, they'd left the hammer there so unless they grabbed another object, I wasn't in too much danger. And also, by then, I'd sort of figured out that the sounds probably came from outside. So I guess, I realised from a combination of these factors that I wasn't in any immediate danger. So I put the hammer down."

"And you said in your statement to the police that you put it down in more or less the same position you found it."

"Yes."

"And what did you do then?"

"Well basically, I ran outside and bumped into a woman whom I now know to be Professor Wallace's wife Soraya. I can confirm her testimony from that point forward."

Nigel then led Calvin through a brief account of what happened afterwards, police arrival, arrest "on suspicion of murder," police interview and how it was only then that he was told that it had not been Professor Wallace who was on the other end of the email communications that had brought him there. However, when asked if he knew now who *was* on the other end of the communications, he hesitated and then turned to the judge to say: "Am I allowed to speculate."

"No," Judge Braham replied firmly. "Tell us only what you know."

Calvin looked awkward at that point.

"In that case, I guess I must comply with your ruling."

Nigel wasn't sure if this was a signal that he *wanted* to say more, or a warning that he didn't. Either way, Nigel had no intention of gambling. Instead he simply said "thank you, wait there" to make it clear that cross-examination was to follow. Then he sat down and waited for Hayden Blair KC to unleash whatever onslaught he had lined up.

"I appear on behalf of the Crown," he said with his by now familiar shuffling on papers.

This was a customary form of introduction, introducing oneself to the witness before cross-examination.

"First of all, should I call you Mr Coffey or Calvin?" he asked with mock politeness.

"Calvin is fine."

"Or should I, perhaps call you Calvin *Conway*?"

Emily froze at the sound of this.

What's going on?

But Calvin said nothing, as if he too were frozen.

"Because that's your real name, isn't it? At least that's the name you went by when you were a maths student at Bristol University. When Professor Wallace got you sent down in disgrace for cheating in your finals."

57

"He swallowed a SIM card!" said Huette frantically to the triage nurse at A&E in University College Hospital.

The stress in her tone was off the scale.

It wasn't just the fear that John-John had swallowed a SIM card. It was the circumstances in which she had come here.

Huette explained how little John had been acting cranky since Sunday evening, some 36 hours ago and what Mike had told her at breakfast. The triage nurse, although limited in what she could say, tried to reassure her, explaining that children swallowing things was common and that small objects, the size of a SIM card, usually came out on their own, but it could take two to three days. She explained also that the doctor would call them, but it might be a four-hour wait. Strangely, this had a more reassuring effect on Huette than the nurse's earlier words. The fact that the triage nurse felt they could wait four hours, meant that it couldn't be all that urgent.

Sitting down in the waiting area, Huette tried to take her mind off it, by playing "I spy" with the children. When it was Mikey's turn, he chose the letter M. When Huette and Ariadne failed to guess, he revealed the limitations on his understanding of the alphabet and the rules of the game, when he told them that it was a SIM card. While Ariadne argued with him that SIM card begins with S, not M, Huette asked him where he had seen one and was concerned when he said: "In the baby."

Now she was beginning to worry.

Had he actually seen John swallow a SIM card. Or was this just a child's fertile imagination?

Certainly John was in discomfort. And there had to be *some* cause. But had little Mike sent them on a wild goose chase? She decided to ask him again, just to make sure.

"When did you see him swallow the SIM card?"

"When we went to Nana."

"And where was the SIM card before that?"

"On the floor."

"You're sure?"

Mike nodded. But she had learned not to trust a nod from a child. It could mean a little fib that he didn't want to say out loud.

"Mikey, are you *sure*?"

"Yes," he said.

Now Huette started wondering.

Why was there a SIM card on the floor? How did it get there? And to whom did it belong?

58

"That's the name you went by when you were a maths student at Bristol University. When Professor Wallace got you sent down in disgrace for cheating in your finals."

Hayden Blair's words had battered the courtroom into stone-cold silence. For the next few seconds, every creak of the wooden benches and every rustling of papers, emphasised the tension that hung in the air. And like a fly on the wall, Emily looked on helplessly as the defence case began to unravel before her eyes.

Suddenly it all made perfect sense to her. Calvin's missing background. His sensitivity over anything that suggested that he was lacking in intelligence. Even his use of sophisticated phraseology that suggested a better education than that of a builder – although this last was a bit of a double-edged sword, as the thought itself suggested an element of privilege and snobbery in her attitude.

And all this because a young man's dreams had been shattered by an accusation.

But what did it all mean? Was it true? And if Wallace *had* got Calvin expelled from university, *did that mean that he had a motive after all?* A motive for *murder*?

But if so, then was it just an unfortunate confluence of circumstances that *led* to the murder? Did Calvin arrive in all innocence? And then what? He saw his old professor and *snapped*? But no... he *knew* the *name* of the man who was asking him for the quote. So did that mean the murder was *premeditated*?

Or did Wallace not invite him there at all? Did he fake the email correspondence and set the whole thing up so he could kill the professor? But how long had he been planning it? And why now?

Hayden Blair was still on his feet. And Nigel – for whatever reason – had *not* got to *his* to raise any objection with the judge. So Emily knew – or at least hoped – that if nothing else, at least she was about to find out the answers.

"So Calvin," said Hayden Blair gleefully, "do you *admit* that your real name is Calvin Conway? And that you were a student of the late Professor Wallace? And that you were expelled from Bristol University because he caught you cheating in your finals?"

"He didn't *catch* me cheating. He *falsely accused* me of cheating."

"Well I'm sure that *every* cheat says that, when he gets caught."

Calvin brushed this off, as he continued his answer.

"Secondly, I wasn't expelled, they merely refused to give me the first-class degree that I had earned, instead offering me a third-class degree, to be delayed for five years, if I agreed to walk away without complaining."

Emily noticed that during this brief exchange, Calvin never once looked at her or Nigel, nor even the judge. He looked at the jury, with the occasional glance at Blair. But Emily looked at Nigel, wondering when he was going to make an attempt to stop the carnage. She realised that he too was stunned, and she was debating with herself whether to step in herself, when Nigel finally rose to his feet.

"Point of law M'Lady?" he said tersely, loud enough to be heard by the judge, but not loud enough to betray his concern or stress level to the jury.

Judge Braham nodded to the jury usher, who knew what to do without verbal prompting. By now even most of the jurors knew the routine and were led out in a swift and orderly procession.

"M'Lady, it appears that once again m'learned friend has breached disclosure rules, by introducing material that was not put to my client in the pre-trial phase. And it is beginning to look like something of a pattern."

"Yes, I'm bound to say prima facie that it is. Wouldn't you agree Mr Blair?"

Blair didn't flinch.

"Prima facie, yes, M'Lady," but there are added details, that might cause the Court to see matters in a somewhat different light."

"Proceed Mr Blair."

"Well firstly Your Honour, there is the obvious fact that the defendant should have informed his own counsel of his true identity, and his background, in relation to the deceased. This is fairly basic. If Mr Farringdon claims that he did not know this background information, then I suppose we must, of course, believe him. However, the failure to apprise him was the fault of the defendant, not of the Crown."

Stop twisting the knife, you bastard! thought Emily.

She had suspected from the beginning that there was something in Calvin's missing past that would be a problem. But she never suspected something quite on this scale. It changed everything – and then some.

Meanwhile, the judge was laying into Hayden Blair.

"The issue here is not defence counsel's *knowledge* or *lack of knowledge* of these underlying facts, but rather that the Crown *was in possession of* such knowledge. The defence is not obliged to disclose a potential motive for the defendant, even if such a motive is known to them, as long as they do not argue explicitly that *no* motive existed. Nor is it a crime for a man to adopt a new name, even without an enrolled – or indeed an *un*enrolled – deed poll. As long as the name change isn't used to facilitate an unlawful act.

"*The Crown on the other hand* had a duty to disclose what it knew of the defendant's identity, and his background, if you were intending to use it. Disclosure goes both to the underlying facts *and* the extent of the prosecution's *knowledge* of those facts."

"M'Lady, perhaps if I could explain. The Crown only found out this information last night, after-hours more or less, and were only able to check it out, this morning. And even then, the CPS could only check out the bare bones of the facts."

Nigel was poised to respond. But he didn't need to. Judge Braham wasn't having it.

"And after you were apprised of these facts by your colleagues at the CPS, did you notify counsel for the defence?"

"Well it was all a bit of a mad rush this morning–"

"Oh *Peleeze* Mr Blair!"

Even Nigel was stunned by the ferocity of the judge's response. It wasn't like Mary Braham to be so aggressive, especially towards a highly respected KC like Hayden Blair. On the other hand, it wasn't like Hayden Blair to resort to street fighter cunning to win a case. He usually relied on solid preparation and courtroom eloquence.

"*I mean*, M'Lady, that it was actually m'learned friend who arrived late this morning. I tried to call him, at about nine thirty, and then again at nine forty-five, but he was incommunicado."

"He could have left me a message," Nigel slipped in quickly, fearing that Judge Braham might just buy Blair's excuses.

The prosecutor kept his eyes focussed squarely on the judge.

"I must admit, M'Lady, that in the excitement at the surprising information, I somewhat lost my presence of mind." And before the judge could respond, Blair added: "I suppose I could have spoken to Miss du Lac, who actually arrived in good time. But I felt that this was a matter that should be dealt with at the highest level."

Oh you dirty bastard! thought Emily. *The old "organ grinder not the monkey" excuse.*

"I suppose you didn't see him in the robing room either," said the judge, refusing to let Blair off the hook quite so easily.

"Indeed not, M'Lady. I saw junior counsel on the steps of the building when I first arrived. But I proceeded to the robing room myself and by the time defence counsel were berobed, I was already in court, desperately hoping to speak to them. Without wishing to imply criticism of any kind regarding opposing counsel, by the time they arrived in court it was barely a minute before ten and your own prompt arrival."

Yeah, yeah, you piece of shit. Keep laying it on with a trowel.

"What was that?" asked the judge, looking straight at Emily.

Emily blushed, fearing that she had expressed her sentiments out loud.

"Nothing, M'Lady."

She realised that she had probably just grunted, subconsciously.

Judge Braham turned back to the prosecutor.

"You know Mr Blair, even accepting all that you have said, when I asked at the start of today's proceedings if you were ready, you *could* have mentioned it then. *That* – and I think you know this – was the proper time to speak. You could have raised the matter with *me* and notified counsel for the defence at the same time. Then we could have held a hearing to decide how best to proceed."

Although the words themselves were uncompromising, Emily was bothered by the judge's conciliatory tone, especially following on from the ferocity of a few moments ago. She now feared that, after all the fire and brimstone, the judge was about to let Blair off the hook with nothing more than a reprimand. But Judge Braham continued.

"At minimum, I could have given the defence a chance to review the evidence. Instead you chose to ambush them in what I can only describe as a rather sleazy fashion."

"But the defendant was subject to the rule on witness segregation. Counsel could *not* have communicated with him on substantive matters once he started his testimony."

"He could, at the Court's discretion, Mr Blair."

For once Blair was silenced, albeit briefly.

"In that case, M'Lady, I can only apologise."

The apology took the sting out of Judge Braham's onslaught. But she wasn't quite finished.

"You said that these facts only came to the Crown's attention after normal working hours yesterday. Can you enlighten me, and defence counsel, as to what was the *source* of this information?"

Again Blair found himself squirming.

"It was an anonymous tip-off M'Lady. A phone call to the Crown Prosecution Service."

"As far as I know, all calls to the CPS are recorded. I take it this one was."

"Yes, indeed M'Lady. The voice was disguised electronically, but we think it was probably a woman. And I have a copy of the recording available for entry into the Evidence Presentation System."

"Then kindly let us hear it."

Blair fumbled around with his computer, until the muffled and distorted voice came through.

"Okay listen – the reason I'm calling is because I have some information about the defendant in the case of Rex versus Coffey that the Crown isn't aware of. The defendant is supposedly a builder called Calvin Coffey. But his name wasn't always Calvin Coffey. And he wasn't always a builder. His name is actually Calvin Conway. He was a student of Walter Wallace at Bristol University. And Professor Wallace caught him cheating in his finals. There was a disciplinary hearing, and Calvin was found to have cheated on four questions. He was denied a first-class honours degree and offered a third instead."

Blair then switched off the recording and described the steps that the CPS had taken to verify the information, using search engines, and the Wayback Machine to find old articles about the case, then calling him just before nine thirty and reiterating his efforts to call Nigel.

Nigel, for his part, came back forcefully, echoing the judge's observation about how Blair could have raised the issue directly with the court. He added that Blair was "no doubt emboldened by the Court's reluctance to grant bail and thus my own reluctance to ask the court to halt the trial and start with a new jury."

He nevertheless proceeded to ask for just such a halt and new trial, with bail granted, or in the alternative for an adjournment till tomorrow and for the Court to exercise discretionary power to lift the rule on witness segregation and allow him to talk with his client.

"I am somewhat conflicted in this matter," said Judge Braham. "On the one hand, as I have said, the Crown's behaviour leaves a lot to be desired. On the other hand, the defendant himself bears some measure of responsibility if he did not disclose this information to his own counsel, though I can well understand why."

If he had disclosed it, then it would have cramped Nigel's style as to what he could say in court.

"But I am also mindful of the tight schedules under which *all* the courts are operating since the Covid lockdown. We face *massive* backlogs, with cases from 2022, and even 2021, being pushed all the way into 2025. And other defendants besides Mr Coffey – or Mr Conway – have been waiting in gaol even *longer*, despite the Custody Time Limit. So I cannot seriously consider restarting the trial. Similarly, I cannot grant bail for reasons already stated. So what I will do, instead, is allow this cross-examination to continue and then adjourn the proceedings until *Thursday* to allow the defence time to look into these matters and, if desired, conduct re-examination on Thursday morning."

So the devastating cross-examination will stay fresh in the jury's mind for 36 hours, you bitch!

"However, in order to preserve the purity of the evidence, I will not allow defence counsel to talk with the defendant before that, unless the defence can persuade me that there is some pressing reason for allowing it."

Emily was fuming. She could understand why time considerations might be at play here. *And, yes, they were worried that Calvin might do a runner. But why tie the defence's hands over talking with Calvin?*

On a piece of paper she quickly scribbled: "Fucking bias – move for recusal."

Nigel saw it, but merely shook his head.

Emily looked up at the witness box where Calvin was standing, looking surprisingly calm. At least he had heard all this and knew to be careful.

59

Huette sat with her children in the waiting area of the children's A&E at University College Hospital, trying to keep them entertained, while the usual chaos buzzed all around them. The triage nurse had reassured her somewhat but kept an anxious eye on little John as the hours ticked by slowly.

Ariadne, with her boundless six-year-old energy, was trying to keep Mike engaged. "I spy with my little eye, something beginning with 'H'," she said, looking around the sterile room.

"H," Mike repeated, scrunching his face in concentration. "Hospital?"

Ariadne giggled. "Yes! You got it."

Ariadne was genuinely impressed, and Mike looked extremely pleased with himself.

Huette managed a weak smile. At least the children were keeping themselves busy. But her mind was elsewhere, turning over the implications of Mike's account of the swallowed SIM card. How did it end up on her floor? She knew she couldn't relax until she had answers.

Finally, after what seemed like an eternity, a nurse called out, "John Shannon?"

It seemed strange that they called out the name of a six-month-old baby, rather than the mother. But that was hospital policy.

"That's us," Huette said, standing up quickly and gathering the children. They followed the nurse down a brightly lit corridor to an examination room where a paediatrician was waiting, a young woman in her late twenties or early thirties.

"Hello, I'm Sudisha Patel," the paediatrician said in a warm tone. "I understand that baby John has swallowed a SIM card?"

"Yes, that's what we think happened," Huette replied, holding John-John who looked pale and miserable.

Dr Patel nodded sympathetically. "Let's take a look at him and see what we can do."

The examination was quick but thorough and Dr Patel knew how to keep a baby amused, even when the little fella wasn't feeling too well. Then she looked up at Huette with a reassuring smile.

"Okay well there's no sign of extreme internal trauma and if it was a SIM card swallowed whole on Sunday afternoon, then it'll probably pass through him. It can take anything from 48 to 72 hours, so that means it could be any minute now or another 24 hours."

"So we've just got to sit and wait?"

"Well a nano-SIM card is small enough to pass through a baby's small intestine without harming him. But because it has corners, rather than a round object, there's a very small risk."

"How small?"

"Small enough that you shouldn't worry. But just to be sure I'd like to do an X-ray."

"Can you do an X-ray on a 6-month-old baby? I mean, is it safe?"

"It's completely safe. The radiation dose is extremely low. In fact, you can even do an X-ray on a new-born baby. And we have a radiology unit, so it won't take long."

Huette nodded, feeling a mixture of relief and anxiety. "Thank you, Dr Patel."

Sudisha called over a nurse and explained what was required. The nurse had a kind smile on her face as she acknowledged Huette.

"I'll take you to the X-ray unit." she said, gesturing for them to follow her. "This way, please."

Huette gathered John-John in her arms and instructed Ariadne and Mike to hold her hands as they walked down the brightly lit corridor.

The radiology unit was only a short distance away. The nurse checked the light to make sure that entry was safe and then opened the door to the room where the radiologist was waiting. They spoke briefly and the nurse handed the radiologist the doctor's request form and then left. The radiologist – a woman about the same age as Dr Patel – explained to Huette that she couldn't stay inside while the X-ray was, taken.

"You can stay with John and keep him calm while we position him and I set it up, but then you'll need to step out while I actually take the X-ray."

Huette nodded, her heart pounding slightly. She told Ariadne and Mike to sit outside and for Ariadne to keep an eye on her brother. Then she stepped into the room. The radiologist guided her gently, showing her how to place John on the table. John squirmed a little, but Huette stroked his head and murmured soothing words to calm him down while the radiologist set up the equipment and positioned the scanner. John may not have understood the words, but he was reassured by Huette's gentle and loving tone.

"We'll take good care of him," the radiologist reassured her with a warm smile. "You can wait just outside."

Reluctantly, Huette stepped out of the room, closing the door behind her. Ariadne and Mike looked up at her with wide eyes, sensing the tension.

"Is John going to be okay, Mummy?" Ariadne asked.

"Yes, sweetheart," Huette replied, trying to keep her voice steady. "He's just getting a picture taken of his tummy so the doctor can see where the SIM card is."

Huette felt a jolt run through her body, as the illuminated sign outside the X-ray room changed to: **"Radiation Hazard! Do not enter!"**

After about a minute – though it felt like an eternity – the radiologist opened the door and smiled.

"All done. You can take John back to the waiting area now. We'll send the X-ray through to Dr Patel electronically, and she'll call you back once she's reviewed it."

Huette thanked the radiologist and gathered the now crying John-John, who seemed relieved to be back in his mother's arms. They returned to the waiting area, where Ariadne and Mike resumed their quiet game of "I spy" to pass the time.

Not long after, they were called back to the examination room. Dr Patel was waiting for them, a serious but reassuring expression on her face. "The X-ray shows that the foreign object is in John's rectum, very near to the anus," she explained. "This means it should pass naturally very soon."

Huette sighed with relief, her shoulders finally relaxing. "Thank you So what happens now? I mean do we just wait?"

Dr Patel smiled warmly.

"I'd like you to try and get him to drink some prune juice or pear juice, or even some pieces of mashed pear. The juices contain sorbitol, a sweetener that acts like a laxative. And the solid pieces of pear contain fibre."

"Where can I do that?"

"There's a café on the ground floor that's more of a restaurant really. They have fruit there for those who like eating a healthy dessert."

Less than half an hour later, Huette was back in A&E, with the nappy in a plastic bag. Dr Patel, wearing blue medical gloves had volunteered to conduct the "search". The search didn't really take much effort. There wasn't all that much stool material to search through.

"There it is!" the nurse exclaimed, as the paediatrician found the SIM card.

Huette felt a wave of relief sweep over her. "Thank goodness," she breathed.

Dr Patel cleaned and disinfected the SIM card before handing it to Huette in a small, clear plastic bag.

"We'll just need to observe John for a little while longer to ensure he's okay."

This made Huette nervous again.

"Wait, so does that mean he's still in danger?"

"On the contrary, he should be fine now. Based on the size of the foreign object, I'd say there's little likelihood of internal injury. But again, just as a precaution, we'll run an occult blood test on the stool while we're waiting, just in case."

Huette nodded, clutching the plastic bag with the SIM card. "Thank you so much," she said, her voice thick with gratitude.

"Let's get John cleaned up and comfortable," Dr Patel suggested, leading them back to the waiting area. As they settled in, Ariadne and Mike seemed to relax, sensing that the worst was over.

"Mum, can I see the SIM card?" Ariadne asked, her curiosity getting the better of her.

Huette showed it to her, still in the plastic bag.

"This little thing caused all that trouble."

"Why did he eat it?" Mike asked, his earlier mischief forgotten in the face of his brother's ordeal.

"I don't know, darling," Huette said, giving him a reassuring hug. "But it's out now, and that's what matters."

As they waited for the final all-clear from Dr Patel, Huette's mind wandered back to the mystery of the SIM card. Who had lost it, and how had it ended up on her floor? These questions nagged at her, but she pushed them aside for now. The important thing was that John was safe.

After another hour of observation, Dr Patel gave them the all-clear to go home. "Make sure John gets plenty of fluids and rest. If you notice anything unusual, bring him back immediately."

"Thank you, Dr Patel," Huette said, gathering her children. "Come on, let's go home."

The trek back to the car was much smoother, with Ariadne holding Mike's hand and John settled comfortably in his carry seat. When they arrived, Huette found the car miraculously untouched by traffic wardens, and they piled in, tired but relieved.

As she drove back to Camden Town, Huette thought about the SIM card, wondering whose it was. But for now, she was just glad to be heading home with all her children safe and sound.

Once home, she put John down for a nap and settled the other children with a movie. Sitting down at the kitchen table, she took out the SIM card, now cleaned and innocuous in a small plastic bag.

60

"So, Mr Conway, let's take a look at these allegations of cheating that Professor Wallace made against you, and your denials of these allegations."

Emily's rage was growing, as the brutal onslaught against her client commenced. No matter how many times Nigel had told her not to take things personally in court, and not to get emotionally involved, she couldn't help herself.

"It started after your final exams, when two of your professors were suspicious of your results. Correct?"

"They raised issues, yes."

"And specifically the issue of cheating."

"*Alleged* cheating."

"The reason being that the results in your finals were so much better than they had been in your first two years. Is that not so?"

"That was the reason they stated," replied Calvin, maintaining his passive-aggressive demeanour.

"The two professors were Walter Wallace and Seamus Harper, is that correct?"

"Yes. Although it was Seamus Harper who was the first to accuse me. Then he brought Walter Wallace along for the ride."

Emily wanted to scream at Calvin: *Don't say anything more than you have to! Just answer the questions Yes or No! Don't you see what he's doing? He's getting you to show your motive to the jury.*

But she couldn't say anything. She couldn't even shake her head or give him a hand signal. All she could do was watch – and silently curse Hayden Blair and Judge Braham. It was painful.

"You'd had several disagreements with Professor Harper, hadn't you? Chiefly on account of your laziness."

"I wasn't lazy. I just didn't attend the university as often as maybe I *should* have."

"Isn't that the *definition* of laziness in a student?"

"I had conflicting commitments."

"Such as?"

"Earning a living."

"You had children? Elderly relatives? Any dependants at all in fact?"

Emily knew that an experienced barrister like Hayden Blair wouldn't normally ask questions to which he didn't know the answer. But he had only found out about Calvin this morning. How much could he have found out?

"I had a wife."

"*Had* a wife?"

"You think a marriage could survive the kind of stress these false accusations put me under. Blowing every penny I had in a futile effort to clear my name?"

"Couldn't she work?"

"She *did* work," Calvin shot back angrily. "But a teacher's salary isn't all that great."

"So your ex-wife is a teacher?"

"*Was*. When we first got married, we had an agreement, I worked at odd jobs supporting her while she trained as a teacher. Then she would support me while I studied maths."

"But it didn't quite work out like that?"

"No. Her pay was too low, so I had to work part-time as well."

"You're not the first student who had to work while studying."

Again Emily bridled at Blair's tactics. He was trying to portray Calvin as having a sense of entitlement, when in fact he was clearly a hard-working and responsible man, with a strong work ethic. But she needn't have worried.

"You were asking me about my poor results in my first year–"

"First *two* years."

"Kindly don't interrupt!"

Blair was too stunned to react to this. Even the judge was knocked for six.

"Now, if I may get back to what I was saying to the jury before that ever-so-adroitly timed interruption. In my *first* year, my results were poor. I initially failed some exams and had to re-take them."

"In fact, you very nearly expelled from–"

"In my *second* year – *let* me finish – my results were *average*. I started working harder and cutting back on the money jobs – and it paid off. My results improved, although that still didn't put me where I wanted to be. Then in my *third* year, I worked my ass off. I was determined to succeed. *And* determined to prove Wallace and Harper wrong. And it paid off. Until they falsely accused me of cheating."

"They thought your answers were too good to be true."

"That was one of their arguments, yes."

"And it started when Dr Seamus Harper noticed the similarity between your answers on one of the papers and one his prepared *model solutions*, as I believe they are called."

"Yes."

"Just to clarify here, the tutors who set the exams don't always mark the exams, but instead they create a set of model solutions which then serve as a template for the markers to follow, is that correct?"

"Yes."

"The markers being post-graduate students or PhD students at the same establishment."

"In many cases, yes."

"And so, with Seamus Harper's suspicions aroused, all your papers were returned to the markers to check. Then at that point, the suspicions of Walter Wallace were also aroused, after he too spotted similarities to some of *his* model solutions."

"I would call it *alleged* suspicion – in *both* cases."

Blair looked somewhat taken aback.

"What? You mean they weren't *really* suspicious of you?"

"I thought they were at the time. But now I'm not so sure."

"So you think they just ganged up on you for no reason?"

"Let's just say, that since then, I've changed my view of then. I sat a total of 13 papers in my finals – five more than required – and I threw in a double project. Those papers were *all* reviewed. Yet *none* of the other tutors or professors accused me of cheating."

"Maybe your results weren't as good in those other exams?"

"Actually, most of them were better! I got 100 per cent for graph theory, 98 per cent for linear programming, 96 per cent for Stochastic processes, 95 per cent for operating systems, 91 per cent for linear models and foundations of mathematics, 90 per cent for computer construction and architecture, 84 per cent for logic, 78 per cent for statistics, 75 per cent for advanced computer architecture and 70 per cent for the project. In algebraic number theory, I answered six questions instead of the required four and was awarded a score of 159 per cent. One examiner wrote on the bottom of one of my papers: 'The best paper I have marked in the last 10 years.' And he never wavered from that, even after I was falsely accused."

"Very impressive. Nevertheless, an inquiry was held at the university–"

"More like a kangaroo court."

The judge stepped in.

"Mr Conway. I can understand your strong feelings, but you must allow counsel to complete his question and refrain from interrupting. Politeness is a two-way street."

Calvin nodded a sheepish apology – to the judge, not to the prosecutor, who brushed off the interruption and ploughed on.

"And they concluded, that four of your answers were sufficiently similar to the model solutions such as to preclude any explanation other than prior knowledge of said solutions?"

"That is what *they* concluded."

"And indeed, in one case there was a mistake in one of your answers that faithfully replicated a mistake in the examiner's model solution."

"The mistaken answers were the same, yes."

"And how do you account for that?"

"I told them, *at the time*," Calvin replied earnestly, "that it was perfectly natural that my answers would mirror those of the examiners, because the examiners had been my lecturers and it was they who taught me how to tackle those particular problems. In fact, there were lecture notes that I borrowed from previous students that had the same mistakes."

"So you're saying that you just happened to make the same mistake as a tutor?"

"I told them that very clearly, first at the original tribunal, then at my appeal to the university council and then again at the university council inquiry, when the matter was returned to them by the courts."

"But they didn't believe you? Or were they, too, insincere?"

Blair's tone was dripping with sarcasm.

"They were… mistaken," replied Calvin.

It was clear to Emily that he was forcing himself to remain calm.

"Now, although it was Seamus Harper who was the *first* to accuse you, at the university council inquiry, it was Walter Wallace who was your main accuser, was it not?"

"It was."

"In fact, would it not be fair to say that he acted as chief *prosecutor* against you?"

"It would be... *eminently* fair to say that."

Emily sensed that Calvin wasn't afraid. Angry yes, but not afraid. She also noticed that he was choosing his words carefully, even if he wasn't always phrasing his answers the way she or Nigel would have advised.

"And at the inquiry, Professor Wallace laid out a number of points, some small, some large, that implied that you had indeed had prior sight of the model solutions."

"That he *claimed* implied such a conclusion."

"And his arguments were accepted?"

"Yes."

"One of Professor Wallace's arguments was that while your examination results were remarkably good *overall*, you occasionally made surprising errors that one would not have expected from a first-class student."

"Exams are taken under time pressure. Even a student who's made the effort to study hard, can make errors under the stress of time pressure."

"But time pressure would hardly explain why your answers coincided so precisely with the examiner's model solutions."

"I never said that time-pressure was the explanation for *that*."

"No indeed. You said that *those similarities* were due to the fact that it was the same tutors who taught you and set the exams. While the fact that you made some clumsy errors as well, were due to time-pressure."

"That is what I told the various tribunals. Yes."

Calvin was still choosing his words carefully. But it may not be enough, Emily realised. Because now, Hayden Blair was building up to asking the "killer" question. She could tell from his body language. Not that Blair was trying to telegraph it by drawing himself up to his full height. That would come later when Calvin had committed to a key answer and taken the bait – when Blair was about to deliver the coup de grace *after* the key question was answered. Right now it was just the calm before the storm.

"Mr Conway, as a... *scientist*, of sorts... could you please explain to the jury the meaning of the term 'occam's razor'?"

Calvin hesitated.

"You mean the etymology? The history? The background? ... Or the definition?"

"The definition will do for now."

"Occam's razor is the principle that when one has to choose between two or more explanations, one chooses the simplest explanation, that is the one that makes the fewest assumptions."

"And this principle is widely used by scientists?"

Again, Calvin was cautious.

"Widely applied, yes. Or widely favoured."

Emily was looking down, sensing what was about to happen.

"So would it be fair to say that if two... er... phenomena... occur at the same time, in the same place, pertaining to the same person – and if those phenomena were unusual or unexpected – then a *single* explanation that subsumes *both* phenomena under a single assumption, should be viewed more favourably than, say, *two separate* explanations or two separate *assumptions*? At least if one is going to follow the strict *scientific* method?"

Oh what a cunning bastard you are! Emily wanted to scream. She looked up at Calvin expecting him to look like a rabbit caught in the headlights. Strangely, what she saw was no such thing. Instead, she saw her client smiling, almost as if it was counsel for the prosecution who had fallen into the trap.

"I would agree with that *precisely*."

"So let's look at the present case. You explain your schoolboy errors in some answers in terms of *time pressure* and the close correspondence between your answers and the model solutions in terms of the fact that you were *following the method you were taught by your tutors*. That's *two* explanations. Your accusers, on the other hand, said that both of these, er, phenomena, were due to straightforward copying... That's *one* explanation. So I ask you, Mr Conway, which of those two is more consistent with Occam's razor?"

"Well you're overlooking some additional relevant details."

"Such as?"

"Such as that copying would require *access to the material* after both the questions *and* the model solutions were finalised. And there would also have to be an opportunity to *use* the material in the exam room. Yet none of the invigilators ever suggested that I had brought any material into the exam room or looked at any material other than the test papers themselves."

"You could have memorised the material beforehand."

"Would that have been any easier than just learning the right methods in the first place? And I would *still* have needed *access* to the answers before that."

It seemed to Emily as if Calvin was actually goading Blair,

possibly trying to provoke him into saying something that might lead to a mistrial. If so, he was barking up the wrong tree. Blair was an old hand at courtroom procedures and highly unlikely to fall into such a trap.

"Perhaps now you'd like to answer my question Mr Conway. Occam's razor. Two *separate* explanations or one that covers *both* points? Which is more logical from a *scientific* point of view?"

"Well obviously *one*."

"In other words copying."

"In other words, copying," Calvin echoed, apparently amused by the irony.

61

With the day's proceedings over, Nigel and Emily took an Uber back to St Jude's, to plan their strategy for the next day. Judge Braham had granted them an adjournment till Thursday to look into the matters that Blair's surprise revelations had raised. That meant they only had tomorrow to get as much information as they could.

"Okay, we're not waiting till tomorrow. When we get back to chambers we're going to pull up everything we can about the name Calvin Conway. Get the other pupils to help you. I'm going to ask Philip Solomon to help. I'm also going to pull some of my old academic contacts to see if I can talk to anyone in the maths department at Bristol."

"You know that none of this would be necessary if that bitch allowed you to talk with Calvin."

"Technically she's correct, Emily. Once the defendant commences giving testimony, the lawyer is not allowed to talk to him outside the courtroom until he's finished giving evidence, including cross-examination and re-examination."

"But she has discretion, in cases like this. She said so herself. There was a blatant material non-disclosure followed by a courtroom ambush. That *has* to count for something."

"It may give us grounds for appeal. But we have to deal with the here and now."

"*Okay, you're right!*" She took a few deep breaths. "You're right," she said again.

She whipped out her mobile phone.

"Who are you calling?"

"Ruth."

Such was the determination in her eyes, that Nigel held off while she made the call.

"Yes, Emily."

That was already a good sign, thought Emily. That meant

Ruth had saved her number. Over the next few minutes, Emily summarised what had happened in court. What Ruth said next, took Emily by surprise.

"I think he stitched him up."

Emily's heart leapt. That was exactly what she *wanted* to hear. But pronouns were ambiguous. She had to be sure there was no misunderstanding.

"Who stitched up whom?"

"Professor Wallace. He stitched up your client."

"Calvin?"

"Yes Calvin."

"You *know* this? Or you just *suspect* it?"

"I *think* it. I think Raymond knew something about it. I think it was weighing on his conscience. And I think Walter Wallace was behind everything, pulling the strings."

This was encouraging. But it was all hearsay.

"Do you have anything that could back this up? In court I mean?"

"There may be something on Raymond's computer. I haven't looked through it. I couldn't bring myself to… "

She trailed off, overwhelmed by emotion. Emily gave her a moment.

"Do you have access to the computer?"

"I know the password. But I haven't looked at it since… I couldn't… I mean I just couldn't."

"Is there any chance you might let *me* look at it?"

"Okay, but you'll have to come down here."

Wednesday 27th March, 2024

62

The following day, Nigel made his way to Frampton Cotterell where he had a meeting with emeritus Professor Herman Whitmore. Frampton Cotterell was a quiet village on the River Frome about 7.5 miles from Bristol city centre, and Whitmore was the professor who had described one of Calvin's papers as "the best paper I've marked in the last ten years." Though retired now, the professor was perfectly willing to meet Nigel and talk about the case. Or perhaps that was *because* he was now retired.

Entering Whitmore's conservatory was like stepping into another world – a less hectic world than the one Nigel was used to in London. Maybe it was no quieter than Nigel's suburban house in Hampton, but at some visceral level, it *felt* like it was. In Hampton he was only a phone call and drive away from central London. But here the day felt like it was a weekend, even though it was a normal working day.

Whitmore ushered Nigel into the conservatory, offering him one of a pair of comfortable wicker armchairs and taking the other for himself.

"Coffee? Tea?"

"Tea please."

The professor's expression was warm and welcoming as they settled in, while the professor's wife went to get the tea. He had a neatly trimmed grey beard and wire-rimmed glasses, giving him a distinguished yet approachable air. Dressed casually in a navy-blue polo shirt, he exuded a relaxed but dignified presence.

As they got underway with the pleasantries, Nigel took in his surroundings. Despite the overcast sky, light streamed through the glass panels of the conservatory, giving it a bright and airy ambience, and offering a view of the well-tended garden outside. Potted plants lined the edges of the room, adding a touch of greenery to the space. A few pictures adorned the wall from which the conservatory extended, including one of a pretty, teenage girl looking a bit like Emily, apart from the platinum curls. She seemed vaguely familiar.

While they waited for the tea, the professor filled Nigel in on the details of his own career and life in Bristol. Every now and then, Whitmore paused for breath allowing the soft chirping of birds or the soothing sound of raindrops to be heard faintly from the garden. And then, at some point Mrs Whitmore brought in a silver tray, setting it down on the small round wrought iron table set between the two men.

In addition to the teapot, milk, sugar, and an assortment of biscuits, Nigel noticed that there were – crucially – only two cups. This gave him the assurance that the professor's wife would not be joining them. That in turn meant that Professor Whitmore could speak freely.

When Mrs Whitmore withdrew, and with the pleasantries completed, they got down to brass tacks.

"I never thought he was guilty, you know," said Whitmore, making it clear from the beginning, where he stood.

"You didn't think there was anything unusual in his results?"

"Unusual yes. Suspicious no."

"What do you mean?"

"Well firstly, he *did* work like a dog in his third year. And even in his second, to some extent. You could see the change come over him. The shock of failure in his first year, and the prospect of nearly being expelled, served as something of a wake-up call. I actually played a role in that."

"You tried to get him expelled?"

"No, I intervened on his behalf to *stop* the expulsion."

"At his request?"

"Not directly. His wife asked me. And I allowed myself to be persuaded."

"He had a wife?"

"Oh Yes. Calvin knew how to pick 'em."

Nigel wondered if there was a *quid pro quo* involved. But he held his tongue.

"So after that near miss with disaster, he redoubled his effort?"

"Exactly. He just morphed into another Will Hunting, if you get my meaning."

"Vaguely," replied Nigel, in a tone of voice that seemed to say: "Not in the slightest."

"*Good Will Hunting.* A film starring Matt Damon. About a boy with a natural flair for maths."

"But Calvin *didn't* have a natural flair, did he?"

"No. Like I said, he had to work like a dog. I suppose it's not really such a good analogy after all. The Matt Damon character was talented but lacked ambition. Calvin didn't take to maths naturally, but he *was* ambitious. You can ask any of the other professors and they'll tell you the same thing. Here was someone who really *wanted* to succeed."

"His accusers would presumably say that he wanted it enough to cheat."

"Maybe he did, maybe he didn't. But I don't think he did."

"But you're not sure?"

"Well let me put it this way. I don't think he needed to, and I don't think he could have done, even if he'd wanted to."

"What makes you think he didn't need to?"

"Well for a start, he got spectacular results in eleven other exams. And they checked those other papers too. No sign of copying. Indeed no *accusations* of copying. It was just four answers that sealed his fate – and all of them were in just *two* papers: Applied Probability, and Probability Theory and Statistical Mechanics."

"You said he couldn't have cheated if he wanted to. Did anyone ever put forward a theory of how he *could* have cheated?"

"Put forward a theory, yes – if one could call it a theory."

"What was it?"

"Well, firstly Conway had often been seen in the mathematics department late at night."

"But isn't that consistent with his claim that he was studying hard in his last year?"

"Of course it is. And that's what I believe he was doing. But there was more to it than that. About a year before that, one of the keys to the filing cabinet got lost. And that was the filing cabinet where the exam papers were stored. So the theory was that he may have stolen the key, then hidden in heating ducts and waited to come out at night to steal the papers, or at least gain sight of them."

"That sounds a bit far-fetched, doesn't it."

"Yes, indeed it does. In fact when it was put to him, Calvin himself said he'd have to have been a cross between Rambo, James Bond and the Invisible Man."

"I'd like to ask you – and this won't leave this room – is there the slightest chance that the theory about the key might be true?"

Professor Whitmore inclined his head back slightly.

"Honestly? No. Apart from anything else, it wasn't just *one* key. He would have needed keys to the office, to the building, and if my memory serves me right, one more key."

"And that's presumably *before* we even get to the question of how he could have memorised all that material or smuggled it into the exam room?"

"Exactly," Whitmore confirmed. And then of course, there's also the question of how he could have known when the model solutions were finalised."

"How do you mean?"

"Well the model solutions that were used by the markers were covered in last-minute corrections in Tipp-Ex and ink."

"Why?"

"You have to understand that academic tutors work under a great deal of time pressure. We have to create courses, mark test results, prepare lectures and seminars and in some cases set exams and create model solutions. The reason for the model solutions is that if the exam is marked by markers, rather than the examiner himself, then they need to all be singing from the same hymn sheet."

"When you say 'set exams' does that mean they set their own exams? The reason I ask is because I've heard that there are question banks where tutors can get their questions from, along with answers or model solutions."

"They sometimes do. But not in this case."

"So about these corrections?"

"Well when tutors draw up their own exams and model solutions, especially under time pressure, they can make mistakes."

"Which hopefully they discover and correct before the students sit the exam."

"Exactly, Nigel. And if they discover the mistakes shortly before the exam, they may not have time to produce a new, clean copy of the corrections. So instead, they might correct them with Tipp-Ex and ink."

"Is that common?"

"No, but it's what happened in this case."

"So for Calvin to get the full benefit of seeing the model solutions...?"

"He would have had to have gained access to them *after* they were finalised."

"And then he would have had to either memorise them or find some way of writing them down."

"Either of which would be very difficult, as I'm sure you're going to point out in your client's defence."

"Yes. But I wanted to ask you, about those theories about him getting the keys and hiding in air ducts. You said that they have no credibility. So why were they believed?"

"Interestingly, they weren't. That is, those theories played no part in the official tribunal report or the findings against Calvin, which looked only at probabilities. The theory was suggested informally, with a nod and a wink. But no one took it seriously."

Nigel realised that this might also have been why Hayden Blair never suggested it, and also why Calvin seemed to be goading Blair into offering a theory as to how he could have done it. That would have led to a mistrial, for sure.

"So the case against him was based entirely on the mathematical improbability of the similarities in the answers?"

"In the end, yes. In fact the tribunal ruled that in the cases of *just four of his answers*, the similarities to the model solutions were too great as to preclude any explanation other than prior knowledge. They didn't even *consider* the break-in theory. But then again, they also didn't consider the evidence of the external examiners whom Calvin brought in to support his case."

"When you say 'just four of his answers'– "

"You have to understand that the case presented by Wallace, was much broader than what the tribunal ultimately accepted. Wallace had recently been appointed a professor, so he wanted to assert his authority and professional competence, such as it was. But his case against Calvin consisted of a lot of nitpicking, and I would even go as far as to say a lot of contradictions. Wallace basically took a 'heads-I-win, tails-you-lose' approach to the evidence. In *psychology*, it's called 'confirmation bias'. For instance, he made a big deal out of the fact that on one question, Calvin turned his page on its side to tabulate some logarithms."

"Is there any significance in that?"

"None whatsoever. And yet Wallace declared triumphantly 'I've never known any student turn the page on its side before.' But now here's the deal: the model solution *wasn't* turned on its side. So what does it prove if Calvin turned his paper on its side? Nothing! And yet when a professor speaks, his peers listen. Even if he's talking a load of codswallop."

"Forgive me for saying this, but it sounds like you didn't rate Wallace too highly."

"Professionally, I didn't. But I have no personal animosity towards him."

"Anything else about Wallace's reasoning? I mean his arguments against Calvin."

"I could give you plenty of examples," said Whitmore. But I'm not sure if they'd help you. They might just give your client more of a motive. But I suppose it's up to you how you use the information. So let me give you a couple of other examples. In one place Calvin started out writing a mathematical condition in one form of notation that appeared in the model solution, then he crossed it out and wrote it with a different form that didn't appear in the model solution. Wallace claimed that this was evidence that he had seen the model solution and then changed it so that he wouldn't be caught."

"Jesus!" Nigel interjected.

"Then there was one case where Calvin crossed out a page of his own working, then wrote a note asking the markers to ignore the crossing out and to reinstate his original answer. Wallace made some snide remark to the effect that 'Mr Conway appears to have had a little accident here.' Yet in the earlier hearing before the original tribunal, had said that Calvin had made *no* false starts – and cited *that* as proof of cheating. It was like Wallace's motto was 'don't let the facts get in the way of a clever theory'."

"And they fell for it?" asked Nigel incredulously.

"They very nearly didn't. The vote was actually tied, and it was the vice-chancellor who had the casting vote."

"There's something that's been bugging me. I thought the usual way of resolving cases like this is to give the student a *viva voce* exam."

In other words a spoken test where they ask the student questions out loud, and he answers them on the spot.

"He wanted to take one at first. But initially they didn't offer one."

"You mean they did, eventually?"

"They only offered it *after* they'd effectively found him guilty. But by then *he* no longer trusted *them*. He said 'I cannot conceive that once those accusations were put to me there could be a fair assessment. I would have been screwed.' He also pointed out that Wallace had already adopted an aggressive and bullying tone, when he first accused him. And he was right. It wasn't an inquiry; it was an inquisition."

"With Wallace as a latter-day Torquemada."

"Exactly! But you know what was particularly galling about it for me? For all the petty quibbling and making mountains out of molehills and having it both ways, it was clear to me from the start that what they really had against him was that he had done so well. They were so vested psychologically in the presumption that he was a bad student, that they took umbrage when he confounded their expectations."

"Did you speak up for him at the time?"

"Unofficially. But I had to be careful about it. There were... certain rumours floating around at the time."

"Rumours about you and *Calvin*?"

Whitmore smiled mockingly.

"No, Nigel. Not rumours about me and Calvin. Just rumours about *me*."

"What kind of rumours?"

"I'd rather not say."

Nigel was trying to get his head round this.

"You'd think that tutors would be proud of a student doing so well. It would surely reflect well on them."

"You'd think so wouldn't you. But let me tell you something else that Walter Wallace said. Maybe I shouldn't be speaking ill of the dead, but this'll *really* give you some idea of the man's character. Wallace's *biggest* point against Calvin – and it was Wallace himself who called it a big point at the inquiry – was that Calvin based one of his answers on an advanced textbook called *A Course in Probability Theory* by Kai Lai Chung.

"Now according to Professor Wallace, the book was too advanced to be used by any lecturer in an undergraduate course and no undergraduate student would want to use it. And yet, not only was there a copy of Chung's book in the maths department library, but Wallace himself had recommended it for further reading, along with six other books, *in his own introductory book about probability theory*.

"So how d'you like *them* apples, as Matt Damon said in that film."

Whitmore seemed to be relishing the moment. It was obvious that there was no love lost between Whitmore and Wallace. In fact, Nigel found himself wondering if Herman Whitmore had an alibi for the day that Walter Wallace was murdered.

63

The first thing Emily noticed, when she stepped out of the railway station in Bournemouth, was the sea air. It brought back memories of childhood. But she had no time for nostalgia. She was here to do a job.

The taxi rank was ten feet from the main entrance, and as soon as she turned her head, she saw yellow taxis lined up by the dozen. Following the same principle that holds sway at the bar, she took the first one in the rank and told the driver the address, reading it off her smartphone.

The journey was picturesque and scenic, and the "lawyer" in Emily couldn't help but wonder if the driver had not chosen the shortest route. With all the twists and turns along the way, she got the feeling that she was being taken three sides of a square.

She took out her phone again and surreptitiously keyed in the start and end points of the journey. Once she looked at the map, the route that the driver had chosen actually made sense.

The moral, Emily? Don't be so quick to judge people. Stay alert, yes, but as Nick Carraway's father said in The Great Gatsby: "Whenever you feel like criticising anyone, just remember that all the people in this world haven't had the advantages that you've had."

The house and street seemed like a pleasant and quiet place to live. She paid in cash and threw in a tip, but insisted on a receipt. Even a privileged girl is entitled to the perks of the job. And St Jude's was going to pay for this trip, Uber car, train, taxi and all.

From the kerb she could see the terrace house where Ruth lived. But through the lace curtains of the front window, she caught sight of something that troubled her. It was just a flash of an image. You couldn't really see into the living room through heavy lace curtains unless it was night-time and the lights in the house were on. But now it was a bright day and the living room was dark in comparison.

Nevertheless she had caught something in her field of vision.

It had looked like some kind of struggle was in progress. She couldn't be sure, but she would know soon enough as she walked up to the door to ring the doorbell.

And then she noticed something else that troubled her: in a curious repetition of what Soraya and Huette had seen, she noticed that the door was slightly ajar.

And then came the scream. Muted and muffled, but a scream, nevertheless.

She didn't hesitate for an instant. She pushed the door open and charged in. The living room was to the right so she went through the door on the right. And then she saw it.

Not a body, lying on the floor, but two figures locked in a life-or-death struggle, one armed with a hammer, trying to hit the other – a woman who was hanging on to the wrist below the hand that wielded the hammer. Not just hanging on, the unarmed woman was *hanging on for dear life*, while using her free hand to fend off blows from the attacker's free hand, a gloved hand clenched into a fist.

And in another room... in *another* room... a baby or a toddler was crying. Despite the blood on the side of the face of one of the unarmed women, it was the crying of the toddler that was the most heart-rending thing playing on Emily's mind.

64

DI Jane Cherry was at her desk in the incident room.

In murder cases, the Major Incident Room may be downsized once someone is charged, and then scaled down further when the trial commences. But it stays open until the trial is over. If the verdict is *not* guilty, then the case file remains open and is assigned to one detective, but the room itself is closed and the staff re-assigned to other duties. The designated case officer remains available to receive any further evidence that comes forward.

But as the trial was still in progress, the police had to be ready to react if the CPS needed any information they didn't have already. Jane had been taken by surprise when the scans of Raymond Morrison showed up and turned out to be the ones that were passed off as those of Walter Wallace. She was surprised a second time when the CPS got the anonymous tip-off about the real name of Calvin Coffey being Calvin Conway and the whole cheating fiasco.

The difference was that whereas it was one of *her own men* who discovered the truth about the scans, the tip-off about Calvin had by-passed her and gone straight to the CPS. In other words, the police were the heroes when it came to the scans – which were beneficial to the defence – but they looked like a complete load of plonkers when it came to Calvin's identity and background.

She was still beating herself up over it and cursing her colleagues over that monumental failure. They *should* have discovered the information. And indeed they should have found it *before* the trial, not halfway through! If it wasn't for reporting restrictions, the press would probably be having a field day about her poor performance and professional incompetence. She wondered if her superiors were whispering about it behind her back.

On the other hand, cock-ups seldom impact adversely on a police officer's promotion prospects – even if they claim the life of an innocent, unarmed man. You just have to stick to the story and play the system for all it's worth – all the way up to the top. Such is the culture of the police in Britain.

In any event, there was but one thing she could do about it. She could find out who was the source of the tip-off. It might seem like petty revenge, but she had plausible grounds for pursuing it. The source might have other information that was relevant to the case.

At least that's how she was going to sell it to Chryseis.

So for the last 24 hours, Jane had been working with the mobile phone companies to trace the phone that the tip-off had come from. If the caller had called 999 or 112, the number could not have been withheld at all, and the location would have been immediately traceable. But because the caller had called the CPS, the police had to work with the phone companies to identify the number.

After three companies came up negative, the fourth confirmed that it was one of theirs: a pay-as-you-go SIM card. It wasn't under contract and so they didn't have a name. It was being topped up by vouchers purchased from local shops. In theory, the police could go to those shops and pull the CCTV footage to try to get an ID. But Jane knew that she couldn't justify the time or the expenditure. And in any case, they could easily trace the phone's location – or at least the phone company could ping it and give an approximate location to the police. Not a precise SatNav position, but at least the nearest antenna.

But if the person was on the move, then catching them would be tricky. It was unlikely that Chryseis would approve the use of police resources for it. After all, reporting information to the police is hardly a crime. And although the information hadn't come through a channel that promised anonymity, like Crimestoppers, it would look bad for the police if they deliberately tracked down a witness who had brought them useful information that they could use in court perfectly well *without* involving the source.

However, Jane had one more thing going for her. The phone company had also given her a list of the numbers that had been called from the phone in question: and several of those calls had been to Ruth Morrison.

65

Emily knew that she had to act and act *fast*. For Emily knew, despite never having met her in person, that the injured woman was Ruth. That made sense, because she was dressed normally, and in any case, why would a person in their own home attack someone with a hammer. More importantly, the figure with the hammer was wearing a burqa covering her – or him – from top to toe.

Not for one minute did Emily think that this was an attack by an Islamic extremist. The burqa was not being worn for religious reasons.

Why wear a garment that restricts your movement if you're trying to kill or injure someone?

The burqa was a disguise.

Emily realised that she had wasted precious seconds by pausing to assess the situation, weighing up the danger to herself. Despite her reputation at St Jude's for recklessness, she still had a basic survival instinct. But she could wait no longer.

Emitting from her throat a loud *kiai* – that blood-curdling battle-cry that martial artists sometimes use to motivate themselves and strike terror into the heart of the enemy, she charged at the figure wielding the hammer and engaged with her, grabbing at the hammer with her left hand, while trying to get the figure in a headlock. The figure responded by swinging the hammer at Emily, aided by the fact that Ruth had now backed off and fallen to the ground in pain, presumably from what had come before.

Reacting to the deadly peril in the last fraction of a second, Emily released both the headlock and the wrist grip and blocked the hammer, with one hand on the handle and the other raised in a defensive gesture, just in case she couldn't stop the impact.

Better an injured hand or forearm than a smashed-in face or skull.

Fortunately, the hand that intercepted the handle of the

hammer was sufficient, possibly because the attacker pulled it at the last minute. Or rather released the hammer altogether. As it fell, the hammer narrowly missed Emily's toes, but the distraction gave the figure in the burqa time to flee via the kitchen at the back.

With the hammer on the floor and the attacker clearly disarmed, Emily was tempted to give chase. But then she heard a moaning sound from the ground, and she looked down to see that Ruth was bleeding more profusely than it appeared at first.

66

Having to adapt to being a worker as well as a homemaker was a struggle for Huette. Soraya was looking after Mikey and John-John, while Ariadne was at school. Soraya would pick her up later and feed her and make sure she did her homework, at least the arithmetic homework, which Ariadne hated.

But still it was hard for Huette to concentrate on work. She had found it easier when she was working from home and the children were running around. But the advertising agency were no great fans of remote work, although they allowed some flexibility and had given Huette the hybrid option of two days in the office and three working from home.

They had used the remote option when they were forced to do so, during the Covid lockdown. But while the workers loved it, the executives did not. The staff insisted that they were working harder than ever because they felt like they were being monitored and timed. But the management's position was never about time management. It was about teamwork. They liked their copywriters and graphic artists mingling together, rubbing shoulders and bonding into a tight-knit group. You couldn't get that from remote working.

So instead, Huette found herself working with colleagues in London's West End, engaging in office gossip round the coffee machine in the kitchen, and spending most of her time thinking about the children. It would have been so much easier just to have them running around at home, and even getting under her feet. That worked fine on the remote days. After a while, the noise of children's play blended in with the background. That's how she managed to take the online course in Adobe in the first place.

Of course, there were exceptions: little John's crankiness and constant crying hadn't blended in. Huette's motherly instinct had prevented her from ignoring it. With hindsight, that was just as well. She felt guilty that she hadn't taken him to A&E sooner. Her mother would have done so, even without little Mikey's prompting. On the other hand, the visit to the hospital was unnecessary. The doctor told her that the SIM card would have passed through his system harmlessly and without any intervention.

The SIM card!

She had wondered about it, but not checked it out. Was it her father's? Soraya's? Or could it even be the murderer's?

She had to find out. And the only way she knew was to put it into her phone. And then what? Phone someone else? She wasn't sure. She knew there was a way to check one's phone number, but couldn't remember how.

But first things first. She managed to get her own SIM card out of her phone easily enough. But putting the new one in was proving to be rather more difficult. She was good with software but was the first to admit that she didn't have a clue when it came to hardware.

Just then a colleague entered the kitchen to throw away a cup.

"Do you know anything about SIM cards?" asked Huette.

"A bit. Why?"

"I was wondering if you know what phone this SIM card fits?"

"That's not a SIM card. That's a memory card."

"Memory card?"

"Yes. You know... for cameras."

67

Emily was pacing the hospital corridor while the police officer assigned to protect Ruth from further violence looked on sympathetically. He wanted to reassure her. But he could tell that she was too tense to listen.

Ruth's two-year-old boy, Liam, was being looked after by social services. But Ruth herself was in A&E. She had regained consciousness but was now being X-rayed.

Emily had wanted to accompany Ruth to the hospital, but the police insisted that she go with them. She was not a suspect, they had explained, but because she had struggled with the assailant, her clothes and even her body were technically a "crime scene" and they needed to take DNA samples from them. That meant swabbing her hands and wrists, and taking her clothes away for tapings that would then be analysed for DNA.

They had been very nice about it, praising her for her courage and thanking her for her cooperation. They had reciprocated her helpfulness by taking her size details and getting a female officer to visit the High Street and buy some clothes for her, which they put on the police budget. When all that drama was over, she made her way post-haste to the hospital, to inquire about Ruth.

"She's not in any immediate danger," the consultant explained. "We did a few X-rays, after she regained consciousness, but we had to sedate her again because she couldn't stay still during the MRI scan."

"An MRI scan *and* X-rays?"

"The X-rays can show broken bones, but we had to do an MRI scan to see if there was any internal bleeding. It gives us a more accurate picture."

Emily forced herself to keep a straight face on hearing the words "MRI" and "accurate picture" in the same sentence. It was just as well that she had done so. She didn't feel like explaining her scepticism to these hardworking doctors and nurses.

"When will I be able to see her?"

"Not before tomorrow morning. And in any case, the police will want to interview her first."

Emily well understood. They needed to get an account from Ruth directly, as she remembered it, untainted by Emily's memory of the events. The passage of time and the blows to the head might affect Ruth's memory. Inserting Emily's thoughts would only taint the evidential value of Ruth's recollections.

Realising that there was nothing more to be gained here, she decided to book into a hotel. St Jude's would cover it. But first she decided to put in a call to Nigel.

"How's it going, Emily?"

He sounded cheerful. But then again, he didn't know what had happened to Ruth. When she told him, his reaction was predictable. He asked about *her* safety first and Ruth's second. Once they had got that out of the way, she filled him in on the details, including her intention to stay in Bournemouth till the morning.

He didn't try to argue with her. The case would be resuming at 10.00 the following day, but he understood her priorities. In any event, he could do Calvin's re-examination on his own. Then she remembered that she hadn't asked him what he had found out from Professor Whitmore. She asked him now and he filled her in too, going into some considerable detail, including Whitmore's caginess about the "rumours" swirling about him and his eccentricities, like using analogies to Hollywood films to explain the background to the case.

"So nothing beyond what Calvin already said," she summarised.

"Apart from the Tipp-Ex corrections, no."

"I wonder why Calvin didn't mention them."

"Maybe I'll risk asking him that tomorrow."

The old rule about never asking a question you don't know the answer to – again.

"Anything else boss?"

She was back to her old cheeky self again.

"Yes. You said you struggled briefly with the figure in the burqa."

"Yes?"

"Were you able to gauge if it was a man or a woman?"

"It was a woman."

"Are you sure about that?"

"Oh yes. No question."

68

DI Cherry arrived at her desk in the incident room when the call came. It was internal from the desk of the Receiver, the team member tasked with receiving all "documents" that came into the room. His job included passing on any important information directly to the Senior Investigating Officer and/or the Deputy Senior Investigating Officer, who in this case was Jane Cherry.

"Inspector, we've just had a call from the Dorset Police. Something about an attack on a woman called... Ruth Morrison."

"What do you mean 'an attack'?"

Jane Cherry wasn't sure if this meant a reputational attack or a physical one.

"Well apparently she was hit on the head with a hammer."

At that point, Jane snapped.

"Why the hell didn't you put the call through!"

"You weren't at your desk."

Jane muttered something incoherent and ended the call. Then she called out to the Dorset Police to get the details. They filled her in, to her growing horror, including Emily's belief that although the burqa may have been a disguise, there was no doubt in her mind that the attacker was a woman.

When the call ended, Jane reflected on the fact that after two decades in the police, she still hadn't lost the capacity to be horrified. Not because the *victim* was a woman, but rather because the violent attacker probably was. And not a drunken woman, but a sober one, in a premeditated attack.

And that gave Jane an idea.

Thursday 28th March, 2024

69

"How are you feeling?"

Emily's voice was gentle.

"Like I've been hit on the head with a hammer."

Ruth's reply was weak. She managed a feeble attempt at a smile to go with the voice.

"Have they caught her?" Ruth added.

"Her." So she agreed! It was a woman.

"Not yet. Do you have any idea who it was?" She knew that the police had already asked Ruth that same question and received a negative answer. Emily shook her head, this time, not even bothering to speak out loud. Her injuries were not life-threatening. But she was weak. The hammer had only glanced her skull. The bleeding had come from the ear when the blow was deflected.

They engaged in some small talk for a while. Emily was dying to know everything that Ruth knew about Raymond and everything that she had surmised. But Ruth was still weak from her injuries and in no hurry to talk about matters and memories that were clearly painful to her. So Emily let the small talk run its course, mindful of the fact that at any moment, the doctors might come in and say that Ruth needed to rest.

Then Emily subtly shifted the subject and got Ruth to start talking.

"You said Raymond was a PhD student of Walter Wallace."

"Yes."

"And you said that there was money going into Raymond's account."

"Yes."

"And you thought it was from Professor Wallace?"

"Yes."

"Hush money, you said."

"Yes."

"But hush money for *what*? And what does Calvin have to do

with it?"

Ruth's tone became earnest, and even somewhat desperate – at least desperate to be understood.

"To start with, Raymond wasn't just a PhD student of Walter Wallace and Seamus Harper, he was one of the markers of those exams."

"The exams where Calvin was accused of cheating?"

Emily's tone may have sounded like one of surprise, but already the tumblers of the lock were dropping into place.

"Yes."

"And he thought that Calvin was framed?"

"More than *thought* it. He may have been part of it."

"In what way? And *why*? Why would they want to frame him? What had he done to them?"

"He was a threat to them. They had to get him first. Before *he* got *them*."

"I don't understand. Got them for what? And why couldn't they pay him off? If they paid Raymond off?"

"I don't have the whole picture. But this is what I've figured out. The student papers are marked anonymously. So the marker doesn't know the name of the student whose work he's marking: only their number. While he was marking the papers, Raymond noticed that one student's answers differed from the model solutions."

"*Differed* from them?"

"Yes, differed from them – differed significantly in some cases."

Ruth began slowly explaining what she had figured out, what she knew for certain and what she had figured out by cold, hard logic – steadily revealing more and more recollections, fragments, and titbits that gradually fleshed out the picture. And as she talked, Emily's mouth began to hang open, her jaw dropping lower and lower... and lower.

70

Jane had taken advantage of Detective Superintendent Chryseis Pines's absence to ping the phone of the person who had supplied the anonymous tip-off and track it, first thing in the morning to a shop in the City – the financial centre also known as the Square Mile.

But Chryseis had returned this morning, a day earlier than she had been expected, and so Jane knew she had to ask permission for what she wanted to do next.

She explained not only about the tip-off, but also the calls from that phone to Ruth and the hammer attack on Ruth in Bournemouth. That part was critical, because it showed that the phone could be linked – albeit obliquely – to a violent crime. But she knew that the next part would be even *more* critical in persuading her boss to agree to what she wanted to do next.

"We tracked the phone to a shop just down the road from the Old Bailey and then it switched off."

"A repair shop?"

"No, ma'am, a shop where people stash bags and things."

"Drugs?"

Jane could see, by the look in Chryseis's eyes, that although her boss had returned physically, her heart and mind were still on holiday. So she elaborated.

"No ma'am. It's used mostly by members of the public who are spectators in cases at the Old Bailey."

"I'm not following."

"It's a luggage storage facility. You see, members of the public aren't allowed to bring large bags, or phones, into the Old Bailey. So they stash them in that shop for about four pounds seventy a day. It's within easy walking distance of the Bailey and so it's quite convenient."

"So you think the person who gave us the tip-off is a spectator at the Calvin Coffey trial?"

"More than that ma'am. We've talked to the owner of the shop, and he told us that it's a woman and he even gave us a description. He said she comes in every morning, puts the phone in a bag and leaves the whole bag there. Then she comes in late afternoon and picks it up."

"And so you want to pull her in?"

"I think we now have grounds."

"The hammer attack on Ruth Morrison?"

"Yes, ma'am."

"Do we know what time she's likely to be there to pick up the bag?"

"It can vary, ma'am. That's why I had another idea."

71

"Okay, thank you Emily."

It was nearly ten o'clock, and Nigel was in the robing room of the Old Bailey, rounding off a conversation with Emily. As soon as Ruth had finished dropping her bombshell, Emily lost no time in leaving Ruth "to rest" and stepping out into a quiet area of the hospital to put in a call to Nigel to make sure that he was fully briefed when he started his re-examination of Calvin.

"Do you think he'll cooperate?" asked Emily.

"I don't know. I mean technically none of this exonerates him from the murder of Walter Wallace. If anything it gives him a motive."

"He already has a motive, Nige. Getting canned from Bristol Uni, remember?"

"True. But he may not see it that way."

"So what are you going to do?"

"I'm just going to go in there and play it by ear."

And play it by ear, he did.

Nigel didn't want to force Calvin's hand on a basis of Ruth's revelations to Emily, so instead he made another attempt to ask the judge to reverse her earlier decision and allow him to meet with his client, despite Calvin being in the middle of his evidence. He argued that he now had new evidence himself from a third party, not previously available, and this necessitated seeking fresh instructions from his client. But Judge Braham stood by her earlier decision.

Her ruling was appealable, and Nigel was confident he would win in the end. But for now, there was nothing he could do. He would probably be better off *not* using the material and keeping his powder dry. Then, at least, he could argue on appeal that he was constrained against using the material by lack of clear, affirmative instructions from his client.

Instead, the way he was doing things now, he was burning his bridges. And if it backfired, he would have nowhere to run. If the whole thing blew up in his face, all he could do would be to step aside and let Calvin seek new counsel who could then appeal on the grounds that Nigel was professionally incompetent by raising the risky material.

But in some ways, Nigel had a bit of "Emily" in him. He was no shrinking violet. He was a fighter. And if he had to put his own professional reputation on the line, so be it.

"Can you please tell the jury, Calvin, if you have ever met Raymond Morrison."

"Yes, I've met him."

"Under what circumstances?"

"He contacted me through LinkedIn on the 2nd of April last year and we met the following day."

"And then he was killed shortly after that. On the sixth."

"Yes. I heard it about it on the 7th. It popped up on my news feed. A brief news report about a murder in Bournemouth. I think because I'd checked him out on my phone, and I opted to allow cookies. So it was deemed relevant by the algorithm."

"Could you tell us what happened at the meeting?"

"Certainly. He approached me, after he had been diagnosed with a brain tumour. And after he had talked to a priest."

"And what was the gist of that conversation?"

"He was tormented by an historic wrong that he had done. A wrong that he had done *me*. And he wanted to put it right."

Nigel was relieved. Calvin was ready to talk about it. He wasn't holding back. It was like a weight was being lifted off Calvin's shoulders.

"This 'historic wrong' that he did you, did it have something to do with the allegations of cheating?"

"Yes."

"And he wanted to put it right by telling you the details?"

"Amongst other things."

"Could you elaborate?"

"Raymond was one of the markers of my final exams. He noticed, when marking my exam papers, that some of my answers deviated from the examiner's model solutions, to use the standard academic phrase. Normally, this would simply mean that my answers were wrong. But as he continued marking my answers, he noticed that even though my answers deviated from the model solutions, those answers were nevertheless right."

"You mean you found alternative ways to derive the correct answers?"

"No. I mean that the *model solutions were wrong.*"

"What, *all* of them?"

"No, not all of them. And indeed not even in all the cases where my answers differed from them. But in *many* cases. Certainly enough to be a cause of concern to Raymond."

"So what did he do?"

Blair rose to his feet for a challenge.

"M'Lady, it seems that counsel is trying to introduce hearsay evidence that falls outside the scope of the common law exceptions allowed by section 118 of the Criminal Justice Act."

Nigel was furious. Blair knew the 2003 act inside out, and he knew perfectly well that this was just plain wrong. His only reason for interrupting was to break the flow and effectiveness of Calvin's testimony. But Nigel had no intention of letting that happen. He was going to rebut the argument now, before the jury was sent out. And if Judge Braham got angry with him for doing so, then so be it!

"M'Lady, this is a *statutory* exception to the hearsay rule, not a residual common law exception: Section 116. Sub-section 2. When the original source of the evidence is dead, the hearsay testimony is admissible. M'learned friend seems to have forgotten the basics."

He was rubbing Hayden Blair's face into the dirt, in full view of the jury and quite deliberately setting out to humiliate him. He had finally had enough of Blair's last-minute disclosures and underhand tactics. Now it was *Nigel's* turn to fight dirty.

But Blair wasn't going down without a fight either.

"I think m'learned friend has forgotten that even under section 116 – if my memory serves me right M'Lady – there is a provision that the party offering the hearsay evidence must seek leave of the court before doing so."

"M'Lady, much as it pains me to say this, m'leaned friend's memory does *not* serve him right. The 'prior leave' requirement applies only to sub-section 2, paragraph *E* where the original source of the evidence is *refusing* to testify due to *fear*. This evidence is being brought in under paragraph *A*, where the source of the evidence is *dead*. Leave of the court is not required."

"And even if it were, Mr Farringdon," said Judge Braham, glancing with disdain at the prosecutor, "I would be minded to grant leave, under the present circumstances."

Yes! Thought Nigel. *She's finally taking my side!*

At that point, Hayden Blair would have been wise to sit down quietly and lick his wounds. Instead, he tried to push his luck.

"But there is still a requirement under sub-section 1 A that the court be satisfied that this testimony be admissible in the matter if it were given by the *original witness*."

"As it is testimony about the alleged cheating, Mr Blair, then it is relevant *by definition*, isn't it? After all, *you* were the one who introduced the evidence of cheating."

Blair was silent. He could do nothing except bow to the inevitable. But Judge Braham wasn't quite finished yet. This was to be a merciless beat-down, with even the umpire joining in.

"Furthermore, what the defendant was told by Morrison, may have motivated his subsequent mental state, so it would then also be admissible under 118 sub 4 para C."

Strangely, this last point didn't seem to bother Blair so much. In fact, as he resumed his seat, Nigel noticed a gleam in his eye. This was a warning sign, a "tell" that Nigel had learned to recognise in Blair. The reason was obvious: "mental state" was another way of saying "motive".

"Okay Calvin. What did Raymond Morrison do, when he noticed the errors in the model solutions?"

As he said this, the door to the spectators' gallery opened and the usher seemed to enter into whispered colloquy with a woman whom Petula didn't recognise. She wondered what it was about. But before she could give it another moment's thought, Calvin started speaking.

"He told the two professors in question: Walter Wallace and Seamus Harper. And they looked at their model solutions again and realised that they had to correct those solutions – and *fast*. They had a stack of exam papers waiting to be marked and no time in which to rework the model solutions. That's why the model solutions were covered in Tipp-Ex and pen corrections. Because it was all done in a last-minute rush. Only more of a last-minute rush than anyone could have possibly guessed.

"But now, here's the deal. They didn't know it was *my* paper that had so many of the right answers that they had got wrong. All they saw was the student number. But they saw that in many cases *their* answers were wrong and those of the student were right. So they took an expedient decision: they decided to use the student's papers – that is *my* papers – as crib-sheets."

A gasp swept through the courtroom as this sunk in. While

the judge told everyone to settle down, the usher signalled Petula to come to the exit.

72

It seemed rather strange to Petula. Why would the usher call her out in the middle of a session? In the middle of someone testifying even? Had she done something wrong?

But the simplest course of action was to comply. So she edged her way past the priest, knowing now full well who he was, and out through the exit, where she found herself confronted by the woman she had seen a few moments ago, as well as two male police officers.

"Petula Gelding?" the woman asked, her voice carrying the weight of urgency as she flashed her police badge.

"Yes?"

The woman whipped out a pair of police handcuffs, seemingly from nowhere and then spoke in flat, passive-aggressive tone.

"The time is eleven forty-three and I am arresting you on suspicion of causing grievous bodily harm."

73

Meanwhile, in court, Nigel was continuing his meticulous re-examination of Calvin.

"Let me get this straight. You're saying that *they used your papers as crib-sheets for their corrections to the model solutions?*"

"Yes. Basically."

"So they just copied your answers? Straight down the line?"

"No, not quite. If they'd done that, then they'd've given me a hundred percent and a lot more of my papers errors would have been copied over into the revised model solutions. No, they used mine as a crib-sheet, but they also ran some quick calculations. According to Raymond, they used a sort of hybrid method. They compared their solutions to mine, and if the answers deviated, they started recalculating the solution. If they spotted a mistake in theirs, they went with mine. If they spotted a mistake in mine, they went with theirs. They didn't recalculate everything – just up to the point when they decided which answer they had more confidence in."

"And that's why so many of your answers matched their model solutions?"

"Yes. Including the one where I supposedly replicated the examiner's error. It was actually the other way round. He replicated *mine.*"

"But why did they turn on you?"

"After they made the corrections, all my papers were handed over to a couple of other markers. And in the case of the exams that were set by Wallace and Harper, the other markers flagged them as suspicious. And once I was in the frame, Wallace and Harper could hardly defend me. It was me or them. The similarities were too great. They had to turn on me to cover their asses."

"But why didn't you speak out about this sooner?"

"Because I hadn't figured it out at the time."

"Why not?"

"Because I was naïve. I was naïve enough to believe that it had to be coincidence. Or in some cases, simply because I was using the methods they taught me. I never once thought they could have been copying from me. I should have figured it out from the masses of Tipp-Ex corrections. But it never occurred to me that they could be so dishonest. And then to blame *me* for it... to *falsely accuse me*."

He was becoming overwrought. Now, finally, after all these years, he was feeling the intensity of the emotions – more so than when they had first falsely accused him.

"So you only found out when Raymond told you?"

"Yes. From what he told me, when he was diagnosed with that brain tumour it brought out his latent guilt feelings. So he went to see a priest and the priest told him that he had to do a penance for his sins."

"And that penance was?"

"Two things. One, to tell the victim of his machinations what he had done."

"Victim meaning you?"

"Yes."

"And the second?"

"To put it right with the authorities. To tell them what he had done and do everything in his power to put matters right."

"And do you know if he did that?"

"I asked him if he was going to the university authorities and he told me he was going to, but he wanted to give Wallace and Harper a chance to come clean first. Then, shortly after that, he was killed."

So that was that.

The evidence purporting to show that Calvin was a cheat lay in ruins. Or at least it was now confronted by a plausible rebuttal. But what now? If it was implausible that Calvin, would turn up at the home of a potential client on the strength of an email exchange without even a single phone call, how much *less* likely would this be if the client just happened to be the former professor who had got Calvin canned for cheating? Even if the cheating accusations were themselves barefaced lies! Coincidence was exceedingly unlikely. And worse still, for the defence, motive was *motive*!

There has to be an explanation, thought Nigel. *But is it one that favours Calvin? And do I dare go there without knowing?*

He couldn't chance it.

Should I end the cross-examination here?

To do so would leave the jury with a thousand unanswered

questions. On the other hand, to probe any further was to risk leaving his client with one very undesirable and damaging answer.

The middle road, maybe? The open-ended question? Let's give it a shot?

"Is there anything else you'd like to say?"

He was giving Calvin the choice.

Calvin hesitated for a moment.

"Only this. I was asked in cross-examination about Occam's razor, and I conceded that deliberate copying, of one party by the other, was more consistent with the principles of Occam's razor than any other explanation – because that explanation subsumed all the unusual events under a single assumption. I stand by that answer now.

"But that still leaves open the questions of access to the material, the ability to use it without getting caught, *and* the motive for doing so. No credible explanation has been offered as to how *I* could have gained access to the model solutions, let alone in their final form. And no explanation has been offered as to how I could have memorised them – or how I could have written them down and used them under the noses of the invigilators. And given that the other eleven tutors never accused me of cheating, despite my achieving even better results in their exams, why would I have needed to cheat in the exams set by Wallace or Harper in particular?

"On the other hand, after I submitted my exam papers, Professor Wallace and Professor Harper would certainly have had access to those papers, via the markers. There were no invigilators watching the markers or the professors. So there was nothing to stop them doing what Raymond *told me* they did. And as for motive, the fact that the exams were covered in last minute corrections *proves* that until then, the model solutions were full of errors. Otherwise, why correct them? Now *that's* a powerful motive! They needed to correct the errors – and they needed to do so *quickly!*

"So to borrow a phrase from counsel for the prosecution, Professors Wallace and Harper had means, motive and opportunity. And the explanation that Raymond told me – the explanation that I now offer the jury – subsumes all the unusual events under a single assumption and a single explanation. In other words – again to borrow an argument that the learned prosecutor put forward – it fits perfectly with Occam's razor."

Nigel wanted to respond to Calvin's answer with a round of

applause. Instead, he simply said, "thank you."

Nigel then looked up at the judge.

"I have no further questions, M'Lady."

Judge Braham looked round at Calvin.

"You may return to the dock," said the judge. But before he could move, a voice rang out.

"One moment, M'Lady."

Calvin froze. It was Hayden Blair.

"I wish to address the court on a matter of law."

74

"The call came from *your* phone."

"So?"

Chryseis Pines was leading the questioning of Petula, while Jane Cherry sat beside her. Jane would have loved to lead the questioning, but even without Chryseis pulling rank, it was obvious that the physically imposing Superintendent would have a more intimidating effect on a female suspect than her junior officer. Not that Petula Gelding showed the slightest sign of being intimidated. So far, she hadn't even asked for a solicitor.

"So we have a simple question. Why did you call the CPS to tell them about Calvin Coff – Conway's past? And how did you know?"

Petula, who had been leaning forward defiantly, shifted to a leaning back and slouching I-don't-give-a-damn posture, as if this "interview" had lost all interest to her.

"That's *two* questions."

She was mocking them.

"Are you going to answer?"

"It also has nothing to do with the charge that you arrested me on."

"Care to elaborate, Miss Gelding? It is 'Miss', isn't it?"

"You can call me Petula. And no, I don't care to elaborate. You arrested me on a charge of GBH and now you're asking me about a call from my phone to the CPS."

"We arrested you on *suspicion* of GBH."

"Same issue. *How* does that relate to a call to the CPS?"

"That's what we're trying to figure out."

"So you want me to help you build up a case against myself? Okay, so let's break it down then, shall we? You think I phoned the CPS and told them about Calvin Conway and his background? Well, bully for you. Damn right I did! Anything wrong with that? Has it suddenly become illegal to report the truth to the authorities? And since when do you go tracking down sources who prefer to remain anonymous? I thought that was against police policy."

Inspector Cherry leaned forward and looked to Chryseis for permission to step in. The superintendent nodded.

"It's not illegal to give information. We'd just like to know why you did it."

"Why? Because I wanted the prosecutor to know the kind of man he's dealing with."

"And how did *you* know?"

Petula was silent. Jane pressed her again.

"Have you got some sort of vendetta against him? Was he your lover?"

"You needn't concern yourselves with that."

"We'll decide that," said Chryseis, her tone harsh, but obviously manufactured for the occasion.

Petula gave her a mocking smile.

"You can decide what you like. I'm not going to answer. And if you charge me with a crime and think that silence will harm my defence, you'll have to establish the relevance of the *alleged* evidence that I'm not responding to. Like your colleague said, reporting facts to the authorities isn't a crime."

Chryseis folded her arms.

"No, but Grievous Bodily Harm is."

"Again – watch my lips – what's the fucking connection?"

Chryseis unfolded her arms again. The menacing approach clearly wasn't going to work.

"You haven't once asked…" This was Jane. But she trailed off and once again looked at Chryseis, as if seeking permission. Again the superintendent nodded. Jane changed tack.

"You know she's conscious and she'll probably make a full recovery."

"Who?"

"The victim of your assault."

"Well, if she's conscious – whoever "she" is – why don't you ask her?"

"She said the attacker was wearing a burqa. But we think it was a disguise."

"So you're saying that someone wearing a burqa attacked someone else, and because you haven't been able to identify the attacker, you've decided that it was *me*?"

"That's what we think, yes."

"I don't even know *who* it is that I'm supposed to have attacked."

"Pull the other one, treacle," said Chryseis. "It's got bells on."

Treacle, as in Treacle Tart. Cockney rhyming slang for "sweetheart". Except that in this case, it wasn't a term of affection or endearment, but rather an expression of patronising mockery.

"Are you going to tell me... Superintendent?"

"You made a number of calls on that phone. I don't mean the call to the CPS. I mean other calls."

"Yes. So what?"

"Including quite a few to one Ruth Morrison, the widow of Raymond. So presumably you know her."

"Yes, she's my friend."

"Really Petula?"

Petula finally showed the first sign of any real emotion, other than mockery and hostility.

"Wait..."

Chryseis hesitated, seeing the tension on Petula's face.

"So are you in the habit of battering your friends with a hammer?"

The next sound that came from Petula was a scream.

75

"M'Lady, in view of the new evidence introduced by m'learned friend, I would like to conduct a further cross-examination of the defendant."

The jury had been sent out, and the lawyers were wrangling, yet again.

"What new evidence is that?" asked Judge Braham, a sneer in her tone.

"Well, for a start, the evidence about Professors Wallace and Harper allegedly copying from his exam papers. The defendant never mentioned this on cross-examination."

The judge pulled a sceptical face at this.

"That might have to do with the way in which you phrased your questions, Mr Blair. But if you wish to challenge the defendant's claims, would you not first have to seek fresh instructions?"

"Oh, I don't wish to challenge the claims. But I would argue that this new evidence isn't exculpatory at all. In fact, I would argue that it gives the defendant an even *stronger* motive for murder."

"Well that's an argument for your closing speech, isn't it, Mr Blair? Hardly a basis for cross-examination."

"I would like to put it to the defendant. I would have done so before, if he had made the claim sooner, instead of springing it upon us."

Judge Braham took in a deep breath and held it for a couple of seconds – visibly trying to keep her temper in check. Slowly, she let the air out of her lungs, and then replied.

"With the greatest of respect, Mr Blair, you're living in a bit of a glass house, when it comes to accusing people of springing surprises on you. In any case, if you accept the testimony as true and don't wish to challenge its veracity, then you have no reason to cross-examine the defendant. If your only purpose is to argue that it is further evidence of motive, then you can do that in your closing speech."

"M'lady, as a matter of *law*, the Crown has surely a *right* to–"

"*Mr Blair*... there is an old proverb: 'sauce for the goose is sauce for the gander.' You have been granted considerable latitude with last-minute disclosures, while Mr Farringdon was prevented from talking with his client. Now the boot is on the other foot. You can argue the case as you please, but you will not be permitted any further right of cross-examination."

Then, looking over at Nigel, she asked: "Any other business?"

"Actually yes, M'Lady," Nigel interjected. "I would like to ask the court to issue a witness summons for Seamus Harper. He has been named by the defendant as a person of interest and he was effectively introduced by the Crown, when m'learned friend introduced the issue of alleged cheating."

Naturally, Hayden Blair was quick to challenge this.

"M'Lady, I too wanted to call Professor Harper, to testify about the cheating issue, but was unable to do so. Sadly, Professor Harper is suffering from Alzheimer's disease and finds it very hard to follow a conversation. I have a letter from a consultant gerontologist at St Bartholomew's Hospital confirming this."

How convenient, thought Nigel, irritated that Blair had seen this coming. After the events of Tuesday morning, Blair had evidently moved quickly.

The prosecutor produced two copies, handing them to the court clerk. One copy was handed to the judge and the other to Nigel, who perused it quickly. A key paragraph in the letter stated that: "The extent of the dementia has been exacerbated by a fall he suffered last September, in which Professor Harper banged his head and suffered concussion. This has led to physical frailty as well as impaired mental capacity. Although he still retains his long-term memory, his inability to understand things that are said to him, or even keep track of his own sentences, renders him an unreliable witness. Furthermore, the whole experience would be extremely stressful to him."

Nigel knew that he could always ask for a second opinion. But notwithstanding the Simon Fletcher debacle, a consultant's opinion would normally hold sway in a court of law, unless challenged by another expert of equal standing. He decided not to push it any further. Instead he had another plan.

"In that case, I would like to be allowed to recall Mrs Wallace. I was not able to complete my cross-examination of her, but I believe she may have some useful information that may be of benefit to the defence."

"Mr Blair?" asked Judge Braham.

"M'Lady, I cannot possibly imagine what evidence Mrs Wallace may have that would be of the slightest benefit to the defence."

Oh yes you do, you old wily fox.

"But if m'learned friend wishes to call her, I have no objections."

"Then I'll allow it."

The judge looked over at the witness area.

"I see Mrs Wallace is here. Mrs Wallace, could I ask you to return to the witness box. I know this might seem stressful to you, but I'm sure that Mr Farringdon will be as brief as he can be."

Soraya returned to the witness box and appeared to be looking at the clerk's desk where the various holy books were.

"You've already been sworn, so there's no need to take the oath again." Then, turning to the jury usher, the judge said, "bring the jury back, please."

76

12.15. Lunchtime. Or was it brunch?

Finally!

Huette had been thinking about this since yesterday. Her computer didn't have an internal memory card reader. But then she remembered that Gerald had a couple of drawers filled with bits and bobs belonging to his various computers, current and old. Memory sticks, external drives, cables with an alphabet soup of names. Aaaaand... most important in this case, an external memory card reader.

She plugged it into her laptop, and then inserted the card, but got a warning:

```
External device not recognised.
```

She wondered if she would have to restart the laptop with the card ready inserted. But before that, she tried something else: unplugging the external reader and then plugging it in again, but with the card already inserted.

This time it worked. The card was recognised, and she was able to find two MPEG files on it. One was just a two-second file. She looked at it first. It was little more than a test of whatever device the memory card was being used in. The other was a much larger file.

She clicked on it and it sprang to life on the screen.

And what she saw surprised her. It was an all too familiar door being opened. But more surprising still was the man who was standing in front of the door: Professor Harper, looking quite tense and very anxious.

"Come in, Seamus," said a voice – the voice of the man who was wearing what must have been a concealed or secret video recording device.

But when she heard the voice, Huette froze.

It was the voice of her father.

77

Soraya Wallace was back in the witness box and the jury were back in their seats.

"We have heard evidence that Raymond Morrison, who was killed on the 6th of April last year, told the defendant on the 3rd of April that he was going to contact your husband in an effort to clear the name of the defendant in an historic case of alleged cheating. Can you please tell the jury if you have any knowledge of the original case or any approach by Raymond Morrison to your late husband?"

"I know nothing about either. But I *do* remember that a couple of days before that – I think it was the fourth, possibly – Walter was acting rather... I don't know how to describe it. I suppose acting oddly."

"In what way?"

"He seemed a bit..."

"A bit...?"

"A bit troubled."

"And that was on the fourth of April last year, you say?"

"I think so."

"A day after Raymond spoke to the defendant and two days before he was killed."

Soraya didn't react.

"Did you know that your husband was paying money into Raymond Morrison's bank account?"

Hayden Blair was on his feet.

"M'Lady, may I enquire if m'learned friend is intending to introduce evidence of these alleged transactions?"

"M'Lady, we will be introducing evidence that money was being paid into Morrison's account in the form of cash deposits into London branches of the same bank as that where Morrison held his account. And we will be introducing evidence that phone calls were made by Morrison to Professor Wallace and vice versa."

Mary Braham looked over at Blair in case he wanted to add anything, but the prosecutor knew already what she had decided and remained silent.

"I think that establishes sufficient foundation for this line of questioning. Carry on Mr Farringdon."

"I'm much obliged M'Lady." Nigel turned to Soraya. "Well Mrs Wallace? Do you know anything about such payments?"

"No."

She sounded defensive now.

"Mrs Wallace, I'm going to suggest to you, that your husband was paying off Raymond, not to reveal that my client was – to put it bluntly – stitched up by your husband."

"Well all I can say is, if he was, I knew *nothing* about it!"

"And I put it to you that this was fine and dandy until Raymond was diagnosed with a brain tumour. Because at *that* point, he wanted to come clean with the authorities and help my client clear his name."

"*I don't know anything about Raymond!*" she snapped. "I never met this Raymond and never spoke to him!"

"And I'm also going to suggest that when Raymond contacted your husband and warned him that he was about to blow the gaff, your husband panicked and killed Raymond."

"Walter never killed..." But she couldn't finish the sentence. She trailed off almost as she was seriously considering the possibility that maybe he could.

"And I further put it to you that your husband in some way contrived to fake his own brain tumour using Raymond's brain scan and your husband's own formidable skills in computational mathematics, to hack the servers at the Royal Free Hospital."

"That's ridiculous! Why would he do that?"

"I put it to you that he did it so that he would appear to be an unlikely murder suspect. Who would suspect a man with a brain tumour."

"Walter did *not* kill Raymond Morrison!"

"You know this for a fact?"

"I... I..."

She was trapped.

"I have no reason to believe it."

"But you cannot rule it out?"

"Mr Farringdon," the judge intervened sternly, "cross-examination – and this *is* cross-examination as I granted you the right to treat the witness as hostile – is *not* an excuse for badgering the witness with unsubstantiated theories. Do you intend to introduce corroborating evidence for these assertions?"

"I intend to ask the court to issue a summons for a person of interest who may be able to shed some light on it."

"That sounds rather vague. Be careful what you say, Mr Farringdon. It would *not* be in your client's interests if I have to declare a mistrial."

In other words, Calvin would rot in pre-trial detention until a new trial could start, which might not be for more than a year. But Nigel was committed now: he had to press on.

"I understand M'Lady." Again, he turned back to Soraya. "Mrs Wallace, I must now put it to you that you thought – rightly or wrongly – that Raymond Morrison's widow Ruth figured out that your husband killed Raymond and killed your husband in revenge."

The look on Soraya's face was a cross between furious and totally befuddled. So much so, that Nigel was wondering if he had got it wrong.

"I never met Raymond or his wife. I never even knew about Raymond. And I certainly didn't know about his wife."

"Then you didn't go to the seaside yesterday and try to exact revenge upon her?"

He was hoping – praying – that she would blurt out something about "Bournemouth", or a hammer, that would show guilty knowledge.

"No I didn't! What seaside? And what do you mean 'exact revenge'?"

"By attacking her with a hammer in an attempt to kill her."

"*You're mad!*" she practically screamed.

But before she could deliver the mouthful on Nigel that she wanted to launch in his direction, Hayden Blair was on his feet in panic mode.

"Point of law, M'Lady!"

"The jury," Judge Braham said to the jury usher. She didn't need to say more.

When the jury were out, Mary Braham unleashed the full measure of her fury on Nigel, without even waiting for Blair to propose his motion.

"Mr Farringdon, you had absolutely *no business* mentioning the attack on Ruth Morrison, in the presence of the jury – at least not without clearing it with the court first!"

She spoke in a tone and language that suggested that she knew about the attack, which was rather strange as Nigel *hadn't* raised the issue with her first. And he was sure that Hayden Blair hadn't either, as that would hardly have been allowed ex parte. In fact news of the attack should probably have come as a surprise to Blair too.

"It was Ruth Morrison that I was hoping to summons, when she recovers enough to testify."

"And what? You think she'll confess to the murder of Professor Wallace."

"It is arguable that she has motive."

"Arguable on the flimsiest of evidence. You are effectively arguing that Walter Wallace killed Raymond Morrison, that Ruth Morrison murdered Professor Wallace in revenge, and that this witness" – she looked apologetically at Soraya – "tried to murder Ruth Morrison. You seem to be trying to turn this trial into an episode of the Hercule Poirot mysteries – and doing so on a basis of a few random unrelated events."

"M'Lady, the fact that all three of these incidents entail murder or violent attack using a hammer and all three involve people who at least in *some* cases are known to one another, suggests that there is a connection."

"And yet you would have the jury believe that these events were the work of *three different people*."

Nigel was silenced by Mary Braham's logic. Looking at it now, he realised how preposterous it all sounded. It was just a wild stab in the dark anyway. The sort of thing that Emily might have done in her immaturity. The sort of thing that he would have chided her for. And yet here he was, a seasoned legal professional, acting like an undisciplined law pupil, going off on a wild goose chase in desperate hope of a quick victory.

And it had backfired.

Hopelessly.

So now here he was standing before a judge with egg on his face – a judge with whom he had once studied law. A judge with whom he had once had a fling.

"All of a sudden you've lost your voice, Mr Farringdon?"

"M'Lady, I can only say that with my client locked away, and with m'learned friend unloading one surprise on me after another, I may have lost my presence of mind, for which I can only humbly apologise."

He was learning fast. But was it enough?

"Well I wouldn't want your client to suffer because of your incompetence Mr Farringdon. I'll adjourn until two o'clock this afternoon and decide over lunch whether the trial can continue."

78

"Hi, Nige. I was just told about your meeting. I'll see you back at the Bailey. Call me if you need me to do anything before that."

Emily arrived back in London by lunchtime expecting Nigel to brief her on what had gone down in court in the morning session. However, not finding him, she called his mobile, but it went straight to voicemail. So she called the offices of the instructing solicitor, Philip Solomon, and was told that Nigel was there for a meeting with a new witness. She asked if they could put her through or pass him a note, but the secretary told her that they had issued strict instructions not to be disturbed unless it was an emergency.

Although she was dying to know what it was all about, she realised that her personal curiosity hardly made it an emergency. So she called Nigel back on his mobile and left a message. By the time she finished her lunch, the meeting was over and Nigel was calling her back.

"Hi Nige."

"Hi, Emily. I'm heading back to the Bailey and I need you up to speed. I recalled Soraya and questioned her about what she knew about Raymond."

"What did she say?"

Nigel filled her in on the gist of the cross-examination, including his reckless suggestions and outlandish theories and the judge's angry reaction.

"Ouch!" was all Emily could say by way of reply.

"Anyway we're in an Uber now. ETA fifteen minutes. There's something I need you to do for me."

"Shoot."

"I need you to call someone and deliver a message."

"That sounds ominous."

79

Because Nigel had cut it so fine, the trial resumed at two o'clock p.m. on the dot. Emily just about had time to tell Nigel that she had delivered the message, but wasn't sure if it would work.

He told her to wait outside and monitor the entrance.

The customary "All stand!" was intoned, followed by the judge's return, the ceremonial bowing. Now seated, Hayden Blair looked somewhat tense, while Nigel, in contrast, was as calm as he had ever been.

Most crucially Judge Mary Braham was herself perfectly calm as she surveyed her courtroom, which itself suggested that her ruling was not going to rock the boat.

"I have decided that in the interests of justice for all concerned, I am going to allow the trial to continue."

The "all concerned" of course, meant Calvin, who had spent over six months on remand.

"I will also allow the cross-examination of Mrs Wallace to continue, but I will direct the jury to disregard defence counsel's comments about the attack on Mrs Morrison. I will also warn *you*, Mr Farringdon, not to make any further statements about the attack, and more broadly not to pull any more stunts like that one. *Is that clear?*"

Nigel rose to his feet.

"It is perfectly clear M'Lady and once again I apologise to the Court. However, in light of certain new evidence that has come into my possession, I have no need to ask Mrs Wallace any further questions. Instead, I would like to introduce into evidence a video that shows certain events that I believe will establish the innocence of the defendant."

"What is this video? And how did it come into your possession? And why was it not entered into evidence before?"

"Well, in a nutshell, I only just received the video from Huette Shannon, Professor Wallace's daughter, and *she* only came across it recently."

Soraya looked stunned. But her muffled cough was drowned out by the judge.

"How recently is 'recently' Mr Farringdon?"

Judge Braham's tone was suspicious, possibly in response to Nigel's coy phraseology.

"It's rather a long story M'Lady, and in parts a somewhat amusing one. But the important thing is that although Mrs Shannon *had* the memory card with the video for a few days, she only looked at its content – and realised what it was – less than an hour ago. And as soon as she realised, she contacted the defendant's solicitors, who promptly notified *me*."

Judge Braham turned to the Crown prosecutor.

"Do you have anything to say Mr Blair? I mean anything that won't be too embarrassing?"

In other words: "you're living in a glass house if you even *dream* of complaining about late disclosure."

"Assuming that what m'learned friend said is true M'Lady – and I wouldn't contemplate suggesting otherwise – I have no objection in principle. However, I'm sure the *Court itself* would like to see the video, in order to reach its own conclusion as to its relevance."

"A good point, Mr Blair."

At that point, Emily entered the courtroom, trying to hold back a smile. But before Nigel could react, the judge turned to him.

"Mr Farringdon, you never finished answering my earlier question."

"I don't understand M'Lady."

"I asked you about the *subject matter* of the video?"

"Ah, yes. Well basically it shows the events leading up to Professor Wallace's final moments."

80

"Check out the bedroom," said DI Cherry to one of the detective constables.

They were searching Petula's home, a rented two-room bedsit. She had refused to tell them her address, but they had got it from her phone's timeline and found the keys in her handbag.

"Governor, I think you need to take a look at this!"

Jane Cherry raced up the stairs. She arrived in the bedroom to see the constable staring down at an open drawer. As she strode closer, she saw that the drawer was full of SIM cards and cheap phones, some still in their closed packets.

Burner phones.

But she hadn't been clever enough – using the same phone to tip-off the CPS that she'd used to call Ruth Morrison, *and* after holding on to it afterwards.

There was also a handheld voice changer. Jane picked it up and tried it on several settings. It easily changed her voice into that of a man. She could also make her voice sound older or younger.

"Bag it all up," she told the constable. "And take the laptop too."

She wondered whether Petula had used the voice changer when she called the CPS.

But it was the computer that held out the most hope.

What secrets do you hold?

She knew they had to get the answers quickly. They could only hold Petula for a maximum of 72 hours, and they'd have to bring her before a magistrate after 24. But she also knew that she could count on Lorraine to find anything and everything worth finding. She liked Lorraine, and this would give her a chance to see more of her.

81

To save time, Judge Braham agreed to allow Hayden Blair to watch the video with her in the judge's office attached to the court. The alternative would have been for Blair to go back to his law chambers and view it, as the robing room was not a secure area for looking at such potentially sensitive evidence.

And if Blair was watching it with her, then Nigel and Emily had to be there too, to ensure that this didn't turn into an *ex parte* meeting or give rise to any suspicion of same. So here they were, huddled round the desk, watching the video on the judge's computer.

"Come in Seamus," said the voice of Professor Wallace.

Seamus Harper shuffled awkwardly into the house and a hand appeared to close the door behind him. It was a man's hand, and probably that of Wallace, given its position and the voice of the man behind the camera.

The image was not particularly sharp, and the movements were jerky. Harper's face did not remain within the frame the whole time. But then again, it was as good as you could expect from a pen camera.

Wallace shut the door behind Harper with a quiet click and led his former colleague down the carpeted hallway, ushering him into the living room.

"Please, sit down, Seamus," said Wallace, gesturing toward the sofa.

"Thank you, Walter," Harper murmured, his voice thin and wavering.

Harper hesitated for a moment before settling down. His eyes flitted around the room, lingering on the books, the fireplace, the window. There was a flicker of confusion in his expression, a hint of someone trying to grasp at threads that kept slipping through his fingers.

"It's... it's a nice place you've got here."

Wallace settled into an armchair opposite Harper. His own body ached from fatigue, his temples pulsing with the dull pain he'd grown used to over the last five months. The brain tumour, diagnosed in April, was taking its toll, and he'd stopped pretending he had the strength to fight it. Today, though, he needed his wits about him.

"You know what I want to talk about, Seamus," Wallace began, his voice steady, but with a gravity that seemed to hang in the air.

Harper blinked, his eyebrows furrowing. "Yes, you told me. I think."

Wallace had indeed told him. That's why Harper had come at such short notice. But it wasn't clear if Harper remembered... or understood.

"It's about Calvin Conway," Wallace said carefully, his eyes not leaving Harper's face.

Harper's lips parted slightly, a look of vague recognition crossing his face. He seemed to search for the name in the fog of his memory, his hands gripping the edge of the sofa as if it might anchor him to the present. "Calvin... Calvin Conway? He was a student."

"Yes. One of ours."

"I remember... He was an American, you know. I hated him. But I liked his wife. She was pretty."

"Seamus, listen!"

Harper recoiled.

"Focus! ... *please*."

Harper seemed to reboot his mind, at least his change in body posture suggested that he was trying to.

"It was a long time ago Walter."

"Yes, twenty years."

"I wonder what became of him?" asked Harper, his eyes narrowing with a mixture of curiosity and apprehension.

Wallace took a deep breath. He had rehearsed this moment a hundred times in his head, each scenario ending with different words, different outcomes. He had to tread carefully, to make sure that he didn't put words into Harper's mouth.

"We have to put it right Seamus."

"Put it... *how*? *Why*? *Why now*?"

"I've got a brain tumour."

"I know... You told me... I'm sorry."

"It's been weighing on my conscience."

"It's not your fault. Anyone can get a brain tumour."

"I mean what we did to Calvin Conway."

"We did..." the thought seemed to go nowhere. Walter was losing him again. "How is Soraya?"

"We ruined his life!"

Harper's expression grew more puzzled.

"But we talked about it already. I remember. We did what we had to do."

"Seamus, listen. Do you even *remember* what we did? What we *actually* did?"

There was a moment of silence, then a flicker of something in Harper's eyes – fear, recognition, maybe even guilt.

"I remember him," he stammered, his voice trembling. "He was a smart alec – a right little smarmy know-it-all. That's what *you* called him. He cheated in his finals."

"No, Seamus, he *didn't* cheat."

"He *must* have cheated! He got all the answers right. Even the ones *we* got wrong."

"Seamus, we both know what happened," Wallace said slowly, gauging Harper's reaction. "His finals at Bristol. You *do* remember, don't you?"

Wallace leaned forward slightly and adjusted the pen in his breast pocket, making sure the camera was pointing straight ahead.

"You remember our model solutions for the exams. You said it just now. We got some of the answers wrong."

"We were under too much pressure. No one can blame us for making mistakes. We didn't do it deliberately. But they were always so quick to judge. And they picked on us, because we were the new boys. But *we* were the ones who caught him in the end. They didn't spot it. But we knew he must have cheated because he was so stupid. And then suddenly it was like he knew everything. It's not possible. You said so yourself. His results were too good to be true."

"Seamus! Just think for a minute, okay! Just think back. Our model solutions were full of mistakes."

"But we corrected them. I remember."

"Yes. But do you remember *when* we corrected them?"

Wallace was leaning forward eagerly now, hoping that Harper would pronounce the fateful words.

"Yes. We corrected them after the exams. And some of the exam papers had to be re-marked after that."

"Yes, but *how* did we correct them?"

"In ink. Your PhD student helped us. Raymond something."

"Yes, our model solutions were full of mistakes. We corrected them in ink. Using Tipp-Ex to cover the old answers. But how did we get the answers so quickly?"

"I don't know."

Wallace shook his head.

Did he really not remember? Or did he retain a spark of cunning?

Regardless, Wallace realised now that he had to lead, and hope that Harper would confirm what he said.

"We used Calvin Conway's answers as a crib sheet. That's when the exam board noticed the similarities. And they came to us for our opinion on the matter. Do you remember that? Do you remember what we said?"

Harper's face paled, his confusion momentarily lifting like a fog blown away by a sudden gust. He stared at Wallace, his breath coming in shallow gasps.

"We... we said he must have had access to the model solutions," he whispered, as if the words were dragged out of him by an invisible force.

"Yes," Wallace nodded, his voice heavy. "We framed him. Claimed he cheated and found a way to access and copy our model solutions instead of the other way round."

Harper's hands began to tremble. "But that was... that was a long time ago. We... we had no choice, Walter. They would have found out about our mistakes. Our reputations... our careers..."

Wallace's eyes never left Harper's face. He needed more. He needed Harper to say it all, to spell it out clearly. "We ruined his life, Seamus. He was expelled, blacklisted. Do you ever think about what that did to him?"

Harper's gaze dropped to his lap, his voice barely audible.

"But even if we copied his answers to make corrections. He must have cheated somehow. He wasn't that clever. Maybe he got access to the *questions* and not the model solutions. Then he could have worked out the answers in advance. He'd've had plenty of time. Or maybe he looked up the answers in textbooks. That's cheating too you know."

Wallace thought about this. It was certainly a possibility. He'd never been entirely sure how Calvin could have done so well. Maybe Harper was right. Maybe he *had* got hold of the questions

rather than the model solutions.
Or maybe I'm just rationalising.
"But we *framed* him Seamus. We framed him when *we* were the ones who copied!"
"It was... so long ago. What's done is done."
At this point, Wallace snapped.
"But it's not done, is it? It's never done. We destroyed a man's life! You think it's over for him?"
Harper looked up, his eyes filled with a mix of anger and desperation. "Why now, Walter?"
Wallace hesitated.
"Because I'm dying, Seamus. I've got a few months left, maybe less."
"You mean the..."
"I can't take this to the grave without at least *trying* to make it right. Not anymore."
"That's what *he* said."
"Who?"
"Raymond. He also had a tumour, you know. And he wanted to put everything right... to clear his conscience."
Something in Harper's tone gave Wallace an uneasy feeling.
"Seamus... do you know what happened to Raymond?"
"He was killed... with a hammer."
The knot in Wallace's stomach was tightening.
"Seamus... was it you?"
"Was it...?"
"Did you kill Raymond Morrison?... Seamus?"
"He was going to tell the university. But we couldn't let him do that. He would have dragged us both down with him. And it wouldn't have helped Calvin. He's probably drifted back into a well-deserved obscurity. That's what *you* said. I remember, you know. I don't forget things. I remember every word you said."
On hearing this, any nagging doubts that Walter Wallace had, fell away. He was looking into the eyes of a murderer.
"Seamus ... *you* killed Raymond... *didn't you?*"
"Well someone had to stop him. He would have destroyed us. *Both* of us!"
Wallace was reeling from this. It was worse than he could possibly have imagined.
"Seamus... listen... *This has to end!*"
"Oh I know. Everything has to come to an end in the end."
Then, quite abruptly, Harper stood up, his body trembling.

"I can't... I can't talk about this anymore, Walter. I need to go."
Wallace didn't stop him.

He watched as Harper stumbled out of the room, down the corridor towards the front door, his movements shaky, his breath uneven. Wallace followed him, and watched as Harper fumbled with the door latch, finally opening it and stepping out.

"Seamus," Wallace called after him softly, "you know the truth. We both do."

Harper turned, his face a mask of confusion and fear.

"We mustn't talk about it," Harper mumbled, almost as if in a daze.

Wallace still had enough mental acumen to know that he would be wise to choose his next words carefully. But he lacked the willpower to rein himself in.

"You're wrong, Seamus. We must."

Wallace watched as Harper stumbled away down the driveway and out of view.

A depressing silence settled over the image as Wallace's hand crossed the in front of the camera, switching it off, leaving a final image of the front garden burnt into the minds of the four people who watched it: the judge and three lawyers.

82

Lorraine Epstein was painstakingly going through Petula Gelding's Google timeline to track her movements. Petula kept her Android SatNav app running at all times, creating a complete timeline for her movements, except when the phone was switched off and checked in to the shop near the Old Bailey.

But yesterday had been an adjournment day in the Calvin Coffey trial and Petula's phone had been on all day. The timeline showed that she had spent most of the day at home, but had gone out to the local shops in the afternoon. Of course she might have left the phone at home and gone down to Bournemouth in the morning.

But the call log also showed that she had *received* calls. The numbers checked out as telemarketers or in some cases private numbers that turned out to be spoofed. In other words, *more* telemarketers – and possibly the odd scam artist pulling one of any number of phone scams like "you owe five thousand to the tax man" or "you can make a fortune with our cryptocurrency advisory service."

The important thing was that the calls were *answered* and conversations were held between the parties. Sometimes a brief conversation, but still a conversation. And to make sure that all the bases were covered, Lorraine also checked the voicemail to make sure that this wasn't simply a case of the callers talking to a machine.

This was enough to satisfy Lorraine that Petula Gelding had been in London at the time of the attack on Ruth Morrison. So there was nothing left to do but call Inspector Cherry and tell her that their suspect in the Bournemouth GBH case was in the clear.

"And there's absolutely no doubt?" asked Jane, clearly disappointed.

"Unless she left the phone behind and got someone else to phone sit, while she went off to Bournemouth to commit attempted murder or GBH."

"Okay, thanks, Lorraine."

"Are you going to let her go? I haven't checked her computer yet."

"I'll talk to Chryseis. We'll probably have to let her go on police bail."

"So I've still got a mandate to check the computer?"

"Oh yes. See what you can find."

Lorraine picked up on the eagerness in Jane's voice. But she wondered if Jane's interest was in finding something incriminating, or just prolonging the connection between them. It was obvious that Jane was into women too. And it might just be fun.

But for now, Lorraine had work to do.

She switched on Petula's laptop and waited for it to boot up. But after only a few minutes she noticed something strange when she opened Google Chrome. It listed two profiles. One was called "Petula" and the other was called "Prof Wallace".

Now THAT'S interesting!

Filled with excitement, she selected the latter. It took her to a Google search page with a circle and the letters WW in the corner, where a thumbnail of the professor might otherwise have been. Beneath it was the hotlink for Gmail. She clicked on that too. It brought up the Gmail sign in page.

She moved the cursor to the Gmail or phone number entry box and left-clicked. As soon as she did so, a drop-down window with the following appeared:

```
petulagelding gmail.com
Passkey from Windows Hello
walterwallace19l gmail.com
Passkey from Windows Hello
Use a different passkey
Manage passwords and passkeys…
```

She selected the latter. The pop-up box was replaced by another:

```
Windows Security
Making sure it's you
```

```
    Sign in with your passkey to google.com as
    Walterwallace19l gmail.com
    This   request   comes   from   the   app   chrome.exe   by
"Google LLC"
    PIN_____
    I forgot my PIN
    More choices
```

This was followed by a cancel button.

In other words she had set up a passkey, which could presumably also work with her phone.

Lorraine knew that she could try various 4-digit guesses for the PIN option first, like Wallace's birth year or that of his wife or daughter. But even if Wallace did not have much of a sense of security or caution, that wouldn't help because this was *not* his computer. It was Petula's. And she didn't know what PIN Petula would have chosen.

So she selected the `More   choices` hotlink and the box expanded at the bottom, showing a square smiley face and the word "Face" to make it clear that one could use face ID as an alternative to the PIN. That was all she needed. Petula's phone had numerous selfies and Lorraine chose the most natural looking among them, holding it up to the laptop's camera at just the right distance to keep the edges of the phone out of frame, whilst keeping the image in focus.

Within seconds she was into the email account!

And what she found was amazing. For there, in plain sight, were the dozen or so emails that had been sent to Calvin, pretending to be Walter Wallace.

83

"M'Lady, in light of the new evidence, I move that the case be discontinued and the charges against the defendant be dismissed."

They were now back in court, where the legal arguments were to be played out. The press and spectators were allowed in, but reporting restrictions were in place.

Blair was quick to respond to Nigel's motion.

"M'Lady, whilst at first blush it might *appear* that Professor Harper confessed to killing someone called Raymond – presumably referring to Mr Morrison – not only was that admission *indirect*, but it also means nothing in relation to this trial, which is solely concerned with the murder of Walter Wallace. Despite m'learned friend's excitement about the video evidence, it clearly shows that Walter Wallace was *alive* when Seamus Harper crossed the threshold *out of* the house."

"But the door wasn't shut M'Lady," said Nigel.

"What's that?"

"The door to the house wasn't closed when Professor Wallace stopped the video. Harper could have forced his way back in. Remember, Wallace was frail from his illness."

"And Professor Harper, quite possibly, from *his*," Blair countered.

Judge Braham thought for a moment and then announced: "Well the evidence is clearly relevant. On the other hand it is far from conclusive. I'll deny the motion to discontinue the case but allow the evidence to be introduced. I understand that Huette Shannon is available to attest to finding the memory card?"

"Yes M'Lady. But if the video is to be introduced, then I renew my request for a summons to be issued to Professor Harper allowing him to be questioned about its content."

"Same objection as before, M'Lady."

"I actually asked Professor Harper to attend court voluntarily, M'Lady. And he is in court and available for examination. However, I will need to ask a few leading questions, and for that I would ask the Court's permission to treat him as hostile."

This time Blair didn't even bother to object.

"Again I will allow it. But it must be done in a manner that does not agitate him, or cause him unnecessary distress."

Without a sideways glance, Nigel announced that his co-counsel, Miss du Lac, would do the examination.

84

"What about my *phone*?" asked Petula.

"We'll arrange for you to pick it up here in 48 hours."

Petula looked Jane Cherry in the eyes, passive-aggressively.

"But I thought you said you'd finished with it. Even if you need it for evidence, you told me at the start of the interview that your expert had downloaded an image of the contents. So you can give the phone back to me. I need it for work. *And* general purposes."

"We don't need it, Miss Gelding, but it isn't on the premises at the moment."

"Then where is it?"

"It's at the Police Intelligence Unit in Colindale."

"And why does it take 48 hours to bring a phone from Colindale to *this* police station?"

More than passive-aggressive now. Just plain aggressive.

"Because we can't spare people to bring evidence on-demand at all hours. These things are usually done on a once-a-day basis."

"Well if it's once-a-day, then you should be able to get it by tomorrow."

"We *might* be able to, but I can't promise. It's already mid-afternoon and we've probably missed the deadline for putting in the request for tomorrow."

She was being released by the police, unconditionally, pending further inquiries. A solicitor would have been more forceful in pushing for the release of her laptop and *all* the electronic equipment they had taken from her. They had effectively admitted that she was no longer a suspect in the assault on Ruth Morrison. And the whistleblowing phone call wasn't even a crime. In fact, investigating her identity after verifying the information from other sources, had been contrary to public policy.

But Petula hadn't asked for a solicitor and instead agreed to give an interview under caution, only to prove incredibly stubborn as to which questions she was ready to answer and the manner in which she chose to answer them.

"Thanks for nothing!" said Petula.

And with that, she walked out of the anteroom, out of the police station, and out onto the street – a free woman.

For her part, Jane Cherry felt somewhat morose as she made her way back to the incident room. But despite the scaling down, since the start of Calvin's trial, the place suddenly seemed abuzz with activity.

"Inspector," said a young constable, holding a phone slightly away from his ear. "I think you'll want to hear this."

He stretched his arm, offering the phone, and handed it to her when she approached.

"DI Cherry," she said, not knowing who was on the other end of the line.

"Jane, it's Lorraine."

"Hi Lorraine," the Inspector replied, surprised to hear from Lorraine again so soon. "What is it?"

"Don't let her go!"

"What do you mean?"

"She's the one who tricked Calvin into going to Walter Wallace's house."

"What?"

Lorraine told her what she had found in the fake email account.

"So she was manipulating Calvin Coffey or Conway or whatever his name was?"

"Yes."

"And she was the one who gave the CPS the anonymous tip-off about his real identity!"

"Exactly! And I found some more, Jane. A lot more."

"What?"

"Well for a start, Raymond Morrison's brain scan, plus a whole load of hacking tools."

"You mean she–"

"Planted the fake brain scan in the records at the Royal Free? Almost definitely. This woman knows what she's doing."

"I've got to stop her!"

"Wait, Jane. There's even more. And you're not gonna believe this. She was manipulating him. Every step of the way."

"Who? Calvin?"

"No. Professor Wallace."

"But how?"

"She was placing advertisements. Search bar advertisements."

"I don't understand."

"Anyone can set up a Google advertising account. Vendors with small businesses, online retailers and such like, can set up advertising accounts. As well as website ads. they can place ads that are seen alongside organic Google search results."

"Okay, but how was she manipulating Professor Wallace?"

"The placement of the advertisements is triggered by keywords in the search terms that a person using Google Search is looking for. Potential advertisers bid for those slots and the highest bids get their listing shown in the search results. So the searches that Petula was placing were targeted on keywords like "brain tumour treatment" and "alternative treatment for brain cancer. Terms that someone in Wallace's condition was quite likely to enter."

"Yes, but so would a lot of other people."

"True. But you can target your adverts geographically too. It says on Google's own website that – listen to this – *'you can choose locations for your ads to show. For example, you can choose entire countries, areas within a country like cities or territories, and even a radius around a location.'* With that degree of specificity, she could select a small radius around Walter Wallace's house and make pretty damn sure that he saw her ads in the listings."

"But how would that manipulate him?"

"Well I've looked at the advertisements she placed, and they said some things that are quite incredible, to put it mildly. And quite nasty."

"What sort of things?"

"Things like 'Clear your conscience now, Walter. This is God speaking' and 'Clear your conscience while you still can, Walter.' Things that would pretty much guarantee that Walter would click on them."

"And then what did she do? Infect his computer with a virus?"

"No, nothing quite so crude. It was his *mind* she was after."

"But you said something about him clicking on the links."

"Yes, well the search results in themselves were already playing on his mind. Imagine being in his position and looking for information about medical treatment and seeing search results with messages saying 'Clear your conscience while you still can

Walter.'"

"So what happened when he clicked on the links?"

"It took him to a website that she'd specially created for him."

"And what was on the website?"

"Well now it's completely blank. I even checked for white text on a white background, just in case. Presumably she erased it."

"But it's definitely Petula Gelding who created the website?"

"Well based on the advertisements linking to it, I'm pretty sure.

"Isn't there some registry where you can check the name of who owns or created it?"

"I checked the ICANN listing. The domain has only been around since last April and it's set to expire in two weeks, but it's protected by third-party anonymity."

"So… what does that mean? She was manipulating Wallace with the phrases in the advertisements *alone*, but she had to have a website to provide the advertisements with a landing page?"

"Oh no, the website was there to enhance the effect of the advertisements."

"But how do you know that? I thought you said she wiped it blank."

"Yes, she did. But there's an Internet archive of past websites called the Wayback Machine and you can look at the past static content of old websites and even defunct websites."

"And you found what was on the website?"

"Yes, and it was quite awful. It was addressed to Walter Wallace personally and it revealed how he had framed Calvin and destroyed his life. It said how God was watching him and punishing him and if he didn't put it right, he would be damned for all eternity in the flames of hell.

"There was also a page, put in later – round about September – suggesting to him that he get someone called Seamus Harper to confess. It even suggested getting a pen camera to record Harper making incriminating statements. And it provided Amazon links to product listings where he could buy such a camera."

"Wow."

The tone wasn't exactly forceful. But it was all Jane could say.

"And I haven't told you everything yet, Jane."

Normally this was precisely the sort of grandstanding that Jane Cherry didn't like. But with Lorraine, she was ready to take it.

"Okay, tell me the rest. But quickly."

"She also placed ads targeting the keywords "Alzheimer's

treatment" and she limited the location for these ads to *another address.*"

Jane didn't need to be told whose address that was.

"What did the ads say?" she asked, her voice still weak.

"Things like 'I know you killed Raymond' and 'Walter will betray you'."

85

The jury were back in court and a somewhat befuddled Seamus Harper had been helped into the witness box by Tina and an usher. The usher had been sympathetic both to Harper himself and to Tina, who looked tense, clearly worried about her father.

But the thing that Emily noticed was that in the section reserved for witnesses who had previously testified, Huette and Soraya were not sitting together. Huette had *tried* to sit next to her mother, but Soraya had rebuffed her, immediately moving away from her own daughter without saying a word or even meeting Huette's eyes.

Has a rift opened up between them?

Presumably because Huette had introduced the video evidence from the memory card. In effect, Huette had exposed her late father to the opprobrium and contempt of the academic world and society at large, by exposing him as a liar and a false accuser.

Emily could well-understand Soraya's anger. It was one thing to argue that the man accused of killing him was innocent. It was quite another to traduce his name and expose him as a liar, a cheat and a bully. But she also understood how much harder it must have been for Huette. To face a choice between discrediting her father and letting one injustice against an innocent man be piled upon another.

And in the face of this stark choice, to do the right thing. That took courage! Thinking about it now, Emily felt guilty about ever having suspected Huette. And now a young woman who had only sought to do right, found herself estranged from her mother.

Emily knew about estrangement to. But her estrangement from her father was her own choice. And it was several orders of magnitude less than this.

Her thoughts were cut short by the proceedings. Seamus Harper affirmed rather than swore an oath and was then given a chair. This was a courtesy because of his age and infirmity.

Witnesses in English courts usually stand while giving evidence.

Now it was Emily's chance to shine. She had to very carefully guide Harper through the video and give him a fair chance to answer questions about it. She had to be firm, but fair.

"Okay, Professor Harper, first of all can you confirm that you were a professor of mathematics at Bristol University?"

"Yes," Harper replied nervously.

"And you were a colleague of Professor Walter Wallace, also a maths professor at Bristol?"

"Yes."

The voice was weak, almost childlike.

"Okay, now I'm going to play a video, and afterwards I want to ask you a few questions about it."

He nodded, as if in some kind of alien world where he was being held prisoner.

She had agonised about whether to play the video in short chunks and ask him about it or play the whole thing through first. In the end, she opted for the latter because the jury had to see and hear the whole thing in order to understand it. In any case, all of her questions concerned the last part.

So she played it through, dividing her attention between Harper's reaction and that of the jury. By the time it was finished, she was already satisfied that she had won over the jury. He had effectively admitted to killing Raymond and they already knew who Raymond was and what his role in this whole sorry saga had been.

"So now Professor Harper, first of all, do you remember that?"

"Yes. I'm very sorry about poor Calvin. I still think he must have cheated. But I suppose we did too."

"Now, I want to draw your attention to when Walter said to you 'But we framed him Seamus. We framed him when we were the ones who copied.' Do you remember that?"

She played it back to refresh his memory.

"Yes."

"And you replied: 'It was so long ago. What's done it done.' Do you remember that too?"

"Yes."

"Was that an admission?"

"What?"

"You said just now in court, that you cheated too, you and Walter. Does that mean you admit that you framed Calvin Conway?"

"Yes. But we never wanted to harm him. We didn't even want to accuse him of cheating. But once other people noticed the similarities, we didn't have any choice."

"But on this occasion, when Walter told you he was dying. He wanted to get it off his chest didn't he? It was weighing on his conscience and he wanted to tell the authorities."

"Yes."

"But you didn't want him to do that did you? You said 'We mustn't talk about it,' didn't you?"

This time she didn't play it back. She wanted to make it clear that he remembered. So that the next part would count.

"Yes."

"And he also asked you if you had killed Raymond. Do you remember that?"

"Yes."

"And you replied: 'He was going to tell the university. But we couldn't let him do that. He would have dragged us both down with him.' Do you remember saying that?"

"Yes."

"And then he asked again."

This time she *did* play it back.

"Seamus... you killed Raymond... didn't you?"
"Well someone had to stop him. He would have destroyed us. Both of us!"
"Seamus... listen... This has to end!"
"Oh I know. Everything has to come to an end in the end... I can't... I can't talk about this anymore, Walter. I need to go."

"When you said, 'someone had to stop him,' what did you mean?"

"Walter would never have stopped him. He was too weak. He didn't used to be you know. Before he got ill. But then he went soft. He used to be strong. He used to say 'a man's gotta do what a man's gotta do' That was from a film. I think it was a western. But then he went soft. Even before he was ill in fact. He told me about Raymond. He was paying Raymond money you know. To keep quiet. He was paying him for years. I only found out when *Raymond* went soft. That was when Walter told me. I don't know why he paid him in the first place. No one likes a blackmailer. Blackmailers are worse than cheats."

"So what did you do? When Walter told you?"

"We talked about what we were going to do. But he kept changing the subject. He couldn't handle the pressure."

"But you could?"

"Oh yes. I can handle pressure much better than he can."

"And then at the end, just before you left, you said: 'We mustn't talk about it.' Did you mean framing Calvin or the murder of Raymond?"

"Well both. I mean he was dying so he didn't care. But it would have destroyed us."

"So when he said 'You're wrong Seamus. We must,' you must have been scared that he was going to tell the authorities."

He looked blankly at her.

"Weren't you? Scared that he was going to tell the authorities."

He looked around at his surroundings, as if he had forgotten where he was.

"Can I go now?"

Emily looked helplessly at Judge Braham, who turned to Harper.

"Professor Harper, I'm going to ask you to go with an usher, for now."

86

As soon as she had finished talking with Lorraine, Jane Cherry raced out of the police station with the slower-moving Chryseis Pines struggling to keep up with her. She arrived just in time to see Petula Gelding getting into the backseat of a car. It may have been an accomplice, but Jane suspected that it was probably just an Uber.

After what Lorraine had just told her, it was obvious that Petula would want to make a quick getaway. She must have known that if they'd taken her computer, the game was up. Even if her computer was password protected, she would have known that they could get in. And once they got in, it was only a matter of time before they found the mother lode.

Jane was talking into her radio when Chryseis arrived, huffing and puffing behind her. While Jane was trying to call for an interceptor vehicle on her radio, the Superintendent was waving her arms about frantically.

"What are you doing, ma'am?" asked Jane.

"Trying to catch the driver's attention. Get the registration number. If he values his operating licence, he'll stop."

"You're in plain clothes, ma'am. He probably doesn't even know you're a copper."

In the car, the driver had in fact caught sight of the large woman wildly gesticulating towards the car as he checked his rear-view mirror, looking for a break in the traffic.

"I think your friends are trying to call you. Did you forget something?"

As she strapped herself in, Petula twisted round and looked back at the two plain clothes policewomen who had been grilling her.

"Oh just ignore them. I'll call them on my mobile."

The driver noticed a lull in the traffic and pulled out while the opportunity was there.

Petula looked at the rear view and smiled at the frustration on the faces of the pair of coppers who thought they could intimidate her.

"You should have stopped them!" said a furious Chyseis Pines. "Instead of wasting time telling me."

Jane had in fact told Chryseis only a fraction of what Lorraine had told her. But Chryseis was too frustrated at being thwarted to care. She just needed to take it out on someone.

"Don't worry ma'am. I think I know where she's going."

87

As Seamus Harper was led away, Hayden Blair asked for a hearing in the absence of the jury, which Judge Braham granted without even glancing at Nigel or Emily.

Normally, the Crown would be given the chance to cross-examine a defence witness, even if the defence had been granted permission to treat the witness as hostile. However, it was clear from Harper's performance in the witness box that he should, if anything, have been treated as a *vulnerable* witness.

Once the jury were out, Blair addressed the judge.

"M'Lady, in view of the incriminating admissions made by the witness, I can well understand why you called a halt to his testimony. Would I be right in understanding that you are going to issue an order for his arrest in the matter of Raymond Morrison?"

"Yes. And I'll issue an order that he be provided with an appropriate adult."

There was a sound of sobbing in the courtroom, and it came not from one person, but two: Tina Harper and Huette Shannon. Two daughters united in grief. The only interested party who remained tearless and silent was Soraya.

"And would I be right in thinking that the court is minded to consider entering a verdict of not guilty?"

"I am certainly minded to consider *arguments* for and against. But as I think I know what the defence arguments are likely to be, let's start with the Crown. Do you oppose dismissal of the charges? Or do you need to take fresh instructions?"

"As things stand now, the Crown is not yet convinced that dismissal of the charges would best serve the interests of justice. Though that position may be open to change, depending on any new instructions from the CPS, I would draw the following points to Your Ladyship's attention. Though it is now clear that both professors were dishonest, and that Professor Harper killed Raymond Morrison, it is equally clear, as I mentioned earlier, that

Walter Wallace was alive when Seamus Harper left his home.

"Furthermore, although Professor Harper expressed *concern* about the possibility of his former colleague taking the matter up with the authorities, he showed no overt hostility or anger towards him. Indeed it was quite clear that not only in this courtroom, but even in the video, Professor Harper was somewhat frail. Whilst the Crown concedes that eleven months ago Professor Harper may have had the strength to batter a younger fitter man to death with a hammer, by *six* months ago – if the evidence of the video is anything to go by – he was in no condition to murder Walter Wallace in the way that the deceased was murdered."

"I'm not entirely convinced of that," said Judge Braham. "However, I *will* say that in the matter of the killing of Walter Wallace, the case against Professor Harper falls substantially short of prima facie. Therefore I shall adjourn for today and consider the matter overnight. I think we can agree that it's been a long tiring day for all of us and we need to go home and get a good night's sleep. I'll deliberate on the matter and announce my decision in the morning."

After the judge had left, Nigel gave Emily an encouraging smile.

"You did very well."

But Emily's mood was somewhat withdrawn. Nigel came at her afresh.

"You stayed calm. You stayed focussed. And considering what Harper did, you showed remarkable kindness. I'm seriously impressed. And so were the jury. I was watching them."

"Then why do I feel dirty?"

Nigel backed off.

"The judge is right. Get some rest. We'll talk in the morning."

As the court emptied out, Emily was watching the two tearful women as they walked out, apparently talking together. She was concerned for both of them.

88

"I'm really sorry about what happened in there, Tina."

Huette and Tina were walking across the grand lobby of the Old Bailey.

"Are you? If you hadn't given them that video, they'd've been none the wiser. You've just destroyed *both* our fathers' reputations. And for *what*? Some cheat who probably–"

"But he *wasn't* a cheat. You heard what your dad said. And mine."

"He was still a cheat. My dad was probably right. He must've seen the questions instead of the answers. But that's still cheating."

"Maybe you're right. But that doesn't mean he killed anyone."

"*Are you kidding?* You think *my dad* killed Raymond? You think my dad killed *your* dad?"

Huette sighed.

"No of course not."

"Then why did you have to hand over the video? When you knew what it would do to their reputations?"

"Their reputations were shot from the moment Raymond blew the whistle to Calvin. After that it was only a matter of time."

"You still didn't have to do it."

"My dad made that video for a reason. I had to honour his memory."

"*Honour his memory? Like* hell, you virtue signalling Goody Two Shoes!"

Huette put a sympathetic hand on Tina's shoulder, trying to calm her down. But Tina just shrugged it off.

"*Don't touch me bitch!*"

"Tina," said Huette, desperately trying to assuage Tina's anger. "I'm not your enemy."

"No you're a toxic friend that's *worse* than an enemy!"

And with that, Tina stormed off. Huette was about to follow, but she caught a glimpse of Emily coming towards her, still wearing her wig and gown.

"What was all that about?"

Huette took a deep breath and straightened her bunched up sleeve.

"Storm in a teacup. Don't worry about it."

Emily let the silence hang in the air.

"I just wanted to thank you."

"For what? Doing the honourable thing? Maybe Tina was right. Maybe I am just a virtue signalling goody-two-shoes."

"You shouldn't beat yourself up about it."

Huette seemed out of breath, as if the exchange with Tina had pushed up her heartbeat and blood pressure. Emily could see that she was still troubled. But there were still a few unanswered questions – a few *unasked* questions, in fact. And Emily sensed that now might be the perfect time to ask them.

"Come on. Let's get a cup of tea. Or a drink if you prefer. I know a wine bar near Smithfield. My treat."

A moment's hesitation. A nervous smile. A reluctant shrug.

"Okay. But not too long. I got a babysitter till six o'clock."

"Give me five minutes," said Emily.

"It must have been difficult coming forward like that – knowing what it would do to your father's reputation."

"When you've been through what I've been through, you learn what's important."

They were seated at a quiet table in the corner of the wine bar, at Emily's request. It had taken Emily, a little more than five minutes to put away her wig and robe, but Huette had waited. Emily sensed that she *wanted* to talk.

"Still, it must have come as a shock."

"Not really."

Something about the way she said it alerted Emily.

"You knew?"

"About dad messing up his model solutions and using a student's paper as a crib sheet? Absolutely. About the fallout? That too. Not at the time, but later. Only I never found out the student's name. And I didn't know about Raymond, till I saw the video."

"Did Soraya know?"

"No. She never had a clue."

"So how did you know?"

"Because he told me."

"He told you, but not your mother?"

"Sometimes a father tells his daughter things that he could never tell his wife."

Emily picked up on something that Huette had said a moment earlier.

"What did you mean before about the things you've been through? Like Gerald walking out on you?"

Huette shifted uneasily.

"That was the least of my worries."

"Your mother seems to have taken it worse than you."

"That's because she doesn't know the half of it."

"And what is the half? I mean the other half?"

"I've got enough troubles of my own."

"Is that what you meant when you said it was the least of your worries?"

Huette stayed silent. Emily sensed that there was something more… something important.

"Huette, after I talked with you and Soraya last Sunday, I did some research."

She was watching Huette carefully now, trying to read her reaction.

"I looked at Gerald's Facebook page, *and* Candy Sweet's."

"Oh yeah. The floozy."

"Yeah," Emily echoed quietly. "The floozy."

Emily let a pregnant silent hang in the air for a few seconds, before adding: "Except that she isn't a floozy – is she Huette?"

"You can call her what you like. She's a bitch and he's a bastard, and quite frankly they deserve each other."

"What I mean is, she doesn't exist at all."

"What are you *talking* about?"

"I'm talking about a fake profile with fake pictures borrowed from a travel blog."

Huette opened her mouth to deny it. But seeing the self-assured look on Emily's face she held herself back. In the next few seconds, she closed her mouth, and her entire body posture seemed to slump. She couldn't even meet Emily's eyes anymore.

But she lacked the strength to get up and walk away.

"Care to tell me about it, Huette?"

89

Petula's two-room bedsit looked all-too-familiar to Jane Cherry. Only this morning, the Detective Inspector had been searching the place with her colleagues from uniform branch, taking away a computer, burner phones and SIM cards. Now here they were again, hoping, in vain, that Petula might have come back here.

Instead, all they found was that the place had been cleaned out. Clothes? Gone. Make-up and personal items? Gone. Shampoo, toothpaste, moisturiser? All gone. She had been thorough. And it looked like the place had recently been *cleaned* as well as cleaned out. That was annoying to Jane because they hadn't even taken a DNA sample from her when they had her in custody, even though they had the power to do so. Nor had they taken her fingerprints.

With hindsight, Jane realised that this had been incredibly remiss of them. But the truth of the matter was they had never really considered her a suspect in any crime. They had merely used the attack on Ruth Morrison as a pretext to indulge Jane's idle curiosity.

And now it was too late.

She put in a call to the superintendent.

"Hi, Chrys – ma'am. Bad news. The bird has flown."

"So much for knowing where she was going to go."

Chryseis was still furious and looking for someone to take it out on. Jane was apologetic.

"I guess she realised her game was up and decided to cut her losses."

"Yes, and in the meantime, we've got another disclosure to make that'll probably blow what's left of our case against Calvin Coffey, or Conway as he now appears to be."

"I know, ma'am. But in view of what we now know, maybe that's the right thing."

90

"Care to tell me about it, Huette?"

The question hung in the air between them, its subconscious echo looming over a long silence.

Finally, Huette forced herself to face Emily.

"Gerald was... he knew how to turn on the charm when he wanted to..."

"Huette... was he abusive?"

"Yes, Emily. He *was* abusive. Sometimes."

Emily's mind filled in the blanks. Finally it was all beginning to fall into place. Soraya's obvious resentment of her son-in-law for abandoning his pregnant wife, while Huette seemed to take it all in her stride.

"So when he walked out on you, it must have come as a blessed relief."

"Look... it wasn't his fault."

"You're not the first battered wife to say that."

"I never said I was. But people like that... like Gerald... they usually have a back-story of their own. And Gerald was no exception."

Emily was having none of it. She'd come across abusers before, while shadowing Nigel and some of the other barristers during her first six.

"Go on, thrill me."

Huette took a moment, and a couple of deep breaths, to continue.

"He was abused himself... as a child."

"Parents?... strangers?"

In the course of her legal training, Emily had learned about many kinds of abuse.

"His mother's boyfriend."

An old familiar story.

"And where was his mother when all this was happening?"

There was a trace of indignation in Emily's tone. Huette may have been forgiving, but Emily brooked no excuses.

"I guess that's what made *me* the target of his anger."

"So... we're talking about a man with latent anger issues." Emily prompted. "A man who was an abuser, yet who hated abusers."

"And abuse enablers," Huette added.

"Like his mother?"

The way she looked at Emily...

"Huette?"

"Yes, like his mother!"

Emily was struggling to process the information. But she was slowly figuring it out.

"And when *you* became a mother, he associated you with that role."

"The abuse started before that... but it got worse after Ariadne and Mikey were born."

"I'm waiting for the other shoe to drop."

"He wasn't a *controlling* abuser. He wasn't a pampered, over-indulged bully with a sense of entitlement. He was a *reactive* abuser."

"So you knew his triggers?"

"I learnt them."

"And you learned how to work around them?"

Huette hesitated.

"Up to... a point."

"Did you try to get him into therapy?"

"Of course."

"But he refused?"

"Yes."

"And?"

"When it was just me, I could take it."

Emily felt a chill running down her spine.

"He was violent towards the children?"

"Not the children, no. But when I got pregnant... I thought it would stop. I thought he wouldn't hit me when I was pregnant."

"Is that why you got pregnant, Huette? To stop him?"

Emily realised – as soon as the words were out of her mouth – that it was a question she should *never* have asked.

"One time, after slapping me around... when the children were asleep... he demanded his conjugal rights."

"Demanded?" Emily echoed tentatively.

"You know what I mean for God's sake!"

"He forced himself on you?"

"If you want the truth from *me* then you shouldn't be coy either. So let's not hide behind a euphemism. *He raped me!*"

"And that's how you…"

Huette nodded, as if she didn't trust her voice.

"But you decided to keep the baby? Or was that *his* decision too?"

"It was *my* decision! Mine alone."

"You thought it would keep you safe. Being pregnant?"

Huette stayed silent. So Emily pressed on, like the effective cross-examiner that she was.

"But it didn't, did it? You said something about him hitting you when you were pregnant."

"That's when I knew he wasn't going to stop," Huette acknowledged grudgingly.

"What did you do?"

Huette still held out.

"Huette? … What did you *do* Huette!"

The tone was intended to frighten the truth out of Huette. Yet it was Emily who was frightened – frightened of the answer she was about to hear.

"The only thing I could do."

"Where is he now?"

In the silence that followed, a change came over Huette, while Emily's mind raced ahead. Throughout the exchange, Huette had looked hurt and vulnerable, as if there was no more fight left in her.

Did I misread her? Or did I just bring out the latent strength of her inner core? Maybe it's those hidden reserves of strength that we all have within us.

Whatever it was, Huette's face had now changed. No longer the fragile flower, she now looked as hard as rock.

"I've said all I'm going to say, Emily. You'll have to figure out the rest for yourself."

And with that, Huette stood up and walked away – looking every bit the strong woman that fate had forced her to become.

Emily sat there for several minutes thinking about what she had just heard. She realised that Huette's confession, if true, would effectively dispense with the theory that Huette and Gerald were in it together to get the house.

But there was just one thing nagging away at her, however.

Earlier in the court proceedings, the blood spatter expert had reluctantly conceded that the attacker was probably *shorter* than Walter Wallace.

She wasn't sure if Nigel had noticed it – or even if she should mention the fact to him – but in the video, when you would assume that Seamus Harper was meeting Wallace's eyes, he appeared to be looking slightly downward. As if he were *taller* than Wallace.

91

Emily was still dwelling on her thoughts about the case as she took the evening commute on the Elizabeth Line to Slough, where she had a two-bedroom, end-of-terrace house, courtesy of a deposit by her dad and a 30-year-mortgage. She couldn't resist a smile at the irony that the station she was departing from, just off Smithfield, was called Farringdon. The train was crowded, and she was hanging onto an overhead strap for two-thirds of the journey.

Seamus Harper had made an incriminating admission regarding Raymond, both in the recording and in court. But that didn't mean that he had killed Wallace. The judge was right: Wallace was alive when Harper left him. And even if the verbal exchange in the doorway about "not talking about it" had an ominous ring to it, one couldn't argue against the hard evidence.

Emily hadn't been in court for the morning session, but the solicitor's representative from Solomon & Co had given her a copy of her notes, sending it to Emily's phone. When she finally found a seat on the long open-plan train, she was able to read up on the morning's proceedings.

Going through the notes quickly, she saw that even before Huette had come forward with the video, Nigel had already sought a witness summons for Seamus Harper, on a basis of Calvin's testimony. But Hayden Blair had ambushed him, producing a copy of a consultant gerontologist's report, stating that Harper was suffering from dementia and unfit to testify.

"The extent of the dementia has been exacerbated by a fall he suffered last September, in which Professor Harper banged his head and suffered concussion. This has led to physical frailty as well as impaired mental capacity."

This was true. Harper was a weak and frail man by the time of the video. He may have had the strength to kill Raymond last April. But he did not look like a man capable of killing someone, using close-combat violence, six months ago, when Wallace was murdered.

On the other hand, the consultant *did* mention a fall... *in September*.

Maybe Harper was pushed over by Wallace *while* attacking him. He seemed more frail in court than he did in the video. So maybe he was *still* capable of murder back in September.

Okay, Emily, focus!

Let's say, she speculated, that Seamus Harper *did* kill Raymond. And let's say he *didn't* kill Wallace? So who did? Calvin?

No! Even if Seamus Harper is innocent, that doesn't make Calvin guilty!

But then again, she realised, maybe that was just wishful thinking.

And then she thought about her old theory: that Huette and Gerald were in it together. That they did it to get the house. This would fit in with the whole business about setting up Wallace to think he had a brain tumour. Trying to pressure him psychologically, and then, when it failed, resorting to more direct methods, like killing him with a hammer – possibly inspired by the method Harper had used to murder Raymond?

Certainly Gerald had the skill-set for hacking. Well, not *certainly*, but probably. And Huette's "confession" was entirely self-serving. It wasn't even a confession. More of a long, drawn-out innuendo, pointing the accusing finger at herself, but never quite saying it outright.

And she had only said it *after* Emily made it clear to her that she was a suspect. More than that, Emily had made it clear that there was specific evidence that Gerald's Facebook page contained faked pictures and that the "Candy Sweet" profile was also fake, with pictures simply lifted from a travel blog.

So was that it? Was Huette's confession just a smokescreen? But for what? Huette had an alibi. She couldn't have done the killing. And as far as Emily could tell, Gerald was as tall as Harper or Calvin. So that didn't fit with what the blood-spatter expert had testified.

These thoughts were still with Emily when she got off the train at Slough, just after sunset, and took the bus four stops to her home.

As she was making this last leg of the journey, another theory came into her mind. What if Gerald really *did* have a "bit on the side"? What if it were Gerald and the unnamed "peripatetic blonde" who were in it together? Creating an alibi with old travel blog

pictures, but still in the UK, lying low after killing Wallace.
But again, why? What was their motive?
The house still? But how could he get the house if he and Huette were separated? Or divorced? Even if Soraya gave up the house to Huette – or indeed even if Soraya were killed or died of some natural causes – the house would go to Huette and the children, not Gerald.

Now a really dark thought was forming in Emily's mind. Assuming, for a minute, that Gerald and the blonde *were* in it together, rather than Gerald and Huette – and assuming that Gerald and the blonde faked the pictures together – what was Gerald's next step going to be?

Were Gerald and the mysterious blonde planning on killing Huette too, once she acquired legal title to the house?

That all made perfect sense, except for *one* thing:
Why would Huette all-but-confess to killing Gerald?

Unless – and this was a critical part of Emily's thinking – what if the information that Emily had given Huette had *triggered* Huette into *forming a plan of her own?* In other words, what if Huette really *hadn't* known anything about it *prior* to that? What if Huette really believed, in all innocence, that Gerald had simply run off with a young blonde to live the life of Riley – or was it Reilly? (She was never quite sure.)

Aaaaaand... what if Emily *telling Huette* about the fake pictures *had alerted Huette to Gerald's plan?*

Emily was still thinking these thoughts when she got off the bus and started walking the last few hundred yards home.

If Huette *had* figured it out, based on what Emily had told her, what would she do *now*? It was obvious that she was no shrinking violet. Beneath that kind-hearted exterior was a steel magnolia. Was Huette planning on pre-empting Gerald? Tracking him down and exacting some kind of revenge? Maybe the murder to which she had so obligingly come close to confessing, was actually a murder yet to come.

It "kind of" made sense and "kind of" didn't. If Huette had figured out Gerald's plan and decided to kill him, why confess to killing him and potentially incriminate herself?

This tangled web of theories was tumbling through Emily's mind in a mass of contradictions and uncertainties when she reached the front door to her house. As she fumbled with the key and opened the door, she was still thinking about the full implications of her theory. She unlatched the door to the house, pushed it open and walked in.

The morning's mail lay sprawled on the floor, way past the doormat. She often wondered how the postman managed to push it in so far. Not bothering to close the door, she bent down to pick up the half dozen letters – probably junk mail and bills – that lay scattered on the wooden floor.

As she did so, she felt herself being shoved hard from behind and heard the door slamming shut. Caught off guard, she lost her balance and landed face down on the floor. As a natural defence mechanism, she rolled over onto her back, still on the floor, only to see a woman standing there, covered from top to toe in a burqa.

Only this time, the woman wasn't holding a hammer. She was holding a kitchen knife.

92

In the ebbing light of dusk, the young black woman walked down the street in Slough, her eyes fixed on a particular house on the other side of the road, just a few paces ahead. A two-bedroom red-brick house, with a paved driveway, it was no different from the other houses, apart from who lived there.

As she approached, keeping her steady, confident gait, she saw movement near the front door. A white woman with chestnut hair, in her early to mid-twenties, was fumbling with keys at the door, her back to the street. The black woman knew all too well who the woman was: Emily du Lac. She recognised her from her picture.

After a brief struggle with the key, Emily finally unlocked the door and appeared to kneel down as she stepped inside.

The black woman kept walking, not breaking stride but still watching. As she drew level with the house, she noticed a second woman walking briskly towards the house, covered head to toe in a flowing black burqa, the only visible part of her a narrow slit for her eyes. Without hesitation, the woman walked right up to the same door, appeared to push something – or someone – very hard, and then stepped inside as if she had every right to be there.

The black woman's heart rate picked up as she heard a muffled scream, quickly cut off, followed by the slamming of the door. She stopped instinctively, her whole body tensing up as her mind wondered what to do. She was not afraid to get stuck in, when the occasion called for it. She was by no means a small woman. Taller than the average man, she was athletic, fit from years of kickboxing and Brazilian jiu-jitsu. She knew how to handle herself in a fight, and she could feel the adrenaline kicking in as she crossed the road to the house.

Through the window, she caught a glimpse – just a brief one – of what looked like a physical struggle. Emily's arm flailed out, reaching for something, before disappearing from view. The woman in the burqa was there too, her movements fast but uncontrolled.

The black woman's muscles twitched, every fibre of her being telling her to act, to move, to do something. She could easily run up to the house, unlatch the door with a credit card – a trick she had learned from her brother – and break up whatever the hell was going on inside. She had a good few inches on the woman in the burqa, and, if necessary, she could easily overpower someone like Emily if it came down to it. She could probably hold both of them apart by the collar, if she had to.

Her body was already angled to move, her feet ready to pivot back toward the house.

But she hesitated.

It wasn't fear of what might be happening inside. If anything, it was the exact opposite: getting involved meant consequences. It meant the police would be involved. And that was the problem. She didn't trust the police.

Her brother had been stopped and searched, twice in as many days. The first time, put in handcuffs and searched for drugs because he was "dressed too warmly" for the weather that day. The second time, the window of the car he was sitting in was smashed by an overzealous constable, and he was physically dragged from the car, through the window, because he and another black man were in a car in an area "known for drug dealing."

She herself had had a run-in with the men in blue when on her way home from a late-night shift. Of course the police had been very nice about it afterwards. But the whole experience had left her feeling powerless and small, no matter how tough she was on the outside.

A black woman busting into someone's house? Even if she was trying to help, there was no way that would end well for her.

The scream echoed in her mind. Someone was in trouble, that much was clear. But was it worth it? She clenched her fists, her heart pounding in her chest, weighing her options. The window gave her another glimpse of the struggle, Emily's body being yanked backward.

She swore under her breath, her stomach twisting with indecision. She wanted to help. But getting involved meant stepping into a mess she couldn't control.

She took one more look at the house before making her decision. With a hard breath, she turned on her heel and kept walking, faster now, but with a gnawing pit in her stomach. Whatever was happening in there, it wasn't her fight. Not today.

93

Emily's heart raced as her mind processed the situation. The surprise of the sharp force shoving her from behind, sending her tumbling forward, completely disorientated her for a moment. But then her Krav Maga instincts kicked in just as she rolled onto her back. Eyes wide with shock, she had seen a woman towering over her – dressed in a flowing black burqa, a glinting knife poised above.

Not a hammer this time, Emily thought with dread.

In that moment, there was no time to think about why someone had attacked her, no time to think at all. There was only one goal – survival.

Emily rolled again, her muscles coiled tight as she sprang to her feet, bolting towards the living room. Her feet barely touched the ground as she tried to slam the door behind her, to lock herself away from the danger, but the woman in the burqa was unnervingly fast. A sharp pain exploded in the back of her legs as the woman's foot connected with the tendons below her knees. Emily collapsed, the impact forcing the air from her lungs in a gasping wheeze.

She hit the floor hard but quickly twisted her body, using her legs defensively to kick at the attacker. Her Krav Maga training came back in flashes, muscle memory dictating her movements. She aimed for the woman's shin with her foot, anything to create distance between them. But the woman in the burqa was relentless, dodging her kicks and closing the gap with terrifying efficiency.

Before Emily could scramble to her feet again, the woman pounced, straddling her in a schoolgirl pin. The weight pressed down hard on Emily's chest, the knife glinting ominously in the low light as it hovered between them. Emily grabbed the woman's wrist, trying to twist the knife away, but the deadly weapon inched closer to her face. Her arms strained, muscles burning from the effort. The attacker was strong – stronger than Emily had anticipated.

"Help me!" Emily screamed, her voice hoarse from the struggle, the panic rising in her throat. Her fingers scrabbled at the woman's wrist while her other hand shot up toward the headscarf that concealed the attacker's face.

The knife gleamed as it inched closer, its deadly point just barely grazing the skin of Emily's face. Her heart pounded in her ears, her breath stuck in her throat as her muscles fought against the weight of the woman's attack. Emily's strength was almost gone.

In the frenzied struggle, Emily's hand latched onto the fabric of the headscarf and yanked it hard. The woman pulled back instinctively, trying to maintain her grip on the knife, but the momentum of the struggle caused the scarf to tear free.

Emily froze, her breath catching in her throat as the woman's face came into view. It was Tina Harper.

But before Emily could fully register what was happening, another figure stormed into the living room, her dark skin gleaming in the light filtering through the curtains. She didn't shout or make a sound of alarm. Instead, she lurched forward, her arm outstretched, as she dropped what appeared to be... a credit card.

94

Petula was unpacking her suitcases, the remnants of her life spilling out, in her new-old place, a terraced house just down the road from St Helier Hospital. She had acted quickly to clean out the bedsit where she had been living for the last six months, because she knew the police would be coming back there for her. As she started taking clothes out of the suitcase and hanging them up, she realised that it wasn't actually necessary. It would all be over soon and she could be on her way to sunnier climes.

She realised now that she had been careless with the tip-off about Calvin's background, using her smartphone instead of one of the burners.

What's the point of having burner phones if you use the same one for two different things? And what's the point of pay-as-you-go, if you pay by traceable credit card, FFS!

But then again, she'd never have guessed that the police would come looking for her after the tip-off. They don't normally trace whistleblowers, unless they need them to testify in person. And in this case, they didn't need her. Once she told them about Calvin's background, all they had to do was trawl through the records and find it.

It was the attack on Ruth that threw a spanner in the works. They assumed, quite wrongly, that Petula's connection to Ruth was toxic. That was presumably because she had called Ruth from the same phone that she had used for the tip-off, and Ruth had subsequently been attacked. So they put two and two together and made five.

In any case, it was ridiculous. Why would she hurt Ruth? She *liked* Ruth. Ruth was a kind, decent, honourable woman who wouldn't hurt a fly. It wasn't Ruth's fault that Raymond had got himself entangled in something too big for his frail conscience to handle. Something too powerful for his weak character to escape from. Ruth was the collateral damage, the innocent bystander whom Petula never wanted to hurt.

It felt all the worse as she knew that she was in some way responsible. She hadn't seen it coming, but she felt guilty nevertheless because she *should* have seen.

Of course it wasn't Seamus Harper who killed Raymond or Wallace. He wouldn't have had the strength to do it.

And the police were quite sure that Ruth had been attacked by a woman. And if it wasn't Seamus Harper himself, then who else had a motive? Soraya or Huette? To protect Walter?

But Walter was killed too. When would they have had the chance to go down to Bournemouth and attack Ruth? They've been in court all the time.

Petula had never really given much thought to Tina. With hindsight it should have been obvious. Harper wouldn't be the one looking up "Alzheimer's treatment" on Google. It would be his carer – his daughter. And Petula could imagine what it must have been like for her, seeing things like "I know you killed Raymond" and "Walter will betray you."

What that must have done to her mind! That and having to face up to the fact that the man who had brought her up alone, when her mother died, had feet of clay.

Of course it had to be Tina who had killed Walter. Who else could it have been?

The height issue, that Nigel Farringdon had introduced in court through his skilful cross-examination, should have made it obvious that the killer was probably a woman. And when Nigel went off on a flight of fancy later on and suggested that the three crimes were the work of three different people, despite the common *modus operandi*, the judge had been quite right to shut him down and point out the absurdity of his position.

And once Ruth was attacked in the same way, that was the clincher. Ruth had been attacked by a woman – albeit a woman in disguise, wearing a burqa. And the motive for the attack was equally obvious: the attacker was trying to silence anyone who might expose Seamus Harper's dishonesty over the accusations against Calvin.

A young woman with an Electra complex. A young woman who loved her daddy beyond any healthy limit. But how far was she ready to go? In the end Tina would be caught. If necessary, it might take a bit more manipulating to trigger that result.

But, in the meantime, Petula headed for the bathroom, with the bottle of hair dye. It was time to say goodbye to the blonde curls.

95

Just as the knife began to press down, a blur of motion slammed into Tina as the black woman jumped onto her with surprising force, knocking her sideways and away from Emily. The knife clattered to the floor, skidding under the coffee table as Tina was tackled to the ground.

Emily gasped for breath, her chest heaving, as she struggled to sit up. The room spun, and the tension left her muscles in waves, but relief was still a distant promise.

The woman who had saved her moved with astonishing precision, pinning Tina down with an arm twisted behind her back. She reached back to Emily.

"Have you got a belt or a scarf or something?"

Emily was confused.

"A belt or scarf?"

"You know. Something to tie her up with."

Finally understanding, but her mind still reeling, Emily whipped off the belt from her formal suit and handed it to the woman, followed by the faux silk scarf around her neck. The mystery woman worked quickly, binding Tina's wrists and ankles with practised ease, all while Tina squirmed and spat curses under her breath.

Emily fumbled for her phone, her hands trembling as she keyed in 999. A few feet away, the woman didn't glance up, focusing only on securing Tina.

"Emergency. Which service do you require?" the operator's voice sounded distant, almost unreal.

Emily's voice shook as she replied.

"Police please."

"Putting you through now."

When she was connected, she started gushing out the details.

"I was attacked with a knife. She tried to kill me. The address is–"

"This person with the knife, are they still there?"
"Yes."
"Is she still holding the knife?"
"No, someone overpowered her. She's being restrained. I mean she's tied up."

As Emily rattled off the details, Tina's muffled voice grew louder, her body thrashing against the makeshift restraints. Her eyes were wild, lips twisting with rage and something else—something darker. When Emily ended the call, the black woman spoke to her.

"Why'd she attack you?"
"It's a long story. Her father framed my client... I'm a lawyer."
"I know."
"I should've killed you before you bitch!" Tina shrieked as she struggled to break free while the woman sat on her. "I should've known you'd go after my dad! You and Walter and Raymond."

Her voice was ragged and hoarse.

"I thought it was your father," Emily rasped, her breath caught in her throat, her fingers freezing mid-air as she lowered her phone.

"Oh you *thought* did you?"

Tina's eyes glowed with a manic intensity, her whole body shaking as she ranted, even under the weight of the woman who was holding her down.

"I know all about you, Emily, I did some asking around and I know what a bitch you are! You don't even talk to your own father anymore."

This was getting personal. What Tina said was partly true. Emily was estranged from her father and had been since he walked out on her mother to shack up with a trainee solicitor not much older than Emily.

But saying that Emily never talked to him was a bit of an exaggeration. They associated in legal circles, and she could hardly *not* talk to him. She did, however, keep it to a minimum. She certainly didn't rush to spend time in his company. On the other hand, listening to Tina now, she wondered what sort of rumours were circulating about her.

"This isn't about me, Tina. Even if you loved your father, you can't just–"

"Can't just *what*? You can't even say it can you? You don't even know what it is to have a loving father!"

"You know what, Tina? Save it for the court! I don't need to hear your self-righteous excuses!"

"Oh I'm sure you don't. People like you don't look beyond your legal fees. What is it they call it? The taxi rank principle? In other words, you go with the first client who comes along and flashes the cash. Like some cheap prozzie strutting her stuff in King's Cross!"

"Tina..." Emily was still finding it hard to breathe. "Tina, get a grip on yourself. Think about what you *did* for God's sake!"

"What *I* did. You go about destroying lives for anyone who pays you, and you preach to *me*."

"Destroying lives? Tina, your father and Walter Wallace *destroyed Calvin's life with their lies*."

"They didn't have a fucking choice. He would have destroyed *everything!*"

Without saying a word, the black woman pulled Tina up and round into a sitting position, the legs tied with Emily's belt and the arms with the scarf. Tina's eyes were locked onto Emily's, as if waiting for her cue. But Emily had no more strength to talk. All she could say was "Why *Ruth*?"

"Fuck Ruth! Raymond was going to destroy everything! My dad told me the whole story. He never told my mum, when she was alive. But he told *me*. He knew I'd protect him. If Raymond had blabbed about Calvin, my dad would've been ruined! He would have been disgraced, maybe even locked away. But I saved him."

Emily's mind raced back to the conversation with Huette.

"Sometimes a father tells his daughter things that he could never tell his wife."

Huette's words from the wine bar echoed in her head, but now they had taken on a darker, far more sinister meaning.

"Your father never wanted you to kill anyone did he? Whatever happened in the past, he didn't want people to die."

Tina's voice grew louder, feverish.

"He had Alzheimer's! He couldn't think straight! But he felt his world crashing down on him, and I could see it in his eyes. The pain. The fear. Everything was unravelling. He couldn't protect himself. So I had to protect him. He knew what I did. He knew I killed Raymond, but he didn't understand why I had to stop Walter. Walter was his friend. He tried to stop me."

"What do you mean?"

"He went to Wallace's house to talk, Walter invited him. But I knew something was up. I knew what Walter was planning. He wanted to salve his conscience before he died. But he would've taken my dad down with him."

"So you went with your dad? Waited outside?"

"I followed him. But he didn't know I was there, waiting. When my dad came out from the front, I was already round the back. I was going to kill Wallace. I had to."

Tina's body jerked under restraint, her eyes wild as she recounted the memory.

"Dad knew I was there – must've sensed it. So he followed me round the back. He tried to stop me, but I…"

Tears were welling up in her eyes now.

"I pushed him. He fell – he hit his head… and I thought he was dead."

Tina's voice wavered, trembling with a mixture of guilt and fury.

"Wally must've heard the noise – probably while he was taking the memory card out of that pen recorder thing – 'cause he came outside via the kitchen door. He saw dad lying there. And he saw the anger in my eyes. Then he saw the hammer, so he turned tail and ran. He was going to try and lock the kitchen door, but I couldn't let him get away. So I chased him back into the house and I killed him. He probably had the memory card in his hand and must have dropped it."

Emily found her voice, barely. "And Ruth? Why Ruth?"

"Once she got involved… once she told the CPS about Raymond… I knew it was only a matter of time. When I got Raymond, I took his phone and did a factory reset. But I couldn't get to his computer. And I didn't know what incriminating stuff he'd saved in the cloud. I knew that sooner or later Ruth would figure it out. It was only a matter of time."

"But Calvin had already blown the gaff in court."

"Yes, but when *he* said it, it was self-serving. He needed corroboration. And the only person who could supply corroboration was Ruth. Soraya didn't know. Huette didn't know. There's no way Walter would've told either of them."

Emily was tempted to tell Tina that she was wrong about that.

"Sometimes a father tells his daughter things that he could never tell his wife."

But she held back.

Sirens wailed in the distance, growing louder, the flashing blue lights of police cars casting eerie shadows on the walls. The black woman, who had remained silent, suddenly sprang to her feet, her eyes scanning the room as if searching for something. Emily blinked, confused.

"Is there a back exit?" the woman asked, trying to keep her voice calm, but sounding urgent.

Emily, still reeling from Tina's confession, nodded weakly. "Yes, through the kitchen. There's an alley at the back. But why?"

The woman didn't wait for further explanation. She turned, scooped up the credit card that she had used to gain entry and darted out of the room into the kitchen, vanishing through the back door and into the night without a word. Emily stared after her, dumbfounded.

"Armed police!" a voice shouted from outside. Moments later, the police stormed in brandishing tasers.

"What happened?" asked one of them looking around and seeing a woman in a burqa tied up on the floor.

"She attacked me," Emily blurted out breathlessly, holding up her hands to show that she posed no threat to the police.

There was only one problem: Tina had just blurted out exactly the same thing.

96

Taking in the situation with a quick visual sweep of the room, the police fanned out. One moved to secure the knife that lay harmlessly on the floor. Two others – both female – moved towards Tina and started untying her. Two others – both male – approached Emily and positioned themselves in front of her, but to the left and right side respectively.

This unnerved Emily somewhat, especially after what Tina had preposterously claimed.

"I'm a barrister working on a case," Emily moved quickly to explain. "I'm defending a man accused of murder. This afternoon we introduced evidence in court that her father may have committed the murder – two murders in fact. And an attempted murder. The judge ordered him detained. And then she came here and tried to stab me. It turns out that *she* committed the murders."

Emily noticed the two policewomen apparently comforting Tina, while the attitude of the two policeman who confronted Emily herself – one of them a sergeant – seemed somewhat less sympathetic.

"So what happened then?" asked the sergeant. "When she tried to stab you?"

"A woman burst through the door, a black woman."

"A black woman?"

"Yes. She saved me. I mean she dragged Tina off me."

"Tina?"

Emily noticed that the two policewomen were gently escorting Tina out of the room, towards the kitchen. She didn't like the idea of Tina loose in her house, even with the police presence.

"Her," said Emily, nodding in Tina's direction just before Tina and the policewomen disappeared beyond the door frame.

"So you know Tina."

"Sort of. I mean we met in the context of the trial."

"And the black woman? You know her?"

"No."

"Is she still here?"

"No. She ran out the back when you arrived. Or just before."

"But who was she?"

"I don't know."

At this point, the demeanour of the police at the scene changed somewhat dramatically.

"You don't know?"

"No."

"Well can you tell us why she came in? Anything?"

"She must've heard me call out for help. I think she used a credit card to open the door."

"And why did she leave when we arrived?"

"She said something about not trusting the police."

The police seemed even more sceptical now.

"So who tied Tina up?"

"She did?"

"The black woman?"

"Yes. With my belt and my scarf. I mean she asked me if I had a belt or scarf and I said yes and gave her both."

"Okay, let me see if I've got this straight. You were attacked in your home by the daughter of a man who was arrested after you offered evidence against him in court in a case you're defending. Then a woman who you don't know, used a credit card to enter the premises and rescue you. Then just before we arrived, she ran away. Is that correct?"

Emily was beginning to tense up at this line of questioning, and the increasingly hostile tone in which the questions were being fired at her.

"Yes. Look I know this all sounds strange. But you can check it out."

"Sergeant!" This was a policewoman calling out from the kitchen. "I think this is something you might want to hear!"

The sergeant had the policewomen bring Tina back to the living room. Emily noticed that Tina was remarkably calm now, rubbing her wrists somewhat ostentatiously. And one of the policewomen was looking at her with open hostility.

"Okay Tina," said the policewoman continued. Can you tell us why that happened? How it started?"

"I came here to talk to her about the case. And– "

"This would be that case that she's defending, in which she accused your father."

"Yes. I just wanted to talk to her, nothing more. And the next thing I know she's having a go at me. Calling me a 'fucking terrorist' and a–"

"You liar! I never said anything! I never touched–"

"Quiet!" shouted the sergeant. "You'll get your turn."

"This is ridiculous! Look this is *my* home. I've got the right to be here. Look, someone who doesn't live here came here and attacked me. You can check out all these facts. My ownership, Tina's identity, the fact that her father was arrested. Everything!"

"Listen, miss, if you carry on like this you'll be arrested. Right now, we're asking her. You can tell us your version when she's finished."

He nodded to Tina to continue.

Emily couldn't believe this was happening, as Tina proceeded to spin her version of events.

"I should explain that I've recently converted to Islam, and I've taken to wearing a burqa as a personal expression of my faith."

"*She's lying! She wasn't wearing a burqa last Saturday at Soraya's place. She isn't even really a f------ a Muslim!*"

"I'm warning you," said the sergeant.

Exploiting the sergeant's current state-of-mind, Tina took a step backwards, as if she was afraid of Emily, limping slightly, although Emily realised that after what the other woman had done, the limp might be real.

"Anyway, I just came here to talk to her about my father and the case. He was secretly recorded without his knowledge or consent. And yes, it's true, he *did* make some incriminating admissions. But he's suffering from advanced Alzheimer's and half the time he doesn't know if he was coming or going. Anyway, as soon as I started talking, she went crazy. Called me a 'fucking Muslim' and a 'fucking terrorist'. And then the next thing I know, she's on top of me, pinning me to the ground and tying me up with her belt and her scarf. If you look at her suit, you'll see that the belt is missing."

"That was the black woman. She asked me if I had a belt to–"

"Last warning!" said the sergeant, still enjoying the power trip.

"Anyway after she had me tied up, she went and got a knife from the kitchen. I don't know if it was just to frighten me or to kill me, but either way, I screamed. And the next thing I knew she threw down the knife and was phoning you lot, pretending that *I* attacked *her*."

"It's not even one of my knives! She brought it here to kill me!"

"Right, that's it!"

The sergeant grabbed Emily's arm and took out a pair of handcuffs."

"*Get off me, you bastard!*" Emily shouted as one of the policewomen rushed forward to help the sergeant.

"Do *not* resist," she said as she grabbed Emily's other arm. Then when the sergeant managed to get the second cuff on, the policewoman added, "Calm down" even as her colleague applied unnecessary pressure, to give the impression that she and her colleague were trying to restrain a violent, aggressive suspect.

"*You people are crazy! Let me go or I'll sue the pants off you!*"

The sergeant took a brisk glance at his watch.

"The time is seven fourteen P.M. and I am arresting you for religiously motivated assault, contrary to Section 28 of the Crime and Disorder Act 1998."

He gripped her forearm, pressing his fingers into her flesh with the intention of causing pain, and started dragging her along. Then she remembered something.

"I said 'help me'."

"You should have thought about that before you–"

"No you don't understand!" said Emily, no longer resisting physically. "I said 'help me' when she was attacking me!"

Friday 29th March, 2024

97

"She clammed up after that," said Hayden Blair, "and answered 'No comment' to all questions at the police interview. However, the police are satisfied that the recording is authentic, and I am instructed that the Crown intends to prosecute her for the murders of Walter Wallace and Raymond Morrison as well as the attempted murder of Ruth Morrison. Accordingly we ask that a verdict of Not Guilty be entered in the case of Rex versus Calvin Coffey, also known as Calvin Conway."

It was 10.30 in the morning, and Hayden Blair was addressing the judge, after Nigel and two different police forces – the Met and Thames Valley – had apprised him of the facts.

The truth would have come out eventually, as Tina's cunning claims, though persuasive at the time, would not have stood up to scrutiny, with the timings of CCTV cameras at the train station, background checks on Emily and a myriad other pieces of evidence. But instead Tina's lies collapsed much sooner than that, because Emily had shouted out "Help me!"

She had previously set "Help me" as the wake-up word for her Alexa, so when she called out the words, Alexa came to life and recorded the entire conversation that followed.

Judge Braham made a show of giving the Crown's motion due consideration, but by that stage, the ruling was never really in doubt.

"I can't thank you enough," said Calvin, as he faced Nigel and Emily in a room that the admin staff at the Bailey had provided him with. "Now I can start my life again."

Emily knew that "start again" was the wrong expression. He could pick up his life from where it had been broken off before his arrest, but not from where it was before he had been framed by

Wallace and Harper. Those lost years could *never* be returned to him.

Before leaving Belmarsh Prison that morning, he had eaten a full breakfast, in accordance with the old prison superstition that if you don't finish your breakfast, you're going back there after court.

"I'm glad we were able to help," said Nigel. "And I know it's not my place to offer unsolicited advice, especially after the fact, but I just want to say that if you'd only told us the whole truth *earlier*, we would have been in a better position to protect your rights. As it was, we struck it lucky with Tina Harper."

Calvin nodded, acknowledging the advice.

"The press are probably hanging around outside," Emily added. "If you want, we can help you draft a statement."

"Or we can draft one for you," Nigel added. "And if you approve it, we can read it out on your behalf."

"No need. I just want to get out of here."

"You'll still have to run the gauntlet of the press," Emily warned.

"I'll ask the staff if I can slip out the way I was brought in, via the car park, where the police vans go."

When they stepped out of the room, they parted ways. Nigel and Emily headed for the robing room. Calvin for the back entrance, away from the prying eyes of the fourth estate.

However, he didn't quite manage to outsmart everyone. For one person had known *exactly* what he was going to do. And when he emerged from the car park, she waited for him on a moped, her helmet covering hair that was now as dark as a raven. She watched with some amusement as he easily evaded the reporters and photographers who had congregated at the main entrance to the Old Bailey. But she waited until he had gone some considerable distance down the road, before she gunned the engine and roared off after him.

The moped was only 125cc, but powerful enough for what she planned. She had some unfinished business with him, and didn't want any witnesses to see what she was about to do.

In the robing room, Nigel noticed that Emily seemed distracted as she folded away her gown.

"Are you still angry with the police?"

"Angry's an *understatement*."

"Don't worry. Even if it was less than an hour, I can get you a lot more than eight-fifty. With the bruising on your wrists and the aggravated circumstances, I reckon I can get you a few thousand."

"It's not that."

"Then what?"

"It's the case."

Nigel was puzzled.

"But we *cracked* the case, Emily! *You* cracked the case!"

"There are a couple of loose ends."

"You mean like who lured Calvin there in the first place?"

"Yes, and who fiddled the hospital records that led to that false diagnosis?"

"Well in that case, I've got some good news for you, because Inspector Cherry filled me in on that before the session."

Over the next few minutes, Nigel told Emily what Jane Cherry had told him about Petula Gelding and what they had found on her laptop. At the end of the explanation, Emily still looked puzzled.

"Yes, but who was she?" asked Emily. "And *why?*"

98

Calvin was packing a suitcase, his mind relaxing to the sound of running water from nearby. It could have been the sound of a waterfall on a tropical island, but for the fact that he was upstairs in the larger bedroom of a terraced house on the St Helier estate in Carshalton, a working-class district to the south of London which he had called home until his six-month stay in Belmarsh prison.

Even the larger bedroom was quite small by American standards, but then again, even the houses in the middle-class suburbs of England were smaller than their American counterparts.

"Hello!" a woman's voice called out from downstairs. "Is anyone home?"

He recognised the voice.

"Emily?" he called back. "I'm upstairs."

"You left the front door open."

"That's what six months in jail does to you."

"Can I come up?"

"Sure."

Emily climbed the stairs and saw an open bedroom door. She walked in to see a half-packed suitcase on the bed, and Calvin's clothes in it, with others on the bed, not exactly strewn, but looking like they'd been pulled out of the wardrobe or a chest of drawers.

"Going back to the US?"

"My life is pretty much over here."

"I wouldn't be too sure. You can probably sell your story to the tabloids. I reckon you could probably get five figures. I could ask Nigel. He won't rep you himself, but I'm pretty sure he *knows* people. And you can make a killing on social media – pardon my French."

"No thank you," said Calvin, continuing to fold his clothes neatly into the suitcase. "I've had more than my share of the limelight."

"You know what they say? Living well is the best revenge."

"Look, just drop it, okay!"

Emily leaned against the doorpost, trying to look "slinky", but not quite pulling it off, looking more like a schoolgirl trying unsuccessfully to seduce her favourite teacher. For a moment she wondered to herself about her reason for being here. Was it personal or professional?

"Look, I *know* you feel bitter. First, you're framed for cheating, and all your plans for life go out the window. *Then* you're tricked into coming to the home of one of the very professors who framed you, and you're framed *again!* This time for murder."

"Oh I'm not bitter. I'm done with the bitterness. I just want to get on with life."

Emily's voice became gentle.

"Calvin, you don't have to pretend with me. And you don't have to hide the fact that you're hurt. I saw how you felt in court when you were talking Raymond."

"What are you talking about?"

"When you were asked about the impact of his death... in court. You almost broke down. Hell, you *did* break down!"

"*Okay so I broke down!* For a moment it was too much for me. But it's over, okay! I'm over it."

"Yes, but I was thinking about what it must have done for you when Raymond was battered to death. You were counting on him to clear your name. So when Tina killed him, that would have put you right back at square one. That must have been frustrating – *monumentally* frustrating."

"It was. But then at least I knew – or rather *thought* I knew – that one of them killed Raymond. I mean either Wallace or Harper."

"Yes, but you couldn't prove it could you? You knew it, but there was nowhere to take that knowledge."

"The authorities? The press? Social media?"

"A self-serving statement by an embittered ex-student who was expelled from the university for cheating? It wouldn't have proved anything without corroboration, would it? And your one and only source of corroboration was Raymond. And he was dead."

"True."

"So you were just going to drop it? Betwixt the cup and the lip? Just let it slide, after you finally found out what *really* went down?"

"What do *you* think?"

There was something about the way Calvin answered the

question with a question that Emily didn't like.

"I think, by that stage, you'd well and truly got the bit between your teeth."

"You read *that* one right. Maybe *you'd* like to fill in the blanks. You seem to be on a bit of a roll, Emily."

Emily bridled in the face of the challenge and decided to push back, Emily style.

"Okay, let's try *this* for size. Soon after Raymond's death, someone hacks into more than one hospital computer, obtains Raymond's brain scans, and uses the scans to trick other doctors into thinking that Wallace has a brain tumour. Then *you* were tricked into entering into an email exchange with a fake account *pretending* to be Walter Wallace, inviting you over to give him a quote for a loft conversion."

In the background, the running water had stopped.

"That same person – a woman called Petula Gelding, according to the police – persuaded Wallace to get a pen camera and try and get Seamus Harper to confess to the murder of Raymond Morrison. And also to confess to framing *you*."

"But Wallace couldn't get an outright confession from Harper," Calvin replied. "At least *not* to the murder of Raymond Morrison, because Harper didn't actually kill Raymond, as it turned out."

"No," said Emily. "It was Tina."

"And who would ever suspect a woman of such a violent crime?" a woman's voice came from behind her.

Emily swung round to see the now dark-haired woman standing there in a bathrobe.

"Who are *you*?" asked Emily, although she already had a pretty good idea.

"My name is Petula."

99

Soraya was pruning the last of her roses when she felt the familiar, unsettling sensation of being watched. Her eyes flicked up from the flowers to see her neighbour, Mr. Lockwood, lurking at his window again, staring at her with that creepy smirk he always wore. She quickly looked away, trying to ignore the prickling feeling at the back of her neck. This was her sanctuary, the one place where everything was supposed to be peaceful.

The person who had murdered Walter had been arrested and although it wasn't the result she had expected, it was, at least, the *right* result. Of course it would be another trial. But the police now had a recorded confession, evidence that the murderer had committed more than one murder, and of course more evidence was certain to emerge as they investigated properly this time. And so, Soraya could at last feel truly at peace.

But the peace didn't last.

The sound of cars coming to a halt nearby, shattered the quiet evening, and Soraya froze, glancing round past the side of the house. The two cars that pulled up outside were police cars, followed by a van marked "Forensic Investigations." She knew this was going to happen, yet her heart started to pound as uniformed constables and plain clothes officers swarmed out and began filing into her back garden. Leading them was DI Jane Cherry, her expression stern and unreadable.

"Mrs. Wallace," said Jane calmly. "We have a search warrant to search your house and garden."

"A search warrant? What for?" Soraya stuttered, her hands trembling. But before she could demand further explanation, a group of officers in Hi-Vis jackets were already unloading what looked like a manually operated lawn mower, with a tablet screen between the handlebars.

"What's that?" asked Soraya, helplessly.

"Ground-penetrating radar."

"Ground...?"

"We use it to look beneath the earth. Unless you'd like to save us all the time and just tell us where to look."

Once the machine was in the garden, an officer switched on and began moving it slowly along the grass. The device hummed as it scanned the ground in slow, deliberate sweeps.

Soraya's breath caught in her throat. Her garden, her safe place, was now crawling with police.

"Perhaps you can tell me just what it is you're looking for?"

DI Cherry looked at her, as if unsure whether to say or wait for her to say something incriminating. It didn't take long before the shout went up.

"Governor! Found something!"

The officer was holding the machine on the spot, looking down at the screen. Jane went over to look and after a few seconds, she nodded to a team of policemen who started putting up a white plastic tent around the spot.

A pit opened in Soraya's stomach as three officers entered the tent carrying spades. They were not wearing Hi-Vis jackets. They were wearing the sterile white "bunny suits" of scene of crime officers.

Another two men, also in sterile white suits, entered the tent. One held a still camera and the other a video camera. They were a photographic officer and a higher photographic officer respectively.

Soraya looked on helplessly until DI Cherry emerged from the tent and approached her.

"Mrs. Wallace," said the Detective Inspector, grabbing Soraya's right arm and clamping a handcuff on the wrist, "It is five forty-nine on the 29th of March 2024 and I am arresting you for the murder of Gerald Shannon."

Soraya collapsed on the ground.

100

"Petula Gelding?"

"My maiden name. For the last twenty years, I've been Petula Conway."

The thing that surprised Emily most, was the fact that she wasn't surprised.

"You were at the trial. I saw you in the spectators' gallery."

"That I was."

"But you were blonde then."

"That I was."

"But you weren't there this morning."

"No I was down the road from the court, on a moped."

"Making a delivery?" asked Emily, with the hint of a sneer in her tone.

"No, a collection."

Emily looked blank.

"Picking up my man," Petula replied, casting a glance at Calvin. "Trying to avoid the prying eyes of the paparazzi."

"You stayed very much in the background throughout the trial."

"A good wife always does."

But the tone was mocking.

Emily felt a note of tension in the air when Petula started moving. But she was relieved when the position Petula took was next to Calvin. Then, when Petula put an affectionate arm around Calvin's waist, Emily was further put at ease. That meant she could talk to both of them, without exposing her back. By now, a more detailed picture was beginning to emerge, but Emily was hungry for the rest of the facts. She wanted the *full* picture.

So she pressed on.

"Hacking an NHS computer takes a certain amount of skill."

"Indeed it does," Calvin replied.

He was being cagey. She would have to play the cross-examiner.

"At first, I thought it was Huette's husband Gerald. He's a computer programmer. But then I remembered Nigel's notes of your testimony. You scored an off-the-scale 159% in computational mathematics. I reckon with grades like that you must have some serious computer hacking skills."

"My boy's wicked smart," said Petula.

Emily was confused, not by Petula's words, but by broad grin on her face.

"What's that?"

"It's a line from a film: *Good Will Hunting*. A friend of the Matt Damon character says it."

Emily remembered what Nigel had told her about his meeting with Herman Whitmore, and the professor's constant allusions to that film. And it was Herman Whitmore who had awarded Calvin 159% in computational mathematics. It was Professor Whitmore who had interceded on Calvin's behalf when Calvin was threatened with expulsion in his first year.

"*I intervened on his behalf to stop the expulsion.*"

Who had been persuaded…

"*His wife asked me. And I allowed myself to be persuaded.*"

Nigel had even mentioned the small, unobtrusive picture of the teenage girl with platinum curls.

"You're Professor Whitmore's *daughter*?"

Petula smiled.

"Not officially. I mean I was never brought up in his household. But he had brief fling with my mum… and I was the result."

"Did you speak up for him at the time?"

"Unofficially. But I had to be careful about it. There were… certain rumours floating around at the time."

"Rumours about you and Calvin?"

Whitmore smiled mockingly.

"No Nigel. Not rumours about me and Calvin at all. Just rumours about me."

"What kind of rumours?"

"I'd rather not say."

"You had to be careful about things like that in those days," said Petula. "They don't like it when professors sleep with their students."

"He paid her off? Your mum?"

"They... made an arrangement."

There was no trace of bitterness in Petula's voice. She seemed to read Emily's mind.

"Oh don't worry. It was all quite amicable."

Emily wasn't worried. But she did feel as if she was wondering down a blind alley. She didn't really care about Professor Whitmore's extramarital affairs – or even about the nepotism that may have played a role in salvaging Calvin's university place after his disastrous first year at Bristol University.

What she wanted to know was about the events with Raymond and Wallace and Harper. The rest was just a diversion.

She looked Calvin straight in the eyes.

"So... the trial is over, and I'm not recording this conversation. Anything you tell me is still under the cloak of privilege. Now it's *your* turn to fill in the blanks. Do you want to let your hair down?"

Calvin was silent for a few seconds. Then he seemed to mentally relax.

"Okay. I suppose, I owe it to you... What happened with Raymond gave me an idea. I don't mean him getting killed. I mean him getting *ill*. I figured if illness could prick Raymond Morrison's conscience, then maybe it could do the same to Wallace or Harper."

"So you reinvented yourself as a builder?"

"I'd worked in the building trades as a student, and when I got kicked out of Bristol, so it was a logical choice. We started work on Wallace as soon as I heard about Raymond being killed. But then I had to change my name and hide my background to take it to the next stage. So I moved to Carshalton and set up shop there as a construction worker."

"What made you decide on Wallace?"

"Raymond told me he'd been getting money Wallace. He said it wasn't blackmail, but bribery. But that meant that Wallace was more likely to use money rather than violence. Otherwise why pay Raymond for years. Raymond said he thought it was guilt."

"Then why didn't he seek *you* out and pay *you* money?"

"You're right, I never really bought it. I guess it wasn't really guilt. But probably a mixture of guilt and self-preservation. But Raymond himself wasn't afraid of Wallace."

"But he was, of Harper?"

"I would say he was... apprehensive. I mean that was just my impression... at the time."

"So you hacked the NHS computers and faked Wallace's illness to manipulate him into coming clean. But when that didn't happen, when Wallace wouldn't budge, you decided to up the ante, by engineering a confrontation between Wallace and Harper. How did you get Raymond's brain scan?"

"That was me," said Petula. "I used social engineering."

"Care to elaborate," Emily replied.

"Bereavement counselling."

Emily's face remained blank.

"We created targeted click-ads for bereavement counselling on a tight radius around Ruth and Raymond's home. I set up shop in Bournemouth and suckered her in. I got enough info to pose as Ruth and request copies of the scans for a second opinion. Then Calvin worked his magic, changing the metadata, and hacked the systems at the Royal Free and planted them there."

"But why would Wallace have a brain scan there in the first place."

Calvin answered that one.

"We used the same social engineering to get Wallace to have the scan. Targeted ads, making him worry about every little twinge in the head, pointing out that the tests were free."

"One of the things we learned from the police was that there were adverts targeted on Harper telling him that Wallace was going to betray him."

She looked from one to the other. Neither answered.

"What was the purpose of that? How would it get him to talk?"

Still not a word from either. Emily's voice hardened. She became her father's daughter again – Emily the cross-examiner.

"The truth of the matter is, you didn't just want to get Wallace to entrap Harper into a recorded confession, did you? You wanted to get Wallace to provoke Harper into killing him, and you wanted to make sure that the *killing* was captured on video."

Petula looked angry at this. Calvin remained calm.

"More than that, Emily. I wanted to catch Harper in the act, personally. Unfortunately, we mistimed it by a few minutes. The traffic on the road was heavier than either of us anticipated."

This time it was Emily who was beaten into silence.

"If you're waiting for an expression of remorse, Emily, you'll be waiting for a long time. After the way they destroyed my life and shattered my dreams... I think I can live with myself."

"Does it matter to you that other people were hurt?"

"I don't know how much Soraya or Huette knew about what Wallace did to me. And I suppose at the time, I thought that even Tina was blameless. But if we start letting wrongdoers off the hook because we sympathise with their family, then where is the justice for their victims?"

"I was thinking of *Ruth!*"

"I had no way of knowing that Ruth would be attacked. At that point, I still thought it was Seamus Harper who was the killer and that he was too frail by that stage to do any more killing."

"You should have realised that it was Tina who would have seen the ads warning that Walter Wallace would betray him. *She would be the one looking for Alzheimer's treatment!*"

Petula opened her mouth to argue. But she couldn't because she knew that what Emily had to say was true. She had had the very same thought herself not long ago.

Emily's mood softened.

"So... I see you're packing... Where are you going? I mean where are you *really* going?"

"Somewhere warm," said Calvin. "Probably the Caribbean. Or maybe the Med."

"Then when winter hits, we might head for Australia," Petula added.

"How can you afford it?"

Calvin smiled.

"I'm a digital nomad. I may not have letters after my name, but in IT, if you have an abundance of skills and a proven track record, you get judged by your results. And for the last twenty years I've been making my living off my IT skills."

Emily realised that since the pandemic, in addition to office staff working from home, a lot of computer professionals had become digital nomads. Like Gerald... *supposedly.*

"As a programmer?"

"That too. But mainly as a pen tester."

Emily knew that this meant "penetration tester" not someone who tests pens.

"White hat or black hat?" she asked remembering the terminology of the trade.

"Grey hat, I suppose. Although I suppose you could even say, Lincoln Green hat. Make of that what you will."

She knew *exactly* what to make of it.
A latter-day Robin Hood.
That was how he saw himself

"So I guess this is goodbye," said Emily, feeling kind of deflated.

"Not necessarily. You never know. Our paths might cross again, one of these days."

EPILOGUE

Friday, 29th March, 2024 – evening

Nigel Farringdon knelt in the damp earth of his garden, the smell of freshly turned soil mingling with the faint fragrance of lingering blooms. In his hands, he held a small packet of forget-me-not seeds – Joanne's favourite flowers. He ran his thumb over the worn packaging, remembering how she used to plant them every spring. Their tiny blue petals had always filled the garden with such life, with the same warmth her smile brought to their home.

But now, the garden was silent, empty except for the wind rustling through the trees. The air was still, thick with memories he couldn't escape. Joanne's laugh echoed in his mind, and the sweet voices of their children: his son with his excited chatter about physics and wanting to save the world from pollution and global warming by solving the problem of nuclear fusion and winning the Nobel Prize, and his daughter's ambition to follow in her father's footsteps and become a barrister, or even stand for Parliament and change the face of British politics.

All gone now. Taken in an instant by a crash caused by a drunk driver who hadn't even tried to decelerate at the intersection, let alone stop. A day like any other for Nigel at work, until the phone call that had shattered his world. He hadn't been there, hadn't been able to hold them, to protect them. He could only picture the scene in his mind – twisted metal, the stillness of their bodies, and the sudden, horrifying quiet where once there had been life.

He dug into the soil, creating small hollows for the seeds. Joanne had always said that planting was a way to look forward to the future, but what future could there be without them? His fingers trembled as he scattered the seeds, the weight of grief pressing down on him, making it hard to breathe.

As he patted the soil over the seeds, the recollections rushed in – Joanne showing the kids how to plant the flowers just right, their laughter filling the air as they competed for the straightest rows. He could still see his daughter's small hands covered in dirt, his son's proud grin as he showed Joanne his handiwork. And Joanne... always there, always guiding them.

A sob tore through his chest, and he dropped the trowel, his hands sinking into the earth. The tears came hard and fast, and there was nothing he could do to stop them. His shoulders shook as he buried his face in his hands, letting the grief crash over him like a wave.

"I'm sorry," he whispered, his voice barely audible through the sobs. "I'm so, so sorry."

The only answer was the wind, and Nigel knelt there, broken and alone, as the forget-me-nots – Joanne's beloved flowers – lay waiting to bloom.

"Didn't they even apologise after that?"

This was Anita Nguyen, a fellow pupil of Emily at St Jude's.

"More like trying to make it seem like *I* was to blame. That mealy-mouthed sergeant kept saying 'but I didn't *know* that' as if his ignorance was an excuse. It was my own home, for fuck's sake! And he assaulted me!"

Anita tried to calm her down.

"You know what they say: don't get mad, get *even*."

The four law pupils were gathered round a cramped table in the London Bridge branch of Honest Burgers, with Emily holding court, regaling them tales of her latest victory. Four was a large number of pupils for all but the biggest sets of chambers. But St Jude's had lost two of their older tenants to Covid, and in any case, the set was planning on expanding under Nigel Farringdon's refreshing, and relatively youthful, leadership.

Honest Burgers was one of their favourite haunts because of its proximity to Southwark Crown Court, as well as to St Jude's.

"Are you going to represent yourself?"

"Nigel said *he* would."

"I'd do it, if they let me. I could be your knight in shining armour."

This was Archie Gaylord, a young, baby-faced Etonian and

her fellow "toff" amongst the pupils. The other two had got there by hard graft and never knew that feeling of having to justify themselves.

"I think we should *all* do it," said Anita. "Like the three musketeers. All for one and one for all."

Anita was always the methodical one among the pupils. Technically brilliant but with a somewhat cautious approach, in contrast to Emily's imaginative but reckless.

Emily was still hyper from what had happened less than 24 hours ago. She had managed to hold it together in court, and through the confrontation with Calvin and Petula. But now, the memory of the incident with the police and Tina was flashing back, filling her with rage at the humiliation and helplessness – even though her cognitive faculty should have told her that it would all come out in the wash.

Back in chambers, she had tried to leave her "office me" behind her and morph into her "party me" for the weekend. To that end, she had changed into a tight-fitting, purple, faux-silk, blouse and form-hugging jeans, in place of the tailored white blouse and loose dark slacks that she had worn under her robes.

On her feet, the smart leather of the courtroom uniform had been replaced by the infinitely more comfortable flat-soled sneakers. The makeup stayed natural, enhancing her features without overpowering them. And she kept the accessories minimal: a slender silver watch and small stud earrings.

But not even "party me" could shake off the negative vibes. She had to try something else.

"Okay what have the rest of you been up to?" She asked, picking up her burger.

"Well, I've just been tasked with trying to persuade a client to drop a hopeless private prosecution."

This was Mark Stevens, a black "yoof" from Carshalton who was vying with Archie for Emily's affections. "My personal corpus delectable," he had once called her in a drunken moment, during a Friday night pub-crawl – a play on the legal phrase *corpus delicti*.

"Since when does St. Jude's turn away a client?" asked Anita.

They could tell from the puerile grin on Mark's face, that this was probably one of his jokes, not an actual case that he was dealing with.

"He wanted to prosecute the band Barenaked Ladies under the Trades Descriptions Act."

Archie was the only one who thought this funny. Emily

nodded grudgingly at the originality of it. Anita kept a straight face.

Emboldened, albeit by the mixed reaction, Mark decided to milk the joke for all it was worth. Putting on his most pompous and effete legal voice, he intoned:

"M'Lud, I must observe, at this, juncture, that if Transport for London displays a poster advertising a band calling itself Barenaked Ladies, an average person of the male gender might be persuaded to buy a ticket. Such a person is surely entitled to hold the reasonable expectation that the band in question consists of ladies – and that said ladies will be disporting themselves in a state of nudity? Accordingly, M'Lud, in my humble submission, a jury may reasonably find the defendants guilty of misleading the public in a commercial transaction, in contravention of the Trades Descriptions Act."

One by one, as Mark continued, they all cracked up at this. Even Anita Nguyen, the most serious among them, finally gave way to mirth. When the laughter subsided Emily excused herself with the words "I have to powder my nose."

As she walked away to the ladies, Mark hooted "We all know what *that* means!"

It was less than half a minute later that the black woman sitting alone, hunched in the corner and wearing a surgical mask, got up and went to the ladies too. Inside, she took off her mask and waited for Emily to emerge from the cubicle.

When she did, she found herself confronted by the same woman who had rescued her from Tina. But this time, the woman had a rather more pugnacious look on her face.

"Yes?" said Emily, surprised, still wondering who she was and what she wanted.

"My name's Chelsey Slater and I've got a bone to pick with you."

THE END

To be continued in...

Best Served Cold

ACKNOWLEDGEMENT

I would like to thank Amanda Sheridan for generously and tirelessly devoting her time and skill to creating the cover design for this book.

Amanda is also an extremely good author in her own right, and I highly recommend her books:-

Rapid Eye Movement
The Dreaming
Dream Catcher
Bad Dreams (Lucy's Story)
Collie Hair Soup

ABOUT THE AUTHOR

Dan Cogan

Dan Cogan is the creator of the Baby of the Bailey series.

Printed in Great Britain
by Amazon